The Rescue Man

ANTHONY QUINN

The Rescue Man

JONATHAN CAPE
LONDON

Published by Jonathan Cape 2009

2 4 6 8 10 9 7 5 3 1

Addresses for companies within The Random House Group Limited can be found at:
www.randomhouse.co.uk

A CIP catalogue record for this book is available from the British Library

ISBN 9780224087278 (Hardback)
ISBN 9780224087285 (Trade paperback)

The Random House Group Limited supports the Forest Stewardship Council (FSC),
the leading international forest certification organisation. All our titles that are printed on
Greenpeace-approved FSC-certified paper carry the FSC logo. Our paper procurement
policy can be found at www.rbooks.co.uk/environment

Mixed Sources
Product group from well-managed
forests and other controlled sources
www.fsc.org Cert no. TT-COC-2139
FSC © 1996 Forest Stewardship Council

'Miss Otis Regrets (She's Unable to Lunch Today)', Words and music by Cole Porter © 1934
(Renewed) Warner Bros. Inc. (ASCAP)
'There's a Lull in My Life', Words and music by Mack Gordon and Harry Revel © 1937,
Reproduced by permission of EMI Music Ltd, London w8 5sw

Typeset by Palimpsest Book Production Limited, Grangemouth, Stirlingshire
Printed and bound in Great Britain by Clays Ltd, St Ives plc

For my father, Peter
And in memory of my mother, Margaret (1935–1997)

PART ONE

Waiting
1939

Present fears
Are less than horrible imaginings.
Macbeth

I

The address he had been given was a road off Sefton Park, just south of the city. Baines, having taken a tram, had stepped off some distance away, convincing himself he wanted to walk through the park. In truth, he was looking for an excuse to delay his arrival. He was becoming more inclined to dilatoriness these days, as if by huddling in the present he could somehow hold back the incoming tide of the future. It seemed that everybody was waiting, tensed and trembling like divers on a cliff. And yet in much else he had to admit that the spirit of business as usual prevailed. The previous afternoon, while looking for blackout curtains at the Bon Marché, he had noticed a young man trying on a top hat.

It was nearly nine o'clock on a cloudless June morning, and the heat seemed also to be collecting in wait. The grass in the park had a withered, yellowish tinge. He was amazed, and vaguely appalled, that individual days could roll on in their oblivious humdrum way. A woman pushing a pram strolled past. Birds were tuning up in high, discordant keys. Only the distant tap-tap of a hammer caused him to look across at the glinting windows of the Palm House, where a team of workmen were boarding up its fragile shell. At the park's perimeter two more workmen were painting the kerbstones black and white, a guide to night-time traffic once the street lamps went dark. Here was urgent work, albeit languidly undertaken: could there be such a thing as languid urgency? he wondered. In any case, somebody had looked ahead, assessed the risk, and made a decision. And the decision was to camouflage as much ground as possible.

Baines stood gazing at the painters as they inched their way around the kerb, their glossy trail of black and white snaking far behind them. As an augury he felt that it lacked poetry. If disaster must be presaged there ought to have been an albatross haunting the seafront, or a comet striping the night sky. He dawdled on. The cobbles of this road were as familiar to him as his own footfall. He must have been ten or eleven years old when he first rode a horse right the way around this park; he could recall the exhilaration of feeling its girth strain beneath him, and later his annoyance when its hooves no longer clattered on the stone; straw had been spread along the road to muffle the clopping and thus spare the slumbering residents of the grand houses an unwelcome reveille.

Lacking inspiration for further postponement, he turned at last into the quiet, tree-shaded avenue and made his way towards a row of terraced cottages, built in the middle of the last century and recently abandoned. He saw Jack at the end of the row, leaning against the wall, a cigarette on the go.

'Give me one of those, would you?' Baines said. Jack pushed himself off the wall and, without a word, tossed over his pack of Player's to Baines.

'Lose your way?' Jack deadpanned, expelling a plume of smoke through his nose. Baines, fishing out a cigarette, accepted the implicit reproof.

'Sorry. Just fancied a walk.'

Jack shrugged, as if Baines's timekeeping were no concern of his. He was a rangy, loose-limbed man in his early forties, with a sallow complexion and fair hair he kept severely cropped; he had the muscular set of a soldier, a profession which he had in fact once pursued.

'After you,' said Jack, pushing open the door and tilting his head by way of invitation. 'The lads have already made a start.' Baines stepped into a room where several young men in blue serge overalls were stacking odd bits of furniture. Damp had colonised the walls, and the floorboards squeaked underfoot. Net curtains hung leprous with dust and cobwebs. Jack ran an antiques business, and often alerted Baines when he had a clearance job that might involve valuing some architectural treasure before it was carted off to the auctioneers: a Georgian fire-surround, a fancily carved newel post, a marble chimney piece. Baines had an instinct for such unconsidered trifles, but looking about this scene of desolation he couldn't foresee a great haul.

Jack, as if reading his thoughts, let out a sigh. 'There might not be much here,' he said. They walked into the next room, which disclosed roughly the same degree of neglect. An old horsehair sofa lolled in one corner, its belly pocked with broken springs. Baines eyed some dull, heavy tables and a sideboard, a rocking chair, a fireguard blackened with use. He thought of how recently these things had constituted somebody's home, had perhaps been cherished – and how quickly they would go straight on to the dump. One of the young lads had followed them in and was now talking to Jack in a low, confiding tone. Jack nodded slowly and called over to Baines.

'We might have found something else,' he said.

The boy led them through a back entrance into a thistly, unkempt garden, and thence to another door at the opposite end of the building. They went through a narrow passageway and up two flights of stairs thickly carpeted in leaves and grime. At the top was a small landing, with a janitor's cupboard on one side and a door on the other, its paint blistered. A heavy, rusted lock barred the way.

'Get Harry up here, and tell him to bring his gear,' Jack said to the boy, who hurried back down. 'I talked to the last tenants here,' he went on, 'they said the upstairs was empty and had been for years.' He shook out another cigarette and lit it, the match flaring against the gloom. Jack smoked with the steady devotion of one who would have liked to make his living from it. Soon they heard footsteps; the boy had returned with Harry, a pensionable fellow who had worked with Jack for years. He carried an ancient knapsack clanking with tools.

'Might have to jemmy this one, Harry,' Jack said, nodding at the door.

Harry, with his rheumy eyes and stooped frame, looked barely capable of cracking a walnut, let alone a locked door; then Baines noticed the old man's hands, beaten and nicked and so long in touch with metalled machinery that his fingertips had been worn to hard, blackened discs, as if they were part of his toolkit. Having briefly picked out a couple of brutish-looking files and tossed them back, Harry now selected a short crowbar and got to work on the door's lock. It took only a few minutes of his cracksmanship before the wood yielded and splintered, a sharp protesting snap announcing that its defence had been breached. Jack completed the job with a brisk shoulder charge, and they were through.

The room, running over the cottages below, was about the length of a tennis court. Long tables, mounted with lathes and punches speckled with rust, revealed it to be a joiner's workshop. Smaller tools were arranged on benches. Wood shavings and fronds of old paintwork littered the floor, and acrid dust seemed to have displaced the air – dust was the element they breathed. Baines and Jack looked at each other but didn't say anything. They had been in abandoned rooms before and were accustomed to the odour of decay. This was different: it was an atmosphere which seemed to rise from the incongruous feeling that they had somehow trespassed, as if at any moment men would return and the sound of sawing and planing would resume. A workman's jacket hung on a peg. A tobacco tin lay on a table next to a sheet of butcher's paper, on which a series of diagrams had been sketched. They walked about the room, as if wary of disturbing the air. Signs of tenancy kept ambushing them. A tin of biscuits, or what the mice had left of them; a framed photograph, askew on a wall, of a football team, arms folded, faces as blank as dinner plates. Baines read a note, in tiny capitals, pinned just to the side of it: REMEMBER MEDICINE FOR DAD.

He looked round at Jack, hoping he'd know what to say. There seemed to be too many questions crowding the room, none of which he felt equal to articulating.

'Like the bloody *Mary Celeste*,' said Harry, finally breaking the silence. The room did indeed feel ghostly, but there was no suggestion its one-time occupants had been abducted, atomised or otherwise spirited away. They had intended, evidently, to return. In the meantime Jack had found something at the other end of the room, and as he examined it Baines knew by the set of his lean features that it would be something quite hard to bear.

'This would explain it,' he said, handing to Baines, almost in resignation, a yellowing wall calendar. It showed the month of August, 1914.

Baines was back at his flat in Gambier Terrace by late afternoon, having helped Jack and his crew clear the derelict building. Jack sometimes offered to pay him, but Baines always refused, deeming the melancholy investigation of abandoned houses its own reward. The terrace, built high on a slope a hundred years ago for the thriving merchant classes, was no longer the fashionable address it had once been. Its veneer of prosperity had chipped and flaked, the stucco had faded from white to a liverish grey, and most of the window frames were carious. What hadn't changed was the vantage it offered over the city. His rooms occupied the top two floors of a house, from which he could gaze upon a vista of soot-smudged buildings, begrimed church spires, smoking chimney stacks; beyond them crowded the warehouses and docks along the Mersey, stretching as far as the eye could see. The view never failed to lift his heart. At this window, its glass smeared and warped with age, he could imagine what it might have been like for some mutton-chopped shipping magnate to stand and survey the dirty, magnificent sprawl that was making him rich – or richer. Baines could not afford to feel possessive; but he did feel protective.

Liverpool. 'Sailortown', as Melville called it. Baines, who was nearly thirty-seven, had never lived anywhere else. What others teased in him as a lack of adventure he now regarded as the earliest stirrings of civic loyalty. Growing up in the outlying districts to the south, where green fields had yet been spared the hand of 'improvement', he first came to know the city as few boys of his age ever had. His mother had died when Baines was three, his father when he was eight; the orphan had been consigned to the care of his father's brother, George, and his wife, May. The couple lived in the suburb of Mossley Hill, where George ran a stable and would allow his nephew to exercise the horses around the circuit of Sefton Park. He had a memory of one blissful summer, it was 1912 or 1913, when he would hurry over every morning to the stables; having helped with the mucking out and feeding, he would saddle up a stately old hack named Charlemagne and go cantering off to the park.

One morning, chafing at the now familiar loop on which his only company would be the occasional cyclist or carriage-and-pair, he turned the horse and crossed into the adjacent Princes Park. Then, hearing a tram rattling north, he decided to follow it – nobody said not to – and soon was ambling down the wide thoroughfare of Princes Avenue towards the city, his accelerating heartbeat soothed by the complacent steadiness of the horse's gait. As the streets called him on, the unwonted height and rhythm of the saddle lent an exhilaration he had never known from the inside of a tram. A shawlie selling flowers outside the Philharmonic Hotel; grubby kids playing hopscotch barefoot on the pavement; the crowd thickening as he passed St Luke's Church and then steered into the narrow funnel of Bold Street, past Lockie's where May had bought him his first jacket and tie, past the stern pillared facade of the Lyceum, the horse's flanks sweating now, the rider too, close-packed alongside the quick flurry of wheels on cobbles, the busy criss-crossing of leisured ladies and boatered gents and boys singing the newspaper headlines. At the corner of Church Street and Whitechapel he paused to watch a commotion – a costermonger's barrow had overturned, its load blocking the way – and then with a mere touch of the stirrup they were heading up Lord Street, choked with trams, past the Victoria Monument overlooking St George's Crescent and down, down again, towards the majestic plateau of the Pier Head, the overhead railway, the amazing novelty of those two green birds atop the Royal Liver Building, its scaffolding recently shed to reveal the gleaming brickwork beneath. Mounted on the horse, with the dark canyons of the business district looming massively behind him, the boy gazed out beyond the liners to the river and the ocean pathways vectoring north. But what did he care for the ocean? Far better, he thought, to be a prince of the city.

Baines knew that his restlessness was partly due to the confused state into which his work had been sliding. A London publishing house, Plover Books, had invited him to compile a study of Liverpool's architectural past, as part of an ongoing 'Buildings of England' series. It was almost a gift to him, but the high hopes and good intentions he had brought to the project two years before now lay scattered around his study, lost perhaps between the pages of the notebooks and scrapbooks on his desk, or else beneath the tottering ziggurats of books which had risen here and there on the floor. Deadlines had come and gone. His natural tendency to postpone had ensured that the commission, if not entirely sunk, had run into the sand.

One diversion he didn't foresee had lately assumed a kind of hold. His interest, always liable to wander, had snagged on a compelling but elusive figure lost in the shadows of Liverpool's mid-Victorian building boom. Peter Eames was a young architect who had briefly flourished in the 1860s when his first commission, an office block named Janus House, shocked the public and provoked damning reviews in the local press. His second building, Magdalen Chambers, was an insurance office of even bolder design and, having suffered a vilification similar to his first, proved to be his last. His proposed plans for a free library, to be built in one of the poorest parts of the city, were eventually abandoned on the grounds of its expense and his already unreliable reputation. After a bitter falling-out with his business partner he appeared to abandon his profession altogether; four years on from the failure of his library scheme he drowned off the shore at Blundell Sands, an alleged suicide. He was thirty-three.

Something about this short life intrigued Baines. For one thing, those buildings for which Eames had been so maligned now looked, seventy years later, very much like the work of a visionary – a man out of time. Their unusual height, combined with their innovative use of curtain-walling and cast iron, anticipated the skyscrapers of Chicago by twenty years. But more than intrigued, Baines was moved, for here was someone who had suffered the slings and arrows of an outrageous press yet heroically refused to back down. Eames had more than mere ambition, he had the unbiddable integrity of a true original. He remembered the words of Delacroix: talent does whatever it wants to do – genius does only what it can. It was sad to think of such a man hounded out of his vocation by people with not the smallest scintilla of his energy and imagination. Baines needed to find out more, and knew just the man who might help him.

Moray Lennox McQuarrie had always sounded to Baines like a company of shrewd Edinburgh lawyers; that a single man should own the whole name deeply impressed him. An early appointment of Charles Reilly's at the Liverpool School of Architecture, McQuarrie had been a noted scholar of Victorian Gothic, an expertise of which Baines as a student in the early 1920s had taken only partial advantage. He could only wonder how his old professor might regard this belated petition for help. The venue for their interview, a gentlemen's club in a side alley off Water Street, might have been regarded as a subtle form of intimidation on McQuarrie's part, but the ancient porter at the door and the cracked parquet in the entrance hall made Baines feel merely sorry. Directed through an upper room where the potted palms looked only slightly more wilted than that flyblown porter, he found McQuarrie in the library, sitting in a wing-backed chair with a copy of *The Times* lying like an obedient dog at his feet.

'Mr Baines,' he said, offering his hand and gesturing at the chair opposite. Time had not much altered the professor, who had appeared impossibly venerable to Baines on their first meeting eighteen years before. Thick, interrogative eyebrows framed a somewhat wolfish face, the chin and neck sporting tiny outcrops of bristle that his morning shave had missed. His worsted suit was too heavy for a summer's day, though it would have been a surprise to see him dressed in anything else. It was a fixture, as was his air of close-mouthed, watchful drollery, which his students knew only too well could suddenly darken into displeasure. His nickname, almost certainly known to McQuarrie, was 'The Flaying Scotsman'. Conscious of paying deference, Baines waited to be spoken to.

'I read your article in the *Engineer* the other week,' said McQuarrie eventually, his basilisk gaze never seeming to flinch. That he declined to elaborate on this declaration was characteristic, so Baines was obliged to fill the void.

'Yes, that piece is about the only thing I've managed to complete all year,' he replied, though even this self-deprecating sally sounded a little garrulous in present company. McQuarrie had perfected a disconcerting tactic of listening and then, by way of reply, silently leaning back and eyeing his interlocutor as if from a great distance. In those few seconds any hope of conversational intimacy would disappear. He was doing it now, so Baines pressed on, explaining his work on the architectural study and his other recent preoccupation. It occurred to him that the publishers had more than likely been recommended his name by McQuarrie himself.

'There's surprisingly little work been done on Peter Eames,' said

McQuarrie. 'A remarkable man. To have produced those designs before the age of twenty-six – you could almost forgive him his, shall we say, overweening arrogance.' He articulated the last two words with disgusted relish.

'I suppose once you become convinced of your own genius, the idea of other people's requirements seems . . . irrelevant.'

McQuarrie nodded slowly. 'I think it was other people's money that became the problem. The library he wanted to build would have cost a king's ransom. He admits it himself in his diaries.'

'Diaries? I didn't know they'd been published.'

'They haven't. They moulder uncatalogued in the Liverpool Record Office. I dare say they'll let you read them – it's not as if there's a waiting list.'

A club underling had sidled over and whispered to the old man, who looked at Baines.

'You'll join me in a sherry?'

Baines readily agreed, and in the meantime listened to his former teacher's laconic update of university news. When the drinks arrived, he sniffed his glass doubtfully.

'It's poor stuff from South Africa, I'm afraid,' said McQuarrie. 'They can't get it from Spain because of the war.'

Mention of one war inevitably brought them round to discuss the abysmal prospect of another. Odd to think it was only last September when they were rejoicing in the streets. The crisis had come, but the disaster had been averted. Or, as it seemed, postponed. Now that Hitler had jackbooted his way through the rest of Czechoslovakia it was impossible to think they could escape a second time.

'Regarding your work on the city,' said McQuarrie, thoughtfully, 'I suppose there's still a great deal to do?'

Baines nodded, and began to describe the multiform nature of the enterprise, how it entailed not merely dating the buildings of note but recording their pedigree and specifying any architectural anomaly or quirk that seemed germane. On top of all that, he was required to make sketches of the major buildings he documented. Baines, the recording angel, had felt his wings begin to droop.

'Well,' said McQuarrie, after silent consideration, 'there's no getting around the historical research. But you could save yourself some time if you leave off the sketching.'

'The publishers insist on illustrations.'

'I'm sure they do. So give them photographs instead – they're going to become standard for that kind of book soon in any case.' Baines could see the charm of the idea but worried that his paymasters might baulk at the expense. There was also a practical drawback to consider.

'I don't know how to take photographs.'

McQuarrie regarded him pityingly. 'For God's sake, man. How difficult do you think it is? You take the cap off the snout, point it in the right direction and make sure nobody walks in front of you.'

Baines fell silent. What he couldn't explain to McQuarrie – what he could barely explain to himself – was this nagging disposition to delay, to postpone, though he now had an inkling that, with the world on the brink, it was perhaps the futility of action in itself that had mesmerised him. His thoughts turned to the discovery of the joiner's workshop earlier that week, those men hurrying off to fight for king and country in the summer of 1914. Did they suspect, did even one of them suspect, that they would never come back? It was intolerably sad. And now, twenty-five years later, he would be following them into – what, exactly? Terror incognita. He glanced down at the newspaper, its headlines the writing on the wall.

'I dare say there'll soon be more pressing engagements than architectural histories,' he said, trying to keep the note of bitterness out of his voice.

McQuarrie looked at him appraisingly, and waited before he spoke. 'That may be so. Which makes your job all the more urgent. A year, two years from now, some of these buildings may not be here. For all we know, "here" may not be here. This could be the last chance to set them down as history. I would advise you not to waste it.'

Baines nodded, his mind's eye clouded with ashes and rubble. He could go for days, sometimes, without thinking about it. But it was always there, a spectral blur, and once it slouched back into view he could think of nothing else.

Their interview was over. McQuarrie rose from his chair, and allowed himself a thin smile.

'I'm sure this will strike you as Presbyterian talk, son, but work is the best defence against worry. I'll search out what I can on Eames, you keep on with this book and, God willing, we'll get through whatever Mr Hitler decides to throw at us.'

Baines took his proffered hand, and thanked him for his time, touched by a suspicion that his old teacher, as undemonstrative a man as he'd ever known, had been trying to cheer him up. As he walked out onto the street he replayed their conversation in his head, and wondered if he had only misheard McQuarrie calling him, with unlikely tenderness, 'son'.

Baines had never sensed the foundations of his life to be secure, for a reason he at first considered obvious: he had not had parents to love. When he thought about his mother all he could retrieve was the image of a young woman sitting on a sofa, tucking a stray lock of hair behind her ear. He had always presumed this was his mother, but he could never be sure. She had died at twenty-eight of TB, and the care of her only child, aged three, devolved upon her much older husband, a dutiful but distant man who seemed at a loss as to what this diminutive stranger might require of him. He was an assistant manager at one of the large city banks, and on his wife's death had buried his grief in overwork. His brother's wife, May, looked after the boy during the day, an arrangement that became permanent when Baines's father died, of a heart attack, five years after his wife.

Now, as he approached middle age, without any prospect of a wife or family of his own, Baines wasn't sure if the fault lay in himself, some hairline flaw in the structure of his personality. It seemed to him he would have been a solitary sort with or without the trauma of orphanhood. It haunted him, when he could bear to think about it, that he had never wept for the loss of his parents. He reasoned that this had been because he had not known his mother, and had barely got to know his father. His only resource had been the unwavering kindliness with which George and May submitted to the role of his guardians. Their first duty in that capacity had been to take him to his father's funeral. Even from the distance of nearly thirty years he could remember the coldness of the church, the smell of candle wax and furniture polish, the mournful wheedling of the organ while the priest droned mechanically through the exequies. Then, at the graveside, George bending down and whispering to him as the diggers waited discreetly at a remove: it was his moment to pick up a handful of earth and throw it into the neatly excavated rectangle. Its pitter-pattering on the wooden box below sounded a kind of farewell. Years later he learned from George that he and May had argued about bringing him to the funeral at all; May had worried that it might be too upsetting an experience for an eight-year-old, but George had insisted.

Were they surprised to see the boy so self-possessed and dry-eyed before his father's grave? Perhaps. But it was surely no less surprising when, a few years later, they did see him break down for the first and last time. One afternoon in the autumn of 1914 Baines had called in at the stables on his way home from school, only to find the place deserted. He couldn't understand it, though the wild heartbeat in his chest as he hurried homewards warned of disaster. May met him at the door, and through his heaving sobs he learned of the horses' fate. It was not only young men who were being pressed into service on the Western Front. George, distraught on his own account, hadn't been able to tell his nephew of the calamitous requisition. When he returned that evening and they read the anguish in each other's face the boy clung to him, and bereft of words to articulate his sorrow he wept – wept out his soul.

The bar of the Imperial Hotel was beginning to hum with a Saturday-evening clientele thirstily catching up with off-duty stewards and deckhands from Cunard – a liner must have recently docked. Through the fug of Woodbines and pipe smoke Baines spotted Jack at one of the back tables; he had evidently just been telling one of his risqué jokes, because the two women he was entertaining had fallen about with shrieks of outraged laughter. One of them was Evie, Jack's dismayingly pretty girlfriend, the other a woman Baines didn't recognise, though she was the first to catch his eye as he approached. He knew at that instant he had been set up for the night.

Jack made the introduction. 'Brenda, this is Tom Baines,' he said, flicking a glance at Baines that might have contained a request to play along. Brenda extended her hand with a coquettish smirk.

'Pleased to meet yer.'

She too was pretty and in her mid-twenties, though made up in a coarser way than Evie; dark, eager eyes greeted him from a heart-shaped face whose pale Liverpool-Irish complexion was offset by alarmingly crim-soned lips. Her powder and paint had been so thickly applied that Baines was put in mind of some rare tropical bird – one that expected to be admired, and perhaps adopted as a pet.

'You've arrived just in time to get the next round in,' Jack said brightly, raising his empty pint glass. Jack was drinking Higsons; the girls, on enquiry, both asked for a gin and French. Baines turned and threaded his way to the bar. While he was waiting to pay, he found Jack leaning conspira-torially against his shoulder.

'I hope you don't mind about this,' he said, nodding back to their table.

'She's an old friend of Evie's, and a really nice lass. Been very lonely since her feller shipped out a few months ago.'

Baines had an intuition, even on their short acquaintance, that Brenda had never been lonely in her life. He didn't know whether he felt amused or aggrieved that this little get-together had been engineered for his sake rather than hers. Jack, something of a swordsman in his prime, was fascinated by Baines's habitual monkishness, and would occasionally take it upon himself to play his matchmaker.

'So, what d'you say?' said Jack.

'I'm lost for words.'

'Come on. We'll have some laughs. She likes you, anyway – she thinks you look like Joel McCrea.'

Baines laughed, and Jack clapped him on the back, joining in.

Brenda, a secretary at a shipping insurance firm, was talking volubly about the sailors whose arrival in port after months at sea would turn the place into a regular boom town.

'They've got wads of money thick enough to choke a horse,' she said. 'But you have to get them quick or else they'll lose it all at cards in a weekend.'

She looked around the bar, as if she were minded to lasso one of their number right then and there. Her voice was fiercely Liverpudlian, containing something droll in its sing-song intonations but also something querulous: it was an accent that carried even in its simplest declaration a note of complaint.

'They can be randy beggars, though,' she continued, giggling. 'I was out with one feller last week, who's tippen back the ale like prohibition's starten tomorrer. We're just there talken about his last trip and next thing I know he's, like, all over me!'

Baines wasn't certain if this should be construed as a warning or an invitation. He thought he must seem very dull to her, despite the professed likeness to Joel McCrea. He looked, covertly, at Evie, who was laughing along with the story of Brenda's amorous assailant. An uncommon girl, really. Jack, as long as Baines had known him, had made a habit of treating his girlfriends with a cordial remoteness; their pleas for attention seemed to slide off him like mercury from a plate. Baines recalled him joking that he preferred women with long faces, because once you made them miserable you wouldn't be able to tell the difference. Evie was not the plaintive kind, yet she also seemed quite indifferent to the wiles of 'keeping a man': it perhaps explained why she and Jack had been together for three years or more. She worked as an editorial assistant at the *Echo*. Baines loved her disarming, old-fashioned air of graciousness, and the way it enhanced her expressive, mobile face and lively almond-shaped eyes. He loved the ease with which she talked to people, friendly with everyone yet favouring no one. Indeed, all he could object to in her was the fact of her being Jack's girlfriend, and there was nothing to be done about that.

Evie was at that moment trying to form a line of communication between him and Brenda.

'Tom and Jack have been friends since they were at the School of Architecture together. Tom's a historian – he's even written a book.'

'Really?!' cried Brenda. 'Must have a look in Smith's for it.'

'Please let me save you the trouble,' said Baines. 'It was a very small print run, and I'm afraid you'll never find it in Smith's.'

'So what's it about then, your *buke*?'

'Anglo-Norman architecture,' he said.

'Tom often keeps us entertained with readings from it,' said Jack, winking at Baines.

'It sounds very . . . important,' Brenda said, gamely, and sensing an end to this topic raised her glass. 'Cheers, everyone!'

They clinked glasses, and discussion turned to their immediate plans for the evening. Evie and Brenda wanted to go to the pictures, and were trying to decide between *Confessions of a Nazi Spy* or *The Hound of the Baskervilles*. Baines wasn't keen on either, but since he had read the Conan Doyle stories he steered the vote in favour of the latter. They finished their drinks, and walked out onto St George's Place, their faces illuminated in the dark by the huge neon sign above the Imperial advertising Guinness. Lime Street was thronged with Saturday-night crowds almost feverish in their quest for entertainment. A gang of sailors, rowdy with drink, passed by and wolf-whistled Brenda and Evie, who smiled complacently.

They entered the packed auditorium and edged their way along the row to their seats. A newsreel was playing, over which a voice fluted with stiff patrician cheeriness. Mr and Mrs Chamberlain were walking in the park; the Duchess of Kent was inspecting something or other; a ship was being launched amid a hysterical outbreak of flag-waving and hat-throwing. The emollient triviality of these non-events seemed to Baines almost wilful, another instance of a collective determination to ignore the one thing staring everybody in the face.

Eventually the picture started, and he found himself lulled by its genteel sense of Edwardian intrigue: Holmes discussing his plan of action while the hansom cab bowls along Baker Street. He could have wished, however, that an actor other than Basil Rathbone had been cast in the lead role: his impersonation felt too brisk, too blithe; it missed the deep-set melancholy of the great detective. Watson was merely a buffoon. Baines cast a glance to his right and watched Jack light up two cigarettes and pass one of them to Evie; their plumes of smoke curled romantically across the projector's tapering beam of light. He shifted in his seat, aware of the rapt stillness around him. Even Brenda's irrepressible tongue had been silenced by the ceaseless sprockety whirr of the reels.

He considered her from the corner of his eye. Well, she wasn't so bad, he thought. Evie certainly liked her – she was disposed to like just about everyone – but he couldn't for the life imagine why she judged Brenda a good match for him. Of course she had a pleasing look, firmly buttressed by a confidence in her own attractiveness. Too firmly. Baines didn't consider himself shy, but his demeanour was sufficiently quiet and inward-looking to be mistaken for shyness. His natural tendency when confronted by a personality as bumptious as Brenda's was to withdraw, to efface himself while louder voices insisted upon their claim to attention. He had a horror of those drinks parties where raucous strangers would dragoon him into talk of 'the international situation' and then gabble their own opinion rather than wait around for his. He had learned to recognise the type very quickly, and would make particular efforts to avoid wandering into their eyeline.

After the film they had called in at the Vines, but finding it even more crowded than the Imperial they took a cab back to Jack's flat in Falkner Square, and on the way sorted out their views on Holmes and Watson. Evie was confused about the reference, in the final moments, to 'the needle' – did Holmes have some kind of illness?

'Not exactly,' said Jack. 'Unless you judge constitutional boredom an illness. He was injecting opium.'

'So you mean . . . *drugs*?' asked Brenda, uncertainly.

'When the mood took him, yes. And spending that much time in Watson's company I expect the mood would have taken him quite often.'

Baines felt an enlivening sense of vindication: Jack had also been irked by Watson's oafishness. He paid off the cab and followed the others into the house. Jack's flat – his 'bachelor rooms', as he called them – comprised a rather poky kitchen and bedroom at the back, and a large, high-ceilinged living room at the front with French windows overlooking the square. Its air of studied informality reminded Baines of a stage set. He examined the spotted glass of the mirror above the fireplace.

'Ooh, look at this one, admiren himself,' cawed Brenda to Evie, nodding at Baines with a pert moue.

'No, not myself,' Baines replied quickly. 'I was admiring this lovely old mirror. It's one I told Jack about a few months ago – part of a job lot from some derelict house we looked at in Ullet Road. See the leaf-patterning on the gilt here, that's called lamb's tongue.'

Brenda peered at the frame, and looked round at Baines. 'This the sort of thing you write about?'

'Something like,' he said.

Jack had come in from the kitchen bearing a tray of bottles and squinting through his own cigarette smoke. He mixed gin and French for the girls, Scotch and soda for himself and Baines.

'It's a bit stuffy in here,' he announced, and Baines endured a secret pang of mortification that he'd been overheard explaining the gilt moulding to Brenda. The remark in fact proved quite innocent, as Jack strode across to the French windows and flung them wide. They moved over to the open doors and gazed out at the velvety black of the night, its enveloping softness now and then pierced by the distant rumble of a tram, or a drinker's voice raised in indecipherable protest. June had a few more nights left to decant. Baines shook out a Player's, lit it and blew smoke rings into the dark. He would gladly have stayed there, silently smoking and gazing, with nothing to interrupt his peace for – for the rest of his life. Save our skins and damn the Czechs.

'Here's how,' said Jack eventually, clinking his glass against Evie's.

He sauntered over to the piano at the far corner of the room, sat down and began playing snatches of different songs. Brenda and Evie collapsed onto the sofa, while Baines riffled through a disorderly pile of sheet music. Jack had been a pianist since his army days, and what his untutored playing lacked in finesse was amply redressed by its feeling. His taste generally dallied at the popular end of the musical spectrum, and tonight he was giving it full rein. He followed 'If You Were the Only Girl in the World' with 'That Old Feeling', and Evie, sensing a cue, joined him at the piano to sing 'I'll String Along With You'. Brenda, not to be outdone, got up and astounded Baines with a beautifully modulated rendering of 'Smoke Gets in Your Eyes', then she and Evie performed what was evidently a party-piece duet of 'Miss Otis Regrets', meeting one another's eyes fondly as they sang the lines,

And the moment before she died
She lifted up her lovely head and cried, madam . . .
Miss Otis regrets, she's unable to lunch today.

Baines, vulnerable to these maudlin tunes, was moved to applaud them. 'What lovely voices you have,' he said, blushing at his own sincerity.

'Oh yeah – bring a tear to a glass eye, that would,' laughed Brenda. 'We were both in Sister Gerard's choir at Holy Child. Remember, Evie?'

'I'll say,' said Evie, smiling. 'There's not a hymn in the book we haven't sung.'

'Those Catholic girls,' sighed Jack, rising from his seat and refilling their glasses. Evie took his place at the piano, and tried out a few uncertain chords of her own. Brenda, recognising the melody, began in her pleading contralto,

Faith of our Fathers, living still,
In spite of dungeon, fire and sword . . .

Jack raised his eyes heavenwards. 'I think we should leave them to it,' he said, backing away from the hymnal ardour as if from the concerted force of dungeon, fire and sword. Baines, born a Catholic, had years ago lost whatever faith he had inherited, though he still felt obscurely stirred by the folk memory of these ancient hymns. Jack, the Protestant among them, treated what he called Evie's 'popery' with steady bemusement.

While the girls continued singing, Baines sank onto the sofa and closed his eyes, humming along with 'Faith of Our Fathers'. Eventually, he said, 'How much do you know about photography?'

'Not a great deal,' Jack shrugged. 'I've got an old box camera that I've not used in ages. Why?'

Baines explained the new direction the Liverpool book might be taking. He had corresponded with Plover Books about the time-saving possibilities of switching from sketches to photographs, and they had been agreeable, with the proviso that expenses should be kept to a minimum. And, as usual, he had been putting off the moment when he would actually have to do something about it. For one thing, he enjoyed sketching, and the idea of abandoning it for the sake of mere convenience pained him: a photograph to him was something fixed and mechanical, whereas a sketch was fluid and individual. But he knew that if the project were ever to be completed it was a compromise he would have to make. 'There's a photography studio down on Slater Street,' said Jack. 'I think they deal mainly in portraits, but you might try them.'

Baines nodded, and sighed.

Jack looked at him. 'What's wrong?'

'I don't know. I just . . . wonder what I'm doing. If what we think is going to happen does happen, what's the point of writing about buildings that might not be here tomorrow?'

Jack considered. 'Well, they're still history, whether they survive or not – you're preserving a record of them. But I see why it might have a lowering effect.'

'Does it ever bother you that people seem to behave as if . . . nothing's happening? I mean, they take the tram, they buy their stockings and marmalade, they go to the pictures, and all the while a country not very far away is planning to . . . bomb us into oblivion.'

'It's not a happy thought,' agreed Jack, mildly. 'But what do you expect them to do? It's just human nature that people get on with things – and they'll still want stockings and marmalade even during a war.'

They were silent for a while. 'What are you going to do – I mean, if it comes to it?' said Jack.

'Enlist, I suppose. I haven't any reason not to.' He was aware as he said this that Jack did have a reason not to. He was four years older than Baines, and had served in France as a lance corporal during the last eighteen months of the Great War. He had been wounded at Amiens, though it was not an experience he talked of much, and Baines was cautious about asking him.

'Word of advice, Thomas – try to avoid the infantry,' said Jack.

The evening was winding down. Baines, slightly nauseous from all the cigarettes, appalled himself by lighting one more. There always seemed to be room for one more. Evie swayed over to him and flopped onto the sofa. Her eyes were blurred from the gin, and perhaps from the spiritual transport of the hymn singing. She dipped her head to his and said quietly, 'You wouldn't mind walking Brenda to the tram, would you?'

'No, that's fine,' he replied, used to performing small gallantries. Evie leaned over and hugged him fondly. As she did so Baines couldn't avoid glimpsing the lightly freckled skin that sloped down from her collarbone and disappeared at the V of her thin cotton dress. He looked away, and coughed unnecessarily; he brushed a speck of ash from his trouser leg.

'You're a lovely feller,' Evie said, laughing. Baines returned an embarrassed smile, and stood up. Her friendliness was almost too much to bear. He briefly imagined reaching out to touch her face, and just as quickly dismissed the idea. Brenda had collected her handbag and fixed him with a look of bright expectation.

'Tanqueray — like the gin,' said Jack, as he was letting them out. 'I mean the name of the photographer on Slater Street.'

'Thanks,' said Baines.

They had said their goodnights. Brenda, somewhat unsteady, shouldered up to Baines as they walked through the darkened streets and put her arm through his. He flinched, and Brenda felt it.

'Don't worry, I'm not gonna bite yer!' she laughed, lightly punching his arm. 'I think I might be a bit tipsy.'

'Sorry,' said Baines, and meant it: he didn't want to seem unfriendly. Indeed, he had rather come round to Brenda in the course of the evening, and felt that a woman who sang that sweetly could be forgiven an excess of boisterousness. It should have been the easiest thing in the world to turn his little flinch into a joke. But much as he wished it otherwise, he had no suavity in the company of women. Brenda was chatting on about a party she and some friends were throwing at their place — she lived in Aigburth Vale — and Baines realised he was being invited to attend.

'That's very kind of you,' he said. 'I'm not sure, though, with work and everything. I'm quite . . .' He let the thought peter out.

'Oh well,' she said lightly, 'I suppose the archaeology keeps you busy. Evie's got the address, anyway, if you change yer mind.'

A tram was trundling out of the gloom towards them. Baines turned to her, and extended his hand.

'It was nice to meet you, Brenda.'

She smiled at him, and put her hand in his. 'You're quite old-fashioned, aren't yer?'

Now it was his turn to smile. 'I sometimes think I was born old-fashioned.'

She nodded, and dropped a little curtsy in reply. 'Ta-ra, then,' she said, stepping onto the tram, and as she waved to him Baines felt suddenly wistful. His company this evening had been, as he thought, reliably unscintillating, and yet this young woman had liked him well enough to extend a friendly invitation — which he could quite easily have accepted. But he had become so used to declining such overtures that to behave otherwise would have required a complete sea change in his own fugitive instincts.

Rain had begun to pimple the pavement as he walked home. He sometimes felt the necessity of simply being himself an insupportable burden. Why was it that whenever the prospect of intimacy loomed he would always refuse? And why, having refused, would he then feel racked by regret? He knew what it was, knew it too well, and whenever the currents of memory tried to drag him under he fought wildly against them, for if he went down he might never come back. It was the silhouette of a woman on a balcony, glimpsed, then gone. He could not look that night in the eye. He would not.

2

The front walls of the Record Office on William Brown Street were fatly buttressed with sandbags, though inside the somnolent atmosphere of a library still prevailed. A clerk directed him to the relevant department, and after a long wait another assistant emerged bearing three slim quarto notebooks, which expelled a fine cloud of dust as they thunked onto the desk. Baines guessed that they had lain undisturbed for years, which surmise the assistant immediately confirmed. He settled himself at a corner desk, where melancholy sunshine was falling through the tall windows in slanting bands of brightness, and slowly began to scrutinise the venerable relics. The dark green boards of each book were stiff and bowed, their edges worn and blunted by the years; one of them was in a worse condition than its companions, its cover drastically bleached by sunlight and some of its pages loosened from the spine. But on examination they proved perfectly legible.

The musty, deadened scent of old paper rose to his nostrils. The journals began in 1860, when Peter Eames turned twenty-one, and stopped, abruptly, in 1869, four years before his death. The entries were fitful, and of varying lengths; sometimes whole weeks and months would elapse without comment, then, as if refreshed from the hiatus, they would start up again with an urgent new rhythm. Breaking up the text at irregular intervals would be a drawing, sometimes nothing more than a doodle, sometimes a precise little diagram or illustration, usually of an architectural nature. The compositional style indicated a fierce and possibly unstoppable energy, an impression amplified by the flowing, confident hand. If the emphatic upward strokes and elegant loops looked to have been the result of careful practice – there were inky hints of experiment in the early pages – they also betokened a very decisive cast of mind. Only in the third and last book did Baines notice a change: the handwriting in the late 1860s lost something of its flamboyance, became more compressed and lean, and the fluency of previous entries was now clogged with his amendments and crossings-out.

Yet just to hold these dowdy-looking books, to read in brown ink the marks that Eames's steel-nibbed pen had scored upon its pages, lent them a kind of reverence for Baines. This was the same hand, the same mind, that had gone against the grain of prevailing certitudes in Victorian architecture and conjured a set of designs that were both of their time and dramatically ahead of it. More than this, however, he hoped the journals would help prise open the enigma of Eames himself. Why did this talented young architect, who could have earned himself a fortune from designing commercial buildings, suddenly change tack and stake his career on the philanthropic but potentially ruinous enterprise of a free library? What had happened in the last years of his life that prompted him to break from his business partner and apparently abort the library scheme? And was it madness or despair that led to the tragic denouement of his self-destruction? Somewhere in these foxed and faded pages he felt sure that a key to the inner sanctum of Eames's life might be found. Returning to the first journal he carefully smoothed down the opening page and began to read.

3rd September 1860

Today I am one-&-twenty. Rode out to Ditton with Chiltern & sat sketching for an afternoon. Weather fine; a continuous armada of fleecy clouds sailing over the horizon – 'as lifelike as Mr Constable's', says Chiltern. His own talents as a draughtsman are of the first order – an excellent line, an accurate & steady hand – but unconscionably slow! In the hours he devoted to catching Ditton Mill, with all his shading, cross-hatching &c., I could have designed such an edifice for myself inside & out, & tell him so. He replies that we are sketching, not competing, & that I only betray my youthful ignorance of human capability – 'You would, without a moment's forethought, take command of the Channel Fleet if called upon.' Indeed I would, I replied, & nothing in my manner or address should betray the smallest doubt of my fitness for the office. He laughed, & agreed that it would be so, even as the Fleet were being knocked into atoms.

I fancy there is about me a bud of something more remarkable than the generality of mankind, but what it is I cannot yet discern. I have done nothing yet for immortality – two years of study in Cambridge, with no degree, & a few guineas earned from the sale of this or that drawing. The difficulty is settling to anything; my brain hums around like a bee flitting from flower to flower. Alas! – to *bee* is not to do.

In the evening Chiltern & later Dalby to Abercromby-sq. for dinner; Ma & Pa in very jolly spirits, & so were we all. Claret to drink. From Cassie & Georgy a gift of a beautiful slender fruit knife, to pare my apples as I sketch. From Will a book of Browning's poems (which he claims to have bought with his own money). After dinner songs at the piano, & convivial merriments.

Only Frank of all the family not present.

14th November 1860

A pleasingly mild & bright morning, so I thought I would walk down to the river. I continued north for three miles or more, marvelling at the immense warehouses & docks that have risen even in the last few years – when I was a boy only a paltry jumble of buildings broke up this shoreline. Ma says that she remembers the town as a seaside resort, with long lines of bathing machines ready to accommodate visitors, who would come hither from miles around to enjoy the briny waters. All gone – even the beach at Kirkdale is swallowed into the giant maw of Commerce. The golden age is never now. But why in Heaven's name should sea-bathing be thought a superior activity to the unloading of the world's cargoes at Prince's Dock? I would sooner look upon that tall forest of masts & spars, & take my constitution around the Goree Piazzas, than idle away an afternoon up to my knees in water. Liverpool is a changing place – has become a busy seat of trade & prosperity – & much the better for it.

27th November 1860

Stopped this morning at the fish market on James-street; prodigious clamour (& a more prodigious stink) rising up from the stalls, close-packed together & slippery with all the creatures of the sea. I stood there entranced by the scene until one of the stall-holders, a withered but bright-eyed crone, broke upon my reverie. Caught off guard I pointed at some cod, & enquired as to whether it was quite fresh. The woman looked sharply at me (I suppose I must have appeared an impertinent youth), & asserted that if her fish were any fresher they should answer that query themselves.

25th December 1860

Another Christmas without Frank. I pray to God that he keeps safe.

30th January 1861

Having patiently awaited messages from Providence that would
summon me to a vocation (or simply to assure himself some peace
& quiet at home) Pa has secured through a cousin a position for me
at Messrs Arbuthnot & Sandham, a company of Architects and Civil
Engineers on South Castle-street. I have begun as an apprentice
draughtsman, in which capacity I may look forward to preferment
of some kind 'after three years'. Three years! In the meantime it
seems I must apply myself to the most stultifying sort of hack-work,
getting up designs for warehouses, breweries & whatnot, that offer
in aspect not the faintest trace of beauty to the eye nor the least
particle of credit to the profession.

Sandham, by whose office I have been vouchsafed the favour of
a desk, is a deaf & somewhat querulous old cove, but benign withal.
His particular genius is for church-building, a demand which has
multiplied through the mighty influx of Irish Catholics since the
Famine. Droll stories circulate the office about his confusion in
regard to these commissions, such a number does he take up at once.
It is said that he has visited a church in the course of erection &
advised on its various faults to the clerk of works, who then re-
directs him to the right church, some distance along the same road.
Another time he has glimpsed a church through the window of a
cab & expressed his sincere admiration of it – only to be told that
it is his own!

25th February 1861

This morning old man Sandham called me into his rooms and set
about explaining a commission that would bring a 'considerable emolument' to the company & be of significant practical value to myself.
A gentleman, recently arrived with his family at a large manor house
near Blundell Sands, requires a portfolio of drawings of the house
in all its aspects, both within & without. The engagement entails that
two days a week I should betake myself to his estate & devote as many
hours as daylight allows to the task, the particulars of each drawing
to be settled between myself & the master of the house. The old man

paused, & I chose this moment to venture that I would be very amenable to such an engagement. He looked sternly over his spectacles at me & said, 'Your amenability, sir, is not at issue – I raise this as an item of business to be transacted, not as a topic for consultation with an underling.' This is not, alas, the first occasion on which I have been reminded of my 'place' (though my own estimation of its whereabouts would perhaps astound my elders & betters). In any event, one of the clerks later owned to me that such a commission is seldom entrusted to the care of a novice, & speaks well of the regard in which I am already held by Sandham &c. As I departed the office this evening I cut a brief caper on the street.

4th March 1861

'Beware of all enterprises that require new clothes,' wrote Mr Thoreau, but Ma said that it behoves a gentleman to dress in appropriate fashion when visiting the house of a knighted worthy. Thus I went down to Lockie's, on Bold-street, to order a suit of clothes. I was accompanied by Dalby, who took leave to offer his advice on my chosen attire. The Lord alone knows why – Dalby is barely qualified to judge as to the rightness of a button – but I suffered his assistance with a show of gaiety. I am to return for a fitting next week.

12th March 1861

I am greatly pleased at the tailor's handiwork, & strut up & down the upper room at Lockie's like a turkeycock. (Today I came without Dalby.) The green velvet frock coat with silk facings is exceedingly fine, & with the checked trousers & waistcoat I look the very picture of a swell. On returning home and exhibiting this finery I am greeted first with rippling ecstasies of laughter by Georgy & Cassie, & then with a look of painful bemusement by Pa, who likens me to 'a magsman on his way to Aintree races'. Only Ma is kind, & says I look decidedly the gentleman – though even she owned that the waistcoat might be deemed a little 'flash'.

Thursday, Twenty-first March, 1861

Of a sudden I feel emboldened & eager to get on. Our span upon this Earth is but 'the summer of a dormouse', as Byron says – there is no excuse for loafing.

Today I walked the few miles up to Blundell Sands & introduced myself at Torrington Hall. Its owner is one Sir William Rocksavage, a merchant who made his name (I am told) in the cotton trade. He lived in America for many years, amassed a fortune & a family (four daughters, two sons), then returned to this country some time ago. His manager, Mr Bowcher, conducted me around the estate, which comprises about three hundred acres & includes a lake, an orchard, summer house & stables. The Hall itself is Jacobean, with later additions, the plan E-shaped with four symmetrical bay windows at the ends of the four wings & two towers in the centre. The building is of red brick with stone dressings & ends in an orna-mental balustrade. It is quite austere & angular, commodious rather than luxurious – a house that one might admire but not love. I was surprised to learn that the master was absent, despite this being the day appointed for my engagement to begin. I am bidden to return tomorrow – such are the whims of the aristocracy. As I retraced my steps down the long drive, I passed a gardener of such ancient & weathered appearance I fancied he might be a relic of the Jacobean period himself.

Saturday, Twenty-third March, 1861

All yesterday spent at Torrington Hall. Had my first audience with Rocksavage, who neither explained his absence on Thursday nor deigned to make apology for it. He is a tall, silver-haired, severely handsome fellow, with a strong square chin on which he wears neatly trimmed whiskers. His eyes are his most distinctive feature, as watchful as a hawk's even while his expression remains a model of indifference. It is far from a genial countenance, seeming to warn that this man does not suffer fools gladly; one imagines he does not suffer friends much more willingly. 'Mr Sandham tells me he has sent one of his ablest draughtsmen,' he said, with a penetrating look. 'It appears he has also sent me one of his youngest.' In reply I expressed a hope that my age would not prevent my giving full satis-faction. He only nodded, & then, paying out his words as carefully as a usurer would his coin, showed me around the house & marked which rooms were to be my subjects.

The hall is two-storeyed, placed at right angles to front & back, & runs right across the building. Above it on the second floor, reached by a wondrously carved staircase, is the saloon, notable for an original plaster ceiling & a grand marble fireplace. Another huge fireplace, this one of stone, stands in the drawing room, itself dominated by a busy classical frieze. A long gallery, occupying the whole north wing, is hung with gilt-framed portraits – perhaps of Rocksavage's forebears. On the ground floor more Jacobean fireplaces in library & drawing room – whatever its owner may lack in warmth, the house will not want for a good blaze. Rocksavage has advised me to start with the summer house, built from a design (he informed me with lofty satisfaction) by Inigo Jones. I doubted the attribution, but knew better than to bandy words with Sir.

19th April 1861

Constant occupation has prevented me setting down a record of my progress at Torrington Hall. The drawings pour forth from my pen so prodigiously that even Sir looks taken aback: I have completed work on the summer house (inside & out), the chapel, & the house itself from south & east perspectives. They are – why should I cloak myself in the false apparel of modesty? – the subtlest & finest things I have ever done.

26th April 1861

A sudden squall drove me inside the Hall this morning, & as I was lounging in the kitchen (whither Mr Bowcher had directed me) a boy of about fourteen sidled in to stare at me. Shyly he asked 'wot I was doin' here' – the accent, I think, is from Yorkshire – & I showed him the drawing of an orchard wall I had recently completed. He looked from the drawing at me, & then back at the drawing, as if in wonder that such a facsimile could be the work of the fellow before him. Indeed, so round-eyed was his gaze – it had something of Will's intensity – I could not help myself from laughing, & the young shaver began to laugh too.

His name is Charley, the younger son of the family, & I confess I found him a good deal more agreeable than his sire. Our talk was interrupted some minutes later by a young lady, perhaps of nineteen or twenty, who scolded Charley for bothering 'the gentleman' & begged my pardon for this intrusion. I replied that her brother – for such I surmised was their relation – had improved the hour very pleasantly, & we talked for some while about the drawings. Her name is Emily, second daughter of Sir W^m, & presently she too was examining the case of sketches I laid out before her. While her attention was so rapt I made a study of her – a tall, very finely made girl, with a beautiful firmness of expression, a pale, scholarly brow, chestnut-coloured hair & eyes of a grey-green hue, the shape of the head decidedly architectural. I asked if she would do me the honour of sitting for a portrait – it did not seem a bold request – but she only blushed, & stuttered out some words of regret, & bade me good-day, taking young Charley with her.

Friday, Tenth May, 1861

Once more I espied the young lady today. She was walking up the drive when I hailed her from where I sat, sketching a line of poplars, & she obliged me by stopping to talk. I first of all made apology for my previous impudence in asking her to sit for me, & graciously did she accept it. I invited her to rest upon the little seat from which I had risen, while I, still holding my quarto sketchbook, sat on the grass verge some few steps behind her, so that she could not easily address me face to face. From this vantage I diverted her with conversation about her accomplishments – she likes to ride, she plays the piano 'but badly', reads French & Italian – & learned something of her personal history. She passed the early years of her life in America, returning to England & her father's native city of Hull when she was nine; he purchased this house two years ago, having wearied of the noise & tumult of Liverpool. Her older sister is married to a clergyman; the two younger ones are supervised by a governess. Her older brother is a scholar at Oxford, while Charley has lately returned to Harrow – 'which he hates, poor boy'. I said I was sorry indeed to be deprived of the young fellow's acquaintance, & she smiled sadly – I think he is the favourite of her siblings. I then delayed her further with idle talk of the weather, & she bore with me patiently, still unaware of my stratagem – for while we were conversing I had, with great stealth, been sketching, & with a flourish presented to her a drawing of her head & shoulders. Once again I begged her pardon for this liberty, but she was too absorbed in the contemplation of my handi-work to respond. Did it please her? Indeed it did, & she thanked me for it with such depth of feeling I was secretly astonished, for was this not a girl whose gilded circumstances might have spoilt her & blunted such niceties as gratitude – especially for a sketch dashed off in ten minutes? It made me think well of her, & as we parted I made my most courtly bow.

22nd May 1861

My mother, who used often to attend the theatre as a girl, at times recovers her predilection for a drama. Pa, on the contrary, has a mortal aversion to it, which in consequence put me under the obligation yesterday evening to accompany Ma to the Theatre Royal – a happy chance, for what transpired there I should have been greatly sorry to have missed. The play was *Macbeth*, which in its earliest scenes was admirably got up & well acted by Mr Trombley as the Thane & Mrs Jennings as his Lady – the audience seemed quite enraptured. But once the play entered into its metaphysical dimension I noticed their mood begin to change, for nothing in it held the smallest shiver of dread – the witches seemed merely a coven of ill-kempt drabs, the thunder & lightning too plainly the mechanical contrivances of workmen in the wings. From the stalls came ripples of laughter which – on the appearance of Banquo's rather substantial ghost – gathered into a roaring torrent of derision. The players, bewildered by this mutiny, looked uncertain as to how they should proceed. At that moment Mr Trombley walked to the front of the stage & with all the dignity at his command stared down the audience – which became quieter. He then took leave to address us in a tone of majestic disdain: 'I have visited this city of Liverpool for many years, have performed in most of its theatres, & have come to know well the proud character of its citizens. This evening, however, has unmasked that other face of the Liverpolitan people, for I see in the jeering mob before me' – & here his eyes flashed with fury – 'all the low, brutish, unprincipled instincts that once motivated your forefathers – so when you dare to condemn & abuse, have a care to remember that every brick of your fine city has been purchased with the blood of a Negro.' Here was boldness. The whole theatre, on an instant, was stunned into silence. I turned to Ma, who looked as if she might truly have seen a ghost – Banquo's or otherwise. Then, as Mr Trombley led his actors from the stage, a very pandemonium broke out, the shouts & catcalls rose up far louder than before, & one or two stout fellows sought to clamber upon the stage with a view to expressing their personal displeasure at this performance. A few minutes later police-men had entered the building & the audience, now a riotous assembly, were baying for the actor's blood. I quickly led Ma away, neither of us quite able to account for what we had seen – though we later agreed that in lieu of drama it may well have surpassed the Bard himself.

Thursday, Twenty-third May, 1861

The theatrical riot of Tuesday evening is reported in today's *Liverpool Mercury*. This *Macbeth* shall be seen no more at the Royal – 'untimely ripped' by the management after Mr Trombley's disobliging address to the Liverpolitan citizenry. I fancy the fellow was lucky to escape with his life, for this city is a powder-keg around the subject of slaving, and only a spark will rouse it to blazes. The report was much on my mind when I encountered Miss Rocksavage in the long gallery, & we fell to talking of the event. She recalled from her childhood in Georgia the slaves toiling in her father's cotton fields, & confessed she was troubled by the memory of those shackled souls. (I thought of Frank and what he might have seen in the West Indies.) But she had hopes that their wretched lot would presently be relieved by Mr Lincoln's fortitude – his refusal to accept the expansion of slavery or the right to secede of the Confederate States has fomented civil war. I privately wondered if her father harboured such sympathy for the cause, his own prosperity being so closely entwined with the South. Their embargo on cotton may prove calamitous for Lancashire mill owners. We thus talked half an hour or more, & for all the gravity of our theme I never felt the time more charmingly beguiled.

6th June 1861

Spoke with E.R. again today – we are now in the habit of talking to one another whenever I am at the Hall.

Friday, Fourteenth June, 1861

Walked today from Abercromby-sq. down to the docks. Such is the pace of building now that the whole city resembles a gigantic construction site. Old Liverpool seems to tumble in the blink of an eye. There is a name to be made as an architect, if only one is shrewd enough to seize the moment.

Yet I find myself preoccupied with Torrington Hall & the drawings, production of which has slowed for reasons I hardly dare admit even to myself. A commission that ought to have been finished in weeks (it nearly was!) has now extended into months; I continue to find pretexts for visiting the Hall, ostensibly to revise earlier drawings that I no longer deem satisfactory. Does Sir W^m suspect what lies behind my dragging? More importantly, does *she* suspect?

Tuesday, Eighteenth June, 1861

Set out very early this morning for Blundell Sands, my nerves in a queer flutter of anticipation. As I walked I imagined what dress she might wear today, & pictured in my mind's eye that delightful hesitancy of manner whenever a difficulty is posed – such modesty being quite out of proportion to her wit & good sense. With my step buoyant from these imaginings I entered the Hall (by the tradesmen's door – which I do not disdain) & asked one of the servants as to Miss Rocksavage's whereabouts. 'Gone,' she said – & my high spirits fell more precipitately than a stone dropped down a well. Gone?! To my confused enquiries came answer that the lady, & indeed the whole family, had removed to the Highlands for the summer (I remembered that hunting & shooting were among Sir's favoured pastimes). Mr Bowcher later handed me a letter, which for one rapturous moment I believed had been left for me by E.R., but on examination proved to be from her father's hand – a terse note advising of his absence & prospective return, by which date (he trusts) the drawings will be complete & my engagement at an end. But why no word of this from her? Perhaps I have deluded myself in fancying an intimacy where only friendliness existed – & yet my recollections of the hours we passed in conversation strongly argue that it had been she who sought me out as often as I did her. No word of unguarded affection ever passed between us, but I must be grievously mistaken if I did not discern the shadow of it across our intercourse. I write these few lines late at my desk, between long periods of sorrowful contemplation – the lamp almost out. Today I have thought only of Emily Rocksavage, & I longed – *longed* – that she too might have thought of me.

*

The journal broke off temporarily at this point, and Baines decided to leave Eames to his forlorn lucubrations. His throat was sore from inhaling the Victorian dust. Having returned the journals to the assistant at the desk, requesting that they be kept to hand – he would be back for them later in the week – he emerged into the afternoon sunshine, his head still astir with the hurrying tempo of the architect's prose. He didn't presume to understand Eames's character from these few pages, but he had caught glimmers, like sparks from a bonfire, of his energy and self-belief. He was struck, too, by intimations of the city's vaunting imperial pride. He had never heard the story of that Shakespearean actor, but he could readily believe the audience's outraged response to his denunciation, for slavery was still, eighty years later, a dangerous subject to raise among Liverpudlians.

He walked across William Brown Street and onto the plateau where St George's Hall stood. If the Pier Head was the heart of the city's romance, here was the purest expression of its majesty. Begrimed with nearly a hundred years of soot, it was nevertheless – to Baines's eyes – the greatest classical monument of the nineteenth century, and the most impressive work of architecture in the north of England. He had sketched it several times, yet never quite managed to capture its soaring, unimpeachable grandeur. Dickens had given readings here several times during the 1860s, and had called the Small Concert Room where the crowds flocked to hear him the 'most perfect hall in the world'. At the foot of the steps, equestrian bronzes of Queen Victoria and Prince Albert flanked the Cenotaph, whose unveiling Baines and Jack had attended some years before. It was a hauntingly simple horizontal block, suggestive of a tomb, with a bronze relief stretching along each side. The relief facing Lime Street depicted mourners in front of a military cemetery that receded into infinity. The other side pictured lines of soldiers on the march, barely individualised, destiny drawing them on. He gazed at it now, waiting for an epiphany – which of course refused to come.

He wished he had brought his sketchbook with him – he felt ready to have another crack at the place. He glanced at his wristwatch. The sultry July temperature was almost inviting him to settle in for the afternoon. But no, McQuarrie was right, urgency was required. He was going to break this maddening habit of procrastination if it killed him. What was the name again? He thought of gin. Tanqueray. Now he'd remembered it, so he had no excuse. He hopped onto a wheezing tram that carried him along Lime Street and into Renshaw Street. The sun was obliging shopkeepers to pull the awnings over their windows, and sweltering pedestrians loitered in the shade. He felt the city stretching out in the heat like a lazy old dog on a doorstep. It was about this time last year they had been bracing themselves for war; he could remember the same brooding atmosphere of anxiety, and beneath it the ill-disguised onset of despair. He alighted at the top of Bold Street and walked down to where Slater Street made a right angle. He patrolled its length without seeing the name – no shopfront appeared to advertise a photographer. It was unlike Jack to have got it wrong – and indeed he hadn't, for there, by a doorbell at the end of a Georgian terrace, he spotted a discreet brass plate: *R. Tanqueray Esq., Photography Studio*. He pushed open the door, setting off a tinkling bell, and entered a room that was empty but for a large canvas screen, a chaise longue and a tripod. Was this it?

'Hullo? Do please come up,' a muffled voice called from above. Baines crossed the room and ascended a staircase at the back. The provisional bareness of the ground floor could not have been in sharper contrast to its neighbour upstairs: framed photographs crowded out every inch of the walls right up to the cornices, most of them individual portraits – brides and soldiers staring hopefully into the lens – though here and there he spotted group photographs of football teams, begowned students, even Boy Scouts. There was no order to their arrangement, they seemed merely to have filled whatever space had become available. A chaotically untidy desk occupied most of the far wall, above which his eye was drawn to a large photograph, evidently a kind of centrepiece around which the motley jumble had congregated. Its sitter was a woman, arms folded across her chest with her face turned confidently, almost defiantly, to the camera. He studied her: the jawline was strong, the cheekbones too, and the glinting obsidian eyes carried the suggestion of a challenge. It looked like a face with character, though Baines wasn't sure if that character would be much to his liking.

A door in the corner swung open and from it emerged a man wiping his hands on an old cloth. His face lit up pleasantly as he caught sight of Baines. 'Hullo there,' he said, striding forward and raising his hand in a half-salute. 'I'm Richard Tanqueray. Sorry, I'd offer you my hand but it's soaked in emulsion – just been stumbling around the darkroom.' Baines introduced himself. 'I haven't made an appointment –'

'Oh, don't worry about that,' said Richard airily. 'We're not overloaded with work at the moment. Though I dare say that'll change once this war starts – soldiers coming in with their sweethearts, and what have you.

Awful to say it, I know, but photographers do a roaring trade when there's a chance people might be parting for good.'

He was about forty, stocky in an athletic way, and seemed to squint as his gaze focused. His neat, toffee-coloured hair fell over his brow, framing a smooth-cheeked, well-fed face of a kind Baines always associated with ex-public schoolboys. He wore about him an air of suppressed jollity, as if in permanent expectation of a joke that might crack his sides.

The bleak echo of 'parting for good' still hung between them, and Richard suddenly looked embarrassed.

'Good heavens, I'm sorry – you're not army, are you?'

Baines smiled. 'No. Not yet, anyway. Nor have I come to have my portrait taken.'

'Phew! Thought I'd put my foot in it there. So what can I . . . ?'

Baines outlined his brief, while Richard nodded with the benign encouragement of a teacher listening to a bright pupil, interrupting with an occasional pertinent question. As he did so, Baines wondered at this new decisiveness. Perhaps something in the air was motivating him.

Richard was proving quite amenable to the idea. 'In a way it's surprising that nobody's done it before – I mean, made a proper photographic record of the city. I suppose in its heyday it must have been quite a place.'

'As grand as any port in Europe,' Baines agreed. 'In the late eighteenth century they compared it to Venice.'

'Hmm. It's changed a bit since then.'

'I should say so. I've just been doing some research at the library,' said Baines. 'Have you by any chance heard of Peter Eames?'

'Afraid not. Ought I to have done?'

'No. He was an architect, little known, worked in Liverpool during the 1860s. He designed Janus House on Temple Street.'

'Ah, now that I do know. One of my favourite buildings – he did that?'

Baines nodded, feeling an almost proprietary pleasure in Eames since his recent investigation of the journals, entombed for years until he had them hauled from the vaults that afternoon. But it saddened him to think of the many people, like Richard, who admired Janus House without having the faintest notion of its creator. He thought of Ruskin's observation: 'In no art is there closer connection between our delight in the work, and our admiration of the workman's mind, than in architecture, and yet we rarely ask for a builder's name.'

'Well, consider me at your service,' said Richard, glancing at his watch. 'How about we shake on it over a drink? I might as well close up for the day – you're the only soul that's been in this afternoon.'

They walked down the stairs and through the echoing ground-floor room. Richard gestured at its spartan furnishings with an air of apology. 'We've been thinking of setting up a little gallery – at the moment it's used for portraits.'

It was the second time he'd used 'we' rather than 'I'. Baines assumed there was a partner in the background, or else a band of assistants who helped out during busier times. He waited while Richard locked up, a routine he had evidently performed too often to have remained quite careful: Baines noticed that while his new associate chatted on he was about to leave one of the smaller keys still inserted in its hole at the base of the door. He plucked it out and handed it to its owner, who mimicked a wince of anguish, like a silent comedian who'd just tripped the alarm.

'Oh, Tanqueray, you bloody fool,' he said, in cheerful self-rebuke. 'Not the first time I've done that – the place got burgled too!' It seemed that he was determined to find something hilarious even in this unhappy memory.

They sat drinking Higsons in the snug of a dusty old pub on Seel Street. Richard smoked a cigar, its roasted, acrid stench poisoning the air quite agreeably. He became even more expansive as he rehearsed a little of his own history. His cultivated voice, naturally amplified by his army back-ground, caused one or two drinkers at the bar to turn and stare. He had been born in London to a military family, and had served as a captain on the Western Front, catching the worst of it at Ypres.

'That was a pretty gruesome scrap,' he said thoughtfully, and then, sensing the inadequacy of the words, shrugged and continued with his story. His father, a colonel who had originally served in India, had been a keen amateur photographer and had passed on the enthusiasm to his son; once he had been honourably discharged from the army, Richard had come to Liverpool and set up his studio.

'Why here?' asked Baines.

'We used to come up here on leave – officers would stay at the Adelphi – and I suppose I just became fond of the place. The people are an odd mixture, they have a sort of aggressive friendliness which I rather like. But it's also something about the quality of the light, I noticed it when I started taking photographs – it's a kind of luminous distance you don't get anywhere else but here. So it suits us pretty well.'

'Us?'

'Ah, I should have said – Bella, my wife. She started out as a painter but lately seems to prefer working with me. And I'm afraid to say she's a better photographer than I am – actually, she's better at everything than I am.' He chuckled at his uxorious remark, and seemed to fall into a reverie. Baines leaned into the silence and drained his pint.

Richard shook off his little trance and turned to Baines. 'I'm so sorry, here I am boring on about my life while you're there dying of thirst. Have another?'

Baines raised his empty glass and smiled in assent. He studied Richard as he waited to be served at the bar. They were not obvious companions, he thought, Richard being a hearty, outgoing, Home Counties type, with a military boom in his voice that he used a little too freely. And yet Baines was surprised to feel something he hadn't in a long time, possibly since meeting Jack back in the old days: it was the curious sensation of instantly liking a man. He warmed to his modesty, his unbullying camaraderie and genial absent-mindedness; he was touched, too, by this southerner's affection for a northern city, so heartfelt that he had actually made his home here. Baines would never have contemplated the prospect of living in London, or the Home Counties, or indeed anywhere other than the place he'd been born. It didn't even seem to him a question of choice – he simply couldn't imagine surviving anywhere but Liverpool. Everything he needed was here, or at least everything he thought he needed.

Richard, resettled at their table, was taking great gulps of his pint, which presently he set down.

'One thing strikes me about your photographic project – if done, then "'twere well it were done quickly", if you know what I mean.'

'Yes, I've left it late,' said Baines. 'I've been rather paralysed by a habit of – putting things off. With certain events on the horizon . . .'

He let the sentence tail off, as though in echo of his inability to follow anything through. Richard nodded slowly, understanding.

'Well then,' he said, 'I think that we could get started very soon. There are one or two things I need to tidy up first, but if all goes well, what d'you say, this weekend?'

Baines, adrift for too long, felt the wind starting to pick up and thump his sails. He hadn't written anything for months, but had explained that away as a consequence of distraction – the news from Europe had knocked him off his stride. Now he thought of a line he had read in Keats's letters: 'if I had the teeth of pearl and the breath of lillies I should call it languor – but as I am, I must call it Laziness.' Yes, perhaps that was more truthfully his affliction, Laziness. With a capital L. He would try one more delaying tactic.

'You do realise the publishers won't pay much?'

Richard smiled. 'If you don't disdain their fees I don't see why I should. Here's to it.' He raised his glass in an imitation of priestly solemnity, and Baines knew now that he had no excuses.

3

Baines climbed gingerly up the last steps and emerged onto the leads, with Richard, more eager-footed, following close behind. They were on the roof of Martins Bank, whose ten storeys towered over the surrounding cluster of buildings. Seagulls wheeled and shrieked overhead, as though alarmed by this unwonted human presence at an elevation they had assumed exclusively their own. At street level the temperature had been mild; up here an importunate wind whipped at their shirts and lifted their hair in comical directions. They surveyed the panorama laid out before them. To the west they could see the Pier Head, the docks, and beyond them the wide curve of the river, the colour of stewed tea. To the east, they looked immediately on to the roof of the town hall, originally an exchange where merchants had transacted business in an open courtyard because the interior was thought too gloomy.

'Marvellous view!' shouted Richard, joining Baines as he leaned over the parapet. Down below the trams and buses seemed to be floating up and down Dale Street, as dainty as tin models, while pedestrians had shrunk to insects beetling across a tablecloth. Richard, briskly methodical, already had his Leica to his eye and was taking shots over the jagged skyline. Baines began to jot down a few notes, then withdrew to a sheltered corner where the wind could no longer riffle his pages. Richard eventually joined him.

'How did you know about this little eyrie?'

'Through a friend of the family. My father was in banking, and there are a few old gents I can still ask a favour from.' He offered Richard a cigarette, and they sat smoking for a while in companionable silence.

'Looks like someone's prepared for the worst,' said Richard, pointing at a pair of enormous searchlights squatting in readiness. 'I suppose it'll be the anti-aircraft guns next.'

Baines nodded, and looked up at the nonchalant blue vacancy of the August sky. It still seemed inconceivable to him that this would be the vantage from which destruction rained. But everyone knew that war would be fought in the air. It had already happened in Spain; now it would happen here.

Richard was peering over at the town hall again.

'The old girl must be Britannia,' he said, nodding at the helmeted stone figure holding a spear and seated astride the dome.

'Possibly – though some reckon it's Minerva, the goddess of handicrafts. Or, if you read Virgil, the goddess of war.'

'That would be more helpful, in present circumstances,' said Richard, drily.

'Well, the building needs a protector – it's had quite an unfortunate history. The town hall they built here in 1673 collapsed seventy years later. Then John Wood replaced it in the 1750s and that one was gutted by fire in 1795. They might have saved it, too, but a winter frost had frozen the water pipes – they just had to watch it burn.'

'Sounds like it's cursed.'

Baines, warming to his tutorial mood, turned back to the Pier Head and pointed out the spire of St Nicholas's, another site of disaster in 1810.

'The church tower was known to be in need of repairs, but the structure was judged safe enough to stand the ringing of bells. One morning a procession of kids from a charity school came in for morning service – the bell ringers had just started when the whole tower collapsed and fell into the nave. Twenty-three children were killed outright, and a handful of adults with them.'

'Good grief,' Richard muttered. 'What a . . . that's horrifying.'

Baines was silent, worried that his zeal for history might have been mistaken for mere ghoulishness. As a boy he would wander for hours through cemeteries, examining the lichen-covered gravestones and their carved inscriptions. *Dearly Beloved . . . Departed this Life . . . Taken to Heaven . . .* Some of the stones had been worn smooth by time, leaving no trace of the names and dates of the departed. He became obsessed with the idea that, once the name on a grave had faded to nothing, the dead person would never be remembered again. Only gradually did his morbid fascination with what was disappearing transfer itself from churchyards and cemeteries to the larger concerns of history and architecture. Now, instead of gravestones, he looked at buildings for the signs of age upon fading traceries, for the dilapidation of pediment and pilaster, for the ceaseless weathering of masonry. He sometimes wondered if he could only love a thing once its doom was certain.

He stole a sidelong look at Richard, who had also fallen silent. His pensive frown was a sufficiently uncommon sight for Baines to assume that something was troubling him. He waited, and eventually Richard cleared his throat to speak.

'I recently met up with an old friend from army days, he's working for Civil Defence now. We talked about what's going to happen, of course, and the measures they had in mind. He said that Liverpool would take a heavy battering, what with the docks, its strategic importance for the Atlantic, and so on. The bombing of populated areas is also inevitable, and civilian casualties are likely to be ... severe. Well, briefly, this friend is involved in mobilising the Air Raid Precautions Services to work in tandem with the fire brigade and the ambulance crews. They need rescue workers, and so to do my bit ...'

'You've volunteered.'

Richard nodded slowly. 'But here's the thing. He also said that for rescue operations they were planning to recruit structural engineers, architects and the like – people who understand about buildings. Those collapses you were describing just then reminded me. You're exactly the kind of chap they're after.'

Baines paused. This was not the way he had envisaged contributing to the war effort. 'I had thought of joining up. Maybe the infantry.'

'Why would you do that?' asked Richard.

He had pondered this too often not to have an answer ready. 'Mostly out of guilt. Unlike you, I've never had to face danger before, I've never known what it is to feel my life might end at any moment. It's that thing Johnson says to Boswell, "Every man thinks meanly of himself for not having been a soldier."'

Richard looked at him, and said gravely, 'Tom, listen to me. For one thing, they'll probably consider you too old to enlist. For another, if it's danger you want – or think you want – then rescue work will provide more than you can bear. Maybe more than any of us can.'

'It's the waiting I can't stand. I'd rather see the worst in front of me than have to ... imagine it.'

'We won't have much longer to wait, according to the papers. Look, allow me at least to give my friend your name. He's a good egg, Jimmy Andrews – I've known him twenty years or more. He'll explain what's required far better than I can.'

Baines was surprised at the idea of being too old for military service. In the accelerating mood of emergency he had assumed that nothing short of blindness would disqualify someone from joining up. He had not relished the prospect, but nor had he seriously considered the possibility of evading it. That the decision might now be taken out of his hands was obscurely disappointing, like waiting with your pads on to go out to bat and then finding your captain had suddenly chosen to declare. It was not that you wanted to face that whippy fast bowler, merely that you had braced your-self to do so.

He had drawn up a rough plan, dividing a map of the city centre into a diamond shape, then marking the major buildings in each quadrant that were to be photographed. The first quadrant, bounded by Chapel Street to the north and Canning Place to the south, Strand Street and North John Street to the east and west, contained such an abundance of Victorian architecture that he feared Richard might feel rather overburdened. When he mentioned this, however, Richard shrugged in his tolerant way and said, 'My father used to say that photographers should be like artillerymen. Aim properly, shoot quick and scram. The advice seems to have worked for me so far.'

Baines admired this straightforwardness in him; it was so different from his own hesitant weighing up of pros and cons. Richard never seemed to waver about anything; once he saw his course of action he simply went ahead and did it. If he was prey to the occasional absent-minded lapse ('oh drat!') he would instantly correct it and move on. Baines assumed that this decisive cast of mind had been forged in the crucible of the trenches; to have been a captain as Richard was, to have had that many young recruits relying upon him every day to keep them alive, in the kind of hell where he had barely learned to keep himself alive – that would surely have been the making, or breaking, of a man. The responsibility of it suddenly reared up before him – vicarious, horrific – and not for the first time he thanked his stars that he had been born too late ever to have known it.

Having finished with the town hall, Baines conducted Richard south along Castle Street, the spine of the business district. He pointed out for attention, amid other looming temples of commerce, C.R. Cockerell's massive, imperious Bank of England, the Adelphi Bank with its copper domes and finials, now oxidised to green, the Renaissance fripperies of Victoria Chambers and Leyland & Bullin's Bank. The confidence and scale of these buildings spoke so clearly of a different age – an age of rapacious mercantile energy. They had been conceived and constructed by men who had thoroughly grasped the power of money and decided that there was no need whatsoever to build small. At the teeming junc-tion of St George's Crescent and Lord Street, Richard conscientiously waited for the buses and trams to pass before he could get a shot of the Victoria Monument. Beneath it a man was emerging up the steps and past the railings. With a half-smile Richard turned to Baines.

'I wonder whose idea it was to position a statue of our dear old Queen over a public lavatory.'

'Only in Liverpool,' said Baines, who happened to know that this was formerly the site of a church, and before that the thirteenth-century castle for which the street was named. Everywhere he looked he sensed the ghosts of time past, their presence insistently alive to him still. The transient landscape of the city, its inexorable susceptibility to change, both thrilled and depressed him.

As they proceeded down South Castle Street, he glanced in the window of a clockmaker's, Barnard Levy, 'Office, Ship and House Clocks in variety'. A handwritten notice beneath apologetically announced the shop's imminent closure. He stopped, sidled into the doorway's embrasure and peered at the owner's name discreetly etched onto the glass, and below it the proud pendant: Est. 1851. It would not make its centenary. 'How wags the time ...' Baines placed his hand on the rust-coloured brick of the wall, warmed by the afternoon sun, and wondered how soon this establishment would be forgotten, its brief candle snuffed out. At moments like this, when he found himself forlorn at the disappearance of a place before it had actually gone, he thought he might be suffering from a kind of pre-emptive nostalgia. It seemed he was better suited to elegy than to history.

'Anything the matter?' asked Richard.

Baines shook his head. 'No, it's nothing important. Just do me a favour, would you – take a photograph of this shopfront?'

Without further question, Richard took a step back, lined up the shot and clicked.

They walked on into Canning Place, where John Foster's colossal Customs House dominated the view. It seemed to have been there for ever, but Baines knew that, as always, it had actually supplanted something else – in this case an enclosed commercial wet dock, the first of its kind in the world.

'There's one more place we should do,' said Baines, 'and then we'll call it a day.' Round the corner stood John Cunningham's astonishing Sailors' Home, a neo-Jacobean fantasy started in 1846 as a philanthropic venture to save impoverished seamen from grog shops and grasping landlords. It had been derelict for some years, but Baines had finagled a key from the nightwatchman to one of the basement entrances. Once inside they navigated a series of echoing stone corridors that led to the kitchens, the air still and frowsy with a hundred years of institutional cooking. It was difficult to resist a sense of trespass as they climbed a winding staircase to the first floor, where a long glazed court stood enclosed by galleries on five storeys, with doors ranged along each level.

Baines turned to Richard. 'Impressive, don't you think?'

'Yes – though it does have the look of, well, a prison.'

'I see what you mean, though the architect actually modelled it on a ship's quarters – they're meant to look like cabins, not cells. It was his way of making the sailors feel at home after their years at sea. And I can't imagine there's a jail in the land that features this sort of thing,' he added, tapping the elaborate cast-iron mouldings of dolphins and mermaids wrought upon the galleries' columns and balustrades.

'Is this place quite safe?' asked Richard, looking up towards the vaulted glass roof.

'As far as I know.'

'Good, because a shot from up there is what we need.' He pointed to the top tier, and headed off to clatter up the iron stairwell. As his steps grew more distant Baines, out of habit, made a quick sketch of a wrought-iron sea nymph, her tail curled suggestively around the diagonal struts; he marvelled at the mind that had conceived this delightful frivolity, and at the hand that had rendered it so intricately. He was still absorbed in it when he was jolted by a call from above, and looked up to see Richard seated vertiginously on a supporting cross-beam that ran along the uppermost storey.

'Ahoy there! Looking fine from the crow's nest, cap'n!' he boomed.

Baines, far from being amused, was riveted to the spot in horror. His first thought – how the hell had he managed to climb up there? – was quickly displaced by a panicky hollowness in his stomach, that awful warning bell of nausea.

Richard, the camera slung around his neck, didn't appear to notice how precariously he was perched; from this distance he looked as nonchalant as a boy in a tree house, his legs swinging freely into the void. Baines felt an instinct to call out and warn him of the danger, but he checked himself for fear of startling his friend and thus precipitating the very thing he wished to avoid. And what would he shout in any case? 'Come down from there' sounded farcically old-maidish, even if it expressed his very particular urgency. As Richard continued to edge around the beam, his progress faintly punctuated by the clicks of the shutter, Baines looked away, unable to hold out against the pressure of memory – that falling figure, arms uselessly grabbing at air while the legs seemed to be flailing away on an invisible bicycle. Down, down it flew. He had kept that image locked away in the vault of his consciousness for years, and suddenly there it was, bursting unbidden into his mind's eye. He kept his head down, and muttered to himself, 'For Christ's sake, don't . . .'

After an eternity, or perhaps a few minutes, he heard footsteps clanking down the stairs, and then Richard was beside him, blithely reporting on the view from the crow's nest.

'The light was falling just so when I –'

'It wasn't the light falling I was worried about,' said Baines quietly.

Richard heard something in his tone. 'Erm, are you all right?'

'No, I'm not. I was just reminded of something, from years ago . . .' He stopped, unwilling to retrieve it. 'What the hell were you playing at?'

'Tom,' Richard laughed, 'I didn't know you cared.'

'I don't. It was just a bloody long way down, that's all. If you want to join a trapeze act, that's fine, but I'm not particularly keen to watch someone break their neck.' In his distraction his voice had become hard and querulous, a tone that was as unpleasant to him as it was unfamiliar. There was silence between them. Richard, chastened, was fiddling abstractedly with his camera lens, and Baines, watching him, felt too relieved to stay sullen.

He sighed with schoolmasterly forbearance. 'You stupid mutt. Let's go and get a drink.'

They turned back through the court's heavy swinging doors and down again into the basement kitchens, leaving the nautical ghosts upstairs to wait out a fresh course of eventless days.

The last Sunday of August was May's sixtieth birthday, and George had organised a gathering of friends and neighbours in the evening to celebrate. The Elms, the house they had lived in since they were married, was a stuccoed Victorian villa set back on a leafy hill road east of Sefton Park. Baines had grown up here and still dropped by, usually on a Saturday afternoon, to have tea and listen to the football results on the radio while George did the pools. Or else he would sit in the living room and listen to May unburden the week's gossip, a digest which might focus on her recent bridge evening or the failing health of a priest whose dreariness Baines could recall even from his own distant years as a churchgoer. Both George and May were severely Catholic, but unlike her mild-mannered husband May combined religious devotion with a brand of indignant socialism – she loathed Chamberlain – which Baines supposed an oddity among the well-heeled parishioners of Mossley Hill. How she squared this outlook with marrying into money and keeping a house with servants had never been clear to him, but he felt it would be the purest impudence on his part to engage her in a debate on political inconsistency.

Baines had brought Jack along, partly for the company and partly because he knew that George and May were fond of him; indeed, they appeared to regard Jack as his saviour from a life of pathetic loneliness. It was baffling enough to them that their adopted son had remained unmarried; that he might not have any friends at all was a misfortune too dismal to countenance, and they would greet Jack with a warmth that contained a quiet but plaintive note of gratitude. This amused Baines, and saddened him, for he realised that his tendency to solitude, however naturally it came to him, would always be a source of anxiety to them.

'Hullo, you two!' said May, almost singing her welcome in the hall. She flung her arms around Baines, who smelt on her a florid new perfume that made him want to sneeze.

'Happy birthday, May,' said Jack, adding with a gallant twinkle, 'Looking quite radiant, if I may say.'

'Ooh, listen to this one,' she laughed, 'trying to charm the old dear! Is he like this with all the girls?'

'No, only with you,' said Baines, confused between teasing and flattering her. May's bun-shaped face glowed with delight. Plucking glasses of dry sherry from a salver, she conducted them through the house into the garden, where people were milling about in small clusters. George, dapper in a checked jacket with a dark knitted tie – it was his uniform – came over and shook hands with them. He was a neat, wiry man, not much taller than his wife, and wore about him a shy, slightly defeated air. He looked at the puny glasses of sherry in their hands.

'I bet you lads would rather be drinking beer. I'll ask Millie to fetch you some from the cellar.'

'Sherry is fine, George,' said Jack, but George was already consulting one of the housemaids. They took in the rest of the greying crowd, several of whom Baines recognised from his Mass-going days.

'I suddenly feel quite youthful,' Jack whispered to Baines.

'Beer's what we need,' he replied, throwing back his sherry very quickly.

The garden, somewhat parched by the August heat, was one of the most beautiful Baines had ever known. He loved its nooks and bowers, the elm trees that thronged protectively around them, the little strip of bald turf where George had taught him how to play a forward defensive and bowled slow off breaks to him for hours on end. He loved the dip in the lawn, and the way it drowsily sloped down towards the fence; he had even come to love the rattle and rumble of the trains below, heading into and out of Mossley Hill station. It was a place inseparable from his child-hood, a refuge of long, solitary afternoons passed in moping, or in his endless drawings, and completely guarded from the smallest obligation to others.

'What do you reckon, Tom?' George was saying, and Baines broke the surface of his reverie to find a circle of politely expectant faces turned upon him. His attention had just been caught by a fallen apple at his foot, its skin showing brown discoloration where wasps had ravaged it.

'Sorry, I was miles away –'

Jack, shooting Baines a wry look, stepped in to help. 'These gents were discussing what sort of chance we stand in an air raid. Walter, I should add,' he nodded at a stout, suety-faced man, 'doesn't even think the Luftwaffe will be able to make it over the Pennines.'

Baines was temporarily at a loss – he had only tuned out for a couple of minutes, it seemed, and now he was suddenly obliged to catch a low one at slip.

'I'm afraid the Luftwaffe are only too capable of reaching here. We know that much from what they did in Spain.'

Walter wrinkled his nose in silent demur and pressed on: 'People shouldn't be worried by the bombing of Spain. For one thing, those peasant houses would have been very poorly constructed. Our bricks and mortar will stand up to that pounding. I'm in the building trade, so I should know.'

Baines, inwardly wincing at the man's self-satisfaction, remembered something Richard had told him. 'I hope you're right, though an army friend of mine says that a direct hit from a 500-pound high-explosive bomb will probably destroy any building you care to mention.'

They were briefly silent. Then another friend of George's, a bespec-tacled fellow named Stan, piped up: 'I dunno about bombs, but if these blackouts get any worse someone's gonna cop it under the wheels of a tram. I was crossing Lime Street the other night and out of nowhere this tramcar suddenly bears down on me – no lights, nothun.'

That the absence of lights was precisely what constituted a blackout didn't seem to have occurred to him. Walter, eager to stoke the fires of grievance, now said, 'What I can't understand is all this practice with the bloody air-raid sirens. I mean, they could just warn us in advance without having to tear us from our beds with that racket.'

Jack chuckled at this. 'You know, I don't think the Germans will "warn us in advance" about their bombing schedule. They'll want the element of surprise.'

Walter and Stan both heard the thin note of flippancy and looked at Jack with pursed disfavour. Baines half hoped that they might challenge him, and then find themselves outmanoeuvred when Jack played the ace, the unanswerable ace, of his own war service. But at that moment May intruded defusingly into their midst, eager to share some happiness with George.

'Look what Tom's given me for my birthday!' she cried to her husband. It was an antique garnet brooch Baines had seen in an old-fashioned jeweller's window on Lord Street; he had gone in to take a closer look at it and been wavering as to its suitability when he noticed the handwritten tag within the box's velvet lining – the maker's name, and the date, 1879. It was sixty years old, like May, though he decided to withhold this pleasing coincidence from her for the present lest she combusted with the excitement. Holding the trinket against her blouse May looked around at her bemused admirers. 'Beautiful, isn't it? Gay as a wasp in a window.' Baines and George had heard this vivid locution before, but Jack couldn't suppress a startled bark of laughter.

'That's a good one, May,' he said, tickled by the line. Walter and Stan had both slunk off in search of an audience more congenial to their peevishness. Baines felt relieved that a useless argument had been sidestepped, and doubly so once Millie approached them with a tray of Higsons.

'Must have cost you a fortune,' May continued, still marvelling at her gift. Baines merely smiled, unwilling to contradict what he deemed close enough to the truth. In the end, he thought, it was better to give than to receive: the feeling of beneficence was more satisfying than that of gratitude.

'I hope I didn't offend your guests just then,' said Jack to George, who shook his head.

'Don't worry, they just like a good moan. I think they're on edge – well, we all are. Old fellers like us don't take easily to change.'

May sighed sympathetically. 'Everyone's anxious, preparing for the evacuations. Dora's going to send her two young ones off to Wales.' Dora was their housekeeper, a large, jolly woman who'd been with the family for years.

George said, 'They offered to build us a shelter in the garden, but we thought the cellar would do for us.'

'Well, I'll be patrolling round here soon with the ARP, so if you wouldn't mind me dropping by . . .' Jack said, raising his beer.

'Any time you're thirsty,' said May, squeezing his arm. She turned to Baines. 'Have they signed you up yet, love?'

He shook his head. 'I'm going to a Civil Defence recruitment at the Municipal Buildings the week after next. I'll find out then.'

The evening drifted on. The shadows of the trees were beginning to darken across the lawn, and Baines watched as a pair of swallows chased one another through the tangle of branches. He and Jack sat on the edge of the garden overlooking the drop to the railway line.

'One more cigarette, and then I'm off,' said Jack.

'I'll join you, I just need to collect something first.'

He stood up, brushed the grass from his trousers and headed towards the house. There were still plenty of guests about, reluctant to draw a veil over the warm, late-summer evening. He spotted Walter in the thick of another heated debate in the living room, so quickly diverted his course round the side of the house and entered via the kitchen. He gained the wide staircase, then stopped to look at the two rows of bookshelves holding George's collection of Wisdens, the earliest dating from the 1890s, most of them still uniformed in their custard-yellow jackets. The hours he had spent poring over them!

He reached the end of the landing and entered his old bedroom, its squared-off neatness and smell of beeswax announcing its faithful upkeep, as if waiting for his return. On the old mahogany chest of drawers stood two framed photographs, the larger one of himself as a ten-year-old boy, jockeyishly small, mounted on a horse, with George – his trainer – holding the reins and gazing off into the middle distance. The smaller one was a sepia portrait of a man standing proprietorially behind a seated woman, their faces slightly stiff and anxious-looking from the long exposure times of nineteenth-century photography. Baines's eye was always drawn to the same details, the woman's sweet-sad expression, and beautiful pale hands folded on her lap; then the glint of the man's watch chain across his waistcoat, and the thick beard worn (it seemed to him) in an attempt at disguise. Two remote Victorian strangers: his mother, his father. He picked it up and stared at them, hoping to detect some trace of himself in a facial contour, in the glimmer of an eye. But they remained to him stubbornly unclaimable.

He heard the door creak behind him, and there was May, her features crinkled in that characteristic smile of sympathy, with something else mingled in there. Fear, perhaps. She scuttled, almost shyly, into the room, and saw the photograph still in his hands. The ghost of his parents, seldom discussed in all their years together, now stood like an awkward secret between them. Baines didn't know what he was going to say until the words were out of his mouth.

'What was she like, May?'

Startled by the question, May hesitated a moment, then recovered her poise. 'Beautiful,' she said, '. . . you can tell. She – she would have been very proud of you.' Would she? Baines tried to see beyond the formula of the sentiment, wondering in what her maternal pride might have consisted. She would hardly have been proud of his achievements, because he hadn't done anything. He supposed May had used the phrase as another way of saying *she would have loved you*. He wanted to believe it, but, doubting Thomas that he was, the unspoken subjunctive *if she were alive* would always block his way. If she were alive. But she had died, before he had known what her love felt like, and before she had known him as anything other than an infant. Would she have loved him as a fifteen-year-old – as a thirty-six-year-old? He looked again at the face on the other side of the glass, and had the queer feeling that he, not she, was the one marooned, helpless.

'You can have that, if you'd like,' May said gently, indicating the photograph.

Baines shook his head. 'No. Thanks. I like the thought of it being here – sort of watching over the room.' He decided that saying anything more would only confuse or upset her, so he adopted a lighter tone. 'I was actually looking for that old box of junk I used to keep under my bed.'

'In the wardrobe. The key's there.' Mary made to leave, then stopped. 'Tom . . .' He waited, sensing their reticence with one another as a bond, and a burden. 'I do love that brooch you gave me.'

Baines smiled. 'I'm glad – really glad.'

He returned to the garden to find Jack flirting pleasantly with Millie. His beer glass was full once more, and he was carving the air with his cigarette in a knowing imitation of George Sanders. He winked over her shoulder as Baines approached.

'Find what you wanted?'

In answer Baines held up an old chrome-plated torch, a trusty companion of his boyhood when he used to pretend to be a secret agent and go sneaking through other people's gardens in the dark.

'Millie here's been telling me she's just signed up for the women's auxiliary ambulance corps.'

The girl looked no more than eighteen years old. Baines felt a sudden dismay at what she might have to endure. 'That's brave of you, Millie. I know George and May would be awfully sorry to see you go.'

She blushed, disarmingly. 'Well, we've all got to do our bit,' she said. There was something rehearsed about the line, but her guileless schoolgirl alto lent it charm.

'I can't think of anything nicer than having you in an ambulance,' said

Jack. Millie giggled uncertainly, performed a little bob and excused herself. Baines shook his head and sighed.

'You sound like one of those McGill postcards.'

'Come on, she's a nice-looking girl. You'd be very glad of seeing a face like hers if you ended up on a stretcher.'

'Hmm. How is Evie, by the way?'

'She's in the very pink of health, I'm pleased to say,' replied Jack, with a smile, 'though it's all hands to the pump now at the *Echo*. Whenever there's a panic they always seem to telephone the newspaper. She's had to take calls from people asking all sorts of odd questions – someone recently wanted to know where they could get a gas mask for their dog.'

'Good Lord. What did she say?'

'Oh, she told them that pets won't be issued with gas masks, and a dog couldn't use one in any case – it relies on its sense of smell.'

Baines chuckled. 'Smart girl.'

Their goodbyes done, they walked through the darkening streets and into Sefton Park, avoiding the trenches that had been dug around the perimeter. The absence of street illuminations meant that moonlight was now working overtime as a guide. The park looked rather haunted in its nocturnal attire of blue-black and silver. For a while they walked in silence across the grass, the night so soft that the only sound to be heard was their own breathing. Baines felt the thickening gloom prompt him towards a confidence.

'I had a moment, just a flash, about that night at the Adelphi – first time in years, to be honest.' Jack looked at him as they walked abreast, but said nothing, so Baines pressed on. 'I was in the Sailors' Home, working with Richard – you know, the photographer – he was perched up high on a beam, and I had this moment, it just sprang out at me . . .'

Jack waited again, and then said, 'I remember talking about it at the time, and what I said then still holds. There was nothing you could have done. You know –'

'Yeah, I know,' Baines cut in quickly, feeling almost reluctant to be absolved. 'I know it wasn't my fault.' But the self-justifying words excruciated him, and he wished he had not raised the matter at all, even with Jack. He looked up, and his eye was diverted by something so outlandish that his confessional mood evaporated as quickly as it had descended. At the west edge of the park he could see a row of barrage balloons, their skins lustrous amid the gloaming; they bobbed with the woozy, graceful menace of jellyfish through a reef.

'Look at that,' said Baines, stopping to contemplate these ethereal globes, and above them the night sky glistening with stars. 'Isn't that the most beautiful thing you've ever seen?'

Jack looked, and nodded slowly. 'As gay as a wasp in a window,' he murmured.

4

The following Friday morning Baines arrived at Slater Street to collect Richard for their next perambulation. On seeing that the blinds had been pulled down over the front windows he wondered if the studio was closed, but he tried the door in any case. It was unlocked, and he walked in to find a little flurry of activity: a young man in a Fair Isle sweater was fixing a light bracket on the wall, while two army officers stood self-consciously against a hessian backcloth. A cluster of arc lights formed an audience around them, the white glare of their inspection harsh and stagy. A woman, with her back to him, was talking to another assistant holding a flash, and only noticed Baines once she had fixed the tableau to her liking.

'Hullo,' she said, 'are you Tom?' He nodded, and she smiled with a sudden reflexive brightness, like a hostess gamely determined to remember every guest. 'I'm Bella – Tanqueray. Richard's gone for the day. Can you bear to wait for ten minutes while I finish this?'

'Of course,' he replied. He recognised her as the haughty-looking woman in the photograph he'd seen on his first visit to the studio, only she didn't seem in the least haughty now. Her face was longish, with notable cheekbones and very dark eyebrows, but instead of the challenging gaze he remembered from her portrait he saw an indulgent readiness to be amused. Her hair was different, too, mid-brown with faint streaks of blonde, and bundled into a loose chignon. More surprising still were the blue wide-legged slacks she wore; he hadn't seen many women in trousers before. He realised he was staring.

He sat down on a window seat and pretended to flick through the *Daily Post*. Bella, having finally coaxed her subjects into eye contact, ducked to the tripod to line them up in her lens. The soldiers, somewhat bovine in their demeanour, now straightened before the camera's judgement. They looked to be in their early twenties, both with their hair cut *en brosse*, spiked like a newborn chick; the jaw of the taller one was shadowed with acne. Something about their eyes, and their unspoken familiarity with one another, made Baines think they might be brothers.

Such callowness – but then he thought of Jack and Richard being packed off to the Western Front, at an even younger age perhaps than these two. There was a sudden explosive crump, and the smell of magnesium permeated the air. Blinking away the flash, he glanced again at the newspaper, its headlines shrill with foreboding from Europe. At the bottom of the page Blackler's was offering half-price bargains – men's worsted suits at 45/-. Was that actually a bargain?

A short volley of laughter brought him back to attention. Bella had said something to amuse the soldiers, who looked quite relieved to be done with the scrutinising lens. She laughed too as she shook hands with them, and he heard her say, 'Good luck.' As they trooped out one of them nodded at Baines.

'Our brave boys,' said Bella, turning to him with a rueful smile.

'They looked like – brothers?'

'They are. Joined up when they turned eighteen – like Richard. Who sends his apologies, by the way. There's a wedding in Formby this afternoon – a friend of his begged a favour after the photographer dropped out yesterday. He felt he couldn't refuse.'

'Oh well –'

' – but he knew there was a lot to do today, so that's why I'm here.'

'You?' said Baines, confused.

'Yes, me. Unless you have strong objections to a woman taking charge of a camera.'

He blushed. 'No, not at all – I just thought . . .' He didn't really know what he thought.

'Good,' she said, with a kind of head-girl breeziness, stacking the photographic plates and handing them to her assistant in the Fair Isle sweater. 'Tim, would you mind locking up the place? I'll be out for the rest of the day.'

She trotted off upstairs, returning almost immediately with a folding camera, somewhat sleeker-looking than Richard's Leica. She saw him peering at it.

'Are you interested in cameras?'

'I haven't a clue about them. I just noticed that marque on yours.'

'You mean Newman and Guardia?'

'No, this,' he said, pointing at a tiny plate beneath the maker's name. 'Sibyl. It's the name of a woman the Greek and Roman gods spoke through. She foretold the future.'

Bella musingly examined the marque for herself. 'That's a useful talent . . . No wonder they charged me thirty guineas for it.'

'Would you like to be able to see into the future?'

'No, not really . . . it would spoil so much of the excitement, wouldn't it?'

Baines nodded, consideringly. Outside, the late-morning temperature was warming into sultriness; vast zeppelins of silvery-white cloud heaved determinedly across the sky, offering swift oscillations between glare and gloom.

'So – let's get started,' said Bella, squinting and shading her eyes against the sun.

Baines produced a little map he'd sketched, marking the area's surviving patches of Georgian housing and shops, much of it abandoned but still handsome for all the neglect. As they walked he felt very conscious of her presence at his side. She was perhaps thirty, tall with a willowy dancer's body, and moved in long, almost loping strides. He noticed people staring at her as they passed by, and imagined them reporting the sight to their friends: 'A woman in trousers, bold as brass she was . . .'

He stopped at a terrace of five houses on Seel Street. 'Those pedimented doorcases are quite rare now, 1790s . . .'

'Shall I do – all of them?' asked Bella, and at Baines's apologetic nod she began photographing. She worked more slowly than Richard, he noticed. At first he thought this might be owing to a lack of confidence, but he gradually realised that hers was a more deliberative style; while Richard's movements were quick and decided, Bella held back and seemed to wait, almost, for the picture to come to her. For the next few hours they toured the once-affluent quarter between Seel Street and Park Lane, a network of tall merchants' dwellings, bonded warehouses and industrial buildings linked to the port. Now the poor dwelt in the grid of narrow alleys and courts thrown up in the middle of the nineteenth century. When children playing in the streets saw Bella with the camera at her eye they would stop and gaze, or else begin capering in front of her. A boy of about six, with dark serious eyes and a smeared face, followed them around for a while. He wore no shoes. Baines felt mortified, as if he, playing host to an out-of-towner, were obscurely responsible for this destitution, but all Bella said was, 'Poor thing's got nothing else to do.' Eventually she turned and smiled at the boy: 'Hullo there.' The boy stared on, silently appraising them; his features, beneath the grime, were delicate, with a girlishly plump lower lip. Bella, shrugging, half knelt and took his photograph – and without a word he turned on his unshod heel and tramped off.

'It can't be an easy life,' said Baines.

Bella shook her head sadly. 'Not many kinds of life are.'

By mid-afternoon, sensing that she might be tiring of the heat, or else of his pedantry, Baines decided to call a halt. They stood on Hanover Street, amid a roiling throng of shoppers.

'Warm work, isn't it?' said Bella, looking slightly wilted.

'May I, um, buy you a cup of tea?' he asked.

'I should say so!'

They retreated from the crowds down the slope of School Lane. Baines, still feeling the spectre of poverty at their backs, looked with relief on the oasis of Bluecoat Chambers, a beautifully proportioned Queen Anne building that enclosed three sides of an old cobbled quadrangle.

'That's the oldest surviving building in the city. It started as a charity school in 1718 for . . .' he heard the pride in his voice falter, 'children of the poor.' There was no getting away from them after all. Without needing to be asked Bella lined up her shot, clicked, then turned to Baines.

'That little barefooted boy . . . have you ever wondered what poverty is really like?' He had, but he never could admit that what he really felt, more than compassion, was fear.

'I'm afraid this place and poverty have always gone together,' he replied. He hated the banality of the line, it sounded pious yet non-committal, and he hated the sound of his voice – that adenoidal Liverpudlian drone – as he said it. But he hated most of all the unconfessed guilt of never having known or helped a poor person in his life.

In search of a cafe they crossed into Church Street, clanging with trams. The one next to Bunney's was nearest, but the room was full to the door so they walked up to the Kardomah on Dale Street. Settled at a corner table, where the low babble of voices was distantly interrupted by the angry hiss of steam from the urn, they faced one another inescapably. A waitress took their order for tea, and Bella added a request for a toasted teacake.

'I've just realised how famished I am,' she giggled. Baines offered her a Player's, and they smoked for a few moments in abstracted silence.

'Thanks for helping out today,' he said eventually. 'I'm sure you had better things to do.'

She accepted his gratitude with a sly smile. 'You seemed a bit doubtful about me this morning.'

'No, just – surprised. I don't know why. Richard reckons you're a better photographer than he is.'

'Don't listen to him. I don't even think of myself as a photographer.'

'He told me that you paint.'

'I was at the Slade for three years. William Nicholson taught me – William Nicholson painted me, in fact. Though it's not one of his best, I'm afraid. Probably a fault with the sitter.' Baines thought again of the unsatisfactory photograph of her he'd seen at the studio; perhaps hers was a difficult likeness to catch.

'How did you and Richard meet?'

'Oh, I'd come up here from London one weekend for a friend's birthday party. He'd got to know Richard through the studio, invited him along and . . .'

'. . . your eyes met across a crowded room,' Baines supplied.

'Something like that,' she said. 'We got married in '34, and I've been here more or less ever since.' He heard something wistful in her tone.

'You don't sound –'

'Well . . . obviously I wanted to be with Richard. But I've not really settled here.'

'Oh?'

'I know, you're like Richard. You probably think it's the greatest city in the world.'

Baines considered this. 'No, not the greatest. But maybe the most interesting.'

'Yes, I can see that, Liverpool is an interesting place. I just . . . don't particularly like Liverpudlians.' She clapped her hand over her mouth and leaned towards him, lowering her voice. 'Sorry, that sounds terrible, I don't mean you – you seem nice, very nice. I'm sure there are others, too. Oh God, I should just shut up . . .'

As she paused, flustered, to drag on her cigarette, Baines stole the opportunity to study her. His eye kept being drawn to a tiny chip on her front tooth, the one flaw in an otherwise even row; it was an imperfection, he thought, that altered the whole character of her face, made her seem more – what was the word? – individual.

'So – you don't like us,' he said, rather enjoying her awkwardness.

'It's not that, really,' she said, shaking her head. 'I just don't know where Richard gets this idea that Liverpudlians are the salt of the earth. Scousers. He thinks they're funny, I think they're rude and aggressive.'

Baines smiled at this. 'There used to be a saying, you know, "Liverpool gentleman, Manchester man."'

'Liverpool gentleman? He must be in hiding. You wouldn't believe the looks I get when I go into a pub – there's a real hostility towards women. Or maybe it's just me they don't like.'

'It could be the trousers,' said Baines, only half joking. 'They might not excite much notice in Chelsea, but around here . . .'

'And it's such a sad city, don't you think? Those streets we walked through today, that little boy we saw – there's such terrible destitution, and everyone seems to turn a blind eye to it.'

'I gather that London has its poor, too.'

'Yes, of course it does, but it's nothing like here. Liverpool feels like a place that's dying on its feet, there's no industry holding it up. If it didn't have the docks there'd be . . . nothing left.'

'Well, if the Luftwaffe have their way there *will* be nothing left.'

For a while they talked about the war. Bella told him about her younger brother, David, who had recently joined the RAF.

'I imagine your parents must be worried,' said Baines.

She shook her head. 'I'm afraid they're not here to care any more.' Her father, she explained, had worked for the Foreign Office, and when he was posted to Egypt he and his wife had taken their three children – there was an older sister, Nancy – to live in Cairo. 'David was a baby at the time. I still remember the policeman turning up at school, and our headmistress calling Nancy and me out of class to tell us that there'd been an accident, and that Mummy and Daddy wouldn't be coming home. And I asked Nance – she was three years older than me – when would Mummy and Daddy be coming home, then? She got furious, and just shouted at me, "They're not, stupid – they're dead." So that's how I found out.'

She spoke with a kind of brave jauntiness, as if the story's frequent retelling might have smoothed the edges off its pain.

Baines, not looking her in the eye, said, 'I'm sorry.'

At this moment the waitress bustled over with the teacakes, which Bella received with the quick 'social' smile she'd used on meeting him that morning. She began eating with schoolboyish alacrity.

'Do excuse me,' she said between mouthfuls, 'I really am half starved.'

Watching her, he was unaccountably touched by her lack of self-consciousness; he had always felt awkward eating in front of strangers. She cleared the dainties quickly, and looked up to find herself being watched.

'Sorry. Richard's always telling me off for bolting my food.'

Baines smiled. 'You looked so hungry I thought you might eat the pattern off the plate, too.' She laughed throatily, revealing her teeth like the half-raised lid on a toy piano. Then she offered him a cigarette and lit one for herself.

'So,' she said, exhaling from the side of her mouth, 'do you have family here?'

'I have an aunt and uncle I'm close to. My parents died years ago, before I really knew them.' She nodded, and waited for him to go on. At length he said, 'I always used to think it was easier, in a way, their being strangers to me. What the eye doesn't see, the heart doesn't yearn for, you know? But just recently I had a pang – I was looking at a photograph of them, and something about my mother's expression made me feel . . . not lonely exactly, but cut adrift. I had this idea that my life had been not just unparented, but – unwitnessed.'

He had never properly spoken about this before, and was surprised to find the words came quite easily. Perhaps it was an instinctive solidarity of one orphan with another.

Bella said, 'No brothers or sisters?' He shook his head. 'That must have been hard,' she went on. 'I mean, Nance and I used to fight a lot, but she was very protective of me. And we both adored David. Adore. I don't why I'm talking about him in the past tense.'

Just then Baines happened to glance over her shoulder, and caught sight of a woman hurrying through the cafe. From the back he thought she looked familiar, and, having collected something at the counter, she turned again to leave. It was Evie, on a break from the *Echo*; in her haste she would have passed right by their table without noticing him.

'Evie!' he called, and she stopped, almost in fright, to look round. 'Hullo,' he said, with a reassuring lift in his voice.

'Tom,' she said, focusing, as if she'd been woken from a dream. Her gaze momentarily shifted to Bella.

'Sit down for a minute,' he said, though he could see she looked quite distracted. Recovering herself, Evie slid into the space that Baines had vacated for her on the banquette. He introduced her to Bella, and briefly explained their association.

'Late lunch?' he said, gesturing at Evie's parcel of sandwiches.

Evie nodded. 'The newsroom's been mad busy all day.' She said it in a way that seemed to assume they would know why, but then she took in their suspicionless faces. 'Haven't you heard? The Germans have invaded Poland. It came over the wire this morning.'

Baines looked across the table at Bella, who was wide-eyed with shock. Evie was talking on about the speed of the German advance and the likely British response, but Baines wasn't quite listening. So this was it, he thought. This quiet afternoon cup of tea would be his final memory of peacetime. But no – they weren't at war. Not yet. Mightn't they pause at the abyss one more time?

Evie said, 'Sorry to be the bearer of bad news. I'll have to be getting back.'

'Righto,' said Baines, forcing himself to sound cheerful. He imagined the scene of gathering urgency Evie would be returning to, as fresh bulletins thrummed down the wires.

'Nice to meet you,' she called over her shoulder to Bella, and hurried out. For a few moments they seemed at a loss, not quite trusting themselves to find a tone equal to the occasion. Eventually Bella said, with a theatrical lightness, 'Well, that's torn it.'

Baines smiled in spite of himself, and pulled from his breast pocket a leaflet he'd just remembered picking off his doormat the previous morning. Its front page announced, SOME THINGS YOU SHOULD KNOW IF WAR SHOULD COME. He handed it to Bella, who briefly scanned the drill on lighting restrictions and fire precautions.

'Thanks. I suddenly feel that much safer,' she said.

Later, as they walked down Dale Street, Bella asked him if his publishers had set a deadline for the book.

'Two, as a matter of fact, and I've missed both of them. But then they'll have to revise it in any case now that it's going to carry photographs instead of drawings.'

'You don't seem all that worried.'

'The irony is that, just as I've rediscovered some of my old enthusiasm, the whole place will probably go up in flames.'

'Oh, but you've got to keep going!' she said, with a vehemence that bemused him. 'Richard is really impressed with how much you know, I mean about the city and everything. He said you were like Mr Memory in *The 39 Steps*.'

Baines laughed. 'Right, and look how he ended up.'

They walked by two men who, idling at a pub door, stared at Bella from beneath their caps. As they passed Baines thought he heard one of them mutter something – it sounded like 'lezzie', though he couldn't be sure. He glanced at Bella, who didn't seem to have noticed. The Friday rush hour was beginning to gather momentum; people were filing out of offices and queueing at tram stops, and motor cars were streaming towards the Tunnel. Bella came to a halt at Old Haymarket.

'I'll be off home, then,' she said.

'Well, thanks again,' he said, shaking her hand, which felt dry and rather bony – she had long painter's hands. He had wanted to finish on an optimistic note, something to restore the convivial spirit they'd established in the Kardomah, before Evie's arrival. But the moment seemed to have gone. Bella looked at him levelly, and said, 'I've a feeling we won't forget this afternoon in a hurry.' She turned and, with a little wave, walked off. He stood watching until her figure receded into the crowds.

He had one more errand to do. A notice outside the Record Office on William Brown Street announced that it would be closed from next week until further notice. At the desk an assistant had begun to explain that it was not a lending library when Baines produced a letter bearing the School of Architecture's crest at its head. Professor McQuarrie had obligingly written requesting permission for his former student to borrow certain materials for 'vital' research purposes. The desk clerk cast a sceptical eye over the letter before he retreated behind the storeroom door, returning some minutes later with the three weathered volumes. Baines signed a release form, and the books were handed over. The journals of Peter Eames were now his responsibility.

He didn't open them that evening, however, and when Saturday dawned he still found himself too distracted to read. Late afternoon he switched on the wireless and listened to the sports results. Liverpool had beaten Chelsea 1–0 at Anfield, the home team having been rounded up from territorial camps that morning to play the fixture. In Hove, spinner Hedley Verity had taken 7 for 9, helping Yorkshire to a nine-wicket victory over Sussex. Life was going on, in its somewhat unreal way. He opened a tin of sardines, but their oily brackishness made him feel nauseous, and he tipped them into the bin. At about nine o'clock he thought he might go for a drink; by the time he had finished moping about the flat an hour had evaporated, along with his plan to venture outside. When he heard the clocks strike eleven, he poured out a Scotch, and flopped onto his bed with the earliest volume of Eames's journal. He lit a Player's and resumed reading.

8th January 1862

News obliges me to consider the possibility that I am, finally, a Genius. Old man Sandham summoned me to his office to announce that the design I have submitted for the Temple-street building has been chosen by the Corporation, with a premium of 150 guineas. In a perfect frenzy of delight – after little less than a twelvemonth engaged at A&S I have secured my first project! Chiltern & Dalby toasted me yesterday evening at the Lyceum with many huzzahs – Chiltern candidly amazed, & asks me whether I am surprised to have won it. I replied that I could only have been surprised had I *not* won it.

Tuesday Twenty-eighth January, 1862

To St George's Hall last night, with Ma & Cassie – both in excitable spirits – to see Mr Charles Dickens on his reading tour of the provinces. Outside the Hall a long line of carriages blocked the way, & on the steps so vast a number of people it seemed that half of Liverpool had flocked thither. (Hundreds were turned away, as I later discovered.) Inside, at the threshold of the beautiful concert room, we encountered more heaving crowds, so rough & unyielding in their eagerness to be admitted that I feared for Ma & Cassie being trampled underfoot – but on the contrary they appeared to thrive in this disorderly cram, & took possession of our seats more swiftly than I could have managed myself. After a good deal of jockeying & jostling, & some adjustment of the gas-light, a hush fell upon the audience at last – & precisely at eight o'clock the Man himself walked onto the stage, to be greeted by a roar of cheering that might have been heard on Brownlow-hill. He looked about the room, seeming to take this applause as his due, & then silence fell, so profoundly that the hiss of the gas jets was all that one could hear. As he began to read I could not help myself scrutinising him, & at first felt surprise to note how aged he looked, his face lined, his hair thin & his neat beard grizzled – a man not yet fifty. But he is a little spit-fire of a fellow withal, trim, well-knit, with a military precision & briskness of movement. His dress was as smart as a carrot – he wore a white waistcoat & white geranium in his buttonhole, with a heavy gold watch chain hung across his chest. His eyes are the most disconcerting, glittering like a cobra's, & apparently able to bewitch a whole room at once, like an actor – indeed he is as much actor as author onstage, for the characters whom he impersonates seem to stand & almost walk about the place. He read from *Nickleby* & Mr Bob Sawyer's Party, & as he performed (only occasionally glancing at the book before him) it was notable how much he was entertained by his audience's responses – their cheers & guffaws – so that he began to laugh with them at the remarks of his own creatures! I was unsure as to what intrigued me the more, Dickens himself, or the people undisguisedly entranced around me. At the conclusion when he took his bow, the noise of the cheering & clapping was more thunderous than that which had met his entrance; Ma & Cassie looked so inflamed with delight I felt a shiver of envy, & considered – what a thing it is to have Power.

Yet this was by no means the end of the evening's astonishments. As we were making our way out through the teeming Hall I came up face to face with my former employer Sir Wm Rocksavage, closely attended by his wife & Miss Rocksavage. As it was impossible for him to pass without cutting me he stopped & with all the graciousness at my command I introduced my mother & sister, & we talked briefly of the performance we had recently witnessed; or rather, Sir W^m talked briefly – my tongue ran twelve score to the dozen in praise of Mr Dickens, the majesty of the concert Hall & I scarcely know what else, for by chattering on I purposed to conceal the one true object of my attention – her. We had not met since last June, nor had I received word of whether my drawings were liked or not – indeed our whole acquaintance might have occurred in some fever-dream, so suddenly & unsatisfactorily did it end. Upon seeing her this evening, however – her pale brow, the grey-green eyes that accord everything its fair weight, the modest and maidenly bearing – I felt a passionate rekindling of all those feelings that assailed me during the weeks at Torrington Hall, & I conceived a determination not to allow this second chance to go begging.

In the carriage home Ma & Cassie could talk only of Dickens (they even sang 'Charley is my darling!') but I could think only of that belle dame Emily Rocksavage, & of how best I should recommend myself to her.

Saturday, First February, 1862

On South Castle-street this morning a lightning-bolt of inspiration smote me. I happened to pass Geo. Philip's bookshop, & spying a large-headed caricature of Mr Dickens displayed in the picture window (his reading triumph this week has blazed through the Liverpool papers) I hit upon the pleasing idea of a present for E.R. The three volumes of his most recent novel sit plump on the desk before me, to be dispatched to Blundell Sands once I have enclosed a note, though the title of the book should perhaps suffice: *Great Expectations.*

10th February 1862

A letter, at last, from her, conveying sincere thanks for the book, with a closely considered evaluation of its merits & its standing in the corpus of his works. Her judgement I cannot fault – she liked the character of Joe Gargery the best, as did I, & owned that she had wept at the note he left for Pip after nursing him back to health – 'fur you are well again and will do better without'. In truth, while I acknowledged her powers of critical discernment, my eye raced on in hopeful search of an avowal concerning the donor of her gift. But inexhaustibly she continued her scrutinising of Dickens & his genius – the felicity of this expression, the fineness of that observation, &c. – until I feared that the stratagem had failed & my great expectations come to naught. O ye of little faith! – There in the very last paragraph of this tormenting epistle the lady, having enquired after my family's health, expressed the hope that I would accept an invitation to dine at Torrington Hall on the fifteenth of next month.

15th March 1862

'Beware the ides of March' – not I, Caesar! Yet I had forecast it to be a day of reckoning ever since I received the invitation to Torrington Hall. For the dinner itself I did not care a rap, my only purpose being to renew my pursuit of *her.* I wore the bottle-green frock coat for the occasion; it felt slightly queer to walk again up the long drive, first because I had not seen the Hall in moonlight before, second because I was no longer a hired draughtsman but a dinner guest – & still I had to check myself when from habit I turned for the tradesmen's entrance. The dining room, illuminated by a great brilliancy of candle-light, revealed a quite different aspect from the one I had drawn last year – it bestowed a lustre upon everything, from the crystal decanters that circulated briskly to the heavy silver on the table. Everything, that is, but the guests, who seemed to be exclusively drawn from the merchant class, & a louder, more uncivilised crowd I never met – jowly, mottled men with short legs & prominent paunches, who talked of little but the counting-house. Their wives even more formidable – a coarseness of feature matched by an outrageous breadth of figure; they sat at table looking satisfied & absolutely immovable, like vast battleships in time of peace.

I discovered, as much to my relief as to my delight, that I was seated next to Miss Rocksavage, we two being, aside from her older sister Francesca, the only persons who might truly be considered representatives of Youth (and Beauty, if I'm not mistaken). She appeared at first unsettled in this boisterous company, but soon we were talking quietly of books, music (she adores Liszt) & sketching, a recent habit to which she owed the inspiration, so she professed, of my example. This was a gratifying disclosure, & I would eagerly have pursued the subject had our colloquy not been interrupted at that moment by a man seated opposite, who had become very expansive under the influence of the hock & champagne. He quickly impressed upon us his achievements: a millionaire, a sugar magnate, a member of the Imperial Legislature – whatever that is – & a man of intellect, of which I doubted none but the last. Clever in a sense he plainly was, having earned his fortune from the refineries & extended his business operations all over Europe, but in manners & address he could hardly have done less to recommend himself. At one point he broke from his orating to enquire as to my profession, & having established that I could be of no use to him, he merely reverted to being a prodigious bore. The man (whose name I have willingly forgot) is typical of the Liverpool merchant, I dare say, embodying at once a pride of energy & an outright ignorance of letters, culture & art. I might have been amused had I been granted leave to argue with him, but no word of mine could pierce his steely self-regard.

Obliged to converse politely with other worthies seated about us, I was unable to resume any intimate dialogue with E.R. until about midnight, when the evening was breaking up.

'I have not said to you the half of what I should wish to have,' I said to her. 'Nor have I to you,' she replied, in a voice that seemed to quiver with unspoken feeling. I took this as my cue, & suggested to her that if she happened to be walking on the beach at Blundell Sands on such an afternoon next week, she might meet there a fellow who would sincerely cherish the opportunity to deepen their acquaintance. She responded with a look that mingled hopefulness & apprehension, but her chance to reply was again snatched away by the circling throng. Will she come?

19th March 1862

The days have been interminable. Tomorrow is the afternoon
appointed to meet. Never before have I so consciously felt my life
to depend upon the affections of another person.

20th March 1862

I had decided to feign a sudden illness at work so as to ensure a day
of liberty, but in truth there was no need for dissemblance – I really
did feel as sick as a horse. I arrived at Blundell Sands at noon, &
paced along the shore for an hour in a miserable effort to calm my
inward flutter. Rain had threatened in the forenoon, but now a pale,
watery sun floated on the horizon, & out of habit I sat down to
sketch. I remembered how, as a boy, I would spend hours at a time
simply staring & wondering at the sea, & later would produce sketches
of the curious toppling motion of the waves. I have them still, thanks
to my mother, most of them untidy scrawls – yet I look upon them,
these untutored boyish efforts, with fondness. Thus was I occupied
with my sketchbook when I spotted her tall, coltish figure in the
distance, & thought of Odysseus meeting Nausicaa on the shoreline.
Silently I prayed that, whatever else Providence had in store for me,
I would not fail in this. She wore a dark brown cape with a matching
bonnet. That she had escaped the attentions of her lady companion
for a few hours was testament to her boldness as much as her ingenu-
ity. We talked, rather skittishly at first, but soon were back in the
old ways of last summer before our acquaintance was inexplicably
curtailed. She said that she was aggrieved by her father's precipi-
tate removal of the family to Scotland, though it was by no means
the first time they had been ruled by his caprice. It took no remarkable intelligence to predict the rest: during their sojourn she was
introduced to a certain Scotch gentleman, with a vast estate in
Inverness & prospects which would happily accord with her own
standing as an heiress. Did she find the gentleman agreeable? I
asked. Yes, she did. And did he take leave to ask for her hand? Yes,
he did – & was refused. Naturally this show of independent mettle
riled her father, whose will was not accustomed to even the mildest
opposition. So why did she resist him? 'Because I wanted to marry
a man whom I love, & who loves me,' she said simply, her eyes
searching mine. This was my cue – & yet my courage failed me! I
could only circle around the question, & asked – Was she not afraid

of exciting her father's displeasure? She saw my feeble delay for what it was, & spoke more truly than I had dared: 'I am afraid of nothing but the possibility of passing our lives apart.'

I have these words by heart.

7th April 1862

A dinner at home to celebrate our betrothal. Ma, in fluttering exultation, thanks Emily for 'agreeing to marry our son' – as if I were some inconvenient loafer to be taken off their hands – though later in the evening she is reduced to plaintive sobs on learning that the married couple will *not* be living with her at Abercromby-square. Georgy & Cassie rather shy around the lady, but melted upon seeing her play the piano. Recalling some of the old songs I begged Ma to give us 'Liverpool's an Altered Town', & she obliged. Two of the verses I here set down:

Once on a time, were you inclined your weary limbs to lave sir,
In summer's scorching heat, in Mersey's cooling wave sir,
You'd only just to go behind the old Church for the shore sir,
But now it's past Jack Langan's half a mile or more sir.
Oh dear oh, for Liverpool's an altered town, oh dear oh.

The spire of famed St Thomas's, that long had stood the weather,
Although it was so very high they've downed it altogether,
& the old Dock, the poor old Dock, the theme of many a sonnet,
They've pulled it up & now have a built a Custom House upon it.
Oh dear oh, for Liverpool's an altered town, oh dear oh.

(To think of washing oneself in the Mersey!)

As I looked upon my betrothed, her face aglow as she talked so kindly with Ma, a fount of pure gratitude sprang up within my breast, & I thanked the Lord God Almighty for the blessing of Emily. To her I owe this happiness, for without that defiance of her sire (now reconciled to the match) we might never have found one another again.

2nd October 1862

Another vexing argument with Sandham today – my hand shakes with rage even now to think of it. Some weeks ago I received a letter from the office of Messrs Daubeny & Rudd concerning the designs of a new bank of theirs which I had been asked to present. The chairman & directors of the bank expressed their pleasure upon seeing the working drawings, & looked forward to 'a bold & imposing edifice that accords with the proud traditions of Liverpool's foremost merchant bank', or some such. Then a more cautious letter arrived last Friday enquiring as to whether I might revise my design with reference to sundry structural alterations, which included reducing the size of the windows! I saw this at once for buffoonery, & replied that I would not suffer the windows or anything else to be tinkered with – & if my work displeased them they were at liberty to engage a more pliant architect. This morning Sandham summoned me to his office & read out a letter from Daubeny & Rudd, who have now withdrawn approval of my designs & threaten to cancel the commission altogether. He asked me why I thought it permissible to provoke their client, & to risk losing a contract that would be an object of envy to every practice in the city. I shrugged, & replied that I should not dare to advise them on how to run a bank – why should they presume to tell me how to design a building? At this he became very angry indeed, & dismissed me from his sight.

17th October 1862

Peace has been negotiated. Sandham has personally overseen changes to the bank drawings, Daubeny & Rudd are mollified, the construction may now proceed. Sandham declares himself satisfied, and no wonder – he will now take the credit for a building to which he has contributed a handful of ridiculous 'improvements' on my own design.

It is nothing to me what he or the client thinks. I would not claim to be a genius in everything – I cannot paint twilight like Turner, or mimic the cockney tongue like Dickens. But I do know how to make a building both beautiful & functional, & it will be of no use to argue with me about it. My mind is not a bed to be made & re-made.

Friday, Seventh November, 1862

Every day this week I have visited the Temple-street site, where building on Janus House – as my design is to be called – proceeds apace. It behoves me to maintain a close scrutiny as it is erected, lest the builders are tempted to bodge or else to make a few pounds by selling off the lead to bluey-hunters. This morning I took Ma & Pa down to inspect the progress. I explained to them the naming of the building – that the Roman god Janus was represented as 'bifrons' – with two faces – symbolic of vigilance in looking both before & behind. Where the common practice in commercial building is to show an elegant façade to the street but hide away a mean court-yard at the rear – Queen Anne in front, Mary Anne behind, as it were – my own shall present identical faces at front & back. The frame will be of cast iron – a substance, as Ruskin says, 'tenacious above all things, ductile more than most' – with stanchions between which oriel windows shall be suspended in multiply repeated patterns. Thus my method of resolving the gloominess of the street – typical of a northern town, where light is so often blotted out by clouds & soot – lies in a simple proliferation of glass. These oriels will allow daylight to flood through the tops & sides of the glass as well as through the front, & the office clerk will thank that architect who saved his eyes from straining.

Ma was moved to raptures of praise, but then were I to show her a house of mine constructed from a child's wooden blocks I fancy she would be no less effusive. Pa more restrained, as is his wont, but in his few quiet words of admiration I felt a sincere delight, for it was from him I learned both the rudiments of draughtsman-ship – the value of a fine point, precision in detail, the simplest means of expressing light & shade – & furthermore the love of all things sound & solid & well-crafted. I pause to consider this bene-ficent patrimony. From my mother's love I have derived my egregious self-esteem; from my father's tutelage – my means of invention. Blessed is Eames!

9th January 1863

Sandham invites a few of his assistants, including myself, to the consecration of the new church in Everton, a district overrun by more of these Gothic monstrosities than it could possibly need or desire. The old dodderer appears to be very pleased with this, his latest design – Heaven alone knows why. The front is stone, with high lancets & some geometrical tracery. The tower & its recessed spire quite drab. The interior is hideously glum & draughty, dominated by thin limestone columns with their sad stiff-leaf capitals & grotesque bases. Not the smallest roguery of detail to be seen. If this edifice has been raised to the greater glory of God then the Almighty has been thoroughly ill-served, & I pity the congregation obliged to worship within its unlovely precincts. The name of the church, it amused me to note, is St James-the-Less: I fancy no one could conceive of a St James-the-Lesser.

The visit only serves to confirm that Sandham is, if not Liverpool's own Pecksniff, a hopeless hack of an architect. For now, needs must, but I fear that a long association with his office must be gravely disadvantageous to my prospects.

Thursday, Twenty-sixth February, 1863

To Torrington Hall for dinner. Seated there at the Rocksavage family table I was troubled — no, not troubled, I was taken hold of — by a peculiar paradox. The triumph of my engagement to Emily a year ago has since been supplanted by a perception of myself as hobbled, like a horse, or else caged & tamed, like a domestic pet. My wings are, at any rate, clipped, while Emily seems to have discovered a new will to power in her pinions. Perhaps this reversal of roles is common to every man & his betrothed. He has done his work, & gained his prize, & by winning has become a slave. She, conversely, by being 'caught', is freed of a restraint that has ever been upon her. Does she rejoice in the knowledge?

What seems certain is that we both perforce put our privacy at risk: to be married is to be under scrutiny. On such thoughts was I brooding when, later in the evening, Emily found me in the library. 'Is anything the matter, my love?' she asked, and when I assured her that all was well, she gaily continued with talk of the house we should occupy when we are married. What was my preference? she wondered. Jestingly I replied that a mansion as commodious as this one would be to my liking, where husband & wife might ensure matrimonial bliss for ever — one in each wing. At this her face clouded, & seeming to believe that I spoke in earnest she upbraided me as cold & unfeeling — if I valued her company so meagrely now, then what possible happiness could we expect in the future, &c., &c. Quickly I had to rescue myself, & seizing her in my arms rained kisses upon her brow & assurances upon her ears. Untimely misgivings, these.

2nd March 1863

To dinner with Chiltern & Dalby at the Cockspur, one of the new restaurants that have sprung up around the Exchange. To see the number of swells thronging the room one might have thought the Cockscomb a better name for the place. I confessed to them my sense of being tamed, like a mynah bird – 'A very minor bird!' cries Dalby, pleased at his jest. Chiltern ponders the question for some moments, & says, 'How can you talk of being tamed before you are even married?' This indeed perplexes me – though the feeling cannot be banished. Then there is the headlong plunge into intimacy that marriage will entail. I have nurtured a friendship with Chiltern & Dalby over a period of years, while Emily I knew barely a twelvemonth before I bound myself to her. I am taking a fearful leap in the dark. 'Aye,' said Chiltern, 'but remember – so too is she.' By the evening's end I had drunk so much hock I can scarcely recall what conclusions were reached, though another joke of Dalby's comes back to me: What fish do wolves generally prefer? Why, lamb-prey of course!

Tuesday, Tenth March, 1863

The town has gone quite mad. Chiltern & I were on our way to the Lyceum in the afternoon when we met a frenzied procession of wassailers pouring down Ranelagh-street, shouting, whistling & crushing any unfortunate passers-by flat against the wall. One might imagine the cause of this rowdiness to be another Trafalgar, with Nelson restored to life & borne through the streets to receive the guerdon of a city's gratitude. Nothing of the sort. The celebrations, it seems, are incident to the marriage in London today of the Prince of Wales & the Princess Alexandra of Denmark. This evening Will (freed from school for the day) leads a party of us through the bustling crowds to see the whole town illuminated, & thence to the Pier-Head where a display of fireworks lights up the river. A splendid & picturesque thing, to be sure, but does the wedding of two strangers, royal as they are, merit these absurd pomposities of demonstration?

Thursday, Second April, 1863

The day of our wedding, & I almost contrived to miss it! In the morning I had visited the Temple-street site, having received assurances from Chiltern that he would collect me in the carriage at noon

& take us directly to the church at Blundell Sands. I talked to Minton, the clerk of works, who now estimates completion of the job within six months; the scaffolding has been removed to reveal the magnificent façade of glass. The builders have nicknamed it 'the greenhouse', he told me, whether out of affection or not I was unable to judge. As the hour struck noon I stepped onto the street in expectation of Chiltern – nowhere to be seen. A half-hour passed, then a clatter of wheels from the direction of Dale-street announced his arrival. He had forgotten our arrangement to meet here & had taken the carriage to Abercromby-sq, where he found the house empty but for the maids, the family just departed, & only then perceived his error. In comical haste we set off, the builders' dust still thick on my coat, & we were halfway to Kirkdale before I realised I had left my wedding attire at the club. No time to turn back, so there in the coach I tore off my coat and shirt, amid much hysterical laughter, & exchanged them with Chiltern's. ('You turncoat!' &c.) We arrived at St Jude's (not one of Sandham's, the Lord be thanked) with ten minutes to spare.

Thus was I wed in another fellow's clothes, though my dear Emily in the frantic toing & froing of the day seemed not to notice. Calamity was averted, we are married, & as happy as cicadas.

The next morning Baines was roused by church bells. They made him think of Eames's wedding all those years ago, and the couple shyly emerging from St Jude's to meet the smiling faces of the congregants who had witnessed them at the altar. Happy as cicadas. As he dressed he looked out on to the steep drop of St James's cemetery, and the half-built cathedral beyond. A few churchgoers were proceeding along Hope Street. Towards the end of the morning the telephone rang.

'So that's that,' he heard Jack say, with a heavy sigh.

'That's what?'

'Have you not had the wireless on? He – the PM – just announced that we're at war with Germany.'

'Ah . . .'

They didn't talk for long. He felt a queer kind of relief: that the worst had happened, and that the waiting was over. They could swim or they could drown, but treading water was no longer an option. His gas mask grinned at him from the mantelpiece. He picked it up, and held it one-handed, like Hamlet apostrophising the skull.

'Where be your gibes now?' he whispered to it.

It was only as he was leaving the flat that he noticed the date on the Sunday newspaper – 3 September 1939. He imagined embassies and government offices in chaos now the news was out, the sudden swell of crisis and the cheerless prospect of flight or evacuation. He thought of the panic that would flood through the city streets, and the inexorable momentum with which it would course from town to village, thence to the open fields and sequestered vales where a farmhand or a rambler might still have a few more hours of blessed ignorance left to him. And he wondered, amid the rising levels of sound and flurry, if there was anyone else in the world who remembered, or cared, that today was the centenary of Peter Eames's birth.

PART TWO

Falling
1940–41

*A life of action and danger moderates the dread of death. It not only
gives us fortitude to bear pain, but teaches us at every step the precarious
tenure on which we hold our present being.*
'On the Fear of Death', William Hazlitt

5

Picking his way over the rubble, Baines caught sight of Richard through the drowning curtain of smoke. At least he thought it was Richard; it was difficult to tell. The standard-issue oilskin capes, gas masks and steel helmets reduced everyone to the same sinister-looking apparition. Suddenly from another direction a whistle blew, and two stretcher-bearers hurried past him in answer to its shrill summons. He sensed a whole theatre of activity going on around him, unseen. When the smoke lifted he could see Richard again, or else the figure who resembled him, waving his arms and beckoning him over to a doorway. He began to move. Beneath the heavy oilskins he was sweating uncomfortably, and though it was only about forty yards to cover it seemed a much greater distance, strewn as it was with crushed masonry and tumbled brickwork. Weighed down by his pack and conscious of his laboured breathing through the mask, he felt like a deep-sea diver lumbering across the ocean floor. Glass crunched under his boots as he sought a secure path through the debris.

He ducked inside the door and moved towards Richard – he could now recognise his outline – standing on the lip of a small crater and stabbing his finger downwards. Baines peered into the hole, and discerned a chaos on two levels, the upper one of shattered joists and plasterwork, while on the cellar floor below it a figure lay motionless. He looked back at Richard, who in dumbshow was indicating that he would lead the descent. Baines nodded, and watched as his friend manoeuvred himself down the broken limb of a door frame to the level of jagged timber about fifteen feet above the sprawled man. Richard moved cautiously but confidently; for a heavy man he revealed a surprising agility in negotiating the unreliable footholds that offered themselves to the climber. There was a kind of fearlessness in him that Baines had first witnessed when they were at the Sailors' Home last August. It was as though he had divined by some unearthly intuition that, whatever the danger, he could not be harmed. Baines wondered where this apparent conviction sprang from, and whether there might be some way he could acquire it for himself.

He had begun his own rather less nimble descent, and had already pincushioned his palm after grasping too eagerly at the splintered door frame. Landing awkwardly from his jump on to the ledge, he had a horrible foreglimpse of embarrassment, wherein Richard would be required to rescue not only the man below but his inadequate partner. Richard had taken off his helmet and gas mask; sweat had dampened his hair and was beading his face. He wiped his brow with a handkerchief and blew out his cheeks.

'Blimey. I'm melting under this stuff.'

Baines struggled out of his mask, and was looking down into the crater. 'So what do we do about our friend?'

Richard wrinkled his nose appraisingly, and trained his torch beam over the far side of the wall. 'Easy. We crawl round the edge and shinny down that length of pipe.'

It didn't look at all easy to Baines, but he had resigned himself to doggedly following Richard's lead, and when the moment came for him to climb down the exposed pipe he did so without even testing it first for support. He reached the bottom with a little leap that Richard acknowledged with a clap on the back.

'Well done, old boy,' he said. 'Now, let's get our man some medical attention.' He was about to put the whistle to his lips when the man raised himself on one elbow and called through the gloom, 'Ey, 'ave one of yous gorra ciggy on yer?'

Richard sighed and looked at Baines, and then they both burst out laughing.

Later, queueing for tea at the mobile canteen, they agreed it was the most lifelike of all the practice responses they had been involved in so far. The cumbersome gear, the heat from the fires and the wide blast area had contributed a certain degree of realism. But, lacking the genuine component of fear, it still seemed to Baines an unsatisfactory substitute for the actual thing – whatever that might be. Around them medical auxiliaries and bomb 'victims' swathed in bloodless bandages now sat smoking, chatting. The day had begun with a huge detonation at a clearance scheme in Bootle, the high explosives intended to simulate a scene of devastation following an air attack. Then a blanket of fake mustard gas was laid down over the area, fires were lit in what remained of the buildings and a posse of volunteers were sent out to secrete themselves in the wreckage: they were instructed to assume a prone position as realistic as possible without endangering themselves, and were asked not to talk to their rescuers. Most dress rehearsals so far had used only dummy casualties, but months of practice had engendered a sense of anticlimax, and the authorities were worried that the stretcher-bearers and ambulance teams dispatched to the bomb scene would become complacent at the prospect of yet another shop dummy to retrieve.

For Baines the anticlimax had passed into a mood of confused agitation. The sense of relief he had felt last September had dissipated in the months that followed – it was now the beginning of May – and the waiting he had initially believed over had merely entered a new phase of rumour and uncertainty. The swirling current of memory carried him back to the week following the declaration of war, and that prickling sense of terrified excitement as he prepared for his enrolment into the defence of his city – his country. He had turned up on the Wednesday morning, nine o'clock sharp, at Municipal Buildings on Dale Street, and been directed through bustling corridors to a long room laid out in rows of individual desks, as if for an exam. A blackboard stood expectantly at the front. Seats were already being occupied, mostly by men of his own age, and he hurriedly found a vacant one at the back. It made him feel like the class dunce. Some minutes later an army officer strode in, accompanied by a nondescript older man who might have been anything from an accountant to a church alderman.

The officer waited for the murmur of conversation to subside and then introduced himself as Major Andrews. His brisk, booming tones resonated so confidently around the room that even from the back row he could be heard loud and clear. It was a voice that reminded Baines of Richard. Andrews began by presenting the War Office's intelligence on the principal types of aircraft used by the Luftwaffe – the Heinkel He 111, the Dornier Do 17, the Junkers Ju 88 – and jotted details of their maximum speeds, ceiling heights and bombloads on the blackboard. He then sketched out 'possible scenarios' of destruction following air attacks on a major port such as Liverpool. Baines felt oddly relieved that Andrews could maintain a level, impassive tone while describing the precise effects of concerted bombing on the city – it seemed there would be at least one man, and perhaps others, who would face these cataclysmic horrors without panicking.

'. . . but I repeat, these casualty figures are only estimates,' he said. 'At this point there are still many variables to be considered. They may be lighter and, of course, they may be heavier.' Baines could hardly believe his ears. How could they be *heavier*? No wonder they were hurrying along the evacuations. Andrews concluded his lecture and handed over to his companion, Pryce-Jones, who turned out to be a special adviser on the Liverpool Air Raid Precautions Committee. He talked in the same matter-of-fact way as the Major, explaining each of the volunteer services that would have to be at the ready in the event of an attack: street wardens, auxiliary firemen, road repairers, demolition and decontamination squads, first-aid parties, stretcher-bearers, ambulance drivers. The inventory was methodical, the delivery unemotional. Baines's attention was beginning to drift when the man broached the subject of 'heavy rescue'. Training for this service, he said, was still at a provisional stage, since there had been little opportunity to make a scientific study of burrowing for bodies in ruined buildings. 'Essentially, we're still learning how buildings behave under pressure from high explosives.'

A deadpan voice piped up, 'They fall down,' and a ripple of laughter followed. Pryce-Jones smiled tightly, but continued without any further acknowledgement of the wag. 'A house can collapse,' he said, 'in three different ways. One – by total disintegration into fragments of rubble. Two – by the curving fall of roofs and floors, held at one side while the other swings downwards. Three – by the collapse of floors in the middle while their sides hold' – here he drew a large V inside a square on the blackboard – 'beneath the arms of which people on the floor below might be preserved alive. Once any fires have been extinguished, it will be the job of the heavy-rescue man to begin the search. This will mean assessing the strength of a broken building and the means of entry, tunnelling through masses of rubble and creating, as it were, a corridor by which he may reach survivors and return them, and himself, to safety. I hardly need add that this will be laborious, and highly dangerous, work. Above ground, there is the risk of a collapsing wall or staircase. Underground, as well as the possibility of the building's entire disintegration from above, one faces the additional hazards of burst water mains, gas leaks from fractured pipes, exposed cables and the all-too-likely recurrence of fire. Working quickly in such conditions will, of course, be absolutely impera- tive. One's survival – and that of others – may depend on split-second decisions.'

Pryce-Jones, with a quick glance around the room, sat down again. Andrews, sober-faced, rose to his feet and nodded his thanks. He turned to his audience. 'Any questions?' There was a pause, then a hand went up: 'What are the hours?' The laughter was much louder this time, and carried in it, Baines thought, a note of nervous bravado. The reverbera- tions of an attack had just been dialled up to unprecedented levels of intensity, and the safety valve of hilarity was all that could defuse it. Once the questions were done with, they began filing towards the exit, where lists of each volunteer service were pinned to a board, waiting to be signed. Baines, among the last to leave, put his name and address beneath the column marked Heavy Rescue. He noticed there were considerably fewer names in this column than in any of the others.

From Bootle they caught a bus back into town. Richard's face was still streaked with dirt and sweat, and Baines presumed his own looked much the same, but nobody on the top deck gave them a second glance. Men reeking of smoke in dark overalls and steel helmets had ceased to be remarkable during the last eight months. Perhaps the sight of them even gave people heart: they were a walking reminder of a city 'at the ready'. They smoked pensively as the bus jolted through the rush hour.

'I wonder,' said Baines, 'was what we did back there of any real value?'

'How do you mean?' asked Richard, with a yawn.

'Well ... I don't imagine they're going to bomb us during broad daylight. How will it be, searching through rubble in the dark?'

'Harder, I reckon, but not impossible. You should try rescuing men from a shell-hole while a sniper's trying to pick you off.' He spoke without bitterness, as was his habit whenever he mentioned his time at the front. Baines had sometimes been on the verge of asking Richard about the bombardments and the shelling – that obliterating payload screaming down on you – and hitherto had always held back. But now that it had been raised he couldn't help himself.

'I suppose it must have been terrifying.'

Richard drew on his cigarette and gazed straight ahead. 'Pretty much. And when you weren't terrified you were just bored to sobs. There wasn't a great deal in between.'

There was a pause while the conductor collected their fares, then Richard spoke again. 'Strange thing, when we found that chap lying in the ruins today, I thought of the first time I ever saw a dead man. We were on the march, but a glance was enough. Half of his face had been terribly mauled and burnt, and his body was twisted in odd ways, like a rag doll. There was this awful smell coming off him, blood mixed with the fumes of the shell that had killed him. I was really that close to throwing up, but somehow I kept walking. Then I looked at one or two of the men, and I suppose my face must have been as sick and grey as theirs were.'

Baines waited, holding back for fear that any interruption might snap this delicate thread of reminiscence. Richard's voice seemed to be coming from a long distance. 'That was the difficult thing, especially when zero hour approached. The men would get this glassy-eyed look, as if they were in a trance, and I felt they were looking to me for comfort – even though I was trembling like a leaf. I just hoped my voice wouldn't quake when I gave the order to fix bayonets. Eventually I got lucky, I was assigned a sergeant named McKendrick – he came from Liverpool, as a matter of fact. He must have been at least ten years older than me. Hard as nails, and his language was appalling, but quite wonderful with the men. He looked after them in a way I never could, kept them going in spite of everything. By the time of Third Ypres I would have staked my life on him, mine and the whole company's. Well, the order had come for an attack – we had to capture a place called Kitchener's Wood – and this indescribable noise was falling around us, shell after shell bursting over the trench. I'd blown the whistle and was climbing up the ladder when I felt a tug at my elbow. I looked round and saw that McKendrick was trying to say something, I had no idea what, the barrage was so deafening it tore any other sound away. But then he put his mouth to my ear and yelled, "Till the very last, sir." I think I patted him on the shoulder, and then we were up and over.'

He fell silent. Baines felt he had been holding his breath for the last two minutes. 'Till the very last,' Richard repeated, as if in a daze. 'For some reason, I knew at that moment I wasn't going to see him again. And I never did.'

Baines bowed his head, and nothing else was said for the rest of the journey.

They alighted at Lime Street, and walked past an *Echo* news-stand blazoning the headline: GERMANY INVADES LOW COUNTRIES.

Richard turned to Baines. 'No hiding from it now.'

Baines was still pondering the story of Sergeant McKendrick and Richard's presentiment of doom. He suddenly needed the anonymous comfort of a pub. 'Have a drink?'

Richard shook his head. 'I've a few errands to do. But we could meet later – or better still, come round for dinner.'

'Grand.'

'See you about eight o'clock.'

Time was when Baines would have felt awkward about such an invitation, but in the months since they had met last summer he had become very thick with Richard and Bella. They had a large circle of friends, he'd discovered, gained either through the studio or else the university, where Bella did some part-time teaching. He assumed that he had been adopted by them, but gradually came to realise that the condescension he had first imagined was in fact a vigorous conviviality. He wouldn't have minded either way. He had never known people with such an appetite for parties and dinners, and he could smile at the irony that wartime had coincided with the most sociable period of his life so far.

Their enthusiasm for the Liverpool book had also had a galvanising influence on him. By the end of October they had finished annotating and photographing most of the city's significant architecture. All that remained to be covered was the seven-mile stretch of docks ranged along the shore, a prospect that once would have daunted him; yet with their help he had taken on this final leg of the study with a renewed purpose. Richard in particular had been a tireless spur, and on his days off would cycle down to the docks to meet him. Needing to work quickly he had even lent Baines a camera and between them they set about recording the brooding mass of warehouses, embankments, swing bridges and gates. Towering castles of brick warehousing stood impassive and apparently indestructible; Baines seemed to be forever craning his neck upwards to identify the names and dates projected high along the line of parapet.

There was one photograph from these dockland ventures he especially cherished. He had been walking past the Goree Piazzas early one winter morning when through the mist that had drifted off the river he heard the sound of hooves ringing on the cobbles. He turned to see an old shire horse pulling a dockload alongside the eighteenth-century arcade that gave the place its name. Something about the animal caught at his heart; he looked down into his viewfinder – it was an old Rolleiflex of Richard's – and clicked the shutter. He hadn't thought of it again until Bella was looking through a sheaf of developed prints a few weeks later.

'You'll like this one,' she said, handing it to him.

The phantasmal light, the mournful heaviness of the horse's movement, the oblivious driver and his load, the rusticated arcade in the background. It was a fluke, he knew, one of those beautiful accidents of composition and timing, but more than that, it was the strange elision of past and present that struck him. There was nothing, not one detail, to suggest the scene might have looked any different fifty or even a hundred years ago.

As the limbo of the phoney war stuttered into January Baines became increasingly absorbed in the book: if it went on any longer he might even finish it! Then a few weeks later came a letter from Plover Books informing him, 'with regret', that due to the war and the spiralling production costs, all projects that were not deemed absolutely essential – that meant his – would be indefinitely postponed. Given that it was his laggardly ways which had delayed it in the first place, he felt unable to work up a sense of righteous indignation. The book would to have wait.

But the photographs were again on his mind when he arrived for dinner at Slater Street that evening. Richard and Bella lived on the top two floors above the office. He felt his way up the stairs, their very tread and creak familiar to him, so regular a guest had he become. He paused on the half-landing, where the skylight had spilt a small illumination, to look at the painting of Bella, signed at the bottom left-hand corner: Nicholson. He was still undecided about it. Perhaps the chartreuse green of her cardigan was unfortunate – it gave her complexion a sickly tint – and he had got the jaw wrong, too, it made her look horsey. But there was something there, the sense of quizzical amusement in her eyes, the confident way she held herself, that Baines found somehow more truthful than the photograph of her in the office below.

'Ah, there you are.' Through the gloom he could see Bella at the top of the stairs and, surprised in front of her portrait, he endured the queer sensation of having been caught spying on her. 'Come up, there's someone I want you to meet.'

He followed her into the living room, where Richard was talking to a gangly, dark-haired youth dressed in RAF uniform. Bella strode over to the boy, who submitted with a blush to her coddling embrace.

'This,' she said, beaming, 'is my baby brother. David, this is our friend Tom.' As they shook hands, Baines for a moment wondered if he was being let in on some dubious practical joke. How could this . . . *boy* possibly have kidded his way into the air force? He seemed no more than seventeen, and the sparse little moustache he evidently hoped would make him look older was having quite the reverse effect. He looked for reassurance to Bella, but she was still gazing proudly at David.

'You're on leave, then?' said Baines.

'Yes, just for the weekend. I didn't have anything else to do, so –'

Bella mock-slapped his arm at this. 'Don't be naughty. What he meant to say was he couldn't bear for another week to go by without seeing his dear old sis.'

A sharp pop came from the kitchen and Richard emerged with a bottle of champagne. 'I think a toast would be in order,' he said, slopping the fizz into glasses. 'Here's to – the young flying ace!'

David smiled shyly as they clinked. To Baines it felt as though they were marking the end of something. The champagne itself seemed vale-dictory – it might be the last they drank for a while if France were to capitulate.

They ate liver sausage for dinner, with semolina for pudding. Richard recounted the day's practice response at Bootle and its bathetic conclu-sion. '. . . and through the dark this voice pipes up, "'Ave you gorra ciggy on yer?"' Baines laughed along, though what really amused him was Richard's hopeless imitation of Scouse. Outsiders never got it right, they confused it with the donkey-bray flatness of the Black Country. Scouse was grating in a different way, he thought, that abrasive nasal whine mixed in with a dose of chronic catarrh. But he thought he might miss it if it ever disappeared. He spent most of the dinner covertly studying David, quieter and more diffident than his sister, though phys-ically their resemblance was strong. He had her dark eyebrows and pronounced cheekbones, and used his hands in the same languidly expres-sive way. He was no longer in his teens, it seemed; his twenty-first birthday was coming up in September. As Baines watched Bella teasing David, her face lit from within by a glow of fondness, he was caught unawares by a sudden piercing jab of envy. It was to do with being an only child, perhaps, with never having known that intimacy of endurance that bound siblings to one another like veterans from a long and diffi-cult campaign. Or so he told himself.

But still he listened to them talking and laughing as he and Richard cleared the plates. They were reminiscing about a holiday together on an island Baines had never heard of, and Bella was gaily recalling a favourite anecdote about their trouble with a local shopkeeper. The irrecoverable nature of this past, as distant as Saturn, suddenly bore down on him, seeming to constrict his chest. If only he had known her when he was a young man – how different his life might have been. He felt quite dizzy, and excused himself. In the bathroom he splashed water on his face, and tried to calm the furious acceleration of his heart. What on earth was the matter? He sat down on the edge of the bathtub for a minute or two, and steadied himself. After a while he heard a tap at the door, and Richard on the other side.

'Tom? Are you all right in there?'

'Fine, yes. I'll be with you in a minute.'

'Righto.' He heard the footsteps retreating.

When he returned to the table he lightly dismissed Bella's expressions of concern. 'I hope it's not the sausages?'

He laughed. 'No, really, it was – nothing.' Just a terrible existential ache, he thought.

'Well, the news today would give anyone a turn,' said Richard, bringing a second bottle of champagne from the kitchen. 'Another German invasion on the same day we get a new prime minister. Quite a comeback for Churchill, though.'

'You're not opening that to toast him, are you?' said Bella.

'It hadn't occurred to me,' he replied. 'But I have to say – the old boy did keep warning us about Germany. He would never have stood for Munich like Chamberlain did.'

'If France falls then we're really in for it,' said David, and a gloomy silence briefly settled on them. Baines looked around the table and cleared his throat by way of announcing a change of subject.

'I've been wondering,' he said, 'about the photographs. I mean for the book.'

'Have the publishers changed their mind?'

'No, and they won't as long as there's a war on. But is there any reason why we shouldn't exhibit them? They're so good, it seems a shame to let them gather dust.'

'I think we should,' said Bella, steepling her fingers as if about to pray. 'We've always talked about turning the ground floor into a gallery.'

They spent a few minutes debating a title for such an exhibition. Baines and Richard both favoured something evocative of the city's grandeur.

'How about "The Glory that was Liverpool"?' said Richard. Bella wrinkled her nose in disdain.

'Pompous, wouldn't you say?'

'We could call it "Liverpool: Venice of the North",' said Baines. 'They say that in the eighteenth century the dock system rivalled the canals. And there's a lot of Italian Renaissance-style buildings around the business district.'

Bella still looked sceptical. 'When I think of Venice I see canals and gondolas. Even Liverpool doesn't get that much rainfall.'

'Very well,' said Richard, tolerantly, 'let's hear your ideas, my darling.'

'I think it should convey both sides of the city, the wealth and the poverty. We could use pictures of the slum courts side by side with the grand public buildings. Something like, I don't know, "A Tale of Two Cities"?'

'Mm. They might notice it's been used before,' said Richard. 'And besides, shouldn't it be celebrating the place rather than highlighting its social problems? Tom, don't you agree?'

Baines did agree, though he knew Bella was right, too, about the divided nature of the city. He thought just then of the barefoot boy who'd followed them around that morning – the morning he'd first met Bella. For her it had been a catalyst. She had continued on her own initiative to photograph not just the inner-city dereliction but the poor, densely populated districts of Scotland Road and Vauxhall Road. Could a portrait of Liverpool really ignore the fact that great numbers of its people lived in chronic poverty?

'I take Bella's point,' he said, carefully. 'But I think the emphasis should be on the architecture.'

'Exactly!' said Richard. 'Let's concentrate on the majesty of the place instead of harping on about the slums and the plight of the poor.'

Bella looked hard at him. 'If showing some photographs of the conditions in which people live is "harping on", as you call it, then maybe we should have more of it. I mean, God forbid that we actually try to show something truthful.'

There was a rising note of anger in her voice that Baines hadn't heard before. Even Richard looked slightly taken aback. Bella's face had flushed, and her eyes glittered like warning lamps from beneath her darkened brow. She seemed about to say something else, but then stopped herself and got up from the table. The atmosphere she left behind was momentarily strained, and Richard continued to pick absently at the foil on the champagne. David, who had observed his sister's flare-up without comment, said softly, 'I don't know the place at all well, but whenever I see Liverpool on the map I always think of it as – the City by the Sea.'

Baines and Richard looked at one another. City by the Sea: it was simple, but somehow affirmative. And the combined sibilance of the first word and the last fleetingly suggested the motion of the tides.

'Sounds good to me,' said Baines, nodding at David.

'We have our toast, then,' said Richard, forcing the cork from the bottle's neck with a mighty blam.

Bella didn't return, and once the champagne was finished David also turned in for the night. Richard and Baines sat on the floor looking through the first sheaf of photographs, which together formed a kind of collage of Castle Street back in that ominous August. They heard midnight tolling from a distant church.

'I'd better be off soon,' said Baines.

'Have a nightcap first. Got some Scotch.' Having risen to his feet, Richard looked like a man trying to keep upright on a tilting deck. 'Sorry 'bout that thing with Bella. She's quite the socialist, isn't she?'

'I suppose she is.'

'Has a whole crowd of lefty friends down in London. All over the place, really. Art school breeds them, you know.' He stopped, and looked round. 'What did I get up for?'

'Scotch.'

'Ah.' He stalked off to the kitchen, and returned with glasses and a bottle of Dewar's. He broke the seal and began to pour.

'Whoa,' said Baines, 'just a finger for me.' The measure Richard handed over was at least three times that.

'But of course she comes from radical stock,' said Richard, doggedly pursuing his theme. 'Not sure about her father, but her mother marched for women's suffrage. Went to prison for it!'

Baines had heard Bella talk of her mother's campaigning spirit, but he hadn't heard anything about prison. For some reason it touched him that she'd withheld that bit of the story. It made her seem at once more human and more glamorous.

Richard smiled ruefully. 'If she ever found out that I drove a bus during the General Strike she'd – well . . . explode.'

'I've not seen her that heated before,' said Baines.

'Tonight wasn't just about that,' Richard reflected, frowning. 'I think she's on edge, worrying about David. They're very close.'

'He seems such a kid. Quiet, too. He reminds me rather of . . . someone I know.' Baines had actually been reminded of himself at that age – reticent, self-contained – but he thought better of confessing it.

'A kid, yes. A kid who's had about twenty flying hours, and now they expect him to take on the Luftwaffe.'

'That's madness.'

'That's war, old boy. Get used to it.'

They talked desultorily for another hour before Baines slipped away, having extinguished Richard's cigar and left its owner snoring quietly in an armchair. He walked out into a night steeped in tall, inky shadows. The streets had seemed emptier, eerier, since the pubs had been forced to close early. The windows along Seel Street, hung with blackout curtains, stared down sightlessly. Under this inky canopy the walk home was strewn with hazards, even with a torch to hand; he kept reading reports of people knocked down and killed by trams or cars spilling out of the dark. It had become necessary to rely on one's ears almost more than one's eyes. He encountered nobody on his way home; even the late-night coffee and pie stall he used to pass on Berry Street had gone.

As May lurched on the news continued rolling from across the Channel like distant thunder. Beneath the mood of apparent calm Baines felt a kind of hysteria about to break. Even when the *Wehrmacht* had crushed Norway and Denmark in April the war seemed to be happening somewhere else. Now it was heading right towards the front door, and every day was bringing fresh disaster. Holland had surrendered, the French and Belgian armies were outflanked and on the run. The hopes of a counteroffensive from the British Expeditionary Force had failed utterly: the Germans were tearing through France, there was nothing to stop them. Only the evacuation from Dunkirk offered a brief respite from the gloom – a miracle in the midst of catastrophe – before the rumours of invasion started up. Hitler would invade, they said, it was simply a matter of when.

Baines saw photographs of the *Wehrmacht* in Paris, marching past the Arc de Triomphe, and he was jolted. They seemed absurd and frightening at once. Now he tried to picture them, as if in newsreel montage, goose-stepping down Lime Street on their triumphal procession towards St George's plateau – he imagined that would be the place they'd stage it. Cut to the Führer emerging from the long motorcade with a salute and that shy smirk, then mounting the steps of St George's Hall, its long portico spiked with swastika flags. Around him would swirl his retinue of ministers and men of war, blankly obsequious, all clad in the goon-squad livery of black and grey; then in close-up you would see the double lightning flash of an SS badge glinting on a collar, or the death's-head on a cap, as party dignitaries craned forward to shake the man's hand. Another cut to Hitler, now staring like a mongoose from the podium, finger slashing the air as he announced the latest step in his Thousand Year Reich . . . and that was where Baines's imaginary film whited out, as if stalled by a faulty projector. He realised this was because every time he had seen footage of Hitler delivering a speech there would invariably be vast cheering crowds in attendance, their arms raised in stiff salute, their faces lit up in a frenzy of obeisance. *Heil, Heil!*

That wasn't going to happen here. Liverpudlians could be a strange, unpredictable lot, but one thing he felt for certain was that nobody could own them. They would never be bullied – he had read somewhere that even the Communist Party had called the city 'an organiser's graveyard'

– and they would never bend the knee to anyone. Hitler would always need a crowd, but Liverpool would not provide him with one – therefore Hitler would never come to Liverpool. And therefore would not invade? Baines wasn't blind to the childishness of this reasoning, but it was oddly reassuring all the same; it encouraged him to believe that, whatever was thrown at them, they would resist it.

The city was still holding its breath as spring lurched into summer. Anxiety had become his companion. It woke in the morning in front of the blackout curtains, hovered by the wireless, read the newspaper over his shoulder, sat on the top deck of the tram, sidled after him into the pub. He heard it within the ticking of his clock, the clanging of church bells, the querulous whine of the air-raid siren. He became used to its presence, until he could no longer imagine his life without it. When Richard started to redecorate the studio in readiness for the 'City by the Sea' exhibition, Baines seized the opportunity to distract himself and volunteered to paint the walls of the office upstairs: they were going to need both floors to accommodate the number of photographs. The disagreement about its social emphasis which had provoked Bella's indignation that night in May had not been mentioned again, though Baines sensed that something was still amiss.

His suspicion was confirmed one afternoon in late July while he was taking a break from painting the walls. He was at the window, staring on to the backs of the houses, with their chipped slate roofs and blackened brick. Bella was working in the stockroom, arranging the photographs in a loose sequence on the huge work table where Richard did the framing, when she put her head round the door.

'Tom, do you want to have a look at this?'

Baines went into the stockroom and saw dozens of the high-contrast black-and-white squares lined in neat rows across the work surface.

'I've arranged them in roughly the order Richard suggested, starting with the docks, then moving through the business district towards the cathedral, the university, and so on. What do you think?'

He hunkered over the table, examining what he had only seen previously in discrete batches. Now, set out in tiers, the luminous monochrome and deep focus seemed to take on a symphonic quality, there was a patterning in the light and dark that absorbed the eye. Whether in the gaunt prosperity of a Georgian facade or the melancholy vista down a cobbled street, the beauty of the place impressed itself anew on him, and he was moved. But something felt wrong, and he realised now what it was. He turned to Bella, who had been fiddling in a preoccupied way with her hair, tied today in a glossy ponytail.

'These look wonderful but, er, they're all Richard's.'

'Not all, there are a few of yours too. Here's that lovely one of the horse and cart at the Goree.'

'No, what I mean is – there aren't any of yours.'

Bella looked down at the table, her mouth puckering slightly. 'Yes . . . I came to a decision. It seemed best to impose a kind of integrity.'

'But I didn't – we didn't mean to throw your stuff out altogether. Honestly, Bella, yours are some of the best photographs of the lot, it would be ridiculous not to include –'

'Tom, please,' she said, holding up her hand to silence him, 'don't fret yourself. I realised that if I was going to stage an exhibition on Liverpool, it would be very different from the one you and Richard have in mind. You both look on the place as this grand seaport, brimming with history and wonderful architecture – it means a lot to you. And that perspective will look odd next to pictures of barefoot children and families in crammed courts with a single lavatory between them. So let's not mix up the two.'

Baines felt a surge of gratitude, and beneath that a needling shame that he had acceded with so little fight. Bella's change of heart in the matter was mystifying, but then he knew he was quite far from understanding this woman at all. He could sense about her an impenetrable force field of sadness; in unguarded moments of repose she could look absolutely forlorn, but then that sudden smile would snap on like a light and she was buoyant once more. Detecting one of these sorrowful moods, he had sometimes been tempted to offer a quiet word of comfort, and had held back. He was too mindful of his own past to make that mistake again.

He said, 'If I could find my hat, I'd take it off to you.'

She smiled. 'Well, maybe one day I'll stage my Liverpool exhibition and invite you along . . .'

'Count on it, I'll be there. But do me another favour, would you, take out those amateur shots of mine. I'd rather it were a one-man show, and Richard probably would too.'

'Are you sure?'

'You said it yourself, better to aim for integrity.' They looked at the photographs a few moments longer, then Bella said, 'We should try to get the press here. Maybe ask that rather pretty friend of yours at the *Echo* to come along.'

'You mean Evie? Yes . . . is she pretty?'

'You seemed to think so. I saw your face light up that time we met her in the cafe.' Her tone was teasing, though Baines was momentarily confounded that Bella had noticed his reaction and could recall it from almost a year's distance. He couldn't help feeling rather pleased about that.

6

The night before the official opening of 'City by the Sea' they had held
a private view to which a great many more people came than had been
invited. It was inevitable, as Baines knew; no one could throw a party in
Liverpool without a raucous cavalcade of gatecrashers rolling up. The
crowd was so large that people had already edged out of the gallery, stifling
under the August heat, and found their way into the Tanquerays' back-
yard. Baines felt a bead of sweat start from his neck and proceed to trickle
down the length of his spine. The hum of conversation had climbed to a
roar, and the mixed odour of cigarettes and perfume and hair oil was
beginning to feel oppressive. He slalomed between the revellers and gained
the relative tranquillity of the yard.

He leaned against the back wall, where long tendrils of wisteria were
scaling the brickwork in an apparent effort to escape. Clusters of people
stood around drinking, one or two occasionally glancing upwards, their
ears cocked for the distant approach of engines. Ever since the reports
came in of Luftwaffe reconnaissance missions over the city they had all
become watchers of the sky. Bombs had been dropped, most of them
without harm. In Prenton, however, one had crashed through the roof of
a house and a maid named Johanna Mandale was killed in her bed. She
was the first casualty of German attacks on Merseyside.

At the first-floor window he saw someone waving and beckoning him
up. It was Evie. He had been rather enjoying his refuge from the crush,
but he thought it might look rude not to join her. Having plucked a beer
from the proffered tray he was retracing his steps through the heaving
press of bodies – there seemed to be an inordinate number of sweaty men
in double-breasted suits, he assumed they were business contacts of
Richard's – when he glimpsed, out of the corner of his eye, a face he
thought he knew but hadn't seen in years. At the same time he was
conscious of it as a face he had felt a commanding urge never to see again.

The crowd shifted and he was temporarily lost to view. Could it have
been . . . ? The startling possibility nagged at him as he climbed the stairs,

which were being swiftly transformed into an obstacle course; some couples were lounging and chatting, oblivious to the traffic passing up and down. He nodded a greeting to Tim, one of the studio assistants, who grimaced comically at the surrounding hubbub: 'Mad, isn't it?'

'Who are all these people?'

'I have no idea,' Tim replied, and they both laughed.

He proceeded to the top, and spotted Evie amid a huddle at the far end of the room. The room still smelt faintly of the plum-coloured paint he had lately used on the walls.

'Hullo, Evie,' he said, stooping to kiss her on the cheek and noting in the same instant that his small infatuation with her was over. He felt a strange complication of worry and relief, 'to mourn a mischief that is past and gone'. Evie, treating him to one of her most guileless smiles, had clearly never suspected a thing.

'I've brought some friends from the paper,' she said, introducing him to an assortment of young women whose names he almost immediately forgot. Just then a doughy middle-aged man in a crumpled navy blazer sidled over.

'And this feller here might be writing something about you for his column. Adrian Wallace, this is Tom – he sort of organised this.' Evie handed him on with a surreptitious wink.

'Ah, the curator,' said Wallace, pink-cheeked and sweating from every pore of his meaty face. His bow tie was wilting like a parched flower.

'I only helped out,' replied Baines, 'Richard and Bella are the people you should talk to. You're the diarist?'

'Oh, diarist, art critic, literary editor – I've done most of them in my time.' He cast a bored, imperious gaze around the room. 'Amazing what a crowd you get when free ale's on offer.'

'Maybe some are here to see the photographs.'

Wallace sighed theatrically and flicked a hand through his wavy, ash-coloured hair. 'That's so naive it's almost charming. The odd thing is, these pictures aren't bad, either – if only people could be bothered to look.' He narrowed his eyes, and pointed a stubby finger at a photograph on the wall in front of them. 'That one, for instance, is really quite striking.'

Baines turned to look at it. 'Do you know what that is?'

'I haven't the faintest,' Wallace drawled.

'It's the front elevation of Janus House, on Temple Street.' It was one of Richard's most arresting shots. He had taken it at such a steep angle that the building was foreshortened into a kind of geometrical abstract, its tiers of windows seeming to soar upwards to a distant apex.

Baines couldn't help adding, 'It's by a Liverpudlian architect named Peter Eames.'

'Never heard of him. Liverpudlian, you say? Looks more like a New York skyscraper to me.'

'He anticipated the skyscraper. That was part of his genius.'

Wallace allowed himself a sceptical chuckle. 'Dear boy, let's not get carried away. Shakespeare, Michelangelo, Mozart – that's genius. A Liverpool architect nobody's heard of, that's . . . quite different.'

'Oh. I was only quoting Ruskin's opinion of him.' In fact, he had read a private letter in which Ruskin had described a visit to Liverpool in the 1870s and merely noted *en passant* 'that great glass enigma known as Janus House'; irritated by Wallace's airy condescension, Baines had decided to gloss the Ruskinian verdict as 'genius'. His scholar's instinct baulked at the misrepresentation, but he knew he wouldn't be challenged on it. Wallace, however, had been distracted by something else.

'Who is that extraordinary-looking woman?'

Baines followed his gaze: it was Bella, dressed in a silk sheath the colour of old gold that rippled and shimmered against the light. A thin headscarf, mixing shades of glinting copper and flame, lent the disconcerting impression that her hair was on fire. Catching his eye she swayed towards them with her long dancer's strides, and Baines introduced her.

'*Buona sera*, Bella,' said Wallace, with emphatic suavity. 'I was just saying what a charming soirée this is.'

Bella fixed him with a bemused smile. 'Have we met?'

'Adrian Wallace, from the *Echo*. Love the show. I'll be saying so in my column – you should pack them in.'

She looked about the room. 'Hmm. I wonder if we could get so many without the promise of a drink. This must be the least "private" view I've ever attended.'

'You've done a great job,' said Baines, with prosaic gallantry, and won a smile noticeably warmer than the one she'd just aimed at Wallace, who was now standing a shade closer to her then he had before.

'Here's my number,' he said, flourishing a card which Bella took and examined with a great show of politeness. 'Come along to Nell's once you're finished here – you may know the place. Just give them my name at the door.' He traced the air with his cigarette as he spoke, and Baines noticed a signet ring flash on his finger: it had the right pompous touch about it.

'That's very nice of you,' said Bella. 'May I bring my friend here?' She leaned pertly against Baines and squeezed his shoulder; he felt the gesture both as a skin-tingling thrill and a sly rebuff to Wallace's familiarity. Here was something to beat quoting Ruskin, or misquoting him, come to that. Wallace glanced at Baines and tilted his head, as if conceding an advantage.

'I'll see you later, then,' he said, flicking at his hair again and sloping off. Once he was out of earshot, Bella turned to Baines and said, 'What a peculiar man.'

'He looks a scoundrel,' said Baines.

Bella laughed. 'Scoundrel. You sound like someone out of Trollope. Good job you were standing between us – I thought he was going to eat me up.'

'Yes, he did have a hungry look.'

'But not a lean one,' she giggled.

At that moment Jack, in his ARP uniform, appeared before them. He had recently been growing a moustache, which had, to Baines's amusement, turned out patchy and incontrovertibly ginger.

'What are you two chortling about?'

'Oh, nothing much,' said Baines. 'Bella just had a close shave with that lardy-looking feller over there.'

'Talking of close shaves, is that a new moustache?' asked Bella.

'Hmm,' said Jack, dabbing at it distractedly. 'I thought it would lend me a bit of gravitas as an air-raid warden.'

'Do you think?' said Baines. 'Seems more like a cricketer's moustache to me.'

'What's that?'

He pretended to count the individual bristles. 'Eleven-a-side.'

'Less of your cheek,' said Jack, looking around. 'Bit of a crush, isn't it?'

'Have you just arrived?' asked Baines, and Jack nodded. 'Did you happen to notice . . . someone, by the door, as you came in?'

'Someone like . . . who?'

'Duncan Heathcote.'

Jack frowned for a moment. 'Heathcote . . . what, chap we were at the School with? No, I didn't.'

Perhaps he had been mistaken. The eyes could play tricks – and would he have recognised him in any case after all these years? He would be better off savouring the pleasure of that moment just gone when Bella had innocently squeezed his shoulder.

'I'll be back in a minute,' Baines said, leaving Bella and Jack talking to one another. He had to know. Quickening his steps he got to the stairs and carefully made his way to the turn. The ground floor was now full to the door, and the drone of chatter had raised a high invisible wall across the room. From this vantage he scanned the sea of faces. He lit a cigarette and waited, like a spy, allowing the smoke to plume down his nose. A few minutes went by . . . he must have imagined it. Somewhere he heard Richard's booming laugh and spotted him deep in conversation on the far side. He descended into the scrum and began dodging his way towards him, preparing in his head a couple of congratulatory phrases: it was his night, after all. Richard, amid a loose cabal of men whose braying voices seemed to compete with one another, saw Baines approaching and lifted his chin in welcome.

'Tom, at last,' he almost yelled – but Baines wasn't listening, for his envelopment within Richard's boisterous throng had brought him face to face with the man he thought he had glimpsed before. Now there was no doubt. His hair was receding, but the weakly handsome features had aged very little, and he apparently surveyed the world with the same humourless gaze. Baines felt an ecstatic sort of menace tightening his chest, as Richard gamely ploughed through the round of introductions. '. . . and this is Duncan –'

'I know who he is,' Baines cut in, sharply enough for Heathcote's eyes to focus and harden.

'Sorry . . . we – know each other?'

'Yes. Of old. School of Architecture, during the twenties. I'm Tom Baines.'

Heathcote frowned as he repeated the name under his breath. 'I don't think –'

'You know me,' said Baines, his tone flat and sinister. Richard, picking up the note of tension, tried to mediate.

'Sounds like someone's got a faulty memory, and if I know Tom, it's not his.'

'I'm sorry,' said Heathcote, still perplexed. 'I was at the School, it's true, but there's heaps of people I've forgotten since then.' He shrugged, almost apologetically, at Baines, and seemed about to turn away.

'You can pretend not to recognise me. But I think you'll remember Alice Thorn.'

Baines saw Heathcote flinch at this, and a faint light of recollection began to glimmer on his face. Richard was looking from one to the other, like a referee preparing to let them box.

'Yeah. I remember Alice,' he said, wary now. 'We used to see each other, years ago. She was – quite unhinged. But what's this got to do with anything? I still don't know you from Adam.'

Baines flushed at the dismissive tone. A little white dot that had been pulsing behind his eyes now flared, incandescent, like a filament jammed with current. He sensed Bella arriving at his side, unaware of the little confrontation in progress. Richard began to say something in his jovial conciliatory way, but Baines ignored him, ignored Bella too, as white anger shot blindingly around his skull.

'What's this got to do with? Let me explain. I wanted to *fucking kill* you.' Now his voice sounded strange and high and mad. He must have stepped towards Heathcote because he felt Richard flailing at him from behind, and a little wave of alarm rippled through the surrounding clamour. Behind him he heard someone say 'fight' just as his fist piled towards Heathcote's nose and made a quick, dry smack against bone.

'Whoa, Tom, what the –' Richard said, grabbing hold of him, and suddenly other tall-shouldered men had stepped in and were hustling him, kindly but firmly, away. Heathcote, he could see, was staggering like a newborn calf. The inside of Baines's head seemed to be caving in beneath some molten avalanche, it was a screaming white-out, and he could feel only the rhythm of his own breathing against the roar.

Out on Slater Street he was calming down, though the blood still pulsed loud in his ears. His hand ached from the impact of knuckle on bone. He leaned his head against a street lamp, its hooded eye extinguished, and took deep breaths, while behind him he heard Richard and Bella talking in urgent low voices. As sanity began to blink on again, he wondered at the sudden way it had just blown its fuses. He felt he had just endured a violent and disabling spasm. After some minutes he turned round to find Bella looking at him, with the air of a doctor assessing a potentially volatile patient.

'Are you all right?' she said, and even as he felt damp tentacles of shame begin to palpate him he was grateful that this was the first thing she said, instead of 'Have you gone mad?'

He nodded, not daring to catch her eye. 'Sorry' came out in a croak. He felt her staring, still. Across the road they heard the door of the studio opening as a couple exited, and the muffled roar from inside indicated that the party was continuing blithely without them.

'I can't go back in there,' he said eventually.

'I know.'

'But you should. I'll push off in a minute.'

Bella shook her head. 'No. We'll go for a drink, and you can perhaps explain to me . . .' She let the sentence hang.

'Look, I don't want to ruin your evening. And there's Richard too –'

'I've told Richard. He's going to meet us later. Come on – you're in no fit state to be left alone.'

They walked in silence through the darkening streets. The pubs were beginning to empty, and the frowzy reek of old beer wafted from their open doors to hang in the night air; snatches of laughter and shouted oaths echoed within. Outside St Luke's Church a chorus of drinkers were stumbling through a ragged repertoire of songs. One would start them off, then after a few uncertain bars his mates would join in, and the tune, doggedly pursued, would gradually subside into bibulous incoherence. Having turned into Hope Street Bella stopped at a tall terraced house, its door overhung by an intricately glazed fanlight. Blackout curtains sealed up the windows.

'This must be the place,' she murmured, and thunked the heavy brass door knocker against its plate. A short wait, then the door creaked open and a woman's face, heavily made up and no longer young, leaned coquettishly against the jamb. Her eyes, raccooned in black, made silent enquiry.

'Is this Nell's?' said Bella.

A pause. 'Who's asken, dear?' The voice carried a satisfying rasp, the sound of a lifetime's kippering in tobacco.

'Adrian Wallace invited us.'

A smirk lifted the corner of her mouth. 'I'll bet he did.' She scrutinised them for a few moments longer, then pulled the door back. Candlelight threw wobbling silhouettes on the wall as they proceeded through the narrow entrance hall, their hostess carrying a gas lamp that illumined her features in a hilariously odd parody of Gothic melodrama. She led them up a staircase, its panelled walls lined with the proprietorial faces of gilt-framed grandees, and then into a large L-shaped room with a bar at one end and a lounge at the other; candle flame wavered on tables where a few shadowy drinkers were hunkering down for the night. They settled at a pair of green plush armchairs and ordered brandy and soda.

Bella took in their surroundings with a sidelong look. 'I used to go to places like this in London,' she said, rather wistfully. 'We'd get soused on gin and discuss the redistribution of wealth.'

'Did you work anything out?'

She smiled. 'Most evenings it would end in an argument about who should pay for the drinks.' Leaning into the candle she let the tip of her cigarette catch the flame. 'Now,' she said, as though a decent interval had been observed, 'can you tell me what happened back there?'

Baines, a natural fugitive from disclosure, sensed his behaviour this evening had been sufficiently extravagant to put him under an obligation to explain. He took a swallow of the brandy and felt its liquid fire slide down his throat. 'That man, Duncan Heathcote –' it only occurred to him now that he might be a friend of hers. 'Do you know him?'

She shook her head. 'He must be one of Richard's crowd.'

'Small world,' he said, consideringly. 'I knew him from the School of Architecture, years ago, but he obviously didn't remember me.'

'I think he'll remember you now.'

He paused, and gazed into his glass. 'There was a girl, Alice – Alice Thorn – she was at the university. A music student. We'd met in our final year and became very close, very quickly. She was bright and funny and . . . different, you know? Quite a strange girl, she had an odd perspective on things. And she had a beautiful singing voice – that definitely appealed to me.'

'Were you – in love with her?' asked Bella.

'I suppose so. But I was too . . . diffident. I told her once, in a round-about way . . .' He sighed, trying to fix an image of her in his mind. 'Next thing I knew she was stepping out with Heathcote. I kept in touch, but clearly I'd missed whatever chance I might have had with her. We left the university, and over the next two or three years I'd spot them together here and there. I heard later that things weren't good between them, that he was having affairs behind her back . . .'

'A scoundrel, as you would put it,' Bella said.

He nodded briefly. 'Whatever he was doing, it had the effect of making her miserable. She was working at a music publisher, and a mutual friend told me that she'd break down in the office, or else not show up for days. I remember seeing her at a party one night, and she looked in an awful state. He was there too, of course, but more or less ignoring her. And then she was in tears, ranting away. I think it was pretty clear to everyone that she was . . . far from well.'

'Poor woman,' said Bella quietly. 'Did you ever think you'd had –'

'A lucky escape? Sometimes, yes. But I still clung to the memory of that funny girl I used to know. It was hard for me to accept how much she'd changed. So . . . then she disappeared, maybe for a year or more. I think everyone realised she'd been taken "away" somewhere. She eventually wrote to me, a rather sweet letter, sort of apologising for – I don't know what. She knew I'd been fond of her, that maybe things could have been different . . .'

He heard something catch in his voice, and waited to compose himself. He'd never recounted the whole thing to anyone before; a few others, including Jack, had known elements of it, but their versions had been gleaned from circumstantial observation and rumour. His throat felt parched.

'Tom,' said Bella, searching his face, 'I'd like to know what happened, but only if you want to tell me.'

'I was just thinking – how can anyone really know what happens between people? I mean, even the people involved don't always understand, so how could anyone else?'

'I suppose people claim to understand one another because it makes life easier. We observe, we imagine, we decide for or against them, but really it's no more than – guesswork. Even husbands and wives can be strangers to one another. Perhaps them most of all.'

Baines looked up from his glass at her. 'Do you not know Richard, then?'

She shrugged philosophically. 'Probably not. I don't know. But I feel quite certain he doesn't know me.' Exhaling a long jet of smoke she stubbed out her cigarette, and seemingly the line of conversation with it. An expectant silence fell, which seemed to prompt Baines towards his unfinished narrative.

'Anyway – I wrote back to Alice, in a friendly way, hoped she was on the mend, and so forth. I steered away from anything . . . dangerous. She was out of the sanatorium and back living with her parents, somewhere down in Sussex. We struck up a correspondence, and slowly recovered something of the old friendliness we'd once had. I didn't know if she'd seen Heathcote in the meantime. I didn't ask. There was some university reunion coming up, I suppose I must have mentioned it in a letter because she decided she wanted to come up and see the old crowd again. I was surprised, it seemed rather soon after her convalescence – but there it was . . . We agreed to meet up beforehand . . . a pub on Lime Street. She had changed, of course, in the year or so since I'd seen her. A sort of distance in her gaze, though she seemed in high spirits. I'd felt rather nervous myself – you have to remember, the last time I'd seen her she'd been rather unstable. She was quite open about what had happened. But it didn't really put me at ease . . .'

He called for another brandy and soda, puzzled as to why he still felt sober after a night's drinking. He needed another to propel him over the finishing line. Bella's dark eyes were intent on him, like a juror's on a witness.

'We eventually pushed off to the party – it was in the ballroom at the Adelphi. I think we were both quite skittish – reunions have that effect

– meeting people we hadn't seen in, what, five years. There was a crowd, and we lost each other, I don't remember how . . . but my heart just sank through the floor when I saw him. For some reason it hadn't occurred to me he'd be there. And of course he was with a woman, who turned out to be his betrothed – God help her. I saw Alice talking with him, briefly, and prayed that it would all be . . . When I next talked to her she seemed perfectly fine, a little drunk, but then so were we all. Once the bar closed a dozen or more of us repaired upstairs – someone had booked a suite on the top floor. Jack was there, probably with a girl. People kept coming in, carrying bottles. A few of the hotel band turned up. I remember someone blaring away on a trumpet. Some were drinking out on the balcony, it was a beautiful midsummer evening, still quite warm . . . One minute everything was fine, the next a cry went up, and there was a sudden rush outside. I saw a woman standing barefoot on the furthest edge of the parapet, and I knew immediately that it was Alice. She seemed weirdly at ease, as if there was nothing remarkable about what she was doing. I was horror-struck, we all were, and one or two friends started pleading with her to come down. I pushed my way through to the front and called to her – she saw me, and seemed almost to smile. I think I said, "For God's sake" . . . One minute she was there. Then she was gone.'

Bella's hand flew to her mouth as she exclaimed sharply, just as if she had been there herself that night and watched it happen. He hadn't seen Alice's plummeting descent, but he had imagined it so often that he sometimes felt convinced that he had. The sickening crack they heard was her body hitting the bonnet of a taxi parked on the hotel forecourt below. A woman next to him fainted as a commotion broke out. His mind had gone blank for a while after that; he vaguely recalled sitting on a sofa, his whole body violently shivering, and Jack next to him saying – he couldn't remember what. He looked again at Bella, whose gaze had nothing in it but pity. He suddenly felt exhausted; he had told the story in the hope of shaking off a ghost, but he sensed it still there, unforgiving.

'Tom, I'm . . . sorry,' she murmured.

'I'm afraid there's a rather grim coda to the story. There was an inquest, and a verdict of death by misadventure was returned. The coroner also reported that she – Alice – had been pregnant when she died. It was not known by whom, though of course I suspected Heathcote. But I had a feeling that I was in some way responsible. I'd accompanied her to the party, I should have been more . . . vigilant.'

'You can't blame yourself for that,' Bella said.

'Maybe not. But guilt has a way of insinuating itself, even when –'

'Even when you know that you're innocent?'

Baines nodded slowly, not looking at her.

Nell's had slowly begun to fill since they had sat down; a crowd of late-night topers stood at the bar. He was aware that he had just revealed more of himself in the last half-hour than he had done in the previous ten years. The story he had told seemed to be reverberating in the space between them. He wondered now if Bella, for all her show of sympathy, didn't despise him a little. Pity sometimes felt like that – the kindlier cousin of disdain.

'I'm sorry for . . . boring on like that,' he said. 'I'd better be off –'

'For heaven's sake, Tom! You haven't "bored on" at all.' She clasped his wrist beseechingly, and Baines was moved, for the second time that evening, by the touch of her hand. 'And in any case,' she added, dropping her voice sharply, 'I'm damned if you're leaving me alone with this character.'

Baines looked round and saw Adrian Wallace swaggering towards them. He was accompanied by one of Evie's girlfriends from the *Echo*.

'Hope I'm not interrupting anything,' he said, looking interestedly at Bella's hand still on Baines's sleeve.

'Hullo again,' said Bella. 'We took up your invitation, as you see.'

'Only happy to oblige you, my dear, and your gallant defender here,' he said, nodding at Baines.

'Sorry?' said Bella, nonplussed.

'I heard all about the fisticuffs at the gallery,' Wallace continued, sinking into a chair and sending his companion off to the bar. 'Sadly I was upstairs at the time and missed all the fun, but those at the ringside say that some cad propositioned you in a lewd fashion – and young Dempsey flattened him with a punch!'

Bella glanced at Baines, then turned back to Wallace with a triumphant smile. 'Yes, that's right. Tom was a real gent.'

'Hmm,' he said, with a measuring look at Baines, 'I should be careful around him.' The remark hung in the air.

'I do like this little hideaway,' said Bella, brightly. 'It's very clever of you to be a member.'

Wallace shrugged and looked about the room. 'It suits me pretty well. I suppose you met Maureen?'

'The lady at the door, with the make-up?'

'That's her. "The Black Widow", as she's known.'

'Oh?'

'She mates, then she kills,' he explained, smirking. 'The second part is metaphorical – or at least I think it is. Since the end of our . . . liaison, some years ago, Maureen has only *looked* daggers at me.'

'I see.'

'*Cherchez la femme*,' he sighed, and flicked at his grey mane again. Baines had never in his life encountered such a degree of campness in a heterosexual man. Wallace had the cultivated poise of a highly experienced male impersonator. 'Talking of which,' Wallace said, leaning round his chair, 'where has that young creature got to with our drinks?'

The creature in question was tottering uncertainly towards them, her progress slowed by the bottle of champagne and glasses she was balancing on a tray. Baines stood and went to her aid, gently extracting the tray from the girl's hands.

'There's a seat for you there,' he said, nodding towards his own vacated chair.

'Don't worry about that, she can sit here, can't you, Rose?'

'Where d'you mean – on your knee?' she giggled.

'Just here,' he said, patting the edge of his chair.

'All right then,' said Rose, wriggling herself in next to him, 'but no funny business.'

'The very idea,' he said, with a horrible leer, and popping the champagne, he poured them each a glass. Baines took a deep swallow and felt the acid bubbles burn inside his stomach – he had not eaten anything all evening. His hand had started to ache again, but he felt drunkenness comfortingly near. Bella and Wallace were talking about the Lisbon, a fancy restaurant on Stanley Street.

'They do a very good fried sole,' said Wallace. 'I took Noël to dinner there once.'

Baines, compelled by a sense of obligation – they were drinking his champagne – took the bait. 'Noël? You mean – Noël Coward?'

'Of course,' he said airily. 'Met him up here when one of his plays was at the Royal, can't remember which.'

'What did he make of Liverpool?' asked Baines.

'"Too, too thrrrilling,"' said Wallace, in a remarkable impersonation of the man's clipped tones. '"Oh to be in Liverpool, now that I'm at the Rrrroyal."' And for the next hour Wallace was unstoppable, apparently able to reproduce every last morsel of conversation he had gathered from the dinner table that night. As he delivered his party piece on Coward – 'Noël' – he seemed no longer to notice his guests, so enchanted was he by his own anecdotal exuberance. He flared his nostrils, he gurned, he rolled his 'r's to an improbable length. At times the mimicry became muddled with Wallace's own voice, to the point where they seemed to be listening to Noël Coward doing a silly but amusing imitation of a northern music-hall comic. As the drinks kept coming the laughter around the table rose giddily, until it had its own hysterical momentum; Wallace could have said anything now and they would have roared. Even Baines was helpless, the tears were rolling down his cheeks. Then he spotted a shark's fin of pale belly flesh peeking through Wallace's shirt front where it had ridden up over his belt, and he laughed even harder.

'. . . so the waiter arrives and puts the HP bottle on the tablecloth – Noël takes one look at it and says, "Sheer sauce".' It came out in two resonant syllables: *share soss*. 'And I said –'

Wallace never got the chance to relate another of his brilliant ripostes. An explosive whump, distant but distinct, had made the windows vibrate in their frames. They had heard an air-raid siren whining about half an hour before, but no one had paid it much attention: there had been that many false alarms. Half a minute later there came another one, nearer now, and the room fell silent. The faint throb of engines could be heard. From downstairs an urgent tattoo sounded on the door. Maureen, ensconced at her own table by the bar, called to one of her staff to answer it. 'If it's that warden on about the blackout curtains again, tell him to piss off.'

The barman hurried off, and returned with Richard, who was bright-eyed and breathing heavily, as if he'd sprinted all the way from Slater Street. Maureen, seeing his flustered state, went behind the bar and poured him a brandy.

'Thanks,' said Richard, as Bella led him over to their table. He sat down and puffed out his cheeks.

'What's going on out there?' asked Baines.

'I'd say there are about fifty planes circling to the south right now. I'd just locked up at the studio and was near the top of Bold Street when I heard their engines. At first I thought it was recon, then the bombs started falling, so I made a dash for it.'

'The barbarians at the gates,' said Wallace. He turned to Rose. 'I don't think it's quite safe for you to be alone tonight, my dear.'

Bella shook her head and laughed. 'You're a caution, Mr Wallace.'

But Rose was genuinely alarmed. 'How am I going to get home? I live in Woolton.'

'You might have to bed down for the night at mine,' said Wallace.

'Rose, don't worry,' said Bella, 'we've a spare room at our place, haven't we, Richard?'

Wallace raised his eyebrows in mock offence. 'Well, I was only offering a helping hand.'

'And I'm sure it's much appreciated. But we can take care of her tonight.' Bella flashed a smile that seemed to clinch the matter, leaving Wallace with the air of a schoolboy who'd been denied his usual cream bun.

Another half-hour passed before the all-clear sounded. Richard glanced at his wristwatch.

'Well . . . I think we should turn in for the night. Tom and I will have to report for duty first thing tomorrow.'

They emerged from Nell's expecting a scene of devastation to greet them, but Hope Street looked to be sleeping peacefully.

'I think the bombs must have fallen over yonder,' said Baines. They walked to the brow of Upper Duke Street, and there, on the horizon, a lurid greenish glow was visible some miles away.

'What on earth is that?'

'Incendiary bombs,' said Richard.

'So what was the one that rattled the windowpanes?'

'I presume it was a high explosive, probably went off a couple of miles away.'

They stood in silence for a few moments. Wallace cleared his throat.

'"'Tis now the very witching time of night, / When churchyards yawn and hell itself breathes out / Contagion to this world." In short, I'm off home. I hope, my dear,' he said, pressing Bella's hand to his lips, 'this is merely *au revoir*.' He nodded briskly to Baines and Richard – 'Gentlemen' – and cast a sidelong look at Rose. 'I'll see you in the office, cheeky.' He sauntered off.

'Is he always like that?' Bella asked Rose.

'Pretty much. I've heard those Noël Coward stories before, and they're still dead funny.'

'He rather fancies you,' said Richard to Bella.

'Hmm, almost as much as he fancies himself.'

As they said their goodnights Baines took Richard aside.

'I'm terribly sorry about earlier this evening. That man – well, it's a long story.'

Richard smiled and said, 'You can tell me it sometime. I've never much cared for Heathcote, to be honest, so it wasn't altogether unpleasant seeing you land one on him.'

'I didn't want to ruin –'

'Just get some sleep. It could be a long day tomorrow.'

Baines was woken from an uneasy slumber less than four hours later by an outrageously parched mouth and a searing spasm of cramp in his leg: the drunkard's dawn. Too restless to get back to sleep, he limped into the kitchen and drank off a long glass of water. In his study the blackout curtains had sealed in an almost funereal atmosphere; parting them slightly admitted a shaft of ashen light, and he saw on his cherrywood side table the Eames journals. They formed a little still life there, dusty and somehow accusing, like Miss Havisham's wedding cake. He had glanced through them from time to time, but had not sat down to read them properly for months. He now recalled his piqued defence of the architect to Wallace last night. He sat down and picked up a stiff-boarded volume, briefly flicking back and forth until he had found his place.

20th April 1864

I see that a year has gone up in smoke since I last wrote in this journal. A year! To the charges of neglect I can but offer the defence of its being the most insanely & productively busy twelvemonth of my life hitherto. What changes have come to pass. First, & dearest to me of all, is the woman whom I now call my wife – moreover, a wife with child. Next is the house to which we have removed, situated in the middle of a fine, tall terrace providentially named Hope-place. Third, another house which I take leave to call my own – Janus House – opened for business last month, & every day the people file down Temple-street to stare & point & declare their astonishment, as if some asteroid had plummeted from the Heavens & landed on their doorstep. The press notices have been, thus far, extraordinarily hostile. The *Mercury* slights it as 'a greenhouse gone mad', while the satirical weekly, the *Badger*, offers this: 'The plainest brick warehouse in the town is infinitely superior, as a building, to that large agglomeration of protruding plate-glass bubbles in Temple-street, known as Janus House.'

Let them scoff – it is nothing to me. I was more surprised by the response on handing my notice to Sandham some days ago. I had expected a blast of indignation, a plague upon all my houses &c., but the old man seemed quite philosophical, shook my hand & wished me good fortune. I know he considers me a youth of overweening ambition – but as the poet wrote, 'a man's reach should exceed his grasp, or what's a heaven for?'

29th April [1864]

Chiltern calls at the club today bearing a copy of this week's *Punch*, & excitedly thrusts a page of it under my nose: 'Read here!' he cries. It runs:

> *Thy streets, fair Liverpool, now turn their face*
> *Upon a human greenhouse, so it seems,*
> *Bereft, alas, of beauty or of grace,*
> *And blame for this abortion – Mr Eames.*

To my surprise he calls for champagne & raises a toast. Has he, I ask him, read this disobliging doggerel? 'Of course,' he replies. '*Punch*, of all things – you're famous, my boy!' If this is fame then it has little savour for me. But I did enjoy the champagne.

May [1864]

The press continue to fire their poison darts. The *Engineer* (which ought to know better) has decanted a whole column of bile upon Janus House. It is really quite astonishing that I should have managed to affront so many; worse, it is alarming that, having set up business on my own, a prospective client may take notice of these assaults. Under the anonymity of Sandham's patronage, I was ever assured of employment, but when my name is hoisted up the flag-pole for all to jeer who will be tempted to offer a commission?

1st June 1864

The crowning insult. The architectural critic of the *Badger*, having vented his spleen on Janus House, now takes leave to write a long panegyric on the recently completed Daubeny & Rudd Bank on Brunswick-street – 'To those who have studied architecture, the merest glimpse of this building is sufficient to demonstrate the true metal of craftsmanship – the goldsmith's mark.' This, the building which I designed & then suffered old Sandham to make his footling improvements upon after D&R cut up rough. Today I visited

Brunswick-street & found that the bank, including the windows of which they had first complained, is almost brick-for-brick the edifice which I set down in the plans. But nowhere is my name mentioned.

In a fury I wrote to the *Badger's* critic explaining what 'those who have studied architecture' signally failed to notice, namely that the Brunswick-street bank is a design of Peter Eames, so lately defamed in their pages &c. &c. That letter is just now burning in the grate. It is folly to bandy words with the press. As an old legal friend of Pa's once said: 'Never engage in a fight with people who purchase their ink by the ton.'

June 9th 1864

A mystery has been solved. During the final weeks of construction on Janus House I had cause to notice a young fellow loitering about the place, occasionally carrying a notebook in which he would appear to sketch the elevation in front of him. I conceived an idea that he was a spy in the pay of a rival practice, or else some other kind of mischief-maker, but so fiercely absorbed in work was I at the time that I did not bother to approach him, & after some weeks he disappeared. It so happened I was on Temple-street today when a fellow tapped me on the shoulder; I turned & recognised him – the rough tweed checks, the twirled cane – as my spy. He said, 'Sir, I believe I have the honour of addressing Peter Eames – allow me to shake your hand.' The manner was courtesy itself; the accent was American. He introduced himself as John Rawlins, & told me a little of his history. He is a native of Atlanta, Georgia, where his father practised as an architect before his death. He had hoped to follow his late sire into the business when the War broke out; he fled the country to avoid conscription, & fetched up here. 'Since my arrival I have been making a study of this great city's buildings, & of them all yours is to me the most inventive & inspiring' – an opinion in which I am entirely disposed to concur. After the calumnies I have recently endured Mr Rawlins' words come as sweet balm indeed.

Tuesday, 21st June [1864]

Dinner with my American friend Rawlins, & more of his gratifying blandishments. He calls me a poet of architecture, who finds 'as much delight in stones as in stanzas'; this idea I know he has got from Ruskin in *The Stones of Venice*, who cites reading a building as comparable to reading Milton & Dante, & demands that we 'wake to the perception of a truth just as simple & certain as it is new: that great art, whether expressing itself in words, colours, or stones, does not say the same thing over & over again; that the merit of architectural, as of every other art, consists in its saying new & different things' – in short, that we may look to an architect, as we do to a poet, to be entertaining as well as truthful. For all Rawlins' pleasant flattery, in Janus House I know that I have written only a sonnet, though it is perfect of its kind. One day, mark me, I shall create something 'new & different' & it shall be my epic – my *Paradise Lost*!

We fell to talk of business at the end of the evening, & Rawlins asked me to consider taking him on as an assistant of 'the company'. I laughed & explained that my company at present consisted in nothing more than a tiny chamber off the Exchange, that I had not a desk nor a chair nor money to pay him. He was undaunted by this news, & said that until the first commission was secured he would work for nothing. (I gather he came into a small legacy on his father's death.) Moved by such enthusiasm, I took his hand, & promised him that this faith would be rewarded. He beamed back at me: 'Sir, I know it.'

8th August 1864

This day my wife presented me with our first child, a daughter: Ellen Frances.

August [1864]

Ma has received a letter from Frank in Jamaica, his first in more than a year. He writes that he is 'hale & hearty', and that he has been getting on capitally in business – a claim one has cause to doubt when he reports a few sentences later that he has left Eames &co. 'for the present' to pursue certain financial interests of his own. It is perhaps significant that he writes to Ma & not to Pa, who had secured the Kingston engagement for him in the first place. Has he found more promising opportunities than the coffee trade can furnish? I hope for the best, yet the news has thrown us into confusion – Frank, though as dear a brother to me as a man could wish, has neither ambition nor any especial power of application, & the prospect of his venturing alone into business causes me (I confess it) great unease.

September [1864]

Pa calls me into his study this morning to confide the burden of a letter he has received from his manager, Mr Boyce, in Kingston, & a sorry burden it is. He writes to say that Frank, innocently or not, had got himself into low company, & that in recent months he had incurred gambling debts of a quite unmanageable nature. Boyce, to our relief, had succeeded in paying off his creditors, & had determined to write to my father advising him of his son's dissolute behaviour when Frank, of a sudden, handed in his notice & promptly slung his hook, to go whither they knew not. Pa, greatly depressed by this intelligence, urges me not to disclose a word of it to Ma, who would only fret herself to distraction. He then asks me what is to be done, to which I propose that I should write to Frank – at his last address? – suggesting that he return home (it will do no good begging) where a position here awaits him, should he desire one. At any rate, to have him back in Liverpool should be our principal object. Pa seems mollified by this, knowing that nothing he should write in that vein would have the slightest effect, for he & Frank have been antagonists for years.

I have just finished composing that letter, & can only hope that its recipient, on seeing the most affectionate & earnest love with which it is expressed, will respond in like fashion.

10th November 1864

What a boon has Rawlins proved to be. His work as a draughtsman, while promising, is not yet of the first order, but his willingness to negotiate business, to seek out opportunities, to pick up the scent of money – in this he is without peer. Last month he arranged the lease on splendid new premises in Tithebarn-street, with an office for each of us, at a rent set astonishingly low. Is this his peculiar talent, or are all Americans so canny? This week alone he has secured new building contractors, designed an advertisement to run in the *Mercury* & made a fair copy of the plans I have submitted for the Chapel-street competition. If that dreadful war comes to nothing, I shall at least be thankful that it has blown this admirable fugitive across my path.

25th November [1864]

A curious letter from Frank. He dismisses my concern without assuaging it, making little mention of his severance from the company

& none at all of his gambling debts. Far from acknowledging any gratitude to Boyce, Pa's manager, he appears to resent him for his refusal to disburse company funds on a certain private 'business venture' he had been pursuing. I can only thank God that Boyce had the wisdom to do so, for any such disbursement would have been immediately & irrecoverably lost.

December [1864]

An early Christmas gift at Tithebarn-street. The winner of the competition for the office building in Chapel-street has been announced – step forward, Mr Eames! A scene of great excitement at our little office; Rawlins is quite beside himself, not least because the premium is set at 200 guineas. Oh, those wretches of the press who pierced me with their satiric barbs & held up my work to ridicule – let them try to injure me now!

Thursday, 9th February, 1865

To walk about Liverpool at present & witness whole streets half-torn down & instantly built up again is a remarkable thing. A week's absence from town will make a man feel a stranger on his return. A frenzy of demolition spreads across the place like some monstrous plague, its dragon-breath a smouldering compound of fire & mortar & brick & iron. The air is permanently aswarm with grit & soot – it is impossible to keep a clean shirt – & the sound of clanking & hammering so violent as to knock one's head askew. Thoroughfares become impassable as steam engines & gangs of navvies establish their own independent republics-old cobbled streets are eaten up by vast trenches & excavations. Beneath it all flows a river of money, swollen & ready to burst its banks. These changing times might cause a gentle soul alarm, but to an architect it is only exhilarating.

Wednesday, 1st March, 1865

Ma arrives at Hope-pl. this morning in a breathless agitation of spirits I misconstrue as portending bad news. But no – her excitement concerns a letter that arrived this morning from Frank, announcing his intention to leave Kingston & return home. He embarks on the 15th of the month. Good Lord. The suddenness of this news is enough to stun me, but when I see the delight writ upon my mother's face I am much affected, & in a burst of exultation I waltz her about the room. 'Oh, to have Francis back with us again!' she cries. Eight years away. He will find the place much changed, I think.

Monday, 27th March [1865]

Today I witnessed something quite terrible. I was walking to the office & had stopped halfway along North John-street to have my boots cleaned by the little fellow who keeps a pitch there. It was a morning no different from any other, the traffic was not unduly heavy & people were going about their business with no particular urgency; the crossing-sweeper was clearing the thoroughfare of horse manure, a coster wheeled his barrow along & whistled away, & the city's bankers & brokers pounded the pavement like so many others towards their chambers of commerce. I had just given sixpence to the bootblack & lifted my gaze across the way, where another huge building was under construction.

At the top of the scaffold I could see two men talking to one another on the parapet, about six storeys above the street, then strolling quite unconcernedly along the narrow wooden platform linking one side to the other. I was still watching them – I cannot explain why – when that platform suddenly lurched, the rope on one side seeming to have snapped, & tipped steeply at an angle. One of the men had already gained safety, but the other had lost his footing & was now clinging for dear life to the loosened plank as it swung off the scaffold. I heard a cry go up as the man hung there, frantically kicking his legs, & of a sudden the traffic around me came to a dead halt, as if an invisible puppeteer had jerked its strings & alerted them to the calamity overhead. I had the queer feeling that the whole street had sharply drawn in its breath, startled by the sight of this dangling figure whose piteous shrieks now carried the full force of mortal apprehension. The man's mate looked down, helpless – everybody else looked up. I was horribly transfixed, & had begun to calculate for how long the man could hang there (what strength might he have in those arms?) when in an instant he was plunging through the air, his body performing a kind of cartwheel, it seemed, but one that could find no purchase in the careless medium of thin air & had as its only end the ground he had not thought to touch so precipitately. I gasped at the sound he made upon hitting the pavement – it was a *thock*, & resonated with a hard, hideous finality. The stillness as he lay there attested to his condition more certainly even than the claret-dark liquid that was now pooling around his head. Shaken beyond imagining I turned away & directed my steps to Tithebarn-street like a sleepwalker in his trance. Rawlins, seeing my pallor, immediately plied me with his brandy flask until I was able to give a stumbling account of the accident – it was but a weak shadow of the real thing.

Tuesday 28th [March, 1865]

A report in today's *Mercury* of the accident in North John-street. The dead man, a labourer named Joseph Tressell, left behind a wife & two children. He was twenty-five – my age. I had thought to tell Emily of it, but she was preoccupied with the infant. Ma & Pa also elsewhere in their thoughts, for Frank arrives on the morrow. Besides, how to convey the horror of that poor creature falling through the air, & the frightful noise that still sounds in my head?

29th March 1865

Casting aside my gloom I accompanied the whole family down to the Pier Head to greet Frank on his return. The sky was heavy with colossal thunder clouds, though the Mersey offered a prospect to delight the eye, crowded as it was with vessels of all kinds – barques, brigs, schooners, cutters, steamers, skiffs, tugs, even rowing boats plied the river, while on the quayside swarmed men hauling loads, sailors shouting to one another, merchants overseeing their cargoes brought from all the shores of the oceans. Show me a seaport to rival this! After a delay of an hour or more we spotted in the distance the red funnel pipe of the Cunard steamship, her masts billowing in the wind, cannon firing to announce her arrival. The ship moored in the middle of the river, & soon a little mail-steamer was puffing its way to the landing-stage bearing such of the passengers as chose to disembark. We eagerly scrutinised the crowd as it came ashore, they numbered a hundred or more, yet nowhere amongst them could we see him; on & on they passed, until the very last stragglers were descending the gangplank. Then Ma cried out, 'There he is!' – & indeed there was Frank, beaming in that familiar way, though in so much else he looked changed. Thinner of face, which now looks quite swarthy ('dusky as a mulatto', I later heard Ma whisper), his hair cropped close & near-blond from the sun, & something distant in his gaze, as if he were still lost in the tropical climes of Jamaica. His coat & trousers were travel-stained, of course, & I noticed his shirt was frayed at the cuffs. He looked tired, but his spirits seemed high. Ma & the girls fell on his neck, & once he had managed to detach himself from their embraces he went to Pa & shook his hand. William & he seemed hardly to recognise one another, and Frank marvelled at him – I suppose Will was only a boy of nine when he left in '57. He came, last of all, to me, & said simply, 'Pete.' I felt tears start from my eyes as I embraced this man whose blood runs in my veins yet who seemed withal a kind of stranger to me. As I introduced him to Emily & the child I raised a silent prayer to God, & thanked Him for the safe return of our brother.

April [1865]

This morning I took Frank to the Chapel-street site, where the building of Magdalen Chambers continues. I explained to him how the three bays of its front would resemble a huge mullioned window, with the middle arch pushed higher to form a curving gable. Then we walked through to the rear courtyard, where a glass curtain wall similar to that of Janus House is to be erected. As I was running on I realised that Frank, far from being swept along by my enthusiasm, was barely listening. I stopped, & waited for him to speak. Presently he turned to me & asked, 'How did you come by all this?' I replied that I had submitted a design in a competition, & that my entry had won it. At the word 'competition' his eyes suddenly lit up – this did interest him, but for a quite mistaken reason. As he construed it, I had made some sort of wager at a gaming table & by sheer nerve, or good fortune, had pocketed the winnings. I avowed that there was, indeed, an element of chance, but as to the placing of bets & the casting of dice ... Having taken in this explanation he fell silent, & I felt conscious of disappointing him. I was not the gambler he thought me after all.

We then went off to dine at the Cockspur. Frank ate little, but we both drank steadily – claret, & then gin. My head was quite thick by the late afternoon, but Frank seemed perfectly unaffected. Hitherto we had not touched on the debts he had incurred, but now I asked him how he proposed to make a living (for he does not wish to work for Pa). At this he looked at me & smiled: 'I've a few irons in the fire, don't you worry.' *But I am worried,* I wanted to say. When the waiter presented our bill to us I took it without thinking, but Frank snatched it out of my hand & to my amazement produced a handful of coins, sovereigns among them. He clinked a couple of them on to the salver. I had heard of sailors on shore leave loaded with blunt, but it had never occurred to me that my own brother would be so flush in the pocket. He winked at me, as if to forestall my asking whence his new wealth had come.

June [1865]

I heard Frank creaking up the staircase again at about two o'clock this morning. Since his homecoming from the West Indies he has been resident with us in Hope-pl., & we have become acquainted, too well, with the peculiar hours he keeps. It remains a mystery to me what he has been at, though whenever I have been working late in the study & caught his return he wears on him the strong smell of grog and tobacco. I hardly mind for my own sake, but his nocturnal crashings have awoken the child, and seeing Emily's piteously drawn face the next morning has induced me to plead with him for a softer footfall on his midnight entrances. Each time he seems contrite, & vows to be quiet as a mouse – but he soon forgets these solemn assurances & returns in the small hours with all the consideration of a thunderclap. Today I had stern words with him (the child was roused from sleep again) & suggested that he should continue here for another two weeks, & in the meantime seek accommodation of his own. He agreed to this, and thanked me for my forbearance in such an earnest, good-hearted way that I felt a dreadful pang of guilt immediately thereupon, & almost called him back to say that I spoke in jest, that our house was his for as long as he pleased. But I did not.

29th June [1865]

Rawlins has come to my aid once again. A friend of his recently vacated rooms in Mount-street, & let slip that the landlord was in need of a tenant. Knowing of our troubles, John secured the lease, & today, after completing negotiations, Frank took possession of the place. The rooms are tolerably furnished, though the walls quite bare, so in the afternoon I brought round some small paintings and sketches from Hope-pl. to hang. As I approached the house I happened to look up & caught Frank staring blankly out of the window: before me rose the vision – I cannot account for it – of a prisoner locked within his cell. He did not see me, but when I entered the room he greeted me with a smile that fleetingly recalled the genial and innocent youth I once knew. He seems to have money enough, the most part of it from gambling I should say, & perhaps he is in his mysterious way happy. Yet I am oppressed with a feeling, justifiable or not, of having abandoned him.

7

As Baines stepped out of the van he glanced up at the sky, where a number of planes were circling. Their formation was so regular that they reminded him of the silvery flying boats he had watched revolving on a merry-go-round as a child. It had just struck midnight, and the thunder of the ack-ack guns was still going strong. Now and then the darkness was spattered with a white enfilade of bursting shells. The shattered pub to which his rescue squad had been called was just off Canning Place, and the scene that met them disclosed a kind of strangeness that was quickly becoming familiar. The front wall of the building had been mostly torn away, leaving it exposed like a doll's house; on the first floor, a toilet stood open to inspection, and next to it a bedroom, with a few pictures still clinging to the walls. Below, the rubble of mangled masonry and charred wood that filled the interior was hissing from where the firemen's hoses had been busy. A staircase zigzagged from the top floor and ended, abruptly, in a puzzle of twisted ironwork about three feet above the bar.

'Right, you lot wait here while I talk to the warden,' said Rafferty, the squad leader, his breath pluming in the chilly November air. He was standing with his hands on his hips, surveying the damage. A tall, square-faced, heavily built man in his early fifties, he carried himself with an air of righteous complacency; Baines wondered if he'd once been in the army. The order was met with sullen silence by the two men who had just emerged from the back of the van. When Rafferty was out of earshot, one of them muttered to the other, 'I'm tellin' yer, la', he used to be a copper. He's got that mean look about 'im, I can spot 'em.' This was Farrell, who, perhaps because he was of an age with Rafferty, resented his authority more keenly than the rest. A thickset, pugnacious-looking builder, he had dark curly hair and a face that seemed in permanent need of a shave. The other man, Liam Mavers, turned to Baines. 'What do you reckon, Tommy? D'you think Rafferty lives in Letsby Avenue?'

'Beg your pardon?'

'It's where coppers come from – let's-be-'avin'-you. D'you gerrit?'

Farrell laughed, as if at an old joke.

'I'd say he's more like a sergeant major,' said Baines. 'You notice how straight he holds himself?'

'Yeah, that's from the poker he's got rammed up his arse,' said Farrell. 'I mean, you 'eard what he just said – "You lot wait 'ere." Like, where the fuck does he think we're gonna go?' He shook his head in disgust. Mavers smiled. 'You should feel sorry for him. I bet he secretly knows we all hate him.'

Mavers generally took this philosophical approach. He was about Baines's age, and had worked on building sites with Farrell for years. His quiet smile and penetrating blue eyes expressed most of what he thought about the folly that passed for the world. Nobody had addressed Baines as 'Tommy' since he was a boy, but in Mavers' sardonic Liverpudlian undertone it sounded all right. Baines was rather intrigued by him. Farrell, on the other hand, he wasn't sure about; it was always the way with moody types. One day he would be cracking jokes and palling up with everyone, the next he had turned darkly, even dangerously, aggressive, and then people would try to keep out of his way. Tonight he seemed somewhere in between.

Rafferty had returned from his consultation with the warden.

'Well, as far as they can tell, there's nobody left upstairs, and the first-aid people are standing by. Ambulances have just gone with the casualties.'

'How many?' asked Mavers.

'Seven dead and twelve injured. The landlord and six of his regulars – seems they had a lock-in and hadn't bothered taking shelter. The warden thinks there might be people in the cellar.'

He delivered this inventory in a neutral tone. It was odd, thought Baines, how only a few months could make talk of death sound so casual.

'There's no chance of findin' the cellar doors under that,' said Farrell, nodding at the ton of debris that had spilt over the street.

'Probably not,' said Rafferty. 'Which means we'll have to look for the staircase inside. There should be one behind the bar, if we can get to it.'

Baines lifted his gaze to the top of the building, where on one side a Dutch gable and a solitary dormer remained intact. It was a late-Victorian redbrick palace on four storeys, a grand old pub that had probably once been a favourite among sailors and dockers. Its brewery signage had split clean in half, so that Warrington Ales now became two: WARRING and, at an angle, TON ALES. Suddenly there was a shivery sound from above, and a warden shouted, 'Everyone back!' Tiles had loosened from the roof and now plummeted down the side of the pub, shattering on the cobbles.

'Watch out for them, lads!' someone called over.

'Yeah, fat chance we've got if one lands on us,' growled Farrell.

The heavy drone of the planes was beginning to fade, which Baines noted with relief. There was nothing a rescue worker hated more than having to explore a building while another attack was going on above them. Rafferty, holding a storm lantern, led the way into the cavernous smoking mouth of the pub. They clambered over the wreckage, the air mingling damp soot with pulverised brick and warm beer, and made it to the saloon bar at the back of the building. The lamp revealed partial devastation: all the windows had been blown out, and the blackened ceiling dripped with water from where the firemen had been at it. But the bar counter itself and the beer taps seemed to have been untouched. Farrell picked up a bar stool, shook off the dusting of glass splinters and sat down.

'All right, who's gettin' the ales in?' he said. Baines and Mavers chuckled indulgently.

'That'll do, Farrell,' said Rafferty. 'Have a look behind there and see if there's a door.'

Farrell swung his huge frame over the counter and disappeared for a moment. They could hear his boots crunching over the glass, and then saw the thin beam of his torch return.

'Nothun 'ere,' he called.

Rafferty took up the lantern again and shone it into the far corner, where a door was partially occluded by a piano that had been hurled across the room and landed, at an angle, against it. They heaved it away and the instrument fell with a crash and a high muffled chord, as if a drunk had just bellyflopped across the keys. The door turned out to be locked.

'Mavers, on you go,' said Rafferty.

Mavers stepped forward, handling the pickaxe that he had kept slung across his back. He gave the door an exploratory tap with the steel beak of the axe, then looked round.

'Give us some room, will yer?' he said, and the other three took a few steps back to allow him a full swing. The pickaxe rang against the wood, tearing and splintering the panel nearest the handle; several more blows made a hole large enough for him to put his arm through and unlock the door from the other side. A staircase dropped steeply into the dark. Rafferty held his lamp out, throwing bulbous shadows against the damp brick wall.

'Hullo? Anyone down there?'

A woman's voice, which sounded as though it came from the bottom of a well, rose in answer. Her words were impossible to decipher, though the distress in her tone was clear enough.

'Could you speak up, love?'

The voice came again, now an anxious gabbled echo. Rafferty turned back and muttered, 'Can't hear a bloody word she's saying. Right then, Baines, Farrell – follow me. Mavers, stay here and listen out for any sounds.' He meant sounds that threatened collapse; by now they all knew stories of rescue workers who had been buried under houses that had fallen during their search for survivors; knew also how little chance they had of escaping a building once it had begun its final disintegration.

As they reached the bottom of the staircase they trained their torch beams over the cellar, a chaos of broken plasterwork and tumbled bricks. The floor was pooled with ale, still seeping from punctured kegs and shattered bottles.

'Over here.'

The woman's voice quavered from behind a sort of barricade of fallen masonry and crates. Baines, who was nearest, pointed his torch in the direction the voice had come from and began stepping, sloshing, through the beery, ankle-deep flood. As he came nearer he realised that something had broken through the ceiling; it must have been a toppled chimney stack, because the damage it had brought in its descent was riotous. His beam swept the littered floor in front of him, and then he spotted it, not a chimney stack at all but a steel cylinder in grey-green casing, snouty and heavy like a prize-winning marrow, its tail fins set at a jaunty-looking angle. He had not seen one in its unexploded state before. His heart, which had been drumming, was now trying to beat down the walls of its cage. He swallowed, and called to Rafferty and Farrell.

'You might care to look at this.' He wanted his heart to stop swelling, it was constricting his chest. He felt Rafferty's sudden halt as he came up beside him. And now Farrell saw it too.

'Oh fuck,' he said, softly. 'What are the chances . . .'

Baines experienced an unbidden cartoon image of them as a trio of pith-helmeted explorers in a jungle, picking their way single file through the undergrowth and popping their eyes, like the Three Stooges, as they came face to face with the beast. The image dissolved. 'If that's a delayed action –' said Rafferty, and stopped himself, as though speculation at this point was useless. They had no choice but to hope it was a dud. Baines felt his legs carrying him on towards the objective that had brought them down there. Tucked into an alcove behind the barricade – he understood its purpose now – were two women and two teenaged children, a boy and a girl, all of them coated in soot and plaster dust. They cowered, blinded by the torchlight, and he briefly forgot his fear as he took in their piteous, stricken faces. Perhaps that was the secret to keeping on, he thought, the sight of people more terrified than you were.

'Hullo there,' he said, his voice steady. 'Is anyone hurt?'

The younger of the two women nodded. 'Irene, me sister, she sprained her ankle when she fell. We can't move her.'

'All right, then,' said Rafferty. 'Let's get you all out of here. Farrell, d'you think you can carry this lady?'

Farrell stepped forward, and crouched down by the woman with the injured ankle. 'Here we go, love. You put your arms round me neck, like that –' As he scooped her up the woman whimpered, and then quietly began to weep. 'Is this yer mum?' he asked the boy and the girl, who nodded.

'Let's get her to the 'ozzie, then.'

Rafferty led the way back, shepherding the children, then Farrell carrying the woman, then Baines with the sister, whose name was Joyce. As they stepped past the bomb, he felt her hands tighten on his arm. She knew how close they were, then.

'I can't understand it,' she said in a fierce whisper, 'I just can't understand it.'

'What is it? What can't you understand?' asked Baines, though an instinct told him that he knew what it was. Joyce wouldn't say anything else until they had ascended the staircase and were hurrying back through the mounds of debris. Out on the street another ambulance had arrived, and the first-aid team were standing by for any casualties. The woman in Farrell's arms was looking around in disbelief at the gutted pub.

'Roy, me husband,' she said, forlornly, 'is he all right? Is he safe?'

'I'm sure he's fine, love,' said Farrell, 'just calm yourself now.'

Joyce, hearing this exchange, whispered again to Baines. 'Her husband's the landlord – is he – ?' He looked at her, trying to compose his features, but she read it in his eyes.

'I'm sorry,' he said, quietly.

She put her hand to her mouth to stifle a sob. After some moments she spoke again.

'We heard such a big blast when we were down there. Then that other one flew down into the cellar – I could tell what it was, but we couldn't move because of Irene. I just kept praying that it wouldn't go off.'

'It was very brave of you,' said Baines. 'Most people would have panicked – you did the right thing, trying to take cover.'

'I can't understand it,' she said, returning to her refrain. 'We heard it fizz. Why didn't it go off?'

'It still might. You – we – were just lucky.'

'Luckier than poor Roy. How am I going to tell them? Those kids don't have a father any more . . .'

A medical attendant approached them holding a blanket, which Baines took and draped around the woman's shoulders. Farrell had surrendered the landlord's wife to the stretcher-bearers, who were now lifting her into the ambulance.

'You might want to go with them to the hospital,' said Baines.

'Yes,' Joyce replied absently, and began walking away. Then she seemed to collect herself, and turned back to him.

'Thanks for –' she started, but was unable to say more. Baines held out his hand, and she looked at him with a tear-stained half-smile as she shook it.

They left the ruined pub just as the bomb-disposal team were arriving, and then answered a number of less dramatic emergencies through the night. They rescued an elderly couple trapped in a house on Great George Street, and later, at a distillery on King Street, they recovered a fireman who had survived a sixty-foot fall from his ladder. As a lavender dawn light crept in over the city and their shift ended, the full extent of the night's raids became apparent. The streets had a gaunt, exhausted look, as if they had just taken a violent beating – windows that had been black-eyed, facades punched through, roofs stamped on and battered without mercy. Rafferty, driving back to the depot, had to keep twisting the wheel of the van to avoid gigantic bomb craters and heaps of debris, the result of a collapsed wall or a blown-out shopfront. Even at this hour people were stoically toiling to clear the rubble, sweeping up glass that sounded like the tide running over a shingled beach. It was cause for a satiric cheer from Farrell that Rafferty had made it back without puncturing a tyre.

They tramped into the depot and found members of another rescue squad playing darts.

'Put the kettle on, la', I'm fuckin' parched,' said Farrell to no one in particular as he flopped into an armchair. Rafferty ignored him and went to the office where he sat to type up his incident reports. Mavers ambled over to the sink and filled the kettle from the tap.

'You wanna brew, Tommy?' he asked.

Baines, his eyes already closed as he slumped on a couch, croaked, 'Yeah, thanks.'

He must have fallen asleep immediately because a few minutes later Mavers was waking him with a gentle tap on his shoulder. A mug of steaming tea had been set on the arm of the couch. Farrell was blowing smoke rings and flicking the ash into his upturned helmet. Baines wasn't sure if he had the energy to lift the mug to his mouth. Farrell began describing the close encounter they had had in the pub cellar some hours before.

'The prof 'ere spotted it first. He says, cool as a cucumber, like, "You might care to look at this —" and 'e's pointen at this huge-fuckin' bomb!'

Farrell, who gave nicknames to everyone as a matter of course, had decided to call Baines 'the professor' after learning that he had written a *buke*. The fluting imitation of his voice was a travesty, but Baines was too tired to care.

'That pub must have had a curse on it,' said Mavers. 'Think about it — what are the chances of two bombs landin' on yer the same night?'

'That's what I said! If that one had gone off it woulda been Goodnight Vienna — for all of us.'

When he next woke Farrell and Rafferty had both gone. Mavers had his feet up on a chair and was reading a book, his brow furrowed in slightly disbelieving appraisal. He looked over at Baines.

'Yer tea's still there.'

Baines looked round at the untouched mug. His eyes itched and his tongue felt horribly furred. 'How long have I been asleep?'

Mavers shrugged. 'Couple of hours, maybe. You looked 'alf dead.'

'Hmm. That's pretty much how I feel. I'm starving hungry.'

'We can go and get some brekky, if you like.'

They emerged into a raw, gloom-shrouded morning and trudged down James Street towards the Pier Head. Great swollen sea clouds were heaving up from the river, and the sky was the mottled colour of pigeon feathers. In the streets around the financial district a skewed sort of routine was taking hold; bowler-hatted men with furled umbrellas were talking unconcernedly outside their bombed-out chambers and office buildings. It seemed that many had decided to continue business hours out on the pavement. Road-repair teams were busily attending to tramlines and overhead cables. The air down by the river had a thick, charred smell from the docks that had been set ablaze, and the burnt cargoes of rum and sugar and pepper added to the fiery bouquet. The cafe Mavers had brought them to was just by the Goree, and had taken a recent hit from flying shrapnel.

One side of its plate-glass front had been boarded up with plywood, on which had been painted a defiant WE'RE STILL OPEN.

They sat by the window, where they could watch the dock traffic rumble by. From the pocket of his reefer jacket Mavers removed a pack of cigarettes and his book, to which he called Baines's attention.

'You ever read this?'

Baines examined the spine: it was *The Secret Agent*, by Conrad. He shook his head.

'It's all right. Not as good as *Lord Jim*, that was me dad's favourite.'

He added, slyly, 'There's a feller in this one called the Professor. He's got a thing about bombs.'

'Sounds dangerous. Maybe that's where Farrell got my nickname from.'

'Nah, Terry doesn't read. Not even sure he *can* read.'

Mavers had the subtly sceptical pride of an autodidact, and he liked to use Baines as a sounding board for his literary opinions. Having left school at fourteen, he had worked on building sites for most of his life. Baines gathered that he had been close to his father, a merchant seaman who had bequeathed to him a reading habit, along with a full set of Conrad.

'So,' Mavers was saying, with a shrewd, measuring look, 'was Terry right about you before?'

'How do you mean?'

'Down in that cellar – he said you played it cool when you saw that bomb.'

Baines shrugged, remembering. 'I don't know why he said that. I was honestly and absolutely terrified.'

It was true, and yet he did acknowledge to himself that something had happened to him since the bombing had started in August, some internal shift that had exposed an unsuspected resolve. It was not that he had found sudden reserves of courage. He still felt a clammy fear seize his innards when he heard a bomb whistling down, or when he heard the foundations of a house he was tunnelling through start to creak and groan. What surprised him was the fierceness of his determination to keep going. It had taken the unambiguous proximity of death to make him comprehend how dearly he prized the sweets of life. And inextricable from this sentiment was a piercing sense of regret, of shame almost, that his life up to this point had not been properly lived. Now, thrust into the eye of a storm, he had promised himself he would not be found wanting again.

Mavers had turned pensive. 'You know, you read in the paper about how brave we all are for carryin' on in the Blitz. But when you think about it, what choice have we got?'

Baines smiled wryly. 'It's called making a virtue out of necessity.'

Their breakfast arrived. They had wanted bacon, sausage and eggs, but the war had quickly seen off such luxuries. Instead they were served a pie filled with meat whose provenance neither of them felt inclined to question.

'Duh,' said Mavers, wrinkling his nose. 'Try maken a virtue out of this, la'.' He forked a gobbet of it into his mouth, chewed, and shook his head. They ate for a while in silence. Through the window Baines watched a dray-horse limp along, an enormous load of crates in tow. Mavers had been watching it too, and said, 'D'you ever wonder about all the traffic that's been through this port? I mean, all the slaves and dockers and merchantmen walken over those cobbles, wearen the stones down . . .'

'Do I ever wonder?' said Baines. 'Liam, I've spent nearly my whole life wondering about things like that.'

Mavers looked at him, and realised he wasn't joking. Baines explained a little about the aborted book he had been compiling on the city, and about the photographic exhibition that was its accidental offshoot. As he did so he wondered how many of the places he had documented had been turned to ashes and rubble by the raids. And what of the ones he hadn't documented?

Mavers, smiling to himself, said, 'Our gran's always tellun these stories about Everton, that's where we live, and how it used to be a village with pasture and tha'. Thee used to run sheep through it! She got it all from her gran, I s'pose.'

'Well, she's right. In 1800 it was a favourite residence for well-to-do families – they built mansions and pleasure grounds there.'

Mavers snorted in amusement. 'They didn't stay, though, did thee? I haven't spotted many mansions on Netherfield Road lately.'

'It was being built up with terraced streets by the middle of the nineteenth century. They had to find somewhere for the Irish to live when the Famine starved them out.'

'Yeah, our grandad was one of 'em. He's still fit as a fiddle, like, eighty-somethin' now, they live round the corner from me and the missus.'

'How long have you been married?'

'Fifteen years!' Mavers exclaimed, as if he found the fact as implausible as anyone else. 'We met when we were kids, like, went to the same school. Sounds a bit soppy, doesn't it?'

'No. It sounds rather lovely,' said Baines. 'And you have children?'

'Yeah, four of them. Our oldest wants to start as a builder, but I'm not havin' it – I just told her straight, it's no job for a girl.'

Baines looked at him blankly, until Mavers spluttered with laughter.

'I'm joken, la'! She's a bright kid, actually, our Beth, bit of an artist on the quiet'.

Opening *The Secret Agent*, he removed a betting slip which he'd been using as a bookmark, and handed it carefully to Baines. On the reverse was a faint pencil drawing of a face – Mavers' face. Baines examined it closely for some moments.

'Pretty good. She can draw.'

'Told yer,' said Mavers, with smiling pride.

Outside, the dust in the air was making Baines's eyes smart again. Having bidden a tired goodbye to Mavers, he rerouted his walk home via Chapel Street, another of the old city streets he knew had been bombed. Across the road fire hoses lay scattered and spent, floored by their exertions from the night before. Baines was muttering a half-remembered prayer to himself as he approached Magdalen Chambers, which, to judge from the wounded building a few doors along, had had a lucky reprieve: hardly a mark on it. It was a small mercy when set against the general panorama of desolation, but he felt nonetheless grateful for its escape. He was about to turn into Temple Street when he heard a motor horn parp, and looked round to see a woman's head leaning out of a van, its engine running. It was Bella, at the wheel of the mobile canteen she drove for the Women's Voluntary Service. Baines walked over, conscious for the first time that morning of his bedraggled appearance.

'Hullo! Fancy running into you. Where are you going?'

'Just finished a shift,' said Baines.

'So have I! Hop in, I'll give you a lift.'

'I'm – well, covered in grime, as you see –'

Bella raised her eyes heavenwards. 'Just get in, you nit.'

He went round the side of the van and climbed into the cabin. They bumped along the streets, crowded with people cleaning up the pavements or else gravely assessing the damage. On the corner of London Road and Lime Street a tram had been flipped on to its side, and a policeman was directing a desultory flow of traffic around it. Glass shards still spangled the setts. Bella eased cautiously on the brake.

'Now, I'd better be careful around here. I've already popped a tyre once this week.'

She was wearing an old overcoat of Richard's and a pair of dark serge trousers, like a sailor's. Remarkable, Baines thought, that even in these drab duds she could look fetching.

'I see women in trousers all the time now,' he said.

'Yes – I don't get so many funny looks any more. I was grateful for them this morning, I can tell you, standing in the cold handing out tea and sandwiches. Those firemen had been hard at it.'

'I think last night's was the worst yet. These huge craters are from the landmines – they come down on parachutes, so you don't hear them before they explode.'

Bella glanced round at him. 'You had a busy night, then?'

'You could say.' He told her about the pub off Canning Place and what they had encountered in the cellar.

'Heavens! You mean you walked right past it? Were you –'

'Petrified? Yes. But as you can see, I've lived to tell the tale.'

'I think it's a tale Richard might like to hear,' she said, as they turned into Berry Street. 'He'll probably be back by now. Come and have a cup of tea.'

Richard was in the living room entertaining a guest of his own when they arrived at Slater Street. The air was permeated with the bitter fug of cigars, and Baines felt a sudden wave of nausea rise in his nostrils and then subside.

'Hullo, you two,' Richard said, and introduced them to a dapper uniformed fellow who had stood up as Bella entered the room. His name was Jimmy Andrews, and as they shook hands Baines recognised him as the officer who had held the enrolment meeting at Dale Street the week after war was declared.

'Ah, so you answered the call,' said Andrews pleasantly, on being reminded of the occasion. 'September last year – doesn't that seem an age ago? Well, we certainly caught it last night.'

'Tom's lucky to be alive,' said Bella, jumping in, and began to describe the bomb as if she'd seen it with her own eyes.

Richard whistled. 'Sounds like a 250. That must have given you a turn.'

'Mm. But so did the meat pie I ate for breakfast this morning – and I had to pay for that.'

'Hard to know what's worse, Jerry's bombs or the want of some decent grub. God, it's like being in the bloody army again.'

Baines noticed Jimmy smirking at this.

'I hate that screaming noise the bombs make,' said Bella. 'It's either that or that awful sound of a sheet being ripped in two.'

'They say you never hear the bomb that's got your name on it,' said Richard. 'It just lands on top of you and – *bouf*.'

There was a brief silence, as if that moment of noiseless death were about to burst upon them. Richard theatrically lifted his eyes to the ceiling, and they all laughed.

'At least it would be over quickly,' said Andrews, drawing meditatively on his cigar. 'When we were being shelled at the front – as Richard will tell you – most of the poor buggers couldn't have known what hit them. There are worse ways to go, really.'

'Such as – ?' enquired Bella.

'Fire,' said Andrews crisply.

Fire. Yes, thought Baines, that would be a worse way to go. He had been at a bombed warehouse a few weeks previously and watched firemen trying to contain the blaze; the brick walls seemed to glow a kind of Halloween orange, and an avalanche of fiery splinters cascaded from the roof. It had amazed him how daringly close the men on the fire hoses came to the leaping flames. If he could feel their furnace heat from where *he* was standing, how much more intense would it have been for them? His mind had turned to stories of martyrs and witches at the stake, the flames crackling, engulfing and finally consuming their poor weak flesh. He must have looked away for a few seconds, because the next thing he saw was a man staggering away from the conflagration, a whirl of flame coursing dementedly about his head and body; the fire had the mad quicksilver movement of a dervish, and in its blind fury was dragging a hapless partner into its dance. His colleagues managed to douse the burning man almost immediately – and saved his life, he later heard – but he had seen enough to know he would rather be blasted to atoms than fry like that.

Richard in the meantime was complaining about the official reporting of the Blitz. 'It's just a farce! Everyone knows London's taken a pounding because they report it on the wireless, but when the Luftwaffe rain bombs down on us the BBC never mentions Liverpool, or even Merseyside – they just say "attacks were made on the north-west". Do they think we haven't noticed, or that we don't care? Jimmy, can you explain it?'

Andrews shrugged tolerantly. 'The BBC is probably under orders from Whitehall. I suppose their argument would be that the Blitz on London can hardly be hidden from the world, but if news gets out that a strategically important target like Liverpool is being regularly hit then they're handing a weapon to the enemy.'

'But for pity's sake, the Germans aren't fools. They know they're battering Merseyside, they can see the place burn! There's no point in censoring news when it's obvious to everyone what's happening.'

'Or else the BBC doesn't think we're that important,' said Baines. 'Maybe to them a city like Liverpool is just "up north".'

'I'm afraid there's more news you won't be hearing on the wireless,' Andrews said gravely. 'There was a shelter hit in Durning Road last night. A junior technical school collapsed into the basement. The last I heard was at least 150 dead.'

'Dear God,' said Richard. 'Shouldn't we be helping?'

Andrews shook his head. 'They've got teams on to it. Direct hit from a parachute mine – I shouldn't think there'll be many survivors.'

Nobody said anything for a while. Bella went out to the kitchen to make tea. The scale of the loss felt suddenly too exorbitant to merit discussion. This really was war, thought Baines; one minute there are men, women and children crowded into a basement listening to the noise of the raid as it gets nearer, the next minute the whole world convulses and their own little space in it is being incinerated. You never hear the bomb that's got your name on it, so Richard said. But what about the bomb that has 150 names on it? Did none of them hear the noise as it hurtled towards that shelter? Did they all die instantaneously, or were some killed by fumes, or fire? In the end it didn't bear thinking about. You just had to keep your head down and hope that the storm, when it broke, would miss you.

'Tom might be interested in helping with this.'

'Hmm?' Baines's attention swam back into focus on hearing Richard's voice.

'Jimmy here has a commission for me direct from the War Office. They want a photographic record of bomb damage on Merseyside, here, Birkenhead, all over.'

'It will be useful,' said Andrews, 'for when we eventually come to prosecute Göring, Sperrle and the rest of them.'

'Well, if you need a hand . . .' In truth, the prospect of recording the city's Blitz damage was far from appealing. He was already far too familiar with the scorched, smoking guts of wrecked buildings to want to spend any more time photographing them. Then again, he had not seen as much of Richard since they had been assigned to different rescue squads, so this might at least serve to renew a companionship he rather missed.

'Have a think about it,' said Andrews, standing up and brushing flecks of cigar ash from his uniform. 'In the meantime I'd better be going. I have a press briefing about last night's raids.'

'I suppose you'll be telling them there were few casualties and some "negligible damage" to buildings,' said Richard.

'Something like that,' he replied, with a wintry smile. He turned to Baines. 'Pleasure to meet you, and – I hope your good luck holds.'

'So do I,' he said as they shook hands.

Half an hour later Baines was preparing to leave when the doorbell rang on the studio downstairs.

'That'll be the postman.'

'I'll get it for you,' said Baines, 'I'm pushing off anyway.'

'Thanks, Tom. Just leave whatever's there on the ledge.'

He said goodbye and ambled down the stairs, glancing as usual at the Nicholson portrait of Bella, and made his way out of the gallery. But it wasn't the postman at the door, it was a boy on a bicycle holding a small orange envelope. Baines felt almost certain of what it contained.

'Telegram for Tanqueray,' said the boy.

Baines nodded and signed for it. He retraced his steps up the stairs, feeling the envelope in his hand like a loaded gun. Bella was clearing up the tea things as he reappeared, and she met him with such an innocent, enquiring look that his heart flipped over.

'Forget something?' she said brightly.

He shook his head and handed her the envelope, and as she took it he saw her expression pass in a blink from bemusement to suspicion. She broke the seal, removed the folded sheet within and began to read. As she did so her eyes flicked up to Baines, who experienced the reasonless pricking of a messenger's guilt.

'It says ...' and she turned disbelievingly back to the text, '"The Air Ministry regrets to inform you that your brother, Flight Lieutenant David Garnett, number——, failed to return from operations over enemy territory during the night of 22nd November ... You will be informed as soon as further information becomes available." This – they must have made a mistake.'

She turned to Richard, who was standing in the doorway, and handed him the telegram. He read it, and the way he kept his eyes lowered was sufficient to suggest no mistake had been made.

'It's not conclusive, these things never –'

But Bella, her face now drained of colour, didn't appear to be listening. She had picked up the telephone and was asking the operator for the number of the Air Ministry. She stood silhouetted against the window, her back to the room, and after a few moments standing motionless she placed the receiver back in its cradle.

'The lines are down,' she murmured, without turning. Baines watched as her shoulders began to shake, softly at first, and then her tall frame was convulsed by heaving sobs.

'Oh, David, David,' she half whispered, her arms braced against the little table on which the telephone stood. Baines, nearest to her, could think of nothing to say, so he laid his hand gently on her shoulder for a few moments, hoping the gesture would carry the sorrow he wanted to express. He felt her body trembling uncontrollably, as if gripped by a chill. Then Richard was at her side, and Baines backed away, without a word, and left the room.

8

In front of his face he could make out nothing but the soles of a pair of hobnailed boots. They belonged to Mike Wo, the best tunneller on the team on account of his short but muscular build and his instinct for finding the safest route through fallen debris. Baines imagined that Mike had once been a miner, so adept was he in confined underground spaces, though on enquiry discovered that he was actually a manager in his family's restaurant on Duke Street. In any event Baines would usually volunteer to go with him on digging operations, and once they were crawling through the shifting masses of rubble he kept as close to Mike's heels as he could.

At the moment they were working a path beneath a row of collapsed houses just off Vauxhall Road. It was four days before Christmas, and the city had just endured a night-long blitz, the heaviest since the end of November. They were still carrying out the dead in the late morning when their rescue team arrived. Even Farrell, who could be relied upon for a macabre quip, had been silent as they surveyed the line of corpses hidden beneath tarpaulin; the ambulances would have to do a second, perhaps a third, run to the mortuary. Rafferty led the preliminary search over the mounds of smouldering timber and brick. As usual they had consulted the warden, who had checked the list of known residents.

'We can't be certain,' Baines heard him say. 'There's a married couple, the Powells, and their son, all unaccounted for, but they may have gone to a shelter.'

Even information as provisional as this would oblige them to begin a search, and so, stumbling, swearing, they clambered about the ruins. It was Mavers who heard the noise first. He called Rafferty over.

'Thought I heard this . . . cryin' sound,' he said, peering downwards.

'Quiet, everyone,' Rafferty boomed, and each of them stopped where he was to listen.

'Could be another cat,' said Farrell. They knew from experience that he was probably right. Baines had lost count of the number of times they had heard a baby mewling and begun a dangerous excavation, only to find a cat trapped in an air pocket. Had it mastered this eerie mimicry on purpose? he had wondered. That would be just like a cat.

'Miaow,' called McGlynn, and sniggered. He was a young bricklayer who had recently joined the squad after poor eyesight disqualified him from army service. Low intelligence may possibly have weighed against him, too.

'McGlynn – shut it,' hissed Rafferty. They listened again, and, straining his ears, Baines heard a distant ululation of distress. He caught Mavers' eye and nodded agreement.

'There's something – someone – down there.'

'It's a fuckin' moggy,' insisted Farrell. 'Come on, you know how many lives they 'ave.'

Rafferty had asked for volunteers, and so Baines now found himself in a tunnel not more than four feet wide. The torch strapped to the side of his helmet offered a dim illumination. Ahead of him Mike Wo was taking a rest, having carefully hollowed out a makeshift passage using table legs and random spars of wood as props. This structure required some delicacy of touch, for whatever the difficulties they experienced getting in they would have to ensure it would still be there when it came to getting out. Mike preferred to use a long plank as a mobile head support, though sometimes a wardrobe frame or a tabletop might be deployed for the purpose. He lowered the wetted handkerchief from around his mouth – worn as protection against a gas leak – and asked Baines if he was all right. Baines lifted his thumb in response, and in a moment they resumed their subterranean journey. It wasn't the mouthfuls of dust or the stink Baines minded so much as the creaks that sounded ominously through the gloom, a reminder that a few tons of debris was poised precariously over his head. He could sometimes distract himself by imagining he was a boy again, crawling in the dead of night beneath the netting of the vegetable patch in George and May's garden. That damp, cold smell of earth in his nostrils came back to him now ... and so did a couplet from a poem he had learned at school:

> Can honour's voice provoke the silent dust,
> Or flattery soothe the dull cold ear of death?

He had always been haunted by that image. Death he could imagine to be dull and cold, but that it manifested itself as an ear was mysterious, and terrifying.

Ahead of him he saw Mike's legs suddenly spasm, and his boots kicked up a gritty cloud of ash and brick dust into Baines's face. 'Jesus,' he heard Mike's voice through his mask, and then saw what had alarmed him. A brown rat, its fur dark with grease, scurried past; it was really getting out of there.

'Did yer see that, Tom?' Mike called.

'Yeah.'

'Fucker had a tail as long as a washin' line!'

He was about to joke to Mike that, working in a Chinese restaurant, he must have seen plenty of them, but then he thought better of it – too like the kind of thing Farrell would say. They kept moving slowly, painstakingly forward, Mike testing every bit of broken timber and masonry in front of them. Behind him Baines heard a shudder as the debris moved, and braced himself for the avalanche to descend on them. When it didn't come they pressed on, like moles burrowing through the dark.

After another ten minutes of digging they could hear the sound quite clearly, and now they knew it wasn't a cat. As far as they could tell the ground floor had collapsed into the basement, but from the middle, so that the floor had created a V shape against either wall. They were into the narrow right angle between the wall and a tangle of broken joists and plaster; it was possible to get up off their stomachs and move about in a stoop. From the far end of this dark enclosure they heard a baby's piercing cries.

'That's the son,' said Mike.

Baines stepped towards the infant, no more than three months old, miraculously preserved in his cot amid the fallen chaos. The smell of faeces and vomit assailed him as he bent down over the wailing bundle. How had this tiny creature not died of fright? he wondered. Looking around he spotted a woman's shoe, and then his beam revealed a leg, poking out from beneath a huge chunk of masonry.

'Over here,' he said.

Between them they managed to heave it away and found, lying side by side on a mattress, the bodies of a man and a woman. Mr and Mrs Powell, he presumed. Apart from a coating of plaster dust and soot there didn't seem to be a mark on them. But they were both quite dead. Baines wondered if they had suffocated. Above them they heard another protesting creak, the sound of a building in its death throes. He turned to Mike. 'I'm gonna say a quick prayer, and then we should get out of here.'

'It seems bad – you know, not givin' them a burial.'

'This *is* a burial,' he replied, looking around, 'and it might be ours too if we don't look sharp.' He found the words forming on his lips. 'Eternal rest grant unto them, O Lord, and perpetual light shine upon them. May they rest in peace – Amen.' He crossed himself, and started uncoiling the rope he kept in his knapsack. Mike was still in a half-crouch, puzzled.

'That's it? That's their funeral?'

'Yeah, that's it.' He was beginning to feel annoyed at Mike's unwonted show of piety. 'What – you wanna sing a hymn? Mike, we're getting out of here, right now, so take this rope and help me strap the kid up.'

Mike heard the urgency in his voice and began winding the rope around the baby, now exhausted into silence, and presently the blanketed bundle was secured around Baines's shoulders.

'After you,' he said as they crouched at the hole from which they'd entered. They had done the right thing, he thought; if another collapse got them and they were entombed down here, at least they would die having tried to save a life, an innocent life at that. Ahead of them lay the journey back, another twenty minutes of crawling through that tortuous stinking wreckage, with only a Chinese restaurant manager's guile – and maybe God's mercy – to protect them. He retied the handkerchief around his mouth, and then he was on his belly again, his face a few inches from the iron-riveted soles of Mike Wo's boots.

Baines always felt hilarious with relief after emerging from a dig. The mug of steaming tea the WVS worker handed to him had the taste of an elixir, and he breathed in the air joyously, no matter how burnt or gritty it felt to his lungs. He was alive, back in the world, escaped from the tomb. Two had gone down, and three had come back: couldn't that be counted a success? He thought of the child's parents still lying down there, as lifeless as a medieval knight and his lady carved in stone. He was sitting on the running board of the mobile canteen when Mavers and Farrell came over.

'Well done, Tommy,' said Mavers, with his odd conspiratorial smile. 'We were starten to worry about yer down there ...' He offered Baines a cigarette, which he lit and inhaled deeply.

Farrell said, with a laugh, 'Should see your face, la'. You look like a nigger minstrel.'

Baines glanced at his face in the wing mirror of the van. Apart from a faint whitish ring around his eyes it was black with soot and smoke. He thought he looked more like the sweep who used to clear the chimney at home. He didn't care: he was alive.

'Bet you were glad you 'ad Charlie down there,' Farrell added. Farrell's nickname for Mike was, almost inevitably, Charlie Chan. Baines nodded.

'It's in his hands. He always knows what can be moved – and what can't.'

'Yeah, well, they start them young down the mines in China. Charlie was probably born carryin' a pickaxe.'

Baines knew he shouldn't rise to the bait, but he couldn't resist. He sighed. 'Farrell, Mike was born in Liverpool. So were his parents. His family's probably been here longer than yours.'

'Yeah,' added Mavers casually, 'you thick Irish git.'

Farrell laughed, pleased that he'd got under somebody's skin. Baines, shuddering for a moment, said, 'We saw a huge rat on the way – moved like lightning, it did.'

'That's cos it'd seen Charlie,' said Farrell. 'It probably knew him from his restaurant and thought – uh-oh, that's the feller who's been drownin' us in the chow mein!'

Mavers and Baines laughed; only Farrell would be so absurd as to voice the mortal fears of a rat. At that moment Mike appeared, but he didn't seem interested in what they were laughing about, which was just as well.

He said, 'Tom, Rafferty wants a word,' and gestured over his shoulder. He seemed annoyed about something. He turned to the woman serving at the canteen hatch. 'You got anything to eat, love?'

Farrell burst out laughing at this. 'Oh, that's just perfect!' he cackled.

Mike looked at him distractedly. 'What?' But he was preoccupied with the canteen woman, who had only sandwiches to offer.

'What's in 'em?' asked Mike.

'Sardines,' she replied.

'That all you got?' he said, with palpable disgust.

'Yeah. Why, what's wrong with sardines?'

Mike paused for a moment, then looked back at her. 'I'll tell yer what's wrong with 'em – they smell like dead people.' Then he turned and trudged off. The WVS woman looked as if she'd been slapped in the face.

'Sorry 'bout that, love,' Mavers said to her, venturing gallantry, 'he's been through a rough time, that lad.'

Baines stubbed out his cigarette and stood up. He found his hand-kerchief and looked in the wing mirror to wipe his face. He really wanted to get home and have a bath, but he supposed it wouldn't be unpleasant to hear Rafferty commend him for his efforts. Farrell had noticed his quick spit-wash, and was evidently not done with baiting. 'There's no need to spruce yourself up for Rafferty – he's not the fucken' prime minister, even if he acts like 'im.'

'I'm not doing it for Rafferty. I just hate feeling this dirty.'

'He'll be in a good mood,' Farrell continued, 'with the kid saved. You should ask him for a promotion – eh, Liam, what's above "professor"?'

'Shut up,' said Mavers, evenly. 'Go 'ead, Tommy, get it over with.'

Baines walked off in the direction of the warden's command post, where he knew Rafferty would be. Most of the corpses had been removed, but at the far end of the blasted street he saw another squad of rescue workers still picking over the debris. As he walked past one of the vans he heard Rafferty call his name. He was sitting in the cabin of the vehicle.

'Step up here a moment, would you?' he said. Baines climbed in. It was difficult to read Rafferty's expression, because his mouth was habitually downturned. He was beginning to realise that it was a face he didn't much like. 'The child has been saved. I gather from Wo that the Powell couple were dead.'

'Yeah, they were.'

Rafferty nodded. 'Obviously it would have been better if you'd brought them out as well.'

This wasn't the paean of gratitude Baines had been expecting. He spoke carefully. 'I didn't believe the structure would hold in time for us to do that. A collapse looked quite possible, so Mike and I decided to save the living . . . rather than the dead.'

'Did you . . . search the couple at all?'

'Search them? What for?'

Rafferty looked measuringly at him. 'For valuables. Did you notice whether they were wearing wedding rings or – other jewellery?'

Baines began to see where this might be leading. 'I didn't notice what they were wearing, and the only time I touched them was to check for a pulse.'

Rafferty nodded again, and then said, 'I ask because, well, there have been incidents of looting among rescue workers. We have to make sure –'

'I've never stolen anything in my life,' said Baines, bridling.

'Yes, but as I say, there have been serious incidents –'

'I've never stolen anything in my life,' he repeated tightly, feeling a dark tide of anger rise in his chest. He opened the van door, then turned back to Rafferty. 'We risked our fucking necks to get that kid out. This is the thanks we get?'

'There's no need to take that attitude –'

'Drop dead,' he muttered, and slammed the door.

He was still thrumming with rage on the bus into town, sitting next to Mike. He felt his hand trembling as he raised a match to his cigarette. The taste was bitter on his tongue. Mike was idly picking away at the blast netting on the bus window. As it happened, Baines had heard of looting after a raid; there were spivs everywhere, and the black market was thriving, even with fire-damaged contraband. But the idea of robbing a corpse repulsed him, and to be suspected capable of it –

'Fucking outrage,' he muttered to himself, and Mike turned to him, half smiling.

'Forget about it, la',' he said. 'We did good today. Rafferty's just watchin' his own back.'

'Yeah, but to be practically accused of thieving . . .'

'You should try workin' in our restaurant sometime. We get people accusin' us of all sorts, thievin' included. And I bet Rafferty didn't ask you to turn out yer pockets.'

'He asked you?' Baines was incredulous. 'What did you say?'

'I told him to fuck off!'

Baines was woken from a dream in which he was trapped underground, alone and unmissed. He'd had the dream so often of late that he was no longer surprised by it, though the panic still fluttered in his chest on waking. The sirens had started their keening wail. He groggily checked the alarm clock on his bedside table: half past six. He'd been asleep for just over four hours. He pulled back a corner of the blackout curtain and peeked out to find the evening sky ominously clear: a bomber's moon. He wasn't due on a shift tonight, but he knew that if the raids were anything like as severe as last night's he would be reporting for duty. There was an immediate problem in that fires still burning in the city from the night before would offer a useful guide to a new wave of bombers. But then there was a permanent marker in the glittering scimitar of the Mersey, and they could do nothing about that.

His jacket was still filthy from this morning's toil, but he hadn't another one to wear. On returning home he had washed his body more fiercely than Lady Macbeth did her hands, and now he was reclothing himself in the acrid reek of smoke and rubble and death. The telephone's ring ten minutes later did not surprise him, though the voice at the other end wasn't immediately familiar.

'Is that the professor?'

'Who's this?'

'We're lookin' for a Professor Baines –'

'Farrell.'

He heard spluttering laughter, and then muffled 'voices off'. Farrell spoke again: 'Rafferty wants you down here quick as yer like. Hitler's sendin' over another Christmas packet.'

There was a click, and the line went dead. Off to the south the heavy broken drone of the Luftwaffe engines grew louder, and closer. He pulled on his boots, put on his helmet and was out of the door within a few minutes.

On Gambier Terrace he looked up and saw the sky lousy with German planes. Evidently a repeat performance of last night was about to start. As he unlocked his bicycle he heard the first bombs falling, a whistle, or a shriek, and then the impact. The ack-ack guns coughed into life, and across the horizon he could see tracer fire brightly stitching the darkness. It reminded him of a Whistler nocturne, the one in which the green-black night is illumined with falling sparks of gold. Fireworks, he presumed. Well, they could depend on getting fireworks tonight. He would usually have made the journey to the depot in Hackins Hey by tram, but tonight he sensed a greater urgency in the air, and the wind against his face as he careened down Duke Street on the bicycle was, he found, rather exhilarating. At the bottom of the street he narrowly avoided a deep bomb crater, harder to spot without the benefit of street lamps. As he rounded the corner into Paradise Street he felt the ground rock beneath him, and the attendant shock wave gusted past his face; a high-explosive bomb had fallen some distance ahead, and he could see a wall slowly sag and topple. It crashed, and from the impact billowed a dense cloud of dust. All the advice suggested that it was better to be under cover, but Baines, as now, could see up close the way bombing transmuted the solidities of the ordinary world – walls, roofs, floors – into pitiful matchwood structures, toy defences against the tearing blast. Outside one felt utterly exposed, it was true, but one could at least cling to the possibility of movement, to the idea, however illusory, that this onrushing menace might be dodged.

Paradise Street now stood stricken in a pall of black dust. In the distance he heard a fire engine clanging its alarm. He turned the bike around and began pedalling furiously into Canning Place. He sailed past the Customs House, its noble facade ruined since the August raids, and took a right into South Castle Street. This was a different gauntlet to run, for a flight of incendiaries was plummeting through the dark; they hit the road with their distinctive popping sound and then erupted in a sizzling halo of greenish-white flame. He saw a fire-watcher emerge from a doorway and begin to stamp them out, a disabling tactic that had enjoyed a brief craze before the Germans got wise to it and began fitting the bombs with a booby-trap charge. The man looked up and saw Baines.

'Give us a hand, mate!' he called.

Baines jumped off his bicycle and began stomping on the fizzing incendiaries, trying not to think of blasted limbs as he did so. The fire-watcher was blowing on his whistle, and soon a couple of wardens were running down the street to join them. One of them, finding his boot unequal to the task, placed his steel helmet over the spark-spitting cylinder. Baines stopped to watch the helmet glow and then melt in the incandescent heat. The man looked up in shocked amusement.

'That's me lid gone,' he said.

Another ribbon of incendiaries tumbled out of the sky. Baines spent a few more minutes helping to extinguish them, but a glance at his watch warned him that he was already late. Remounting his bicycle he began slaloming past men who were carrying stirrup pumps towards a blazing shopfront; incendiaries had evidently fallen on rooftops and burnt their way through. On St George's Crescent an empty tram had been overturned, and ignored. Towards the docks he could hear the shrieking descent of bombs, and now he could see them too, falling, almost ambling down across the glowering sky. Fear seemed to propel him faster along the street, and by the time he reached the depot he was pouring with sweat. They were just leaving the building as he arrived, and Farrell called out, 'You know there's a war on, don't yer?' He quickly locked up his bicycle and fell into step with them as they made for the van on the street. He sensed Rafferty fixing him a look, but he refused to catch his eye; he wasn't going to talk to him if he could help it. He nodded over to Mike, who was also ignoring Rafferty. In the van he sat next to Mavers, hoping to absorb some of his stoical calm while the random thump of explosions fell around them.

'Trouble getten here?'

Baines nodded. 'An HE in Paradise Street and then incendiaries on South Castle Street.'

Mavers lifted his chin in acknowledgement. 'It's another one like last night, they reckon. About a hundred bombers, with more on the way.'

'Where are we off to?'

'The docks. There's a load on fire right now. We've gotta clear a shelter that's right in the middle of 'em.'

At the foot of Chapel Street they happened upon a scene of pandemonium. The Church of St Nicholas, the sailors' church, had taken a direct hit, and fire could be seen devouring the roof. The van juddered to a halt and they climbed out. Baines looked up at its tower, and remembered telling Richard the story of the schoolchildren who had perished there one morning in 1810. Firemen were grappling with hoses, but their long arcs of water were unavailing in the battle against the blaze; the flames seemed to dance higher in mockery of their elemental foe. Across the road Baines caught sight of a man in a dog collar watching the place burn, the vicar, he supposed, dumbstruck by the spectacle of this house of God being consumed in hellfire.

'There's nothing we can do here,' said Rafferty, 'let's get along.'

Back in the van McGlynn was shaking his head. 'Me mam and dad got married in that church.' His softly bewildered expression was rendered more pathetic by his protruding teeth. Poor eyesight and buck teeth, thought Baines: this kid really had got the booby prize.

'See that priest?' said Farrell. 'He looked like someone'd gobbed in his collection plate.'

'He was in shock, for fuck's sake,' said Mavers. 'You'd look like that if they burnt down the Bevy.'

'The what?' asked Baines.

'The Bevington Bush – his local,' Mavers said, nodding at Farrell, who turned to Baines.

'Bet you've never been in a pub down Scottie Road, 'ave yer?'

'No, I haven't.'

'Just as well. You'd stick out a mile.'

'Don't worry,' said Mavers to Baines, with a wink, 'you're not missen much.'

The van had pulled in at Wapping Dock, and Rafferty was on the street talking to a fire officer. In front of them a long line of warehouses were burning, and across the waterfront flames seemed to be gorging on every rooftop. He heard a warden shout to a messenger, 'Tell them to bring all the pumps they've got – the whole place is goin' up!' The firemen were fighting the blaze in pairs, braced over the hose as if it might at any moment leap out of their hands. From the warehouse nearest to them could be heard continuous metallic pops, which turned out to be drums of paint exploding in the fire. A sickly sweet odour had infused the air around them – burning sugar. He saw one fireman close to the leaping flames remove his mask and retch on to the cobbles. Even from this distance Baines could feel the tremendous heat of the conflagration, it seemed to be cooking his blood. They were standing there in a line – Mavers, Farrell, Mike Wo, McGlynn, himself – their faces illumined by this fiery spectacle; it was appalling, and yet none of them could look away.

Rafferty, his brow beaded with sweat, hurried back towards them. He seemed almost dazed by the chaos.

'The shelter's been cleared, but the warden says there's a nightwatchman who's not been accounted for. We need to do a quick sweep of those sheds to check he hasn't been trapped.'

Farrell said, 'Shouldn't the fire brigade be dealin' with that?'

'The fire brigade are dealing with the fire,' said Rafferty.

Carrying a stirrup pump, they stalked down a narrow alley that ran between Duke's and Wapping Dock, their shadows looming monstrously against the wall. At the bottom of the alley they found a fire door that was unlocked. On entering the warehouse they could instantly smell smoke, mixed with something potently aromatic; incendiaries had burnt right through the old Victorian timbers and started a number of small fires. Baines glanced at crates stamped with the Lipton's trademark, and realised that what they could smell was burning tea.

'Get that pump working over here,' called Rafferty, and soon, in a reverse of the traditional process, they were pouring cold water on hot tea leaves. They continued down the vertiginously stacked corridors, calling as they went, but no answer was returned. Turning a corner they found lead-covered timbers that had been brought down by an incendiary and were now melting like wax on the floor. There was no more water left to put them out.

'This place is tinder,' said Mavers, gesturing at the barrels of rum packed solid against a wall. 'I reckon we best be gettin' out.'

Rafferty looked around, evidently dissatisfied. 'We've hardly covered the place. We should split into teams –'

'No, we shouldn't,' said Mavers. 'It's gonna blow to hell. If we stay here we're just gonna get roasted.' There was conviction in his voice, and Baines knew that in the event of a confrontation Mavers would carry the day. From the way Rafferty hesitated it seemed he already had. They began to retrace their steps, but the fires had moved with disconcerting speed and were now scything across the aisles down which they had come. Black smoke was rolling towards them. Blinded, they turned back, and now they were moving without any distinct idea of an exit. Their pace quickened. The warehouse was suddenly a labyrinth to be escaped, and the minotaur that lurked behind them was white hot and roaring.

Baines was alarmed. How on earth had they got caught in this? One minute they had been searching for a notional nightwatchman, now they were running for their lives. As they sought a corridor that was clear of smoke they could see the torrent of flames coursing along adjacent corridors. Behind them they heard a huge explosion, and then another. The rum barrels, igniting one by one. They were heading towards the opposite corner of the building, and now the smoke had begun to envelop them. Baines took out his handkerchief and tied it round his mouth.

'There's a door,' shouted Mike, pointing to the end of a corridor that vectored off to the right. Within moments they were upon it; it was locked, but Mavers already had his pickaxe and was hacking into the wood. Farrell removed an axe from the webbing on his belt and the pair of them fell into a steady rhythm, each landing a blow at a time. The door was splintering, but slowly, and the heat had become so intense that when Baines took a breath it felt like burning fire itself. Seeing Mavers begin to tire he snatched the pickaxe from his hands and tore at the wood. He felt maniacal, possessed, as he swung the axe; he was not going to die in this place, he was getting them out of there, and Farrell's grim rictus of concentration as he swung in time spurred him on.

Meanwhile Rafferty, perhaps conscious of his part in exposing them to this inferno, was convinced he had seen a trapdoor at the far end of the corridor.

'I'll have a quick look,' he called.

'I wouldn't if I was you,' Baines heard Mavers tell him, but Rafferty was already gone. Their blows rang heavily against the door. Baines felt the smoke stinging his eyes. They were all coughing like hags. Hearing a terrible wrenching noise he glanced behind; iron girders had begun to buckle under the heat. Mike Wo put his arms through the space where the axes had made a hole, and started straining at the wood, his face twisted in a grimace like a circus strongman's. Baines could see a vein bulge on Mike's temple as the door cracked down one side, and now they could see – relief! – a rift large enough to crawl through. When he tried to recall it later Baines wasn't sure if it was the noise of falling timber or Rafferty's cries that alerted them first, but when they turned to look they saw him engulfed in a whirl of flame, its wild energies fed by whatever material had been spilt in the collapse. The flames licked hungrily around his body and made an aureole about his head. Mavers took a few steps towards the burning figure, and as he did so the whole corridor seemed to flash in molten rage, and the figure and the fire could no longer be separated. Mavers staggered back, his arms raised against the furnace blast of heat. By the time Baines had heaved himself under the mangled door, the last man out, the building was a lost cause, a house of flames.

'We should never have been there in the first place. It was a job for the fucken fire brigade.' This was Farrell, who still carried in his voice the shock of what they had escaped, and what Rafferty had not, the night before. He, Mavers and Baines were walking up Church Street, where firemen were still training long loops of water over the blackened crusts of buildings. The second raid had lasted from midnight until just after five in the morning. A lurid glare now hung across the sky. Everywhere people stood about watching the smouldering ruins.

'Rafferty knew the risks,' said Mavers.

'Did he, though?' asked Farrell. 'When we were inside that place 'e didn't seem to 'ave a clue. Any of us coulda done better – you, the prof, McGlynn . . .' He paused. 'All right, maybe not McGlynn.'

They laughed in spite of their weariness. The corpse, what was left of it, had been recovered from the charred wreckage a few hours ago. Baines thought of the last two words he had spoken to Rafferty in the van the previous afternoon. He didn't feel guilty – he was still euphoric with survival. Rafferty would have died whether he'd said the words or not. But he couldn't deny feeling glad that nobody had actually overheard them.

At the curving end of Ranelagh Street Lewis's department store had had all of its windows blown out. In the street opposite, Blackler's was a ravaged husk. Christmas shopping would have to be scaled down this year, he supposed. Not that they were expecting much in the way of festivities; the heavy-rescue squads would be on stand-by for as long as the attacks continued, and they had shown no signs of abating. He parted with Farrell and Mavers on Lime Street, and, seized by an urge to get clear of the grit and smoke, he began to walk. He would usually have spent Christmas Day with George and May; realising that he might be on duty for the rest of the week he decided he should try to see them today. He stopped at Gambier Terrace to change his clothes – he would burn this filthy jacket once he could get hold of a new one – and set off south. There was no possibility of a tram, for the roads were either cratered or blocked with debris, and the road-repair teams were already overstretched. On Princes Avenue he passed children playing on bomb rubble. Outside certain ruined houses boards had been left with forwarding addresses painted on them.

He was grateful to reach Sefton Park, a refuge from the chaotic damage on the streets. The barrage balloons still swayed around the perimeter, and the lake had been drained by the Fire Service for auxiliary water supplies during the last raids. But these reminders of war were set against the tranquillity of matutinal birdsong, of wide green spaces, and of couples strolling by without apparent regard for the desolate atmosphere beyond.

He had recently come across the phrase 'London can take it', a tribute to the capital's resilience in the face of the Blitz. If that were so, then Liverpool could take it, too. The Luftwaffe might knock them about all they wanted, but in the end the streets and houses and pubs and churches would be rebuilt in new and better ways. It would be changed, but it would be the same. What would survive any amount of bombing was the spirit of the place, the unshakeable honour in belonging to this ancient, altered town.

These optimistic thoughts were still stirring his blood as he turned down the avenue that approached the Elms. He was smiling at the memory of a scabrous joke of Farrell's the previous night when he saw George standing in his driveway talking to a man he'd not seen before. Both were wearing funereal black. George saw his confusion and came to greet him.

'Hullo, son,' he said quietly. 'I'm afraid it's poor old John, Dora's husband. Their house got a direct hit – I've been trying to telephone you the last couple of days.' The man he'd been talking to was one of the undertakers.

'I've been . . . out,' said Baines, in a daze. He hadn't known John well, but Dora, their housekeeper, had been a fixture in his life since he was a boy. She and her family lived on the other side of the park.

'I know you have,' said George, patting his shoulder. 'Why don't you go in and see May, she's been worrying about you.'

He entered the house, which seemed to have partaken in the mood of mourning; the blackout curtains hung like a mark of respect. He opened the door and peered into the living room, where, huddled around Dora on the sofa, sat her two boys, returned from evacuation. A few other mourners stood around in attitudes of stiff unease, as if they had been hired for the occasion but not given anything to do. Dora didn't look up, so immersed was she in her grief, and the boys, hollow-eyed and pinched, directed a faintly accusing glance in his direction before their heads dropped again.

He found May in the kitchen, and as he embraced her he felt absurdly relieved that he'd put on a suit and tie for his visit. She cupped his face with her hands, in a way she hadn't done since he was a boy, and as he looked at her the tears stood in her eyes.

'When George couldn't get you on the telephone I was that worried.'

'We've been kept busy,' he said, as lightly as he could. 'I've hardly been home the last three days.'

May didn't seem to have heard him. 'Do you know how precious you are to me?' Baines, not sure whether an answer was required, could only muster what he hoped was a reassuring smile.

'What happened?' he said, lowering his voice.

'It was the raid the other night. Dora was in the Anderson shelter, John had gone back into the house because he thought he'd left a light on, then ...' She shook her head slowly, unwilling to put the moment into words. 'They said he wouldn't have known a thing about it. The whole house has gone.'

'At least she's got the boys back. Where are they living?'

'Here, of course,' she said, almost surprised by the question. 'We weren't having them go to a rest centre. This is their home until they're rehoused.'

Just then George came in. His air of flustered decency was somehow even more affecting than May's capable solicitude. Spry in his late sixties, he had recently begun to look older, and thinner; anxiety did that to you, Baines thought.

'I've just had a word with the undertaker,' he said. 'They can't get enough men to dig the grave – there are too many others waiting to be buried.'

May looked distraught. 'Mother of God, that's just – how long are we meant to wait?'

'They said it could take a week, maybe more, just to clear all the mortuaries.'

'A week?' cried May. 'We've got his funeral mass in an hour.'

Baines considered. 'Where's the burial?'

'It's in the cemetery just down the road,' said George.

'Right then. George, can you get hold of a couple of shovels?'

'I should think so. Why?'

'Because I think I can get you a couple of gravediggers.'

'Who?'

'Don't worry about that. But I'll also need the telephone number of a Chinese restaurant on Duke Street.'

George had lent him a pair of overalls, and by the time Mike arrived at the cemetery Baines had already made a start on the grave. He smiled when he saw the expression on Mike's face.

'You've got a nerve, la',' Mike said. 'Me 'ead had just hit the pillow when you rang.'

'Mike, I'm in your debt. Honestly. But I couldn't think of anyone who reveres the ceremony of burial like you do.'

Mike shook his head, and picked up a shovel. 'I don't know what you're talking about,' he said, and began to dig.

They worked mainly in silence, their breath frosting in the chill December air, and with the help of a corporation digger who had just finished at another plot they had prepared a reasonably neat hole in time for the arrival of the funeral cortège. Bone-tired, he watched as the undertakers lowered the coffin into the ground while the priest intoned the exequies. He could hear the murmurs of lamentation among the family, but he kept his eyes averted from Dora for fear that he might just crack himself. Sometimes it was harder to face the ordeal of the living than it was to ponder the fate of the dead.

9

There was another funeral to attend before the year was out. None of the rescue squad had conceived any friendly feeling towards Rafferty on their short acquaintance, and three of them would have admitted to an intense, if not implacable, dislike of him. But now he was dead, and with the horrific circumstances of his demise still vivid in the memory, his former colleagues had duly assembled at the church on Ullett Road which had been Rafferty's place of worship. Baines listened to the priest's eulogy of his late parishioner 'Dennis' with astonishment, for he had not expected to hear the morose, suspicious, unamiable man he had known talked of in such sorrowing tones of loss. Orotund phrases – 'man of deep faith', 'beloved father and husband' and even 'pillar of the community' – echoed startlingly around the cold vaulted space, still adorned here and there with baubles from the dismal Christmas just gone. Baines stole a glance at Mavers, seated just along from him on the varnished treacle-brown pew, but if he felt the same surprise his expression betrayed nothing of it. He didn't dare look at Mike, who he imagined would be less circumspect about the obligation of keeping a straight face.

The organist wheedled on aimlessly, almost tunelessly, as they carried out the coffin, and the mourners, muffled in their coats and hats, began to edge out of the pews and followed in sombre procession. Nobody had invited them to the wake, so they walked back through the wrecked streets of Toxteth towards the city, a smoking necropolis since the last raid on Christmas Eve. Settled at the corner table of a pub, they brooded in silence for a while, as if cowed by the reverential mood that had tagged along from the church. Bleary sunshine slanted through the frosted glass, and motes of dust shimmered in the slender parallelograms of light. It was Farrell, of course, who finally popped the bubble of solemnity.

'Is it me, or does it feel like the Pope's just died?'

Mavers shook his head. 'Dennis – we hardly knew yer.'

'Oh, and by the way, I was right about 'im bein' a policeman.'

'A military policeman,' Baines corrected. 'I guessed he was in the army, so we could call that one a draw.'

'Did you see his missus?' asked Mike. 'Not bad-lookin', really . . .'

'Too good for 'im,' said Farrell. 'Poor cow, imagine bein' married to Rafferty all them years. Bet 'e ordered her around like 'e did everyone else – "Right, Mrs R, I've just discussed it with the warden. Stand by yer bed and I'll take down yer – details. We're gonna proceed wit' what's known as a bit of 'ow's yer father."'

They stifled grunts of guilty laughter. Mavers took a deep swig of his pint, then said, 'Rafferty's one of them fellers who 'as to be a boss, it's just the way he is – I mean, was.'

'Yeah, but he was only that way cos there's other fellers willen to be bossed,' objected Farrell. 'I reckon he must have 'ad that priest in his pocket, too, all that guff he talked about 'im. Pillock of the community and what 'ave yer.'

McGlynn, who had been dreamily preoccupied in one of his long empty silences, perked up at this. 'Did the priest call Rafferty a pillock?'

Farrell groaned. 'God, who woke up Grandma? No, he didn't, but he should've done.'

Mavers clicked his tongue in mock reproach and turned to Baines. 'What's that thing you said the other night, Tommy?'

'*De mortuis nil nisi bonum* – don't speak ill of the dead. Though in Rafferty's case . . .'

'Listen to the prof and his fancy phrases,' sneered Farrell.

'It's Latin, Terry.'

'I know it's fuckin' Latin. *Caesar adsum jam, Pompey aderat!*'

Baines laughed, oddly tickled that Farrell should remember this doggerel at such a distance from his schooldays.

'He was somebody's father anyhow,' Mavers murmured. 'You see his kids there?'

'What a fuckin' awful time to be alive,' said Mike, with sudden feeling. 'Funerals everywhere, the streets on fire, food and coal rationed – and knowin' that any minute those fuckers are comin' back to kill us.'

'Yeah,' said Mavers, and after a pause added, 'I wouldn't miss it for the world.'

Later, when the ale had made them expansive, they began swapping stories – some already of mythic status – about the blood, sweat and tears of heavy rescue. Farrell was shaking his head in frowning disbelief.

'Think about it, la' – we actually volunteered for this. What does that make us?'

'The stupidest fucks alive!' said Mike, snorting beer down his nostrils as he laughed.

McGlynn, himself cackling like a hyena, turned to Farrell.

'Tell 'em about the old woman you dragged out the other week, Terry. None of yous was there.'

Farrell, who had half adopted McGlynn as his stooge, pretended exasperation. 'I told you not to mention that, you soft git.'

'Go 'ead, then,' sighed Mavers, sensing that Farrell was only too pleased to tell it. Farrell took a preparatory swig of ale.

'Yous 'ad all knocked off. I was still with these other lads in a house on Blackstock Street, and we'd taken about three hours to tunnel through the back to this old dear's bedroom. None of the others were up to it, so I said I'd get her out. Soon as I crawl in, the smell 'its me – fuckin' terrible it was. The old dear's been lyin' there, covered in her own shit. I swear, I was gaggin' on it – not that she could care.'

Groans of disgust, mingled with a rising hilarity, had started up around the table as he continued.

'So, I've followed basic procedure – tied her hands, put her arms around me neck and now I'm crawling along with her on me back. You know how sometimes they hang on so 'ard they almost strangle yer – not this one, she was light as a bird. But that smell just gets worse, and now I can feel this, like, dampness on me back. I realise – fuck, she's just shat herself again.'

'Fuck's sake. What d'you do then?'

'What could I do? Just kept on crawlen. By the time I got us out of there we must have looked like – I dunno wha' – a shit sandwich!'

A ragged chorus of guffaws. Baines was caught up in them – it was difficult not to be – but he watched curiously as Farrell leaned back and enjoyed his audience's mirth. What Farrell didn't know was that Baines had been there when he emerged from the wreckage; he had remembered the smell, too. But what had really struck him at the time was Farrell's extraordinary gentleness as he lifted the old woman from his shoulders and, ignoring the stretcher-bearers, carried her over to the waiting ambulance, murmuring assurances as he did so. At no point had he betrayed a hint of revulsion at this befouled bundle of humanity. Now he had transformed the incident into the stuff of horrid laughter – but what harm could it do? The old woman had been saved by his courage, and she would be none the wiser that her rescuer had finessed the memory into a scurrilous anecdote. Baines had accepted that he more or less disliked the man: Farrell was a brute and a bigot, and he knew they would never properly be friends. Yet he would not forget his gruff gallantry that evening. In the end Farrell, and all of them – Liam, Mike, McGlynn, even poor dead Rafferty – had proved themselves capable of heroism. Perhaps the noblest kind of heroism, because it went unsung.

The sun was just about to set as they were leaving the pub. It was only half past four, but they knew the blackout would be imposed in an hour, and the world of peace would elide once again into the world of war. The minutes of twilight separating the two worlds cast a melancholy shade over the city, the time when the trees became dark imploring silhouettes against the sky; Baines thought of it as 'the desperate hour'. By seven o'clock this evening he would be reporting for duty again. Mavers accompanied him on the walk back to Gambier Terrace.

'I'd ask you in for tea,' said Baines, 'but all I've got is powdered eggs.'

Mavers smiled. 'Don't worry, I should be on me way – the missus'll wonder where I've got to.'

Just then Baines remembered something, and told Mavers to wait while he dashed up to his flat. He returned a minute later carrying a block wrapped in brown paper, which he handed over.

'It's for your daughter, just a pad of drawing paper – I know it's hard to come by at the moment . . .'

'I can't take this,' Mavers said, suddenly shy. It had surprised him.

'Of course you can. It's . . . a Christmas present. She's a better artist than I was at fourteen.'

Mavers held the parcel for a few silent moments, then looked at Baines.

'Thanks, Tom,' he said quietly.

'I'll see you at the depot.'

'Yeah. Ta-ra.' He walked off, then looked over his shoulder and, almost boyishly, waved goodbye. Baines wondered if he too had fallen prey to the desperate hour, because that small gesture of Mavers' made him want to cry.

On New Year's Day Baines called on Richard and Bella at Slater Street, but there was no answer when he rang the doorbell. He supposed they were visiting Richard's parents in London. He had not seen Bella since the morning she had received the telegram, and he felt his conscience jolt him for it. True, he'd had the excuse of being on duty almost every night of the last four weeks, and Richard had promised to keep him informed of any news concerning David. But he knew he had been avoiding her, either because he didn't know what to say or else because he couldn't bear to see her as unhappy as she was that morning. He had thought more than once of writing to her, but then reasoned that a letter of commiseration would be tantamount to admitting that David was dead. So he fretted, uselessly.

He returned to his flat and, vaguely stirred by the seasonal call for resolutions, went into his study. It seemed even more sepulchral since the blackout curtains had become a fixture. A pot plant that May had given him some months ago had withered and died. Library books slouched in stacks, their truancy no longer monitored amid more pressing circumstances. Still open on his desk lay a volume of the Eames journals, which at any other time of his life he would have raced through but now could afford to give only the most desultory attention. It was a minor but regrettable side effect of war that he would come home too exhausted to read. He sat down, turned on his desk lamp and began to skim the second volume.

September [1865]

For some weeks I have been puzzling over the back elevation of Magdalen Chambers. It seemed to me that it was not quite complete – that something was wanting – but what it might be I could not discern. The rear wall is made almost entirely of plate glass, in much the same way as Janus House; so close to it, indeed, I should have been thought to repeat myself, & thus to have failed Ruskin's architectural precept of 'saying new & different things'. This morning I happened upon Emily delighting Ellie with the effects of a 'magic' lantern, its bulbous spiral encased by slender lead rods. When it had been put aside I snatched the mechanism up & carried it to the study, where I made a number of sketches. I felt myself to be in the grip of a very singular inspiration, & all but cried 'Eureka!' – for using the lantern as a model I envisaged a staircase constructed of glass on a narrow spiral frame, cantilevered from the back elevation with thin cast-iron mullions to receive the panels.

Undecided as to whether this were foolery or not, I rolled up the sketches & hurried with them down to Tithebarn-street, where Rawlins, mine own familiar, had lately arrived. In a kind of impetuous flurry I explained my notion, & begged him to examine the hastily drawn designs.

Could such a structure be realised? – Rawlins bent his head over the scrolls & stared hard for some moments, while in my own head I suffered a dizzy oscillation between hope & unease. First he puffed out his cheeks – 'Damned if it isn't the queerest thing I ever saw,' he declared, then paused – 'It will be a sensation.' We set about revising the plans this very day.

3rd October 1865

The House of Eames flourishes – Emily is with child again, & Cassie is to be married next March. In the evening I ventured out to Mount-street with these glad tidings, & was met at the door by a raw-boned youth I did not recognise. He appeared civil enough, & I proceeded up the stairs to find Frank sitting on the floor with his back to the wall next to a large Negro, both smoking clay pipes from which pungent clouds emanated – the odour was akin to burnt rope – not unpleasant. He greeted me with a wave, & the distant smile of intoxication. The Negro he introduced as Jess, who merely raised his chin in salutation; from Frank's somewhat slurred talk I gathered that Jess was a prizefighter, that they had known one another from Kingston, & that Frank occupied a managerial position in their partnership. I endeavoured to conceal my astonishment, though after some minutes in the room I perceived that neither of them had the smallest interest in my outward demeanour. Frank offered me his pipe, which I declined – though I was curious to know what strange weed they might be smoking. The youth who admitted me now returned with a sheaf of bills & handed one over – it was a notice of a forthcoming prizefight between 'The Jamaican Hammer' (the Negro before me, I presumed) & one 'Slugger Morrison'. I folded it away, nodded my thanks & left the house – the mystery of Frank's occupation is resolved, though why he scrupled until now to reveal it I cannot fathom.

29th October [1865]

A night to open my eyes. I had wavered these past weeks over the prizefight notice, now tacked on the wall above my desk, & was still in a muddle of indecision about it. I do not care a rap for the sport (if sport it be) yet stirrings of curiosity about the event, & Frank's part in it, were not to be subdued. When Rawlins happened to catch sight of the bill some days ago & confessed himself a devotee of the pugilist's art, the matter was decided, & we bent our steps in

the direction of a low neighbourhood hard by the docks. I had seen
this district by day, when costers & women of all ages throng the
streets & sell their wares – baskets of fruit or oysters, cheap trinkets, flowers, or the Devil knows what – while at every ten steps
there would be an ale-house or spirit-vault into which women &
indeed children might disappear. A dismal sight, though as nothing
to the dense, seething crowds at night, lent a terrible aspect under
the glare of gas lamps. Those who have lain-a-bed all day now come
out & swamp the streets – drunks, beggars, night prowlers, swells,
& prostitutes in eager solicitation. From every corner one hears
curses, shrieks, bursts of music from an organ grinder, as if orches-
trated for some crazed pantomime. Even Rawlins, who has visited
New York, seemed taken aback by the roaring tumult. We finally
gained the public house at which the fight was to be held, & were
met at the door by the same boy who had been at Frank's lodgings
– Jem, by name. On payment of a shilling each we were led through
a crowded saloon, its walls hung with sporting prints & glass cases
that displayed not stuffed fishes or birds, as is the custom, but *dogs*.
I asked Jem about this repulsive anomaly – he explained that the
canines had been champions of another house entertainment,
rat-killing, on which men wagered hundreds of pounds in a single
evening. Thence we proceeded down a reeking passage into a courtyard, where a ring had been set up and a large crowd, many of
them sailors & swells, was milling about, the smell of cigar smoke
thick in the air. 'Mind your pockets, gents,' said Jem, 'I've seen a
few prigs about.' He left us, & returned shortly afterwards with
Frank, in a peacock silk waistcoat such as the Fancy like to wear.
He looked rather prosperous. 'Evening, boys. I hope you've got ducats
with you – our Jess could make you rich tonight.' There was in fact
a frenzy of betting around us, & men yelled & remonstrated with
one another in a spirit of jocular aggression. Rawlins, at least,
seemed to be enjoying the scene. A lusty roar went up as the two
fighters were led in, & I quailed at the size of the brute 'our Jess'
was to face – Slugger Morrison was not as tall as Jess, but he did
appear twice as wide, & his arms were powerfully muscled. His
phiz, I should add, was that of an ogre, & no light of common
humanity shone from his eyes. I had heard that these bare-knuckle
contests might last as long as a hundred rounds, for the rules allow
a man to be knocked down repeatedly & still continue. As soon as
the fight began Morrison made a lunge at Jess and caught him a

tremendous blow on the side of his face; a long plume of blood spouted from his nose – he staggered back against the ropes & closed. The ogre then advanced upon him & threw his meaty fists at Jess's head and body – the sound he made recalled the dreadful thock of that falling man I had seen in North John-street. The next few minutes were an agony to witness as Jess took one whip-crack blow after another, blows that seemed to shiver from the top of the head down to the very toes in one's boots. I noticed that one of the Negro's eyes had swollen over like a huge bruised plum. My stomach lurched, & I retreated to the tap-room that I might not endure another moment of this sickening exhibition. Even there I could hear from the courtyard the shouts and cries of the spectators, as piercing as a screech-owl, & prayed that Jess might be spared mortal harm from those pitiless hands. I stood at the bar drinking porter for perhaps twenty minutes, until another great roar went up from the vicinity of the yard, & I rushed back through the passage to ascertain the outcome. 'e's done him, 'e's done him!' I heard someone shout, & there beheld an astonishing sight – Jess standing in the ring, his face horribly bloodied but his arms held aloft, while his awful antagonist was being carried insensible out of the ring. A 'knock-out!' Frank, his face bathed in sweat & eyes ablaze like coals, appeared to take a desperate kind of relish in the victory. As a confused throng of corner-men & swells & bookmakers jostled around the ring I noticed Jem, at the side, cut a little caper of delight, & I laughed – possibly with relief. I eventually found Rawlins, & we left the wild revelries to play on. As we retraced our steps through those teeming streets I remarked that it had been a strange night. 'And a profitable one, too, I should say,' replied he, producing a wad of grimy bank-notes from his pocket & counting them. 'Your brother was right – that fighter could make a man rich.'

December [1865]

Our first Christmas dinner with Frank at Abercromby-sq. (for eight years) did not pass off without alarm. I had not seen Frank for some weeks, & knowing him to be less than dependable I purposely called at Mount-st. three days before; there a man, who turned out to be a letting agent, admitted me. He said that the rooms were empty, & the tenant gone, which my own investigation quickly confirmed to be the case. The tenant had four weeks' rent in arrears, the agent informed me – did I know to whom bills might be sent? I paid the man off & departed in a state of perfect confusion: Frank, I knew too well, would have enjoyed this moonlight flit, but if he truly was in difficulties why had he not told me, & where might he have gone? Bafflement then gave way to anger, for I had (with the help of Rawlins) been diligent in securing the lease & helping him to settle, & indeed had paid the deposit out of my own pocket. A fine reward for my fraternal solicitude! Having not the least clue as to where he might have fled, I spent the days immediately preceding Christmas in frantic turmoil, sensible of Frank's capacity to ruin the occasion altogether – my mother, I knew, would be inconsolable if her favourite son, after all those years of absence, failed to present himself at the Eames hearth. Christmas morning arrived, we attended the service at St Catherine's, & still we had received no communication from him. My store of seasonal goodwill was almost exhausted by fretting when, just after noon, a knock came at the door & there, resplendent in his best togs, stood Frank, bearing gifts for one & all. The scenes of familial joy that ensued were something to behold as Frank, his charm in full blossom, enchanted the company with his tall tales & mischievous sallies. Even Rawlins, to whom I had confided some of my trouble, was beguiled when he arrived at the evening festivities (Georgy had made a punch that somewhat accelerated the flow of conviviality). As is his wont, Frank consumed a prodigious quantity of spirits without ever seeming to be intoxicated, though I was pleased he saw fit not to smoke that confounded pipe in the company of Ma & Pa. At a quiet moment of the evening – there were very few – I took Frank aside to ask about his recent disappearance, & why he had abandoned the Mount-st. lodgings. 'Ah, Pete, they were too quiet, those rooms – I need a place that's got a bit o' life about it. Found meself a crib down Greenland-st. by Queen's dock. You don't mind, do you?' What in Heaven's name could I say? His manner was so affable, & his conscience so plainly innocent of the anxiety he had caused, that the acerbic speech I had been rehearsing all that day dissolved on my tongue, & we were once again caught up in the joyous mood of the occasion. Yet even in my relief I could not quell deep misgivings as to Frank's erratic behaviour; during those dark hours when I speculated upon his sudden disappearance I had a ghoulish presentiment that he might one day be found lying dead in a ditch. Am I my brother's keeper? These intimations of dread persuade me that I must be.

Wednesday, 17th January, 1866

Today I visited Frank in his present 'crib'. The walk from Hope-pl. to Greenland-st. measures but a half-mile, yet between these addresses lies a chasm. Liverpool has hitherto seemed to me a city of which one might be proud to be a citizen – its temples of commerce, its vast docks, its gracious thoroughfares, its fashionable shops. To declare oneself a Liverpolitan I believed comparable to Cicero's defiant proclamation, 'Civis Romanus sum'. Intimations of a quite different city had disturbed me before – the squalid district Rawlins & I walked that evening of the prizefight – but I continued indifferent by the simple expedient of ignoring them. Whenever a hansom happened to carry me through these wretched streets I chose not to let my gaze linger, & thus could live untroubled.

But today, on foot, in broad daylight, I passed men & women in the direst grip of poverty, & barefoot waifs carrying pitchers of ale, their faces pinched by the cold & emptied of the light of childhood; I saw crowds spill out of taverns, & people wandering drunk, but drunk despairingly, joylessly, as if to drown the misery of this netherworld they inhabited. I felt many pairs of eyes upon me as I walked, & none of them friendly. Frank's lodgings were on the upper floor of a grim-fronted doss-house, & I was admitted, as before, by his young factotum Jem. The smell of grog & fried fish hung thick in the air. I found Frank & Jess sitting together mutely – Jess's hand was heavily bandaged, & it took no wild surmise to discover that something was gravely amiss. 'Gone & broken his damned flapper,' muttered Frank, gesturing at the boxer's hand. 'And such a tuppenny-ha'penny fight it was. He'd already knocked him down twice, this feller looked ready to tumble again – so Jess roundhoused him & next thing his fist goes crack.' Jess merely stared, impassive as a Buddha. Grievous as this news was, of more concern to me were the abysmal surroundings in which we held our colloquy. 'What is this place?' I asked him, failing to conceal the note of dismay in my voice. 'Home,' he shrugged. I could scarcely believe my ears. It was piteous enough that drunks & paupers were obliged to call this neighbourhood home, but to see my own brother settled in amongst them was insupportable. Right there I asked him – implored him – to give up this pathetic accommodation & come back to Hope-pl. with me, we would put old troubles behind us & begin anew. Frank looked at me sadly & said, 'And where should Jess live?' That silenced me. I had no inkling that their companionship extended to such ... He perceived my confusion. 'Don't worry, we get along here very well, & Jem here's our trusty mascot!' At which the young shaver smiled & gave an absurd salute.

Useless to argue. My spirits utterly depressed, I bade them farewell & left the house. As I turned on to the street Frank followed after & called me back. I thought for a moment he had reconsidered my plea & was prepared to come home – but all he said was, 'Pete, could you lend me some money?'

February [1866]

The staircase at the rear of Magdalen Chambers is complete, & today as I gazed upon it the enigma of its creation struck me anew. From what recesses of my teeming brain did I glean this iron-wrought astonishment? My sketching work I have always done as quietly & fastidiously as a carpenter at his bench, secure in the dexterous play of my hand & the accuracy of my eye. But then I was merely capturing the perceived surfaces of the world before me: an aspen, a windmill, a wave toppling & creaming on the shore. Once I ceased to be a student of architecture & became its master, unsuspected vistas of possibility began to unfold, & whatever principles had been absorbed I knew I could now transform into something that was indisputably mine. Yet why this inventive faculty would express itself in one way rather than another I could never rightly tell – & still cannot.

Thursday, 8th March, 1866

Cassie's wedding day. My beloved sister, having endured a number of disastrous suitors, has at last found a fellow – a lawyer, Thos Jackson – who loves her dearly & appears sensible of his good fortune in making her love him. At Abercromby-sq. I was surprised to see Frank arrive in good time & attired as neatly as a guardsman, though he did not scruple to ask for a stirrup cup ('a medical necessity before a wedding', he said) before we set off for St Catherine's. Ma clung to Frank's arm & cried silently as her older daughter was led up the aisle & thence (one must hope) to matrimonial bliss. We proceeded to the reception in the Concert Room, where Pa's speech expressed all that we should have liked to hear about our dear Cassie. Indeed, the day appeared blessed, not only in the radiant happiness of the bride herself but in the crisp spring weather & the gaiety of the wedding breakfast. Alas, the occasion was to have a sting in its tail; Cassie & most others did not witness it, thank Heaven, but it utterly quashed the merriment of those who did. Will quietly reported the matter to me late in the evening. It seemed that some light-hearted remark Pa had made in his speech about children being a 'trial' to their parents had offended Frank, whose long antagonism with Pa had lain mercifully dormant since his return last year. I felt grim forebodings as I sought out Frank in one of the Hall's upper rooms; it seemed too likely that he had been drinking, & indeed his slurred speech & face as red as a Chinese dragon confirmed the worst. He was angrily denouncing Pa as a 'miser' who had refused him the preferment that was his due when at Eames & co., then had compounded the offence by humiliating him in a public speech. The small crowd of guests who gave him ear seemed utterly confounded, & I feared that they might be kinsmen of the groom. Unable to suffer this drunken tirade any longer, I took Frank aside & spoke to him sternly, more sternly than I ever had – whatever his grievance with our father (I argued) this was not a fit occasion on which to raise it. Frank even in his cups saw the justice of this & fell to brooding, while I promised to have a private talk with Pa on the subject. But this only started him off again. 'Why should you or anyone else intercede on my behalf? Am I not entitled to fair treatment from my own father without another prompting his conscience?' & so on – he could not be reasoned out of his deluded indignation. It pains me now to remember Frank as he was, the genial schoolfellow of my youth who saw what other people got angry about as merely a humorous part of the nature of things. Time was when my older brother's gentlemanly ease in the world was an inspiration to me. But the man I saw this evening is not the same one who left us nine years ago.

18th March 1866

Emily gave birth this morning to a girl, now 'mewling & puking' in her mother's arms, & very beautiful she is. Evangeline Rose is the name we have given her, for her face was as pink & delicate as that bloom when she emerged into the world. Sir W^{m}, the child's grandfather, called at Hope-pl. in the afternoon to inspect her, pronounced himself satisfied & departed in his carriage twenty minutes later.

July [1866]

Triumph & disaster. Rawlins & I celebrated the completion of Magdalen Chambers today with a luncheon of Chablis & oysters at the Cockspur. We merrily reviewed the troubled history of the building, begun in the wake of my trial by mockery in the press, then continued in the face of financial reversals & my own doubts as to its originality. The late addition of the spiral staircase I now see as its most vital component, & I thanked John for his faith in this & other architectural oddities of mine that many would have disdained as outlandish. As I toasted the fine fellow I noticed an untypical awkwardness in his manner, & in truth I imagined he was about to request of me a partnership in the practice. How happily I should have obliged him! – but no, this was not his meaning at all. He has lately been in correspondence with a cousin who has started an architectural business of his own in Chicago, Ill., & has been eagerly urging John to return to America & take up a position there. This news fell like an axe upon me. As he related it, John's eyes never met my own & his voice hardly rose above an undertone; he seemed quite mortified, & mumbled something to the effect that I must think him 'an ingrate'. I laughed at this, assuring him that nothing could be further from the truth. He had cheered me when my spirits had been most afflicted, & he had brought to bear his practical assistance & indefatigable energy at a time when they were most needed. Indeed, I was the one at fault, for I had forgotten how much John – still only two-&-twenty – had left behind when he fled his country; his mother still lives, so too a brother & sister. Heart-stricken as I was, I told him simply what a friend he had been to me, & what a true companion in hardship. This seemed to have the opposite effect I had intended, for tears now stood in his eyes, & he seemed bereft of the capacity to speak. Poor John! I decided not to oppress him any further, & instead held out my hand, which he took sadly but warmly.

27th July [1866]

A footman came early this morning bearing a note from Pa. His message was to the point – 'Pandemonium here. Be kind enough to come immediately.' Minutes later I was hurrying along the street, my footsteps light with trepidation. My father, of a naturally equable temperament, would not have issued such a summons without grievous cause, & I feared that Ma had been taken ill, or worse. On arrival at Abercromby-sq. I found Georgy & my parents unharmed (Will away travelling in Italy) though this relief was tempered by the egregious spectacle of the house turned upside down. They had returned from a dinner late last evening to discover that the back door had been jemmied & the place ransacked. Intruders had made off with whatever they could lay hands upon – candlesticks, ornaments, the silver, an ormolu clock that had stood on the chimney piece for years, a gold hunter of Pa's; his desk had been forced, & a sum of money taken. I found Ma slumped on the couch in the piano room, weeping inconsolably while Georgy looked about the disarray in shock. The burglars had tossed about the furniture so savagely it seemed as though a tornado had suddenly whistled through the house. A police inspector who had just concluded an interview with Pa tipped his hat to me on his way out.

'Mark of a proper cracksman, that back door,' he said, almost admiring the handiwork.

I went to talk to Pa in his looted study, books & papers strewn about the floor. The servants had already been questioned, & were plainly innocent of any implication in the robbery – two of the maids had been overpowered & locked in a cupboard. The policeman had told him certain suspected housebreakers had attracted the notice of the constabulary on the streets hereabouts, & were at present being watched. Small comfort to us, I replied, & Pa nodded absently. The single consolation he could entertain was that none of Ma's jewellery had been stolen, although to have broken the locked drawer of the dresser where it lay would have been the work of a moment. My response to this news passed rapidly through three distinct stages, bafflement at first, then curiosity, & finally distant but horrible tremors of suspicion that the author of this outrage might – No, inconceivable – I cannot bear to write it. Too late, the vile thought has taken root. I dared not mention it to Pa, for even to voice it I feared would pollute the family hearth for ever. My brain in violent turmoil, I felt obliged to take my leave, having promised to call at the house again the next day.

August [1866]

Several days passed & still I waited for news that the police had apprehended someone – anyone – & thus have my suspicions rebutted. But no such intelligence came. I returned to Abercromby-sq. to supervise the replacement of the locks, stouter than the previous, & to help Pa compile a thorough inventory of all the stolen items. Still the fact of my mother's untouched jewellery tolled though my head. I dearly wanted to believe that the thieves had in their haste over-looked this treasure, & that we should be thankful for a small mercy. But their diligent rapacity elsewhere argued against such careless-ness: they had deliberately omitted to raid that dresser, I felt certain of it.

With heavy heart I set out for Greenland-street, taking a life-preserver with me; the ruffians I saw thereabouts the last time would put a man on his guard. Through that mean district I walked once more, trying to order my thoughts the while. The summer season had not improved the aspect of those streets; indeed, they seemed more poisonous than when I first made acquaintance with them in January. Again, it was shocking to find so many children plying the squalid trades of adults; one girl, aged no more than twelve, brazenly tugged at my sleeve & begged me to come with her – to what end I dread to imagine. That people should have to abide in such wretchedness –

I should have learned my brother's ways by now. On reaching the doss-house he called home I enquired within, & was told by the sour-faced landlady that Frank had 'slung his 'ook' some weeks ago, & his two companions gone with him. Naturally no forwarding address had been left. On the one hand I was worried & depressed about this latest disappearance; on the other I admitted to myself a kind of relief. It is no enviable duty, after all, to ask a man whether he has burgled the house of his own parents.

That was the final entry of the journals' second volume. Baines realised his view of Eames had changed in the course of his reading. The cock-sure young fellow of the early 1860s had fascinated him, but he had not much cared for his tone of strutting braggadocio and the slightly tiresome acclamations of his own genius. Once his brother's volatile behaviour had begun to make itself felt, however, and Eames took on the responsibility of minding him, he suddenly appeared a more human and sympathetic figure. He wanted this story to end well for the architect, and at the same time had an inescapable sense that the gathering storm clouds prefigured tragedy. The third and final volume awaited him, but for the moment he felt unable to press on to the denouement. He wanted to preserve the faint possibility of Eames's salvation for a while longer.

10

Meanwhile he was preoccupied with more immediate demands of salvation. Rafferty's death had left them without a squad leader, which none of them minded, but being a man short had imposed a heavier workload and longer hours, which all of them minded. One night in the second week of January they were sitting around the Hackins Hey depot when the sirens began to sound. Farrell, who had been playing darts with McGlynn, raised his eyes heavenwards.

'Fuck's sake! Has Hitler got some personal grudge against us or wha'?'

'London's had it worse,' said Mavers, nodding at the photograph of St Paul's, wreathed in smoke but defiant, which some patriotic soul had clipped from the front of the *Daily Mail* and pinned to the wall. Stoically they hauled on their winter coats; McGlynn was absently, buck-toothily winding a knitted blue-and-white scarf around his neck, which somehow made him look even younger. He saw Baines watching him.

'Me mum made it for me,' he explained. 'For when I go to Everton, you know?'

'Yeah, fat chance of that,' said Farrell, who was in one of his bitter moods tonight. 'Another thing to add to early closen we can thank the Germans for – no footie.'

'You red or blue, Tom?' McGlynn asked.

Baines shrugged. 'Neither, I'm afraid. I listen to the results when my uncle does the pools –'

'*Wha'*?!' said Farrell incredulously. 'You're tellin' me you come from Liverpool and you don't like football?'

'I imagine there are others. Besides, it's not that I don't like football – just that I never got interested. I was keen on cricket.'

'I've heard it all now. So, like, yer dad never took yer to a match?'

'No. I suppose he might have done, but he died when I was eight.'

Farrell, silenced but plainly peeved to have his flow of indignation stemmed, kept shaking his head. Mavers tactfully stepped in. 'If they do open Goodison again, you'll 'ave to come with us one Saturday.'

'I'd be honoured,' replied Baines.

A few hours later, they were on their way to a fire in Virgil Street when a bomb screamed down thirty yards in front of them, bounced off a watchman's shelter and flew through the window of a shop. For an instant nothing happened, then Baines saw the building shiver for a split second before it exploded. He had been riding shotgun next to Mavers, and both of them turned away as the force of the blast rocked the van. Fragments of debris rained down on them as Mavers twisted the wheel sharply and collided with a parked tram. The vehicle had not been travelling quickly – he was a cautious driver – but the front radiator had buckled and black smoke poured from the engine. Farrell, Mike and McGlynn had jumped out of the back and come round to survey the damage.

'Are yous all right?' Farrell asked. Baines stepped down from the cabin, his legs weirdly hollow. There was also a smarting pain just below his right eye. He touched it, and felt something sharp lodged in the flesh. Farrell was now pointing the torch beam into his face.

'Jesus! Hold still a mo,' he said, and carefully plucked out a fragment of glass the size of a shilling. He showed it to Baines. 'Lucky lad – an inch higher and that would have taken yer eye out.'

The van was a smoking wreck, so they abandoned it and walked the remainder of the way to Virgil Street. They had turned the corner of Cazneau Street when they were startled by a sight so freakishly horrific that Baines for a moment thought he was dreaming. A horse was bolting towards them, its head and mane on fire – a biblical apparition. They scattered and watched the animal career past them, its screams piercing to their ears.

'What the fuck –' said Mavers, who broke into a run. The others followed close behind until they reached a stable, engulfed in flames; on the street an old man stood in a daze, watching it burn.

'Bloody vandals,' he shouted, without looking at them. His voice sounded wild, unmodulated. 'Bloody Nazi vandals.'

The smell of burning horseflesh suffused the air: an incendiary must have landed on the stable and turned it into a raging slaughterhouse. Baines, reaching for his handkerchief, felt his gorge suddenly rise, and just managed to keep himself from retching. In the light of the fire he could see the creases in the old man's face, the patchy bristles on his chin, his jaw working furiously. Above them the planes were still circling, and suddenly the air was alive with a vicious whistling noise that portended what they knew too well.

'Watch yourselves,' called Mavers, and as one they turned and started for the doorway of a pub opposite. Baines glanced back and, seconds before he threw himself to the pavement, saw the old man still standing there. Flattened against the kerb he didn't hear the blast so much as feel it, right through his teeth, the shock waves sucking monstrously at the atmosphere around them. The windows of the pub shattered in an instant, and the roasting horseflesh was now mixed with a choking sulphurous stench. When the smoke cleared, they stood up and walked out into the street, or what was left of it. Adjusting their eyes they could see a deep crater about the length of a bus in the very place they had stood less than two minutes before. It was spewing out smoke and ash like a dying volcano.

It took him a while, but eventually McGlynn lowered the handkerchief from his mouth and said, 'Where's the old feller?'

They looked at each other, not speaking, not willing to be the one who had to explain. He had disappeared, atomised by the one that had his name on it – 'the one you didn't hear'. But then Baines remembered how the old man had not responded to Mavers' warning, had not even turned to see them all running for cover. He had seemed transfixed by the flames.

The truth was now dawning on McGlynn. 'So the bomb – ah no ...' He stopped, confusion and horror chasing around his features.

'Yeah,' said Mavers, and gently patted McGlynn on the shoulder. In the distance they heard the bell of a fire engine approaching. The stable was still burning, but the sounds they had heard from within on first arriving had, mercifully, ceased. There were hurrying footsteps behind them; a man and a woman, neighbours, it seemed, had come to inspect the damage. Baines saw them talking with Mavers, who was evidently explaining what had happened to the old man. The woman had raised her hand to her mouth in a reflex of shock. The man simply hung his head. A warden who had just arrived called over to them.

'Are yous the rescue squad?'

In answer Farrell pointed to the white 'R' stencilled on the front of his helmet. 'What does it look like?'

The warden wisely decided to ignore his insolence. 'There's a collapsed shelter round the corner, a load of injured – they need help bringing them out.'

'We'll get going then,' said Baines.

As they walked away, Mavers rejoined them. He looked troubled by something, and Baines asked him what it was.

'The couple I was talken to, they said the old feller had looked after that stable for years. I told them about the bomb.'

'Did you say how he didn't bother taking cover?'

'Yeah,' said Mavers, his eyes downcast, 'and now I know why. He was deaf – had been all his life.'

They worked through the night, dragging bodies from their premature burial chambers. More squads arrived and they had formed lines, passing buckets of debris from hand to hand. They found a few survivors, lucky ones who had been trapped in air pockets and managed to make themselves heard through the sprawling tonnage of brick and plaster. But most of the time they expected the worst, and they had learned to recognise a corpse before they had even touched it. Sometimes it was the colour of their skin; sometimes it was a smell. Baines could tell just from the way their limbs lay disposed. Nothing looked more absolute than the dead. By the morning they had dug out fifteen corpses, and a grisly assortment of body parts, which put an edge of horror on their dark mood.

Mike had returned from the mobile canteen bearing a tray laden with steaming mugs of tea. They were sitting against a damaged wall, their heads hung low in exhaustion. Baines, looking around, assumed that his own face looked as ashen as everyone else's.

'Here you go,' Mike said, handing him a tin mug. 'Gorra say, there's a smashin'-lookin' bird serven the tea.'

'Any food there?' asked Farrell.

'Sandwiches 'n' that. Dunno how you can eat anythin' after a night like this.'

Farrell shrugged. 'Just somethin' to keep me goin', like. I'm not after curried dog or anythin'.'

Mike heaved a long-suffering sigh. 'Where d'you get the idea we eat curried dog?'

'Don't start this again,' pleaded Mavers. 'Mike, ignore him. Terry, go get us a sandwich, will yer?'

Farrell, chuckling, walked off, taking McGlynn with him.

'He's an arsehole,' said Mike, shaking his head.

Mavers took out a cigarette and lit it. 'He just wants an audience. Ignore him an' he'll stop.'

Baines shivered against the dawn cold. He felt dirty and depleted, and what was worse, the unignorable taste of death filled his mouth. He cadged a cigarette from Mavers and blew smoke down his nose, hoping to rid himself of it. He thought of the bombs whistling down, the crump as they landed, the compacted fury of detonation. They had been lucky last night, two near-misses within an hour of one another. He should be feeling grateful to have survived, he knew, especially after a night dealing with those who hadn't, but fatigue had emptied him of nice considerations.

Farrell had returned with the sandwiches. 'Charlie's right about that bird at the canteen.'

'The gear, isn't she?' said Mike, surprised at last to have located common ground with Farrell. Baines, still shivering like a whippet, rose unsteadily and stamped his feet, trying to get the circulation back into them. He thought he might go and inspect this paragon for himself; after last night it would do him good to look on something beautiful. He trudged past the ambulance crews and the geysers of water springing where the mains had burst, rounded the corner and spotted the canteen parked against the kerb. Its hatch faced in the opposite direction, and when he walked round it he saw her, busily pouring out tea. Bella. He stopped in his tracks, stunned, and experienced a moment's indecision. His first instinct was to duck away, so unprepared was he for an encounter with her – but, too late, she had lifted her head and caught him in the spotlight of her gaze.

'Tom!' she called, her voice almost shrill with surprise. He walked over, certain of nothing but his guilt in avoiding her these past weeks. She excused herself at the hatch and came out to greet him, though concern darkened her features once she was up close.

'Heavens – you look awful! What's this blood all down your face?' she said, peering at his cheek.

'A lucky escape, actually. Do I look as bad as all that?'

'You look exhausted. Let me get you some tea –'

'No, I'm fine,' he cut in, catching her sleeve as she was turning. He wanted to get his apology out straight away. 'Bella, I'm sorry I haven't called you –'

But she interrupted him. 'Did Richard not telephone you?'

Baines shook his head, though now he did recall hearing the telephone ring as he left the flat the previous evening. Bella was smiling, and gripping both his arms fiercely.

'He's alive! David – he's alive. We heard it yesterday, the Swiss Red Cross finally found him. He's in a prison camp in Germany, near Leipzig – but he's unharmed.' She told him how they had kept telephoning the Air Ministry, and how the weeks had felt like months – years – as they waited for news. 'You know, I think I went slightly mad for a while. I couldn't do anything, couldn't sleep, couldn't read a book. Anything! Poor

Richard got the worst of it. I went down to London to stay with Nancy, and then she had to listen to me crying the whole time. I just imagined him lying dead in a French cornfield, and our never knowing . . . God, I feel awful about it now. I mean, David's her brother too.'

She had been talking excitedly – he had never seen her face so animated – and now she turned the full beam of her attention on to him. 'I'm so happy to see you again!' she exclaimed girlishly, and threw her arms about him.

He felt his heart skip a beat – this was more affection than he felt able to handle. He said, by way of diversion, 'I ought to tell you, you've won some admirers round the corner. One of them reckons you're a "smashing-looking bird".'

'Really?' she said, with an abrupt laugh. 'Who are they?'

'Just fellers I work with in rescue. How's Richard getting on?'

'He's working with a squad down in the Dingle. They say there've been dreadful raids there last night.'

'Yeah, I heard that.'

She was examining his face again. 'That's a nasty cut you've got under your eye.'

He shrugged, feigning nonchalance, and then noticed that her gaze had shifted somewhere beyond his shoulder.

'I think your friends . . .' she said, and he turned round to see Mavers and Farrell ambling towards them. Farrell's expression mingled curiosity, admiration and faint disbelief. This was not an encounter Baines had planned for, and he felt a potential awkwardness in the air.

'Bella, these are my – colleagues, Liam and Terry.'

His apprehension dissolved as soon as she turned her smile on them and shook their hands. Her forthrightness, her way of meeting a person's eye, was of a kind that had a disarming effect on men, even men who habitually imposed themselves on company. She had an irresistible geniality, he thought, the way she communicated a vivid interest in whoever happened to be standing in front of her. She was asking Mavers and Farrell something about rescue work, he wasn't exactly listening, but he registered how they responded to her attention – how they became eager to please. He remembered it now from the first time he saw her at the gallery and she had joked with the two young officers. He felt once again how lucky he was to know her.

His reverie was broken by Mavers. 'Tommy? We're knocken off for a few hours. Might be an idea to get some kip.'

Baines nodded. 'I'll see you at the depot, then.'

'Nice to meet yer,' Mavers said to Bella, who smiled back: 'Likewise.'

Baines expected Farrell to make some saucy remark, but Bella's charm seemed to have left him – unprecedentedly – at a loss. He said only, 'Ta-ra,' and glanced at Baines, who felt briefly lit in the reflected glamour of the woman standing next to him. When they had gone, she looked round at him and said in an amused tone, '"Tommy"?'

'Yeah. Suits me, don't you think?'

'Mm, I suppose it does . . . in a boyish kind of way.'

'What did you think of those two?'

'I liked them! The older one – Terry? – seemed a little shy.'

Baines allowed himself an incredulous laugh. 'If only you knew.'

Bella glanced at her watch. 'Look, my shift finishes in about half an hour. If you can wait I'll walk back into town with you.'

An hour later they had almost reached Gambier Terrace when the bruised, slate-coloured clouds that had been amassing finally closed over them, and the rain, spitting at first, was suddenly crackling over the cobblestones. They began to run, but the drowning curtain swept over them obliviously; by the time they reached the shelter of the terrace's colonnade Baines could feel the drops of moisture leaking down his collar and the bottoms of his trousers were clinging damply around his ankles.

'That was quite . . . unpleasant,' he said, wiping his face with a handkerchief which, he now saw, was streaked with dirt and blood from the night before. Bella was giggling as she glanced at him.

'You look like you've just swum here! Sorry – I'm in such a PollyAnna-ish mood even the rain seems funny.'

They stood watching the downpour for a few moments longer; there was something about its headlong intensity that you couldn't tear your gaze from. *Let it come down,* he thought, remembering *Macbeth*.

'Cup of tea?'

While Baines busied himself in the kitchen, Bella looked around his flat in an unabashed display of interest.

'I always wondered what your rooms would look like,' she called. He watched through the door as she studied the prints and photographs that hung on the living-room walls.

'It seems strange that you've never been here before,' he mused.

'Well, maybe I was waiting to be asked!' He thought he heard a sharp note beneath the playful tone. She continued her wandering examination of the room as he laid down the tea tray. 'I like this,' she said, peering at a William Herdman pencil-and-sepia sketch.

'Mm. St George's Hall, about 1867. Dickens did a few readings there – said it was the finest concert room he'd ever known. Eames saw him read from *Nicholas Nickleby*.'

'Ah, your architect. Still interested in him?'

'I've just finished the second volume of his journals. Things have started to go wrong for him – seems his alcoholic brother burgled his parents' house, and his great friend Rawlins is leaving him to return to America.'

'John Rawlins – the Chicago architect?' she asked, and Baines nodded. 'Isn't he quite famous?'

'Yeah. Rawlins did most of his architectural apprenticeship under Eames, then went to Chicago and designed office buildings that were self-confessed tributes to his teacher. He became a great success – unlike poor Eames.'

Bella returned to scouring the assorted photographs of Victorian Liverpool that lined the mantelpiece. 'This room, it's like ... a little museum to the city.'

Baines smiled, and handed Bella a mug of tea. 'Sorry, I seem to have no milk.'

'That's all right. Do you have any whisky I could put in it? I need a bit of warmth.'

'Of course. And I'll get some coals, too.'

As he went to the drinks cabinet to fetch a bottle of Dewar's, he caught a glimpse of his face in the little Venetian mirror above it.

'Good God! What a fright –' Although the cut below his eye had been stitched by an auxiliary nurse the blood was congealing in an unsightly black scab around it. Bella stood at the mirror behind him.

'I told you! Do you have any iodine here?'

'Er, there might be some ...'

She followed him out into the bathroom, where he began rummaging around the tiny mirrored cabinet. It was a narrow, windowless room, and he sensed the closeness of her presence behind him. She was now staring in puzzlement at something pinned next to the cabinet.

'Why do you have a calendar from 1914 on your wall?'

'Oh ... it's something I retrieved from a clearance Jack and I did a while ago. We found this old workshop that had been completely un-disturbed for, um, twenty-five years. It was pretty eerie, actually – they'd obviously just downed tools and gone to join up.'

'And never came back?'

'That's what we assumed.'

Bella pondered this, then said with a faint smile, 'You are peculiar. Do you ever think you live too much in . . . the past?'

He paused, considering, and said, 'I used to, I suppose.' He plucked out a bottle of iodine. 'Here we are.' She took it from him and with matronly briskness began to wash her hands.

'Right, if you could just sit there,' she said, pointing to the edge of the bathtub. He sat on the uncomfortable roll-top and watched her soak a corner of a flannel in the solution. Because she was tall he had the impression of her looming over him. Then she was bending down and her face was a few startling inches in front of his.

'This might –'

'Fuck!' he said thickly, wincing from the sharp bite of the iodine.

Bella reared back, with an apologetic grimace. 'Sorry . . .'

'No, I'm sorry, for my – language.' Since he had begun working in heavy rescue he had noticed himself slipping into the same everyday profanity that Liam and the rest of them indulged in; yet he still considered it brutish to swear in front of a woman.

'Nothin' I 'aven't 'eard before, dearie,' she cawed in the cockney-charwoman voice she liked to use, and he laughed. Once again she lowered her head towards his and began gingerly to dab the wound. Her face was so close he could smell the cold cream she had put on however many hours before, and could discern tiny flecks of amber he had missed till now in her olive-green eyes. Then he felt the awkwardness of staring into those eyes, so he looked at her mouth instead. Her teeth gently bit on her bottom lip as she concentrated, and he saw up close the tiny indent on the front tooth he had noticed on first meeting her.

'That chipped corner, on your tooth – what happened there?'

'Oh . . . David did that when he was a baby. I was holding him when he jerked up and accidentally butted me in the mouth!'

There was something about this reminiscence that called to him – it was sad and fond and comical all at once – and before he had time to stop himself he tilted his head and put his mouth on hers. He held the kiss until she drew away. She looked surprised, and yet not surprised.

'What are you doing?' There was less accusation in the question than curiosity, and perhaps the hint of a challenge.

'I'm sorry,' he said, wondering if his nerve would hold. 'You looked so . . . lovely, just then . . .'

He stood up to face her. She was staring hard at him, and as the silence lengthened between them he knew this might go terribly wrong.

He decided to speak and have done with it. 'Actually, I've wanted to do that for ages. I know, it's unpardonable, you're married, but I just didn't want to die without knowing what it was like to kiss you. You can hate me for it if –' The sentence went unfinished because now she was kissing him, cautiously at first, and then, as her mouth found an answering heat in his, more urgently. Seconds passed that felt as long as minutes: he was amazed that his tongue should be inside her mouth, feeling the tiny grooved notch on her tooth that had provoked it all. He had a sudden thrilling sense of reciprocated intimacy, and felt the contrasting familiarity of a face he had yearned over and the absolute unfamiliarity of touching it with his hands, his mouth. She pulled back, her eyes seemingly blurred by the accelerating momentum of what was happening.

'I could never hate you,' she said, but there seemed more meaning in her voice than that simple declaration could contain. He took the bottle of iodine she was still holding and placed it on the sink, then without a word held her arm as he guided her out of the bathroom and down the corridor. A shaft of daylight had poked into the bedroom where the blackout curtain was imperfectly hung. They could hear the gusting rain against the window, the shivering of its frame. Bella looked for a moment at the bed, the unambiguous implication of it, and with a sidelong glance at him she stepped with her languid dancer's strides on to it and quickly twisted herself round to face him. He unlaced his boots and kicked them off; when he saw her watching him in the dreary half-light he suddenly felt the presumption of undressing and instead climbed on to the bed, and then on to her.

She laid her hand on his chest, and whispered, 'Your heart is racing.'

'Is yours?'

She nodded. The next minutes seemed to evaporate in an ecstatic fumbling of underclothes. When he thought about it later he found the narrative of it had splintered into momentary images and sounds. He couldn't quite put it all together in his head, the trickle of retreating silk, the vivid counterpoint of pale skin and dark hair, the sudden reveal of livid flesh; and then his own questing hardness within her, the broken, quickening breaths as they moved together, and the sudden high scalp-tingling release, like a flare going off behind his eyes. He desperately wanted to hold on to that moment, but it was already gone, as moments tended to be.

* * *

Later, when he brought in a fresh pot of tea and the forgotten bottle of Dewar's, she was lying sideways with her head propped against her fist. Her eyes were on him, but he couldn't properly read her expression. He sat down beside her, and while he pondered what to say he lit two cigarettes and handed one to her; she took a long reflective drag on it and exhaled with a little sigh.

'So . . .' she began, 'did you have this planned?' The question rather disappointed him, it implied calculation on his part when he had acted – more dashingly, he thought – on impulse.

'No. Though I'd wanted to do it for a long time.'

'When? When did you realise?'

'I think it must have been that night David was at your flat for dinner, back in May. I remember you talking about your family holidays with him, and I suddenly thought of all the years I wished I'd known you. It made me quite ill – with longing.'

'Was that the night you had that sort of turn?'

'Yes. I tried to hide it – not very well, it seems.'

He wanted her to reassure him in similar vein, but he couldn't bring himself to pose a direct question in case her answer was too honest – or not honest enough.

Bella spoke musingly: 'I kept thinking about the night you punched that fellow's lights out at the gallery. That surprised me! Till then I'd always regarded you as rather' – and here she smiled – 'remote.'

It was not what he had been hoping to hear. True, he had been in her thoughts, he had even surprised her, but that confessed misperception of his character was very far from his own passionate avowal. He felt himself retreating into self-appraisal.

'I've changed, I suppose. You were right when you said I lived too much in the past. It was only when war came and I started doing rescue work that I sort of . . . woke up.'

Bella nodded slowly, and then sat up in the bed, facing away from him. He gazed at her back, its creamy, elegant curve and the knobby little ridge of bones at the base of the spine. He loved the very tallness of her – it made her beauty more imposing.

'I'll be thirty soon,' she said. Her voice sounded distant, preoccupied.

'Why do you mention that?'

For a long time she didn't answer, and he began to wonder if she'd heard his question. But eventually she spoke: 'Because I should be old enough to know better.'

A shadow had fallen across her. When he leaned over to touch her back she flinched, and then tried to make amends by offering him a smile. But it felt brittle, there was something mechanical and willed in it that dismayed him. Her euphoric mood of a few hours before had dissipated, and in the tense line of her shoulders he seemed to read a shocked reckoning of what they had just done. Neither of them spoke, but he knew that they were both thinking of the same person.

I I

19th October 1866

A letter from Rawlins, now established in partnership with his cousin in Chicago, Ill. Just to see his handwriting on the envelope caused my heart to turn over.

'... My thoughts still carry me back to that morning at the Pier-Head when we shook hands for the last time. I had fled to England from that terrible war – whose effects, I need hardly tell you, still linger dreadfully. For a long time I felt lost. Yet I never thought to leave my place of exile with so heavy a heart, for in Liverpool I truly found the sweets of life. This poor scrap will not suffice to convey my gratitude, either for your diligence as a tutor or for your unceasing kindness to me as a guide, philosopher & friend. Wherever destiny may take me I will always count it a privilege to have known & worked alongside you. Please remember me to your wife, & to your family, whose convivial hospitality I was so fortunate to share. Goodbye, my dear Friend!

Believe me, ever yours affectionately, John Rawlins.'

Good, honest John! How keenly I have felt his absence – I can never replace him. He arrived at a time in my life when I most needed a friend, supported me without thought of recompense, & transacted so much of the business that was dreary & incomprehensible to me. Is it not an unkindness of fate that so often it snatches from us those we can least afford to lose?

October [1866]

Months have passed since the completion of Magdalen Chambers, yet not one single line has the press seen fit to bestow upon it. An admirable escape, one might suppose, after the avalanche of opprobrium that nearly buried my first building. It seems I am either to be pilloried or else ignored entirely, & feel at a loss as to which I should prefer. When the *Badger* &c. took up cudgels against me I was affronted, but I perversely rejoiced in the consciousness that my work had *provoked* them. Now, alas, I cannot claim even this small satisfaction.

17th November [1866]

It is hard – grievously hard – to abide in the knowledge that my own brother, the companion of my youth, chooses to avoid associating with me. When Frank was away in the Caribbean for eight years we would write to one another, & thus maintained our fraternal bond by proxy. Now, he lives in the selfsame city as I, yet we are further apart than ever. We have none of us seen hide nor hair of him since Cassie's wedding day in March. I dread to imagine what undiscoverable slum he calls home. Does he ever think of us, I wonder, or is he too deep in befuddled oblivion? It seems another age when we stood at the Pier-Head & welcomed him off the gangplank – the joy of that day! Since then I have been obliged to learn a bitter lesson – that a family is only as happy as its unhappiest member.

Friday, 14th December, 1866

My father's thoughts have evidently been tending in the same direction, for this evening after dinner at Abercromby-sq. he invited me to his study for a private colloquy. He looked in some degree older, wearier too, no doubt from shouldering the burden of Ma's now-constant anxiety in regard to Frank. Confounded by his disappearance she has taken it into her head that he must have been kidnapped – else why has he ceased to visit her at home? 'Perhaps she is right,' sighed Pa, though we both knew this to be unlikely. Without any prompting on my part he began talking about the long-enduring antagonism between himself & Frank, which he traced back to a time when Frank hoped to assume the management of Eames & co. in Jamaica – an appointment my father withheld, believing Frank's temperament to be unsuited to the task. His inclination was to set Frank to work in Liverpool, where he might supervise his progress at close quarters. He confessed now that this had been a mistake, not because he thought his instinct unsound but because it was seen to betray a lack of confidence in his eldest son – it was, he added, the only occasion in their married life on which he & Ma had argued. Frank duly marked the slight, damned his father's eyes & set sail for the West Indies without delay – a leave-taking I sadly failed to witness, having but recently gone up to Cambridge. Pa belatedly arranged a position for his disobliging son, but by now the canker was in the bud.

All of this I had in some degree suspected, but I was taken by surprise when Pa then asked whether I believed Frank to be the culprit in the burglary of his house. When I confessed my misgivings Pa merely nodded, his expression betraying no anger, or even disappointment – only a profound sadness. The stolen property was of little concern to him, he said, & I believed him; what he dreaded to lose was his son. I tried to assure him that I would do all in my power to find him, though in my heart I have but little confidence of doing so. Frank does not wish to be found.

Christmas Day, 1866

A subdued dinner at Abercromby-sq., the first of its kind I can ever remember here. Cassie & Jackson present, & Will returned from his travels, so the house was full. But of course there was a ghost amongst us, & although Ma put on a show of gaiety I could discern behind her trembling lip an anguish that grieved me terribly. Thank Heaven for Ellie & Rose, whose lisping innocence provided such distraction. Noting Emily's looks of fond absorption I felt, as doubtless many a father has done, a curious compound of love & estrangement – the latter accountable to an entirely natural sense of being *usurped* by one's children. However devoted a wife to a husband, once she conceives a mother's love her spouse must learn his pre-eminence will never again be secure.

Friday, 1st February, 1867

Seized by restlessness this afternoon I left the office, not caring where I walked, & found myself hard by Queen-square. There was a small tavern there I used to visit years ago, & nostalgic tenderness had prompted me before now to visit the place – which I never did. Too late, alas, for the wrecker's ball was at that very moment loudly pulverising it. Odd that I should have been there to witness its dusty death. It used to amuse me that Pa would break off a conversation at dinner to lament the destruction of this or that ancient building – he would look so stricken that one might have supposed he had designed the thing himself. I understand him better now.

11th April 1867

At a guild dinner I happened to meet Edward Urquhart, whom I knew a little at Trinity in '59. He had been employed for years at a broker's, which had lately been ruined in some injudicious foreign scheme. This epidemic of speculation! He recounted the story of his misfortune with no expressions of self-pity, though he admitted that the collapse of the house could not have happened at a less timely moment – he was married only last year. We talked very amiably with one another until after midnight, & before parting I took his card, that we might meet again. He seems an honest & capital fellow, & his dignity under straitened circumstances impressed me deeply.

25th April 1867

To dinner here Urquhart & his wife, Euphemia, or Effie as she calls herself – a vivacious, apple-cheeked creature with long chestnut-coloured hair & a brightness about her eyes that I found wholly enchanting. Emily liked her, too, & our little gathering proceeded in high congenial spirits. When the ladies retired I ventured a subject which I had been turning over these past days with Urquhart, to wit – whether he would oblige me by assuming the post of my business manager. (I had previously recounted to him the departure last year of my faithful friend Rawlins.) I had begun to express a regret that the remuneration would be in no wise comparable with his previous employment when Urquhart broke in, his face lit with gratitude, to say how deeply he esteemed the offer & that he accepted it right willingly. We shook hands on the matter straight away, then called the ladies back to share the good news. I hope the appointment brings me as much luck as John did.

June [1867]

I begin to despair of entering architectural competitions, so familiar has rejection become. My designs seem to be out of joint with the times, or else they are admired but shunned on grounds of expense. The winning entries of these competitions, by the bye, are of such a dreary & unreflective kind I should be ashamed to put my name to them. Emily tells me that I must persevere, that an architect of my calibre cannot be overlooked for long, but I have really come to wonder if Magdalen Chambers might be the last building I will ever be allowed to make.

Thursday, Fifth September, 1867

Yesterday on Bold-street I happened to be standing idly at a shopfront window when I spotted in the glass reflection a figure I recognised – or thought I had. He had passed by so swiftly that it was hard to be certain, but I turned & began to follow him at a discreet distance. As we walked through the massing crowds of Church-street & thence into Lord-street I became convinced by degrees that the person whose footsteps I tracked was Jem, the young shaver who used to keep company with Frank. He seemed a good foot taller since I had last seen him, & though I had yet to look him properly in the face, something in the jauntiness of his gait inclined me to think it was he. At the junction of St George's-crescent he stopped to look about, & I feared my shadowing presence had been discovered, but he then continued unawares down into the warren of narrow lanes between Red Cross-st. & Canning-pl. & disappeared into a squalid-looking spirits-vault. Conscious of a business engagement set at five o'clock, I paused for a moment, undecided. I was tempted to let deuce take the boy – his identity was yet far from certain – & make for the office, but then if it were indeed Jem I would have spurned the slender possibility that he might lead me to – a certain errant kinsman of mine.

Drawing down the brim of my hat I descended into the vault, & found its interior to be quite as deplorable as its front had promised – a subterranean cavern of sawdust on bare boards, spotted looking-glasses, an atmosphere reeking of grog & inexpressible gloom. Yet the dim gas-light allowed me to pass almost unremarked through its rooms, crowded even at this hour, & in the large saloon at the back I caught sight of my quarry once more, & now there could be no doubt. Jem was seated amongst a loose crowd of drinkers, most of them navvies & old salts, whose entertainment – aside from the bibulous sort – was presently being addressed by a barefoot girl of about ten or eleven, who stood pertly on a table, a curious little slouch hat set atop her lustrous auburn hair. The men gazed on at this sprite who, meditatively lifting her finger as a conductor might his baton, began her performance. The piece was some mawkish folk lament, yet she sang it in a quaveringly sweet alto that held her audience rapt; my attention was riveted by the girl's eyes, which were quite plainly conscious of her effect upon the listeners – it was not innocence one discerned in them, but an impersonation of innocence. I never saw anything so daintily, or disquietingly, calculated. As she finished her song she dropped a grave curtsy, & the room exploded into applause. Our little friend, with barely a pause, set about collecting the men's coppers – I now saw the purpose of that hat.

I was standing at the bar, my face turned away from inspection, when the sprite came round to me, her expression still ingratiating, & held forth her hat. When I dropped a sovereign in it her eyes briefly flickered, & she bobbed another little curtsy by way of thanks. I wondered at that moment how long she would be able to maintain this form of income before some bawd got her claws into the girl (she was extraordinarily pretty) & set her to work at more than singing. In the meantime I kept an eye out for Jem, who was thoroughly settled in with the gang of topers at the back, & stayed for a full two hours – when he did finally make to leave a chorus of drunken oaths and yells rose to serenade him thither. Then I was once more on his tail as he sauntered through the darkening streets, where, to judge by his frequent salutations & saucy exchanges, he appeared to be well known. Presently we came to a terrace, where he mounted the steps of a tall old house, perhaps once the property of a shipping merchant. We were close now to the docks – close enough to smell the river – but I had no clue as to what this place might be. Still I kept to the shadows as Jem knocked at the door & a few moments later was admitted. Some instinct prompted me onwards; I did not carry my life-preserver, so I should have to rely upon my wits if trouble lay ahead. I waited for ten minutes before crossing the street & knocking on the door. For some reason I had expected the doorkeeper to be a hulking brute, but instead an old, delicately featured Chinaman answered my summons. I was momentarily at a loss – how to announce the purpose of my visit? – but I dare say the man had quickly surmised from my attire that I was a gentleman, & that a gentleman would probably be carrying money – with a bow he invited me within. He held a lantern, for the hall was unlit, & beckoned me with quick little gestures up the staircase. I presumed myself to be in some den of vice, but as I proceeded upwards I saw no brightly painted doxies, heard no raised voices. I was led into a first-floor room lit with a few mean candles, its windows blacked out by thick curtains; after some minutes a crone, possibly the Chinaman's wife, entered carrying a copper kettle which brimmed with some strong infusion. I was left alone to wonder whether this place was merely – a tea-house? I tried the door on the far side of the room & found it gave on to a back staircase, which servants would have used in bygone days. It was Stygianly dark, & I had to feel with my hands along the walls as I ascended. Below my feet I heard the scratching of mice. Two doors I tried on the way up were locked (the house was more commodious than I had thought) but the one at the very top opened on to a narrow corridor, & I walked, arms held blindly in front of me, until I saw a faint light spill from beneath another door. My pulse was racing as I turned the doorknob & entered. The smoky, candlelit room was shrouded in muslin veils, like a field hospital, & through them I dimly discerned figures lying stretched on divans. A sweetish scent permeated the tenebrous fug. The first face I saw, peering through the gloom, was Jem's; he sat on the floor, resting his head against a low divan, whereon lay a frail apparition. It was Frank, almost insensible, the effects of whatever drowsy opiate he had been smoking evident in his heavy-lidded, unseeing gaze. Jem, his expression briefly clouded, now recognised me, & taking the pipe from his mouth he raised his chin in salutation. Perhaps he saw shock in my expression, for he gestured casually at Frank and said, 'Yer man's just had a big hit – not up to sayin' much, you know?' I knelt down to look in his face. In the year or more since I had last seen him Frank wore the evidence of a most dismaying physical decline: his cheeks were sunken, dark rings smudged his eyes, & his teeth looked brittle with decay. 'What has – happened to him?' I asked. Jem frowned, & shrugged. He seemed not to understand the question. At that moment I became decisive, & told him to help me get Frank to his feet. The boy demurred at this, & I thrust my face close to his – would he prefer to discuss an unsolved case of burglary with the police? 'Dunno nothin' about that,' he replied. 'So you'll not mind helping me with my brother,' I said, & with that he saw his hand was forced. We had got him between us on to the stairs when the Chinaman reappeared, barking out fierce, rapid remonstrances which Jem sought to defuse – certain large Oriental gentlemen then emerged from below, the strong arm of the operation, yet my eyes must have carried murder in them for we bustled past them down the stairs, with foreign imprecations ringing in our ears.

Out on the street I held Frank as he slumped groggily against me, & I gave Jem a couple of shillings to go & fetch a cab – I expected the boy to take to his heels, but minutes later a coach clattered round the corner, & Jem darted out to hold the door. I directed the cabman

to Tithebarn-st., where I made up a couch for Frank in my office –
I did not dare bring him home lest his cadaverous aspect frightened
Emily & the children. While he slept I had a desultory conversation with Jem, still sulking over the interruption of his evening. I
gathered a little of Frank's recent history – the squandering of his
money, the gambling debts, his surrender to drink, & now to opium.
Finally I asked what had happened to Jess – 'Ah, they've fallen out,
them two – that's why Frank's on the fuddle all day.'

8th, September 1867

I endured an uneasy night. As dawn seeped in I woke from fitful sleep
& began to ponder whether I should take Frank to Abercromby-sq. &
risk terrifying my parents, for his appearance was indeed more alarming
in daylight than it had been at the Chinaman's den. Then I reasoned
that they would prefer to see him even in this state than not at all, &
I was leaving to hail a cab when Frank lifted his head in a daze from
the couch. I explained to him where he was, & what I intended to do.
He rubbed his face, & smiled in that guileless way of his youth. 'Pete,
you're such a good son. You always have been.' I replied, lightly, that
I would only deserve the tribute if I restored him to the care of those
who loved him best. He looked away then & said, quietly, 'You know
it was me, don't you?' I nodded, & we held silence for a few moments
before he said, 'I can't go home.' I then spoke to him very earnestly,
arguing that whatever he had done was forgiven – that all Ma & Pa
wanted was to have him near – that nothing else in the world mattered
to us but his being well again. He did not reply for a long time, his
face turned to the window. Presently he said that he didn't feel quite
well enough to move, but that if I went down to fetch a cab he would
accompany me wherever I wished to take him. I asked him for his
word that he would be here on my return, & he gave it. I hurried down
into the street to find the early-morning traffic starting to thicken,
first on Tithebarn-st., then Moorfields, until I almost threw myself
before a cab coming down Dale-st. & bade the man make haste to my
office. The errand had taken me no more than five minutes, but I
returned to find – *mea culpa* – the door open, the room abandoned.

I write these words three days later. I should not have let him
out of my sight, not even for five minutes. It seems as though I have
hauled a drowning man from a river who directly has thrown himself
back in again.

October [1867]

I took a walk south yesterday down Princes-road, & spent some hours wandering the edges of the new park being laid out on land purchased from the Earl of Sefton. It is to be the largest public park in the country outside of London. New houses are to go up around its perimeter – & so the town will extend itself yet further. This building delirium rages on, yet it seems that I, alone of architects, am untouched by its symptoms. I continue to pursue commissions, & meet with failure so often that I have become inured to it. Urquhart tells me that our finances are in good order, for the last revenues from Magdalen Chambers have recently been disbursed. I must count it a blessing that money has never been a trouble to me – such is the accident of birth – yet truly I could bear to be poor so long as I were acknowledged for my talent.

November [1867]

It has been intensely cold. Yesterday at the Goree I saw a horse slip & fall on the icy cobbles, throwing its rider. When I returned to the scene later, the blood from the man's head wound was itself a frozen puddle.

28th November 1867

I was at home & about my breakfast when I heard Joanna, our maid, answer a knock at the door – there followed a startled shriek. I hurried out into the hallway to see what had alarmed her, and there, outside, loomed the figure of Jess. I suppose the appearance of a six-foot Negro at the door could not be considered an everyday occur-rence, but I told the girl to apologise to our visitor in any event, which she tremblingly did. I invited Jess to come in, but he shook his head & said, 'Your brother – he's ill.' I realised some time later that these were the first & only words I ever heard him speak. I hurriedly donned my coat & hat, & we proceeded without a word across Upper Duke-st. into St James-rd. A few minutes more & we had gained Chesterfield-st. which abuts the courtyard of St James's Church. Jess's footsteps slowed at this point, then paused at a narrow, dank, gloomy little court between nos. 9 & 10. Still he said nothing, but his expression seemed to prepare me for what lay ahead. I knew these were poor dwellings, & I had some experience of their interiors from when I visited Frank in Greenland-st. It was a shock never-theless to see the desperate squalor in which people were sunk – whole families I saw occupying a single room, their faces like ghosts at the soot-smeared windows. The sanitary arrangements of the place I could smell for myself. Jess led the way into one of these wretched enclosures – we started up a staircase, & then entered a room on the first floor back. Let me describe it – a chamber, with a tiny fire-place – unlit – & a single chest of drawers, the walls leprous with damp, a single window so mean & dirty there was barely light enough to see. On a bed in the corner lay my brother, his face spectre-thin & pale; his eyes were closed, & I might have thought him dead were he still not drawing breath in ragged, piteous gasps. I took the single chair & sat down by him. Jess had quietly closed the door & stood watching. I turned & asked him if he had called a doctor, & he nodded. Sick to my heart, I went down to buy a sixpenceworth of coals from the landlady, & returned to make a fire. Then I took Frank's shrunken hand in mine, & lowered my head near to his. I spoke his name, but he gave no sign of having heard. For the next hour as we awaited the doctor I remained in that attitude, my eyes a salt blur. Every rasping breath he took seemed to announce the end, but then another, slower than the last, would come. I prayed – I hardly knew what for – that he might live, that he would not suffer. But the one prayer seemed to contradict the other.

At last came the doctor, a brisk but not unsympathetic fellow in his fifties. His examination was brief, & I read the worst on his grave countenance. We left the room together to speak privately – he told me that congestion in Frank's lungs was advanced. I urged that we remove him immediately from this terrible hole, but the doctor shook his head – he was much too weak to be moved; he knew of a nurse who might be engaged to come, if I were willing to pay. I assured him that I was. 'He should never have been allowed to get into this state,' he said, sombrely. 'You are his – brother?' I heard his faintly accusing tone, but was much too anxious to begin defending myself. Might he be saved? I asked him. He replied that Frank's condition was too precarious to offer any assurances, but – an ambiguous shrug – one had to trust to the mercy of God. Then he left, having promised to send the nurse.

For the rest of the day I kept vigil by his bedside. Jess had vanished as mysteriously as he had appeared. Under the bed I saw a clay pipe, its bowl cracked: I picked it up & hid it in my pocket. The nurse arrived just before nightfall, & her capable solicitude kindled a thin flame of hope. As the evening wore on Frank vacillated between waking & dreaming. The gas-light showed sweat beading on his brow. I addressed him quietly, & he spoke, but they were no words I could discern. He was in a delirium, & as the shadows in the room thickened, his tongue fell to confused muttering – he appeared to be earnestly addressing some invisible interlocutor, first in heated tones, later in a more conciliatory manner. I watched in an agony of remorse. Then, of a sudden, Frank seemed to waken fully & looked about the room, as if for the first time. His gaze met mine, & he said, 'Pete,' & then, 'Am I dying?' Hot tears stood in my eyes, as they do now, & I croaked out, 'No, no, you'll always be here with us.' Whether he knew it to be a lie I cannot say. He sank back into unconsciousness, his harassed breathing a torment to the ears. I heard the midnight bell of St James's, & at intervals I drifted into sleep myself. At just after four in the morning the nurse shook me gently awake & whispered, 'I think this is the end.' Frank's breathing had all but given out – now only a dreadful rattle in his throat could be heard. We waited, listening to the life slip away, until he was gone. The nurse held a small looking-glass above his mouth, examined it briefly, then turned a face of honest sympathy to me. Good-bye, my brother.

30th November 1867

I am benumbed with exhaustion, but must complete this sad narrative. I left the nurse at seven in the morning & sent for the doctor, who gave me the death certificate, & then for the undertaker. I paid the landlady the rent owed to her by Frank – he had taken the room unfurnished for 2/- per week. Then I took a cab home to tell Emily the news, & on seeing her at play with the girls I broke down & wept – nothing to be done. I feared that if I were to stay there I should be for ever paralysed, so I took a clean suit of clothes with which to dress the corpse & returned to Chesterfield-st. & that miserable back room. Neighbours who had seen the arrival of the undertakers were now thronging the stairs – nothing draws a crowd more quickly than a death – but the nurse (bless the woman) had warded them off. I stepped into the room – the bed had been stripped & on it lay Frank, in a coffin. I went about the chamber & collected the paltry evidence of his occupancy. On the mantelpiece stood a row of his cherished books – Marryat, Scott, Byron, Keats, a pocket volume of Shakespeare – I opened this last & found on its flyleaf a plate from our old school, St Jude's, & written in faded ink. *June 1849 – Presented to Francis Eames for First Prize in the School Poetry Competition.* I had quite forgotten what a versifier Frank used to be – to think that he had kept this tattered volume with him right to the end. I went to the chest of drawers & drew them out – in one I found a number of pawn tickets, disordered clothes, a few mementoes of his time as a boxing manager. In another I found all of my letters to him in Jamaica, & all of Ma's, too. In the last drawer were a few broken fragments of ship's biscuit – a more pitiful thing I never set eyes upon. I asked the undertakers to leave me alone for a few moments – when they had gone I looked long at Frank's face, the eyes sunken deep, the awful rictus of his mouth. I cut a little lock of hair from his head (why, I could not say) – bending down I kissed his cheek, & left the room.

12

Weeks passed, and Baines heard nothing from Bella. At first he felt a dismal ache of sadness, for he could only imagine that their encounter, while momentous to him, was now a source of mortified regret to her. When he heard nothing from Richard either he began to feel stirrings of alarm, and envisaged scenes in which Bella was confessing her infidelity to him and imploring his forgiveness. It was not that he feared the retribution of a wronged husband: the possibility of a violent reaction on Richard's part would be much easier to endure than the hurt he knew he had caused, and the inevitable sunderings that would follow. Bella would resent him for allowing herself to be seduced; Richard would loathe him for the shabby betrayal it was. Yet when he replayed in his head that fateful morning on which Bella had returned with him to Gambier Terrace, he found that he was not of a mind to wish that it had been otherwise. The goadings of conscience were as unignorable to him as a stone in his shoe, but had they been doubled, trebled, in severity, he would not have renounced the memory of what had happened between them.

He had had more time to brood because the raids had thinned out. Bad flying weather in January and February had limited the Luftwaffe to reconnaissance missions and the occasional attack, with nothing of the savagery that had characterised the Blitz of late November and December. He still reported for duty at Hackins Hey, and in the absence of serious rescue work he did periodic stints of fire-watching, usually with Mavers. The city had battened itself down for the winter, and some nights they would patrol the blacked-out streets without meeting another soul. Liam had finished reading *The Secret Agent* and had moved on to *Heart of Darkness*, which he was describing to Baines as they sauntered down Whitechapel one evening.

'You've not read it?' he asked. Baines shook his head.

'I've not read any Conrad, actually.' He noted the surprise on Mavers' face; it flattered and slightly embarrassed him that Liam assumed he was au fait with English literature, for his expertise encompassed little more than the poetry he could remember from school. Most of his reading life had been consumed with architecture and history. And *Wisden*.

'I've just read this great bit,' Mavers continued, removing the little volume from his pocket and riffling through its pages in the gloomy reflection of a shop window. 'Here, listen to this – "He cried in a whisper at some image, at some vision – he cried out twice, a cry that was no more than a breath – 'The horror! The horror!'"'

'There's a line for the times,' said Baines, with a bitter laugh. Mavers looked at him curiously, then closed the book and returned it to his pocket. For a while they walked in silence, and Baines wondered if his response to Liam's enthusiastic reading had been too brusque. Eventually, without looking at him, Mavers said, 'Is somethin' wrong?'

'Why do you ask?' he replied, buying time.

'Well . . . the last few weeks you look like you've been – somewhere else.'

Baines was always unsettled to learn he had been the subject of study. 'I suppose . . . I've been out of sorts,' he said, trying to keep his tone light.

Mavers nodded, and seemed about to speak. The pause felt like his apology for prying. Finally he said, 'Would it 'ave to do with that woman we met the other week?'

Baines was so surprised that he laughed in spite of himself. He knew that Mavers was a close observer of other people, but this had to be guesswork of the most outrageous inspiration. Flustered, he stopped and took out his packet of Player's.

'Cigarette?'

Mavers took one, and Baines struck a match. In the light that briefly flared he saw Mavers watching him, waiting. He could bluff his way out now, bury the thing completely . . . but then he liked Liam, and trusted him; if only he could – his inward vacillating was brought to a halt by his companion's interruption.

'I thought so,' said Mavers, nodding to himself. 'The way she kept lookin' at yer . . . '

Baines felt utterly outmanoeuvred, and said nothing.

'You only have to watch people,' Mavers continued, shrugging. 'I could tell there was . . . somethin' goin' on.' Baines wondered how Liam had intuited this when it had taken him so long to recognise it for himself. He thought of Bella now, of the way she would seek out his company, of the way he had sometimes caught her looking at him. Could he really have been so obtuse?

'I noticed she was, er, wearen . . .' Mavers held up his wedding-ring finger by way of illustration.

'Yeah, I'm afraid so.' He valued Liam's good opinion too highly to admit what he had done. 'The awful thing is . . . I think I've fallen in love with her.' He hadn't dared say it before, but as soon as he did he knew it was true.

Mavers sighed quietly. 'You wouldn't wanna lose a woman like that.'

They had reached the depot and, by unspoken agreement, the end of the conversation, though not before Mavers turned to him and said, in conspiratorial admonition, 'Don't go doin' anythin' stupid.'

'I'm not sure I should be here,' said Baines to Jack as he looked up the open well to the top of the staircase they were ascending.

'Thomas,' Jack replied, clapping him on the back, 'consider it a favour to me.'

They were inside the North Western Hotel next to Lime Street station, a large, lavish memorial of the 1860s building boom, now partly given over to a club for officers of the armed services. Voices echoed off the pillared halls above them, and there was a pleasing thrum of joviality in the atmosphere. Tonight was an old soldiers' reunion, and shoaling placidly amid the waves of eager young men in khaki were grizzled veterans of the Somme and Ypres, chests ablaze with ribbons; around them drifted survivors of even earlier campaigns in Spion Kop and Ladysmith, some of them stooped and supported by canes, some being steered around in wheelchairs. The air hung thick with reminiscence and cigar smoke as they entered the long room on the second floor. Shouldering their way to the bar they passed a trembling beribboned cove with a walrus moustache of magnificent droop. Jack leaned towards Baines and sang in a whisper,

'"Old soldiers never die; they simply fide a-why!"'

'Maybe you should ask him for some tips,' said Baines, fingering his upper lip. He had maintained a steady barrage of disapproval against Jack's moustache, and its owner had responded with an equally steady indifference. Jack had handed him a Scotch and was chatting to a couple of his regiment pals when Baines felt a tap on his shoulder. He turned and found Richard grinning at him.

'Tom! What are you doing here?'

'Ah – guest of Jack's for the evening. Shortage of numbers.' Baines hoped he sounded more relaxed than he felt. By the rubicund glow of his cheeks he could tell Richard was a few drinks ahead of him, but he nevertheless sensed a need to be on his guard. Their talk quickly turned to rescue work; Richard was recounting a story of the casualties his squad had sustained in January.

'... you try to limit the risks, but they're brave as bloody lions, all of them.'

Baines smiled. Richard sounded even more like an old soldier when he was among the regimental colours.

'Bella said you saw each other a few weeks ago,' he continued. 'She mentioned that cut of yours – nasty one.' Baines listened warily for an ulterior meaning, and found none. How much had Bella told him? Richard wasn't given to sly insinuation, but he might know more than he was letting on.

'Yes. She'd just got the news about David, so she was ... you know.'

Richard nodded vigorously. 'My God, that was a relief! She was so distraught during those weeks – Christmas was a disaster. Between you and me, I didn't know what to do with her.'

'I'm sure you were – a great support.'

But Richard had fixed a measuring look on him. 'Actually, Tom, I wanted a word with you about Bella ...' His tone was not instantly readable: had he been leading up to this moment all along? If so, it would surely be best if he came out with it himself rather than wait for an interrogation. He looked down and mentally prepared the first paragraph of his confession, but Richard got in before he could speak.

'She's going to turn thirty in April, and I thought after what she's been through, well, a birthday party might be the thing. What d'you think?'

Baines felt as one who had pulled back from an abyss. He looked at Richard whose face now wore the innocently enquiring expression of one friend to another, instead of the cuckold's suspicion that should have clouded it. How could he have done such a thing to him? He deserved – he didn't know what – a horse-whipping, probably, but he had got away with it, and now Richard need never know. Their friendship was safe. As for Bella, he imagined that she would be only too willing to forget. It would be their guilty secret, locked down in memory's darkest and stoutest vault.

'I think a birthday party's a fine idea,' he said, and received a beam of approval from Richard that should have broken his heart.

The food was a shambles, the wine was filthy and the diner to his left was a near-deaf octogenarian colonel whose conversation tested Baines's interest in cavalry manoeuvres to the limit. Yet he endured it willingly enough, for he was still too stunned from his narrow escape with Richard. He looked down the long white runway of the table they were seated at, and let his gaze drift from one unknown face to another. Once the aproned waiters began serving the cheese and port he decided to turn in for the night. Jack was far gone into the bibulous absorption of old camaraderie, and would not miss him. Richard was on the other side of the room – he could hear his laughter booming over the ambient drone of other loud voices.

On retrieving his coat from the cloakroom, he stepped out into the wintry stillness of the night and managed to catch a tram that was heading south. The unilluminated interior was occupied here and there by single passengers, their pale, illusionless faces just visible through the gloom. He had the impression of riding a ghost train: even the conductor seemed frozen at his station. His eye was caught by a poster that had been tacked upon an advertising board: WALLS HAVE EARS – the usual wartime caution against gossip and loose talk. He looked down the length of the silent, swaying car and the handful of impassive occupants. These walls didn't appear to have enjoyed much earwigging in a while.

Alighting from the tram, he walked along Hope Street and had turned into Gambier Terrace when, out of the shadows, a figure loomed towards him. He knew her by her silhouette alone.

'Bella? What are you doing here?'

He could see her mouth shaping a characteristic moue of ironic self-awareness – it was her way of saying, 'Would you believe it?' It seemed to be the only answer he might get until she said, shruggingly, 'I had a night off.'

'How long have you been here?'

'Oooh . . . a couple of hours?'

'What?! But, you should have . . .' He didn't really know what she should have. 'You must have been freezing.'

She nodded. 'I still am.'

'Sorry – I mean, come in –' he said, hurriedly fumbling for his door key and guiding her up the steps. Once inside they ascended the dark staircase in silence; when Baines snapped on the light in the living room the air felt abruptly charged, as if they had made an entrance at the beginning of a play. It felt too exposing, so he killed the light and lit a couple of candles instead.

'Richard has been out all evening, so . . .'

'I know he has. I talked to him.'

Her expression darkened. 'How – at the dinner?'

'I was a guest of Jack's. Richard came over to say hullo . . .' He wondered if he should tell her how close he had come to giving them away. In the meantime he poured her a Scotch and started to prepare a fire in the grate. Bella, still in her coat, had sat down on the sofa, and he sensed her watching him as he lit the fire. Eventually he stood up and said, with a levity he didn't feel, 'I thought you'd decided never to see me again.'

Bella looked away. 'That's what I thought. That morning here ... I kept telling myself it was a mistake. I'd been so relieved about David – do you remember? – and when you – when we ... – I thought it was just that rather giddy mood I was in – it didn't really mean anything.' She stopped, and seemed to blush. 'Sorry, that sounds awful ...'

Baines waited a few moments, not sure how to construe these stuttered sentences. 'So – that's what you came here to tell me?'

She shook her head. 'I came to see you because ...' Her voice had dropped to an undertone – '... it was killing me not to.'

Doubt, which had been asphyxiating him, let go its grip, and thus released he felt his heart begin to lift and swell. Those days and weeks since they had last met, she had been thinking – of him! It seemed a marvel, a miracle. He didn't want to do anything that might break the eggshell fragility of this moment. Stalling, he turned to gaze at the fire that was just starting to crackle and spit. The candle flame wobbled on the mantelpiece. He heard the clink of glass as Bella put the tumbler of Scotch down on the low marble-topped table, and looked over to see her eyes still fixed on him, her head enquiringly tilted. Her face ... it really was the most agonisingly lovely thing he had ever seen. He walked over and sank onto the sofa beside her, and their faces met one another in a kiss. It was astonishing all over again to feel the firmness of her mouth, astonishing and strange and exciting. After some minutes she pulled away and gazed very seriously at him. Her voice came in a whisper.

'What are you thinking?'

'I'm thinking ... of all the things I'd like to do to you.'

Pressing her down so that she lay lengthways on the sofa, he unbuttoned her coat, but didn't remove it. He felt her body's warmth through the layers of clothes; slowly, he unbuttoned the woollen cardigan she was wearing; he kissed her stomach through the silk blouse underneath, and the sweet embroidered vest beneath that. Then he pushed these back too so that he could taste the pale skin, and felt her trembling against his mouth. His hands caressed the sharp jut of her hip bones, and fingered the buttons at the side of her skirt which he anticipated trouble with, unless ... He had the sensation of journeying through veils, of a headlong descent towards disclosure, and the prospect of pausing to fiddle with more buttons was not to be borne. Her breathing had become shallower, and her face was turned distractedly to one side. His head had drawn level with her lap, and as he lifted up her skirt he recalled an image of Bella at Slater Street casually flipping back the dark hood from her camera and removing the plate. Feeling the snaps and entanglements of her underclothes as a delay to his progress, he placed a kiss, quite reverently, on the ivory-coloured sheath of her pants; through the material he traced smooth skin, then the wiry tussock below. The thin silk felt like water purling through his fingers. His hands squirmed beneath the cool curve of her buttocks and stroked the dimple at the base of her spine. Then he dipped his head lower until his mouth grazed the tip of the inverted white triangle that ended between her legs; he brought a hand around and, parting her legs slightly wider, allowed his finger to draw back the pouched silk. It felt to him as if he were tending a delicate weeping wound, and as he probed it with his tongue he heard her moan quietly. Excited by the oysterish intricacy of her he sucked and licked the salty folds until they became sweet, and slowly she arched her back to heighten the angle of provocation. As her gasps grew more urgent he glanced upwards and saw her face almost angrily flushed and straining, his mouth now breathing in the wetness of her until, with an agonised cry, she stiffened and shuddered down the length of her torso.

Obeying a vague chivalrous instinct to give her a few moments alone, he went into the kitchen to fetch some water. When he returned he was amused – and aroused – to find her lying in the same half-abandoned state, her uncovered flesh almost electrically white against the gloom. He went over to the fireplace and stirred the coals, glowing peaceably in the grate, then brought a candle from the mantelpiece to the middle of the room, the better to light her face. Bella's eyes appeared to have changed colour, their olive green transmuted into an inky opacity. Recumbent on the sofa, her mouth a bruised-looking smear of red, she had the sated look of a beautiful vampire. As he handed her a glass she seemed to waken again to her surroundings, her eyes focused and she smoothed the skirt back over her hips. She took a sip of water, and noticed him gazing at her.

'What's wrong?' she asked.

'Nothing – nothing at all,' he said, and chuckled. 'You're so beautiful it's frightening.'

'Am I?' she said doubtfully.

'Yes! I look at a woman sometimes and think, well, God did a good job there. But you . . . He must have been – *showing off* when he made you.'

She laughed, not in the deep-throated way he had sometimes heard, but the relaxed, giggling tenor of a schoolgirl. Different laughs – that was another thing he loved about her. She plucked out a cigarette from his proffered pack and lit it, then said, 'D'you remember that day we met? We went for a cup of tea at the Kardomah on Dale Street, and I found out you were an orphan, like me.'

Baines nodded. 'And you said that you didn't really like Liverpudlians.'

Bella placed a hand over her eyes in a mime of horrified embarrassment, then peeked at him through the lattice of her fingers. 'What an appalling thing to say. You must have thought I was so . . . *rude.*'

'Not really. I took it as a challenge. I thought – I'll have to charm her.'

She smiled archly, and fluttered a hand at her dishevelled state. 'Looks like you succeeded.'

'In a way I could understand your view of us. Liverpudlians – they're a curious lot, so belligerent and cocksure, and yet with that fierce Irish streak of sentimentality. I used to think they – we – were hard to like . . .'

'What changed your mind?'

'This war, I suppose,' he shrugged. 'Adversity seems to bring the best out in people here. You come across such courage – such kindness, and in the most desperate circumstances. This may sound potty, but it's made me quite proud to . . . be among them.'

Bella squinted through the smoke. 'It doesn't sound potty at all. I liked that shy way you introduced me to those fellows you work with.'

Baines smiled. 'It's odd, you know, how quickly you can become close to someone. When you're dodging bombs and crawling through wreckage you come to depend on the feller next to you. There's a couple of them . . . well, they're like friends for life.'

'The one who called you "Tommy"?'

'Liam, yeah,' he said with a chuckle. 'You've never met such a stoic, he has this wonderful cool-headed common sense about everything – sort of keeps the whole squad together.' He was now remembering the last time Mavers had spoken to him, fire-watching on Whitechapel. 'He said something about you, as a matter of fact . . .'

'Really?'

'Mmm. He said, "You wouldn't want to lose a woman like that."' Bella inclined her head graciously. 'How nice of him.'

'It's true, though,' he said, and something prompted him to add, 'I imagine Richard thinks so, too.'

He watched her, and she didn't flinch. 'I sometimes wonder if Richard even sees me.'

He felt perversely goaded to speak up for the absent party. 'I'm sure he loves you.'

'Oh, of course he does,' she said impatiently, 'that's not what I mean.'

He very much wanted to know what she *did* mean, but he sensed that closer questioning would be impertinent. Ever since the moment his relationship with Bella had changed, they had not talked about Richard, but even in his absence he was a presence: a needling one.

Bella shifted on to her side, and drew her long legs beneath her. When she spoke again the words came out slow and measured. 'I was young when we met – twenty-one, still at the Slade. Richard seemed so grown-up, he'd fought in the war, seen the world. He would always . . . take charge of things. He was dashing!' She laughed at the old-fashioned sound of the word. 'When he asked me to marry him it came right out of the blue. I didn't think very hard about it – and I'm not sure he did either.'

'He's . . . such a good man,' said Baines, as if he were searching for his own defence of her choice.

Bella nodded, her mouth shaped in that rueful half-smile. 'Yes. But one doesn't love a man for his virtue.'

'You loved him enough to move up here.'

She paused before answering. 'That was a mistake. I mean, he knows I've never really been happy here. But it's more than that – he thought I was going to be this jolly sort of helpmeet, the wife who bakes and breeds and doesn't complain, and doesn't have a career, either. Richard didn't expect me to be an independent type, and I think it shocked him a little when I took up photography.'

'But he once told me – I distinctly recall it – that you were a better photographer than him.'

'Well – he's always been charming. But I did think he resented me for it at times. I was sneaking onto his territory, wasn't I? And then there were moments when I realised we hardly knew one another at all. You remember that night we talked about the Liverpool photographs, and the way he dismissed my suggestion about showing both sides of the city – he just thought I was being a mad socialist. "Like mother, like daughter" – that's what he used to say.'

'You mean, he doesn't now?'

'We don't really have arguments any more – we're too aware of the things we might say to one another. Honesty would be the ruin of us.'

Listening to her talk, Baines monitored guilt and relief grappling for purchase within. On the one hand, he was glad to learn that he was not the lone assassin of Richard's happiness. The fact that Bella had already strayed as far as she had suggested deep faults, on both sides, in the structure of their marriage . . . On the other, he knew he was actively helping to sabotage whatever insecure base it remained upon, and the monstrousness of what he was doing suddenly lurched up at him.

A brief shiver came from the fireplace as a coal slid off its perch. They listened to the fire's dwindling crackle for a few moments until Baines felt moved to say, 'I suppose marriage is . . . quite hard to do.' He hoped the vague generality might coax her to say more.

'I've found it so,' replied Bella, softly. Then she fixed her gaze back on him. 'You've never been . . . tempted by it?'

Baines shook his head, and heard a distant squeak from the door of his conscience . . . He had one more secret to tell. Was it worth exhuming now after all these years?

'I've never . . .' He stopped, and began again, more carefully. 'It's only ever come up once before.'

'Really?' said Bella, in a tone that implied she had never suspected such a thing of him. Baines, amused, continued. 'You recall the night I told you about Alice?'

'Tom – I would hardly forget that, would I?'

'Well . . . I didn't quite tell you the whole truth.' He paused, and swallowed. 'The night it happened, at that reunion, Alice came up to Liverpool, as I mentioned. But we didn't meet in a pub beforehand, we met here, at this flat. It seemed the friendly thing to do, we hadn't seen one another for a year or so –'

Bella looked alarmed. 'You didn't –?'

'No! God, no,' he said, hearing the implication in her question. 'Nothing like that happened. We just talked, for hours . . . Of course she was in a very vulnerable state, that's what must have prompted it.'

'Prompted what?'

'She asked me to marry her,' he said, with a shake of his head, almost disbelieving his own words. Bella was startled.

'*No* . . .'

'It could only have been because she was pregnant – though I had no idea of that at the time. At first I thought she was joking, and I just laughed. But she wasn't laughing, she was deadly serious. I couldn't get over it. We hadn't spoken for a year, and all of a sudden, this . . .'

'I can understand her anxiety. But would having a child really have been so terrible?'

'Her parents were quite religious, I gathered. But who knows what was going through her head?'

'So – what did you say to her?'

Baines looked away, the memory of it clawing inside like rats at a pantry door. 'I told her – as gently as I could – that it didn't seem the right thing to do. And I remember thinking, if only she'd asked me the same thing a few years back, when I was in love with her . . . In any case, it turned out to be the last serious conversation we ever had.'

He thought of her again, her statuesque poise on the balcony of the hotel, the silent movie of her stepping into the void – one moment there, the next gone. Might he have saved her by agreeing to her mad proposal? He would never know, and he had carried that uncertainty with him ever since. As he sat there, drained by his story, Bella took his hand between hers and pressed it fiercely against her cheek. She didn't say anything, but he felt her touch more dear to him than he could have thought possible.

In March the weather cleared, and the bombers returned. Birkenhead and Wallasey caught the worst of it; from across the Mersey Baines could spot flares going up and the distant silhouettes of bombs tumbling down. The ack-ack guns roared blindly into the night. He knew that the pity people felt for their Wirral neighbours would recede as soon as the raiders turned east and their own homes were targeted again. They didn't have to wait long. One night he returned with Mavers and Farrell from an emergency call at the docks to find that the streets around their own depot had been set on fire, and they had worked into the small hours helping the auxiliary services deal with incendiaries. A huge conflagration at the Cotton Exchange was occupying most of the emergency workers. On the Edmund Street side the huge windows that faced north – designed to admit the light necessary for examining cotton samples – were exploding in starbursts of glass fragments. They were returning to the van when Baines stopped, his ears pricked by the distant tinkle of breaking glass on the narrow cobbled lane running off Old Hall Street; it sounded like a single window being smashed, quite different from glass bursting under heat. Through the curtaining smoke he could make out shadowy figures loitering around a terrace of shops, though some instinct told him that these were not fire-watchers. He called over to Mavers and Farrell.

'What d'you reckon?'

Mavers, his hooded eyes squinting through the murk, turned to Baines. 'I'd say they're up to no good. Terry?'

Farrell nodded. 'I'll lay odds they're standen outside a jeweller's.'

They began to walk down the lane, and gradually the figures resolved themselves into a couple of men, one of them in uniform; on seeing their approach the pair slipped into the shadows of the building they had been casing. Farrell was right: it was a jeweller's shop, which had evidently suffered bomb damage from a previous raid and was now vulnerable to attack from the ground. The brick they could see against the emptied window display was, Baines knew, the one he had just heard being heaved through the plate-glass front. Mavers unhooked the pickaxe from his belt, and twirled it briefly in his grip, like a batsman about to take guard.

'There might be more of 'em inside,' warned Farrell, loosening his collar. Touching his finger to his lips he led them quietly through a door that had been forced off its hinges, and thence into the front salesroom, strewn with emptied drawers and broken cases. Mavers swept his torch beam over the rifled premises; even the gas meter had been cracked open for its shillings. A blade of light shone from under another door at the back, and within they could hear murmuring voices. Farrell beckoned them on, and at the threshold turned to whisper, 'Let's give 'em a fright.' There was relish in his voice.

Then he rapped curtly on the door and called, 'Police!' flinging it open to reveal two men crouched around the contents of a strongbox, the lantern next to it illuminating their frowns of surprise. Baines thought of an ancient *Punch* cartoon in which a burglar, caught red-handed, was offering his pathetic excuse to the policeman – 'I wuz only lookin' after it for 'im, sir!' These two didn't look capable even of that much wit. Farrell was staring at the one in uniform, and shaking his head in a mime of disappointment. 'Oh, an' you a warden, 'n' all.'

Baines realised that this was probably how the looters had known the building was empty. The man stared back at them, his eyes narrowing.

'Yous aren't the police.'

Farrell laughed nastily and said, 'Nah – we're fucken *worse* than that.'

In a flash the warden picked up a chair and flung it across the room at them. Farrell ducked, and the other man, seeing his partner bolt for the side door, decided to make a break for it himself. Being a stout eighteen-stoner, he was plainly intending to bullock right through them, and Baines, standing nearest, braced himself for the impact. Mavers, however, was quicker than both of them, and with dexterous aplomb swung the flat of his pickaxe across the man's knee. He collapsed as heavily as a stunned boar, and lay moaning in pain. Farrell had disappeared in pursuit of the warden.

Above them Baines heard hurrying footsteps, and ran back through the salesroom towards the staircase. Another man was halfway down when he saw his path of escape blocked, and turned back as Baines took the stairs two at a time. He followed the retreating figure into what was apparently the jeweller's living quarters. He looked first into a bedroom, where bomb damage had left a blanket of soot and feathers in its wake; he could already smell the neglect. The sound of a window creaking open came from the bathroom, and he entered to find his quarry standing on the edge of the tub with one foot on the window ledge. The man must have heard his advance because as Baines went to grab him an elbow swung round and caught him sharply on the nose. For an instant he saw stars and fell back, the coppery taste of blood filling his mouth, and as he staggered towards the sink he saw the man's shadow in the mirror dart behind him and out of the bathroom door.

Smarting, he stumbled after the man, who was now clattering down the stairs with a bag slung over his shoulder. So desperate was his flight that he hurled himself at Mavers, who was coming up the other way, and the two of them went flailing down to the foot of the staircase. The looter was just struggling to his feet as Baines arrived and on instinct nutted him full in the face, in return for his own bloody nose. The man reeled but stayed on his feet, so Baines grabbed Mavers' pick and rammed the shaft into his midriff, and now he did go down.

'You all right, Liam?' he asked as Mavers rose unsteadily.

'Yeah . . . 'e landed on me like a sack of spuds.'

A few moments later Farrell returned, his breathing heavy and his expression thunderous. 'Gave me the slip – fucker moved faster than a squirrel.'

He went off to the back room to deal with the burly man Mavers had dropped. Baines picked up the looter's bag of swag and emptied its contents onto the floor. Among the ropes of pearls and rings and brooches was a handful of medals from the Great War, their coloured silk ribbons flopped on the floor like tropical fish; they had been lifted from the jeweller's personal effects. He imagined their owner as one of the doddery old soldiers he had dined among at the North Western a few weeks earlier. It was one thing to have your business premises looted; quite another that the old boy's service medals, earned in the valorous defence of his country, should be so wantonly tossed in as trinkets to be fenced. The sight of them triggered a sudden rage in him, and he walked over to the looter, still motionless on the floor.

'You *bastard*,' he muttered, and on that word aimed a savage kick at the untidy heap. He heard the crunch of bone and cartilage as the man whimpered under the blow. Without thinking Baines caught him with another, and then another, until his assault was interrupted by Mavers hauling him away.

'All right, la', that's enough,' he said, as Baines tried to push past him. The blood angrily rushing past his ears had deafened him to reason. Their struggle continued until he felt Farrell's chunky arms pinion him from behind, and further resistance became pointless.

'What the fuck's wrong with you?' Mavers eventually said, looking almost hurt. Baines, released from Farrell's grip, hung his head, at a loss to know whether it was anger making him tremble still or the shock his own violence had provoked.

'I dunno – just seeing that stuff lying there . . .'

'Yeah, well, we can let the police deal with that.'

Farrell had rolled the looter onto his back to examine the damage, and whistled as he took in the bloodied nose and swollen eye. 'Whoa,' he said, grimacing, and looked round at Baines. 'He won't be out on the nick for a while.'

'He won't be up to *anythin'* for a while,' said Mavers, with a note of accusation in his voice. Unable to meet their eyes, Baines bent down and began to sort the medals from the tangle of jewellery. Mavers eventually withdrew to go in search of the police, leaving them to guard the two miscreants. Still absorbed by the battered face of the looter, Farrell glanced at Baines and said, with a dry chuckle, 'Hope I never take a bite out of yer.' His tone was amused, but Baines also detected something he hadn't heard from him before: it sounded, horribly, like respect.

It had been more than two weeks since Bella had been at Gambier Terrace, yet he could feel her still permeating the atmosphere of his flat; he would take the cushion from the sofa on which she had lain that evening and hold it against his face, inhaling her scent. It was blissful to him. He had picked up her lipstick-smeared cigarette ends from the ashtray and gazed at them as he might have done at a religious relic, thrilled to think that the lips that had touched them had touched him, too. He began to have dreams about her, vivid, sexual, very seldom reassuring: in the last one he had found himself back in the jeweller's shop where they had discovered the looters, only this time he and Bella were being stalked through the upstairs rooms by some shadowy, faceless figure. He kept promising that he would protect her from this mysterious pursuer, but she was crying inconsolably, convinced that they were about to be caught, and hurt. Sleep had become no longer a respite from exhaustion but an invitation to it.

He answered the telephone one morning and jumped slightly when he heard the voice at the end of the line. It was Richard.

'Our depot got hit last week – nothing to be done with the place. So what d'you know? – we've been relocated to Hackins Hey. Looks like we'll be working with your lot!'

'That's – good news,' said Baines, hoping his bright tone would cover for the lie. Richard was the last man he wanted to be working alongside.

'Something I meant to ask you, Tom.' Baines heard a devil's voice rasp in his head: *Would you kindly stop fucking my wife?* Richard continued, 'You remember that birthday party for Bella I mentioned? I've invited a few pals to the flat on the twenty-fourth of next month, but I'm keeping mum – it'll be a surprise for her.'

'Oh ...'

'– which is why I need a favour. Would you mind keeping her occupied for the afternoon while I get the place ready?'

Baines swallowed. 'Of course.' He really has no clue, he thought, and experienced a shocking flare of contempt for his friend. If a man could not read the signs that his wife was straying then he didn't deserve to keep her. In these rare moments he felt reconciled to his deceit. Then the moment dissolved and he would wake from this illusory justification to the ferocious acid of self-reproach burning in his stomach.

13

War, they were not the first to discover, was a friend to romantic furtiveness. Its sudden alarums and emergencies provided ideal camouflage for late-night absences that in peacetime would have aroused immediate suspicion. A wife could pass off an abrupt telephone call as a summons from the auxiliary service to which she was attached, while the preoccupied moods and bedraggled appearances that followed a desperate tryst might assume the guise of war exhaustion. When the air-raid sirens started to wail they signalled a return to a life in which the contingent and provisional ruled: under cover of darkness anything was possible, deception included. Deception most of all.

At first they were careful, and met only at Gambier Terrace. The flat itself seemed to have become a mute witness to their secret, offering neither approval nor reproach; Baines was pleased that Bella seemed to have adapted so easily to its configurations, like the side of the bed that had become hers, or the admiring way the mirror in the living room held her reflection. One afternoon towards the end of March she invited him over to Slater Street after Richard had gone out for the day to photograph bomb damage. The prospect of taking off their clothes in her own bedroom both excited and appalled him. He who had once indignantly claimed never to have stolen anything would now, on top of everything else, be guilty of – what? Breaking and entering, he supposed. His behaviour was unforgivable – but then he didn't want to be forgiven. He was still bewitched by the realisation that his most passionate feelings for this woman were unambiguously reciprocated. She wanted him, and nothing outside of that thrilling fact mattered.

Bella came out on to the landing as she heard his footfall on the stairs. 'Tom,' she called excitedly, 'the tulips are out!'

That she could be thinking of tulips at this critical juncture in their affair rather surprised him, but then he realised that a woman like Bella would always be a surprise to him.

'That's wonderful,' he replied, entering the living room.

She must have heard the uncertainty in his voice, because she switched to a more explanatory tone. 'Whenever the tulips appear I always think that spring has properly begun.' She paused, than added, 'Would you like a cup of tea?' – and now he actually laughed. This was hardly the atmosphere in which adultery could proceed.

'What's funny?' she said, about to enter the kitchen.

'Oh, nothing.' He looked about the room, with its familiar stack of magazines and books, *The Times* folded to the crossword, framed photographs and paintings propped against the wall, a camera in a half-assembled state on the coffee table. He knew this room and its contents intimately, down to the very pattern in the carpet, but it felt subtly altered now that he was there as more – and less – than a friend. He hadn't yet told Bella about his last conversation with Richard, and he sensed that once he did she might not be quite as insouciant as she now seemed. He saw the faintly farcical element in Richard's confiding to him about her surprise birthday party, but indecision gnawed at him. He was already in cahoots with Bella against Richard; he couldn't enter a similar arrangement with Richard against Bella, however harmless the deception. She came in and set down the tea tray, glancing at him as she did. 'You're looking rather worried, my darling.' The last two words were blithely spoken, but he felt a shiver of delight in hearing them.

'I have something to tell you,' he said, trying to keep his tone light.

'Oh?' She arched her eyebrows. 'Not sick of me already, are you?'

'No', he replied, smiling, 'not that . . . Richard called me – he's throwing a birthday party for you.'

Bella plonked down the teapot she had just picked up. 'Oh, *please God*, no.' Her tone mingled vexation with weariness.

'Sorry for ruining the surprise, but I thought you should know.'

She was silent for a few moments, her face shielded by her hands. 'Why on earth would he do that? He knows I'm dreading thirty.'

'I imagine he thinks it's a loving gesture,' said Baines, with useless loyalty.

'Don't make me feel worse about it. I wish you'd told him just to drop the whole idea.'

Baines took out his Player's, handed one to her and lit one for himself. 'It's hardly my place to tell him what he shouldn't do. Besides, there is one small compensation involved. He's asked me to occupy you for the day while he gets this place ready.'

'I see . . . and what d'you propose?'

'Well, I thought I might spend it ravishing you, actually.' He expelled a jet of smoke. 'Or else we could just have lunch.'

'Hmm,' she said, with a considered moue. As she was pouring the tea she caught his eye, and a smile played over her face. 'While we're on the subject ...'

'Of lunch?'

'No – of "ravishing" as you so nicely call it. Why don't you go upstairs and prepare yourself ... I'll be up in a moment.'

'That sounds like an offer I shouldn't refuse.'

'You'd be mad to,' she agreed.

He had not been in their bedroom before. He had never had a reason to. In the small bathroom next door he saw Richard's straight razor and a badger-hair shaving brush amid the casual disarray of Bella's creams and pots and unguents. The mirror above the sink caught him in its sights. He turned away and went back into the bedroom. He had imagined that as photographers their dresser would be a shrine of family portraits, but it turned out there were only two. The first was of a young couple marinated in Edwardian sepia, and a brief examination of the woman convinced him he was looking at Bella's mother; she was nearly as beautiful, with the same frank incontrovertible gaze. The other was of Bella, thoughtful and seated at a cafe table on their honeymoon. For some reason Mavers' words came into his head: *You wouldn't want to lose a woman like that.* He backed away, and sat on the bed. Looking down, he saw a pair of Oxford brogues, neatly aligned and polished. He could imagine Richard's look of merry industry while he buffed the leather to its parade-ground sheen.

He heard Bella walk in, and he stood up.

'I really don't think I can do this,' he said. 'Not here.'

He couldn't properly explain to himself, let alone anyone else, why the sight of those shoes had thrown him off his stride. After some moments he heard her flop down on the bed and sigh.

'I'm sorry,' she said, eventually. 'You must think me such a ... *hussy* – I mean, for asking you here.'

'No, I was rather thrilled by it, actually. But it just feels – spooky.'

'We could – I don't know – go for a walk instead?'

He turned to her, and nodded ruefully. As they were going down the stairs Bella said, 'There's something I quickly have to finish,' and he followed her into the darkroom, bathed in its sinisterly alluring red light. While she was busy with her tongs and trays of emulsion, he examined the photographs that were pegged and hanging on a line, like laundry. One of them held his eye: he could just make out the profile of the Pier Head at night, though what dominated the picture were the white dots and dashes of light that sequinned the horizon. He took it off its peg for a closer look.

'That's beautiful,' he said, handing it to Bella.

'Ah – that's tracer fire, I was out during a raid one night and happened to have my camera with me. It looks like –'

'– fireworks.' They said the word at the same time, and laughed. The closeness of her, and the enveloping intimacy of the darkroom, stirred the atmosphere between them. For the first time since he had arrived that afternoon Baines felt aroused, and he pulled her towards him. She giggled responsively, slowly tilting her head as he kissed her throat and neck. He loved the feel of her, from the softness of her cheek and mouth to the yielding firmness of her chest – loved too the poignant boniness of her hands that he could feel on his skin where she had pulled up his shirt. He had undone the buttons on her trouser front and had slid an exploratory hand into her knickers when, abruptly, she tensed. He saw quickly enough that her expression betrayed not annoyance but alarm, and she was now cocking an ear to a sound he hoped was imaginary. Then he heard it, too, the muffled footfall on the stairs that could only presage the arrival of one person.

'I thought you said he was out,' Baines whispered, but Bella was too frantic with rebuttoning her trousers and smoothing her ruffled appearance to answer. Of all the wretched luck – They were suddenly breathing the air of bedroom farce, only with the laughter sucked out of it, and the crimson-dark enclosure that had so recently felt seductive now lit them in a dangerous glow, like the ops room of a submarine that had just taken a shuddering hit. Richard could be heard moving about the office next door. They stared at one another for a moment like cornered animals. Then Bella leaned over and whispered low in his ear, 'Stay here – don't make a sound.'

She composed herself, as if she were about to walk onstage, and slipped out of the door. Baines heard the feigned note of surprise as she greeted her husband, and then some casual remark about not hearing him arrive. He held his breath as the voices drifted out of earshot. The width of a door stood between him and calamitous exposure; if Richard decided to enter the darkroom right now – and why should he not? – then all was lost. He had to trust to Bella's nerve to clear an escape route for him ... Minutes passed, and then the voices receded down the stairs. They were out of the office at least. He strained his ears trying to determine whether they were still in the house. When he could stand waiting no more he silently opened the door a crack and looked out; the fug of Richard's cigar smoke hung in the air, and with a cracksman's light-footedness he sneaked over to the far door. His heart was thumping wildly against his ribs, but his wits were in cold command. Rescue work had taught him this much. As he stole silently down the stairs and out of the empty house he could feel a familiar surge of relief, only something was different. He wasn't the virtuous rescuer now – he was just a housebreaker who had got away with it.

He had yet to square things with Mavers. He was conscious of destroying one friendship unavoidably; he didn't want to let another fall into disrepair. His vicious behaviour on the night of the looting incident had gone undiscussed, and, he sensed, unforgiven. In the last couple of weeks there was not the same ease between them, and though they maintained their professional front it was apparent that Mavers regarded him in a different and altogether less flattering light. Baines kept hoping that the clouds would suddenly disperse and his friend would talk to him again as of old, but the *froideur* he had detected didn't thaw. He realised that he would either have to make an appeal to him or else keep silent and risk losing him for good. That both of them wore their reticence like a badge of honour made a reconciliation doubly difficult.

One morning in the middle of April the squad was carrying out a routine investigation of damaged houses in Garston. The warden on duty had told them he was 'fairly certain' that all the occupants had been accounted for, so Mike Wo and Farrell had gone to help another squad with a big excavation nearby. Baines was searching a half-destroyed house with McGlynn and Mavers when he thought he heard a voice deep below the rubble. He stopped to listen, and it came again, high and querulous. 'Help – get me out!' Mavers looked over to where Baines was standing.

'Did you hear that?'

Mavers nodded. 'Sounded like an old woman.'

Baines told McGlynn to go and fetch the warden. While they waited they heard the voice again, saying the same words, and now they knew they would have to start digging. Half an hour later they had created a makeshift tunnel with the aid of some old furniture that had survived the blast. As they inched along through the rubble they called reassurances to the old woman, who simply repeated her plea, 'Get me out!'

'She can't hear us,' said Mavers.

'Maybe she's deaf.' Baines was remembering the old man who had stood outside the burning stable that night. As he continued to dig he mused on how it would be to experience the Blitz without benefit of hearing, the way a deaf person would *feel* its vibrations, its violent rending of the air, perhaps the knowledge that their last moments were near – and that the genetic injustice which had blighted their life was now conspiring in their certain death, or else –

Mavers' voice interrupted his morbid reverie. 'I can't work out where she is.' They had excavated a tunnel roughly to the point where they thought the woman's voice had been coming from, yet their torches revealed nothing beyond cataracts of rubble and smoking timber. Baines called out again, and received no reply. He looked at Mavers.

'D'you suppose she's – ?'

The word hung between them, unspoken. They had tried to save her. Now they would face another wretched hour searching for a corpse to drag out. He heard Mavers' weary exhalation – and then the voice: 'Help! Get me out!'

'What in the name of fuck . . .'

Baines pointed his torch into the crevice beneath a broken door, and twisted himself round to look beneath the splintered wood. He smelt it before he could see it.

'You're not gonna believe this,' he said, and carefully drew from the stinking darkness a buckled metal birdcage, its beaky occupant intact. It cawed, 'Help! Help!'

'Ah, that beats the lot,' said Farrell, wiping tears from his eyes. 'A fucken parrot!' The stentorian roar of his laughter had eventually calmed to a contented snigger. He shook his head as Mavers and Baines sat on the pavement, the battered cage between them. Now that the bird had been rescued it had fallen silent, a dusty fluttering of its feathers aside. Farrell continued, 'Yous could go into business – pet rescue! Cats up trees, stray dogs and tha' . . . parrots a speciality.'

McGlynn was explaining to Mike what had happened, which started up another little ripple of shared hilarity. Baines could see this story becoming a real favourite back at the depot. As Farrell was leaving he called over his shoulder, 'Eh! We've just heard on the wire – Long John Silver's on his way over, said yous'd know what it's about!' His laughter receded into the distance. When the others had pushed off he handed Mavers a cigarette, and cleared his throat.

'D'you think we'll ever hear the end of this?'

'Doubt it.'

He stole a glance at Mavers, trying to gauge his mood. 'Liam – are we, like, straight . . . with each other?'

'How d'you mean?'

His tone was not encouraging. Baines took a deep breath, and exhaled. 'I wanted to say, you know, sorry for that thing the other week, at the jeweller's.'

'Don't say sorry to me, la'. It wasn't my head you were stoven in.'

'Maybe so, but . . . I'm apologising anyway.'

'Why?'

'Well . . . because I regret it – and because I don't want to lose your good opinion.'

Mavers looked at him, then shook his head and smiled. '"Lose your good opinion . . ." – you should hear the things you say.'

Baines shrugged. 'Just – forgive me, and I won't pester you again.'

'All right,' Mavers sighed, 'I forgive yer.' Then he turned and picked up the cage. 'Better go and find Polly a new home.'

The pianist was languidly fingering the melody of 'It Had to Be You' in the far corner. The notes drifted and echoed around the high-ceilinged dining room of the Lisbon, one of very few restaurants in the city that was still serving a full à la carte menu. Baines had been here once before, years ago, and had preserved a particular memory of a fellow in white toque and apron standing at a table to carve the saddle of mutton, and of the diner whose plate had just been loaded handing this carver a tip for his trouble. It seemed the most perfectly old-fashioned thing Baines had ever witnessed. The room was beginning to fill with a lunchtime crowd of lawyers and other *hommes d'affaires* who he supposed ate here as a matter of course, whether there was a war on or not. A pair of ladies, both wearing elaborately structured hats adorned with feathers, were twittering away at a nearby table. For some reason he thought of the rescued parrot.

He spotted Bella a moment later waving from across the room, and then she was striding towards him, leaving a diminutive waiter almost hurrying to catch up with her. Baines rose from the table as she arrived, and, momentarily thrown by a sense of caution, he extended a hand. Bella laughed it away and kissed him on the cheek.

'This is a treat!' she said, folding herself into the banquette seat and smoothing a napkin on to her lap. 'Gosh, I've forgotten what it's like to have *linen* on the table.'

She was wearing a damson-coloured woollen jacket with matching skirt. Above the collar of the jacket a loop of tiny pearls glimmered on the narrow column of her throat, matching the refulgent liveliness of her eyes. He found himself smiling helplessly.

'What's so funny?'

'Nothing – I was just admiring your pearls.'

'Oh, they're nothing but paste, I'm afraid.'

'Well . . . they look awfully nice on you.'

A bottle of champagne arrived; when they clinked their glasses Baines said, 'Happy birthday,' and then pushed a slim package across the table towards her. She looked at him with humorous disapproval, having previously insisted that she didn't want presents.

'I told you –'

'I know you did. But open it anyway.'

It was a silver cigarette case with a mother-of-pearl inlay. He had gone back to the jeweller's on Lord Street where he had bought the garnet brooch for May. He had baulked at the idea of giving Bella something to wear – rings and necklaces, anything that touched the skin, seemed to trespass on the uxorious – but a cigarette case, he felt, carried in it both the straightforwardness of friendship and the ulterior associations of intimacy.

'Tom, it's beautiful. Really.' She opened it, and saw the inscription, something else that he had hesitated over. The usual formulations seemed either presumptuous or else dangerous. Even to have it inscribed with his name seemed to court trouble, so he directed the jeweller to engrave, hidden beneath the band, BT-TB. He was pleased with the mirror image their initials created. She held his hand beneath the table until the arrival of their waiter obliged her to release it. They both had the consommé – as the restaurant preferred to call it – and the lemon sole. At one point their heads were turned by the complaints of a diner at the next banquette, who called sharply to the waiter, 'Do you call this rare?' 'Yes, sir.' 'Well, I *don't*. Take it back.'

Bella looked over to Baines, her eyebrows conspiratorially hoisted. 'What a disagreeable man,' she said, sotto voce. 'And to think he's eating food most people could scarcely dream of . . .'

Baines looked about the room. 'To sit here you wouldn't know there's a war on. It doesn't seem to belong to the world outside.'

Bella nodded. 'Or maybe *we* don't belong to *it*. I have a vague memory of my parents taking us to a restaurant like this in London, it must have been just after the last war ended. I suppose with Daddy being in the FO they dined out a lot.'

'Do you still remember them clearly?'

'Oh yes, Mummy in particular. She was quite a firebrand, with the suffrage movement and so on – did I ever tell you she went to prison for it?'

'Um, no.'

'*I* didn't know until my aunt told me years later. She said it was quite a scandal among the family – though Mummy was very proud of it!' She laughed, but she sounded sad. 'I do so wish she were still here. I always imagined we'd be great pals . . .'

'I saw the photograph of her on your dresser. You look a lot like her.'

'Do I?'

He nodded. 'I'm glad she named you Bella. You've lived up to it.'

'You're sweet to say so,' she said, with a blushing smile.

They were just finishing their coffee when, seemingly out of nowhere, a figure loomed over their table.

'Well, well,' said Adrian Wallace, looking archly from one to the other, 'if it isn't love's young dream.' He was looking at Bella, though the remark seemed to be intended for both of them. Wallace was wielding an ivory cigarette-holder, a dandyish prop to go with his pinkie ring and florid bow tie, and he had not lost his habit of standing too closely. The aggressive scent of his cologne perfumed the air.

'Hullo, Adrian,' said Bella, with notable composure. 'How are you?'

'Oh, tolerably well, in the circs.' A smirk began to form on his fleshy lips. 'I had an intuition I might run across you one of these days.'

'Well, I suppose this would be the place. Wasn't this your lunching venue with Noël Coward?'

'Yes – though I gather Noël has run off to America. Not very patriotic. Must introduce you to him – if he returns. He might like to put you in one of his plays.' He flicked his hair back and waited to see if this little sally had made its mark, but Bella refused to be ruffled.

'And how is it at the *Echo*?'

'Oh,' sighed Wallace, with a theatrical roll of his eyes, 'dying, Egypt, dying. We were recently affrighted by a dread visitation from on high –'

'You mean the bomb that fell through your roof?' said Baines, deadpan, and Bella giggled.

'What I'd like to know, Adrian, is how you can afford to eat here the whole time.'

Wallace shrugged in seigneurial fashion, as though the opulence of the surroundings had not even occurred to him. 'A journalist and his expenses are seldom parted – and after dining here you can't really go back to the Kardomah.'

'But I *like* the Kardomah,' said Bella, with a twinkle in her eye that caused Baines to smile. Wallace then noticed the empty champagne bottle lolling in its bucket.

'Celebrating, I see. Now let me guess what that might be . . .' His eyes were glittering malevolently.

'It's my birthday, actually,' said Bella, before he had a chance to say anything else. 'My husband's busy this afternoon, so he asked Tom to look after me.'

Wallace nodded slowly, as though he understood more about this arrangement than he was being told. He prattled on for a while, then glanced at his watch.

'My felicitations to you,' he said, bowing his head slightly. 'I'll leave you to enjoy the rest of your – afternoon together. Cheer-o.' And he strolled off, leaving behind him an air thoroughly poisoned with insinuation.

'Oh God, what a *weasel* that man is. All that smirking and hinting and eyebrow-raising – you know, I'd rather he'd just come out with it and call me a – I don't know – a Jezebel.'

Baines chuckled. 'Yes, that's exactly the word he would have used.'

They had left the Lisbon and walked down to the Pier Head. The pavements glistened from the showers they had missed at lunch, and the sky was the familiar Mersey shade of watered-down milk. A train on the overhead railway chuntered in the distance, and the dockside traffic stoically worked its way around the scattered bomb debris. They leaned against a rail overlooking the ferry landing stage. The wind gusted off the river, bearing the whiff of tidal salt water, with a bouquet of mudflats and old seaweed in its tow.

'I do like this waterfront,' said Bella. 'It must have been amazing in its heyday.'

'It was. I rode down here once when I was a kid.'

'You mean, on a bicycle?'

'No, on a horse. George, my uncle, used to run a stable.'

'Gosh, you're full of surprises. A horseman!'

Baines turned about to the Royal Liver Building behind them. 'I remember when they unveiled this building – before it got so grimy – and I saw the Liver birds for the first time.'

'What *are* they exactly?'

'Well, they reckon a medieval draughtsman tried to draw a cormorant for the coat of arms, and it gradually metamorphosed into that.'

'So the city's symbol is . . .'

'Entirely bogus. Or mythical, if you prefer. And talking of birds . . .'

He related the story of the parrot, and was rewarded when she threw her head back in a paroxysm of mirth. How wonderful it was, he thought, to see a woman laugh, *really* laugh – the sort where she forgets herself and opens her mouth so wide you can see the ribbed pink cavern and the horseshoe curve of teeth at the back. They continued to gaze out at the river, past the funnels and derricks, past stricken battleships that had sought refuge from the Atlantic conflict. Seagulls screeched ignorantly overhead. Clouds were shouldering their way across the horizon – there would be rain again. He suddenly saw the pair of them as two explorers standing at a summit, looking out on the wide unreadable expanse of their future, with a decision to be made: press on, or turn back. When he offered her a cigarette she didn't respond, for she was still lost in abstraction. Eventually she broke in on her own train of thought.

'I suppose that's why it's always felt so sad . . .'

'What – Liverpool?' asked Baines, trying to pick up the connection.

'Mm . . . because people have always been leaving it behind. This was the last of England they saw, before sailing for the New World.'

He thought he heard a wistful note in her voice. 'You sound as though you'd like to be among them,' he said, with an uneasy laugh.

'Wouldn't you?'

'Honestly – no. I don't think I could survive anywhere else. It'd be like a polar bear leaving his ice cap.'

She smiled, but didn't say anything for a while. Then: 'I envy you, really. I've never felt rooted to a place. For the first ten years of my life we moved – all over. Then after my parents died Nancy and I were sent to an awful convent school in St Leonard's. In the holidays we stayed with our aunt in Wimbledon.'

'So London became your home.'

'Only by default. I never felt especially happy there, either.'

Baines sensed a distance opening up between them, and wanted to close it quickly. Trying to keep his tone as nonchalant as he could, he said, 'If you ever go looking for a place where you might feel at home . . . wherever it is, would you – take me with you?'

'You mean, you'd leave here? What about the polar bear in the Arctic?'

'I'd try to adapt.'

She looked at him appraisingly, then leaned in and kissed his cheek. 'Well,' she said, 'I suppose I could make some room in my luggage for you.' There was a smile in her voice as she spoke, but he found no comfort in what she said.

* * *

He had left the party early, too nervous of being in the same room as Richard and Bella, and now had the final stretch of Eames's journals in front of him. The architect's handwriting was more cramped than of old, and the last twenty pages or so featured more drawings than actual entries: traceries, ornaments, arches, pediments, mouldings and a certain style of capital to which Eames returned obsessively. There were drawings of foliage, and what seemed to be the Nine Muses of mythology. These gradually gave way to sketches of a cormorant – or was it a Liver bird? he wondered. But the final pictures were the most interesting, for they were all of a single figure, a man in an armchair reading a book, with the foot of his crossed leg resting at an angle, just so. He counted around twelve variations of this figure, each subtly different from the last. He turned back to his place in the journal and began to read.

March [1868]

I have lately found myself returning to the earliest entries of this journal – only seven years stand between then & now, yet what changes have they wrought upon me. I wonder at the lightness of spirit, the gaiety, that sports through those first pages, & seem hardly to recognise myself. In that time I have gained a wife, two children, a house, & a reputation of sorts. I have lost, alas, a beloved brother, whether through my own negligence or else some fatal weakness in his character I cannot say – only that the sorrow of it sits heavily on my soul.

Tuesday, Seventh April 1868

Searching through a drawer of my desk I came upon the pawn tickets which I found in that last dismal room of Frank's. I had hidden the things away, but now felt able to recover whatever it was he had staked in those final weeks. The pawnbroker's was a narrow slice of a shop on Parliament-street, wherein the dingy odour of all the clothes & sticks of furniture still awaiting reclamation polluted the air – the very miasma of poverty. I paid the clerk the pitiful interest & received across his counter a box of half-forgotten sundries – some Herdman sketches I had once loaned to Frank, his own topcoat & riding boots, candlesticks taken in the burglary at Abercromby-sq. – & a pair of old silver nutcrackers, which I now recalled from a time when Ma and Pa allowed us two, as very small boys, to come

down to dinner and crack walnuts for our guests. I replaced them in
the box, tied a knot upon it & carried them out. But I had walked
no more than ten yards along the street before I had to stop, & leaning
my head against the wall I wept – wept tears of hopeless misery.

Thursday, Thirtieth April [1868]

Urquhart rushes into my office this afternoon in a state of high excitement. The new building about to begin on Paradise-st. has run into
trouble & the architects (I know not which) have been dismissed. Now
Urquhart has it on good authority that the developers, in search of
a replacement, want 'the fellow who made the glass house'. This, it
would seem, is myself. I know that I ought to embrace it as a good
omen, for opportunities seldom come my way, and the emolument
from such an enterprise might be tremendous. Yet I have little relish
for it. Those speculators may offer a good premium, but I have a
certainty they will not be satisfied with merely contracting their architect – they will demand to know the cost of this or that, & whether
a certain material cannot be substituted for a cheaper one. They
will *not* ask the important, necessary questions: Is this a well-made
building? Is it graceful & pleasing to the eye? Is it speaking the truth
about itself? But Urquhart, the good fellow, seemed so enthused by
the prospect of work that I had not the heart to make objection.

May [1868]

Rumour is, of all pests, the swiftest. A report in today's *Mercury*
avers that the Paradise-st. consortium has entrusted its new building
works to the care of Mr Eames of Tithebarn-st. As I remark to
Urquhart, this is a revelation both to them & to me.

8th May [1868]

On my desk lies a letter requesting my services as architect on the
Paradise-st. enterprise. A decision is required by the end of next
week.

11th May [1868]

This morning arrived a hastily scribbled note from my old employer,
Sandham, whom I have encountered from time to time at guild
dinners & suchlike. He begged my pardon for the short notice, but

would I oblige him by coming to dinner at his house this evening?
– for he had just received notice that he would be entertaining a
'renowned personage' whom he felt certain I should 'particularly'
like to meet. I was intrigued & replied in the affirmative, then passed
the rest of the day idly wondering who this personage might be.

I duly presented myself at Rodney-street, & was led into a drawing-
room thronged with august-looking gentlemen, many with beards as
thick as rooks' nests & all talking at immoderate volume. Some few
ladies present. There was, I should say, a palpable excitement in the
air, yet I could not ascertain its source. Sandham came over &
expressed his delight at my attendance, but any expectation that he
would reveal the mystery of his honoured guest was dashed, for
almost immediately he broke off to welcome some others. I supposed
it characteristic of the old dodderer to have forgotten altogether his
reason for inviting me. I circled the room, nodding at acquaintances
here & there, until I saw standing at the fireplace another fellow I
believed I recognised, but could not place – slowly it dawned upon
me that I knew him only from portraits. Perhaps I had been staring,
for the man had now turned his penetrating gaze directly upon me;
it seemed at first a rebarbative countenance, there was something
fierce around his bushy eyebrows, but a gentle smile suddenly altered
his aspect & invited me to approach. I knew before we had even
shaken hands that I stood in the presence of John Ruskin. Let me
describe him: rather tall, with a thin face & prominent nose, a slight
hang to his bottom lip. His large side-whiskers flecked with grey.
He wore a smart greatcoat with a brown velvet collar, & at his throat
a blue neckcloth – the effect at once formal & quite raffish.

As if in a dream we began to talk, & I heard myself answering
his enquiries about my work. (I told him truthfully that the iron
frame of Janus House was indebted to his inspiration.) There was
about him such a kindliness & humility that I felt most oddly at
ease, though I sensed withal an effort in his manner – there was
no true gregariousness in him. He told me that he had been visiting
a favourite school of his in Cheshire, & that he would sail the
following day for Dublin, where he was to deliver a lecture. He
added, confidingly, that he also had hopes of seeing a 'young friend',
very dear to him, who was resident in Kildare. He smiled again as
he said this. I was flattered to have been a recipient of this little
disclosure, & hoped he might say more. (The scandal of his broken
marriage is still whispered about.)

Dinner was served, & I found myself seated at the other end of the table from my recent interlocutor. I confess I was poor company to the lady on my right, for it was all I could do not to keep spying on the great man as we ate our pork & applesauce, & wondering whether, behind that benign but clouded phiz, he actually listened to old Sandham's ceaseless prattle. I had resigned myself to passing the remainder of the evening at such a distance, but when the ladies withdrew & the port was passed around I found – *mirabile dictu* – that Mr Ruskin had occupied the vacant seat next to mine, & we resumed our talk as if we were friends of old. He asked me whether I enjoyed the port (his late father, he said, was a wine merchant) & laughed when I said I would prefer a pint of champagne. Talk turned again to architecture, & emboldened by his show of interest I told him about the speculative building on Paradise-st., & confessed how little enthusiasm I had for the thing. He looked at me very earnestly, & said, 'You ought only to build that in which your heart can rejoice.' I replied that the emolument would be substantial, but he shook his head. 'You cannot set an emolument against your instinct – money will not buy life. Work should be done with a will, or with a delight; otherwise it were better that it were not done at all.' By now I sensed others crowding in, awaiting their turn with the sage; I rose & thanked him, & he bowed his head graciously. I wished him a safe crossing to Ireland, & bade him good-night.

As I sit writing by this lamp, I wonder at my composure during this interview. To have met the man, an idol to me for years, is a landmark in my life – I trust this will be useful to my biographer!

12th May 1868

I poured all of this out to Urquhart at the office – 'Ruskin? – *John* Ruskin?' he asked, with a look of wonderment he could not have outdone had I reported a colloquy with the shade of Socrates. He was much less impressed, however, upon learning that I had declined the Paradise-st. speculation this morning. I quoted a wise man's words to him: Work should be done with a will, or with delight – or else not done at all.

3rd June [1868]

A curious thing happened today. I was at Abercomby-sq. talking to my mother when of a sudden she smiled – the first I had witnessed since our sorrows of last year – & hurried off to fetch something.

She returned with a sheaf of papers, which on inspection were revealed to be drawings & sketches which she had preserved from my youth. Most of them poor untutored stuff, & I laughed to see them; but one, which I had quite forgot, gave me pause. It was a pencil portrait I had done of Frank, at about one-&-twenty, seated & profoundly absorbed in a book, one leg crossed & his head resting on his hand. I stared long at this sketch, only now recalling my brother's youthful habit of hiding himself away to read. I thought then of those travel-worn books I had found in his room at Chesterfield-st. I asked Ma to loan the thing to me, & it sits propped on my desk as I write these words. An idea has taken root –

8th June 1868

I break off at this midnight hour – I have barely slept these last three days – to record the precipitous heights of fancy I have been scaling. Having taken to heart Mr Ruskin's precepts I fell to imagining what building I should most *like* to design, if there were only my will to consult. The pencil sketch of Frank had begun to haunt me, & I conceived of a building that might be raised to his memory. What else but a library? – designed not for the entertainment of the exclusive leisured few but for that indigent mass to whom it might provide a refuge from care & a solace to the soul. It would be, moreover, a building infused with the spirit of the people, a means of reflecting all that is good & noble in them.

The despondent torpor of the last twelvemonth fell away, & a vision rose before me – if a library should express a kind of human sympathy it would necessarily require the counterpoint of light & shade. For as a great poem cannot hold us if it propounds only a lyric jauntiness, but must be sometimes serious, & grave, to strike at the truth of this sad world of ours; so there must be in a great building some equivalent expression for the sorrow & mystery of life – & this can only be achieved by the subtleties of shadow and the nuances of gloom upon its surface. Thus my plan: a library situated in that part of the town that stands most in need of a light in the darkness, a spur to hope, & a source of beauty.

20th June [1868]

Notes on a proposed library.

The façade to be iron-framed, tripartite, symmetrical, the centre a portal with trumeau; a pair of oriels, recessed, set above reading-room window. Left & right two bay blocks ending in octagons. Along the sides two-storey tiers of oriels.

Within, a vaulted main hall dominated by wrought-iron stair-case. Eight columns of red granite, placed in front of piers, with arches between the piers. Plasterwork on the vault (?) – ornamental detail to be carefully managed, integral to the building – banish all irrelevant crusting & flouncing.

Intermediate landings are below the octagon, with a gallery running round. The effect of extravagant space vital to this. Top landing, reading-room (70 feet?) arranged with bays left & right, divided by vaulting piers. Each bay has to the outside an oriel, below & above. (See sketches.) Cupola above, octagonal to echo the end bays, supplemental to the light from the oriels.

At the back elevation, glass curtain-walling, with mullions.

22nd June 1868

Blazing away to finish accurate designs of the building. Once done, I wrote to my father, then carried the scrolls to the office & unfurled them for Urquhart's inspection. When he had finished I asked him if he had forgiven me on the Paradise-st. business. 'Gladly,' he cried, 'if this is to be our replacement.' He then suggested that we draw up a list of private subscriptions. I shook my head, & explained that this was to be a free library, a gift to the city – & that every poor man should find a welcome in it. But how did I propose to pay for it? he asked. In answer I showed him the drawing I had made of Frank as a young man, absorbed in his book. 'I have a good hope that this man's father will help pay for it.'

June [1868]

My hope has not been in vain – Pa confessed he was deeply affected by the plans, & vouchsafed his entire approval. He even suggested a name: The Francis Eames Library. (I omitted to tell him that this was to have been my own choice.) With the help of certain business associates he is confident of raising money for the purpose. I am quite preposterously delighted, & feel a revival of energies I have not experienced since the design of Janus House fully six years ago. In honour of the man who inspired me then & now, his aphorism shall be carved above the door: THERE IS NO WEALTH BUT LIFE.

July [1868]

Library plans proceed apace. I spend so many hours at the office that Emily claims I have become a very stranger to them – 'Ellie & Rose will barely know they have a father,' she says. There is a humorous note to her plaints, I think, though there is justice enough in them; I leave home before they wake, & return long after they are abed.

2nd August 1868

Urquhart met with our bankers today, & returned with a troubled expression that I could not tease away. The issue stands at this – Pa, true to his word, has organised a philanthropic fund that will raise the sum of £40,000. All well & good – but Urquhart says that the cost of the library, once the land has been purchased, the builders hired &c., will now certainly exceed £65,000. The bank is prepared to lend only £5,000, leaving a shortfall of at least £20,000. He presented our dilemma thus: either we seek the money elsewhere, or we cut back the costs of the building. Urquhart knows that I am adamant on the latter – it shall be made as I have designed it, or else not at all. But savings could be made, he argues, & instances the use of ash for the shelving as less expensive than walnut. No, I insist, walnut it must be. He throws up his hands as if to say, 'The Devil take him,' & I smile – he knows I can bend the matter to my will.

19th August [1868]

Loath as I am to drag her into the business I broached it with Emily this evening, enlightening her on the excess costs of the library scheme, the parsimony of the bank &c., & enquired as to whether she supposed her father might look favourably on a request – £20,000, while no small sum, would not unduly tax a man of Sir W^m's means. She considered the matter seriously for some moments, & presently admitted that she had little confidence in his acceding to my petition – it is long acknowledged between us that my father-in-law holds me in no great esteem. 'But he might be brought round to the idea,' she continued, 'if *I* were to approach him.' It shames me to confide here that this was the solution which I had secretly purposed – whether Emily was deceived by my surprised expression of delight

I could not say. 'You might prove your gratitude,' she said, as I whirled her up in an embrace, 'by devoting a little time to your wife and children.' I accepted the reproach, & promised her all the uxorious attention at my disposal if she succeeds in convincing Sir to open his coffers.

25th August 1868

This is the day upon which Emily has made an appointment to see her father at Torrington Hall. I had suggested that Urquhart accompany her thither, for if I know Sir W^m he will not be tempted into munificence without the guarantee of a sound business plan – on which subject, I feel assured, Urquhart will be most persuasive. Emily agreed to this, & they left an hour ago by carriage from Hope-pl. I set down these words now to distract myself from anxiously pacing up & down my office carpet – the matter is out of my hands. Still I fret.

3rd September 1868

My twenty-ninth birthday, though the true fount of this evening's celebration sprang from the pockets of my father-in-law, the estimable Sir Wm Rocksavage – never again shall I slight the fellow! We have our £20,000, & I raised a toast in tribute to Emily & to Urquhart at dinner here. Effie, Edward's wife, also present, looking remarkably pretty – though I sense a melancholy about her of late. Edward, in truth, makes a habit of ignoring her on such occasions, as if he had brought the woman along on compulsion & quickly tired of her. It is perplexing, for Effie seems to me all that a wifely companion ought to be, affectionate, attentive, convivial, & blessed with a humorous acuity of observation – I am reminded of Cassius, who 'looks quite through the deeds of men'. But where marriage is concerned I deem it best not to enquire too closely – it being difficult enough to understand one's own without making another's the object of study.

September [1868]

Library. The cost continues to spiral upwards; I look away and another thousand has crept on to the account. At present it stands at £85,000. The builders with whom we had drawn up a contract have now seen fit to offer their services elsewhere. Such is the demand for bricks & mortar at present that many hold back for the highest bidder – & previous loyalties go up in smoke.

November [1868]

Library. It is proving really the most vexatious project I have ever undertaken. No sooner do we dispatch one problem than another rears up, Hydra-headed. Now the Duke-st. site is judged unsuitable to our purpose, & we must go scouting for another location. Yet my determination to see it through will not waver – I owe this much to Frank.

29th November 1868

My brother's anniversary. Pa had organised a service at St Catherine's – the first reading was from Psalms: 'As for man, his days are as grass: as a flower of the field, so he flourisheth. For the wind passeth over it, & it is gone; & the place thereof shall know it no more.'

Wednesday, ninth December, 1868

Library. Today I was talking with one of the uncomprehending apprentices (I have a small collection of them) when a caller was announced at the office – 'a lady', said the boy, & thereupon entered none other than Effie Urquhart. She had come on the expectation of a luncheon engagement with Edward, it seemed. I was sorry to disappoint her, & explained that her husband was gone from the office on business, not to return until evening. She looked crestfallen at this, so I quickly added that – being at leisure myself (if only) – I would be greatly obliged if she were to accompany me to luncheon instead. She declined at first (I had an inkling that she perceived my invitation as mere charity) but a little cajoling won her around. We walked over to a respectable dining-room on Dale-st., where the appearance of a lady provoked only one or two of the more ancient heads to turn. Settled in a booth, we talked amiably of something & nothing – when I ordered champagne Mrs Urquhart betrayed a look of surprise. 'I count every day lost that does not occasion at least one glass of it,' I said truthfully, & I persuaded her to join me. She recounted a little of her history – born & raised in Alderley Edge, had met Edward through his acquaintance with her father,

& migrated to the city on being married. She confessed herself ill-suited to Liverpool after her years in Cheshire – 'I still imagine myself to be a country girl,' she said, rather sadly. I begin to see the truth of this, for there is about her an innocent gaiety not commonly associated with the bustle of city folk & the roar of thoroughfares. A loneliness haunts her – she seems to have made few friends in her time here. Had she talked of this discontent to her husband? I asked. – Now & then, came her smiling reply, 'but Edward is not much given to listening'. (This was no surprise to me.) As we proceeded merrily through luncheon I pondered an oddity, for though we had met on but a few occasions I felt a closer companionship with Mrs Urquhart than I have ever done with Edward, whom I see nearly every day.

Just before we parted she enquired as to the progress of the library, & remarked – without any trace of asperity – that Edward was more at the office than he was at home. I owned that I had neglected Emily in like fashion, & by way of apology assured her that once the actual building had begun both he & I would make good the deficit of attention that was long owed to our wives. She smiled at this, & as we shook hands she said, 'I acknowledge the respect of being properly addressed – but would you do me the kindness of calling me Effie?'

Christmas Day [1868]

Dinner at Abercromby-sq. All the family present, & I invited the Urquharts for our evening party. It pleased me to notice how well Ma & Effie liked one another – perhaps they recognised the fellowship of country girls. ('A lovely lass,' Ma whispered to me later – an estimation in which I readily concurred.) While I played at cards with Georgy, whose Christmas punch is ever popular, Emily & Urquhart played duets at the piano – I asked for 'Liverpool's an Altered Town' but neither knew it, & Ma says that she has quite forgotten the words.

Later I talked with Pa about the Library. I confessed my exasperation with the delays, & with the stupendous absurdity of the builders' caprice – one moment they make an oath to start on this or that date, the next they make footling excuses as to why that date is now 'impossible'. (Invariably because another client has tempted them away.) Pa is sanguine, however, & bears it with a patience remarkable in one who has invested a cool £10,000 of his own money. 'All shall be well,' he says. 'The place shall be built.' I hope to Heaven he is right.

10th January 1869

Library. The Toxteth site has been approved, copies of the plans have been made, the builders are ready to begin – in March. All that remains is to decide upon the plasterwork of the vault; the designs of the capitals I have sketched here seem satisfactory. Yet I have an abhorrence of things that are merely 'satisfactory' – they must be outstanding, or else I should forbear to put my name to them. My first scheme was to have stiff-leaf mouldings, such as ornament any building one cares to visit – therefore unsuitable; Liver birds, as sketched, another possibility.

Wednesday, 20th January, 1869

St Agnes's Eve – 'ah bitter chill it was!' I rec'd at the office this after-noon a note marked *Private*, in a lady's hand. It was from Effie Urquhart, asking very earnestly to see me. I had not the faintest notion what the matter might be, but readily answered her request & set off for her house in Canning-st. On arriving I was conducted to the drawing-room, where I found her alone & in great distress – it was apparent that she had been weeping. After some awkward efforts on my part to comfort her, she addressed me quietly; she ventured to hope that I was a friend to her, & I replied – Of course. Then would I speak truthfully to her? Again, I assented, still uncer-tain of where she was leading. 'Did Edward have a meeting with you yesterday afternoon?' We saw each other yesterday afternoon, I replied. 'At two o'clock, at the Adelphi Hotel?' she asked. No, later, I said, at Norfolk-st. At this, she lowered her head in her hands, & began to sob. I begged her to tell me her meaning, but for a long time she could not speak. Presently she collected herself, & said, 'You will think me foolish, I am sure, but I have reason to believe – these last few weeks Edward has been so often away from the house –' 'You know too well the library has occupied us both insanely,' I offered, but she shook her head. 'Not this time,' she replied. 'He told me he was to meet you, yesterday, at two. I had suspected something was amiss for a while – you recall the day I came to meet him for luncheon, & he was gone? – so I decided to put the matter to the test.'

I was dumbfounded. 'You ... followed him?' She nodded, distractedly, her kerchief crushed in her hand. 'I saw him enter the hotel,
& I waited, pacing up & down the street outside. He did not emerge
until half-past four. I kept to a doorway & observed him leave –'
'Alone?' She nodded. There might be an innocent explanation, I said
– Edward was frequently obliged to meet with our financial
committee, building managers &c. – the Adelphi would be a likely
place to do so. (But I did wonder – why would Urquhart lie to his
wife about meeting me?) Reluctant though I was to investigate any
further, only a brute could have ignored the silent appeal of Effie's
woebegone face. I assured her that her fears were almost certainly
groundless, but I would pursue the matter & settle whatever doubts
remained.

23rd January [1869]

Whatever doubts ... Effie's story has fastened itself upon my brain
as unyieldingly as a limpet. Now suspicions goad me that Urquhart's
absences from the office might not be so blameless – has he been
engineering mischief on behalf of a rival speculator? It would
explain why the builders have so often played false with us, & why
financial assistance promised to the Library is later mysteriously
withdrawn.

I determined to establish the truth for myself, & when Urquhart
had left for the day I slipped into his office & examined his business diary. 'Meeting with E' was a frequent entry – E being myself.
I scoured the later pages & read, under 19th Jan (the day of which
Effie had spoken), 'Adelphi – 2 o'clock – E.' So he *had* arranged to
meet me, it seemed – I had no memory of the appointment, but then
the Library has so preoccupied my thoughts there would be nothing
unusual in that. Looking further I noted that he had marked another
meeting at the Adelphi for 28th Jan – with whom was unspecified.

28th January [1869]

I have just now visited Effie to tell her this news – for such it is,
to both of us. My own calmness as I sit here astounds me, though
I fear it shall not last. How to begin? – This morning (that seems
another age already) I called on Urquhart at his office & with a
show of friendly indifference enquired as to his appointments for
the day – would he oblige me with his company at the Cockspur?

226

Alas, he replied, he had made another engagement for this after-noon – but (he continued) might we have luncheon tomorrow? I spread my hands as though to say, Of course. At half-past one he left the office, & moments later I was out on the street, following him, down Moorfields, into Stanley-st. – the bright bustle of the passers-by keeping a distance between us. It seemed absurd at first that I should be shadowing my own friend in this way, but as his pace quickened an ominous lightness entered my own steps; I could not account for it, but felt as one who might be stalking towards disaster – I shall not forget this walk for as long as I draw breath. On, on, I pursued him, up Leigh-st., across Clayton-sq., Cases-st. and then into Ranelagh-st. where the old hotel closes the view at its top. (This too is soon to be demolished.) Carriages clattered by & for a moment I lost my quarry in the crowds milling around Ranelagh-pl. I entered the hotel by a side-door, & hugged the shadows – there were people enough in the vestibule to afford adequate concealment. Then I espied him, seated at one of the tables & looking about in expectation of someone. I continued to wait – oh for those last minutes of *not knowing* – when at the far side of the entrance-hall I caught sight of Emily, looking quite lost amid the press of porters & guests & other hotel-haunters. Emily! Marvelling at the coincidence of her being there I was about to present myself when I saw her face light up & she walked towards the man she had come to meet – Urquhart. *Meeting with E* . . . But I am not E.

He stood, they talked – then with a furtive glance about the hall he led her towards the staircase, his arm hovering proprietorially at the small of her back. Up the stairs they walked, deep in conver-sation – & disappeared from view. For one preposterous moment I thought of his declining my invitation this morning – 'but might we have luncheon tomorrow?' he said. No, I thought sadly, we shall not dine with one another again . . . Emily, Emily – I have neglected you, truly I know it now –

I hear a key in the latch – her key. We are husband and wife still. For how long did she imagine it could last? My heart knocks so violently against my ribs I wonder to think she does not hear it. I could not –

There the journals of Peter Eames came to an abrupt halt. Baines felt a number of things in quick succession: surprise, outrage, disbelief, pity, and then a maddening sense of anticlimax. Eames had exited his own story just as he was beginning its denouement. The bare details of what lay ahead were well known, at least to those who had ever taken an interest in this obscure provincial architect. He and his wife Emily had separated early in 1869; she had taken her daughters, Ellen and Rose, and moved back to Blundell Sands with Edward Urquhart. Eames, who also lost the William Rocksavage endowment as well as his business manager, continued to work on the library scheme in defiance of mounting costs and his own near-bankruptcy. Building began on it in autumn 1869, but when the money dried up three years later it was abandoned. His premonition that Magdalen Chambers would be the last building he would ever complete had proven correct. In July 1873 he was drowned while swimming off Blundell Sands. He was thirty-three years old.

'I could not' – the last words he wrote – would stand as his melancholy epitaph. Could not build his library; could not fulfil his potential; could not see that his marriage was in crisis; could not finish the last sentence of his journal.

14

It was the soft clicking sound that he couldn't get out of his head. Of all the terrible noises he had known during the Blitz – the uneven drone of the Heinkel, the scream of a bomb falling, the maniacal roar of a fire – it was the clicking that haunted his dreams now. Weeks later he read through separate incident reports, trying to piece it all together. The broad outline was clear enough: from 1 May, a Thursday, the city had endured seven consecutive nights of bombing, in which 1,453 people died and 1,065 were injured. Nobody had yet calculated the exact number of buildings destroyed.

It seemed to him that the whole city was on fire that week. Night was turned into a continuous day by the brightness of the flames. The Saturday would be recalled as the white-hot centre of this inferno, a night when an airborne armada of hundreds of German bombers rained destruction from ten thirty until five in the morning. Baines and the rest of the squad had been kept busy by an incident in Mill Road Infirmary, where a huge HE had wiped out three large hospital buildings. It was the worst that any of them had yet seen – seventeen members of staff, fourteen ambulance drivers and thirty patients had been killed outright, with at least seventy injured. The mortuary vans could not cope with the numbers, and by dawn rows of bodies wrapped in tarpaulin shrouds were lined along the cobbles in a nearby courtyard.

When Baines walked through town on Sunday afternoon he could not properly take in the level of the damage. He had become inured to the sight of tumbled masonry, glinting carpets of tiny glass shards, streets choked with pumps and the intestinal coils of rubber fire hoses. But at least then there *were* streets. His first inkling of what had happened to the centre came when he saw the view that closed the south end of Basnett Street. The grand old Victorian block facing him on Church Street now resembled a flat stage set, or a silhouetted elevation painted by de Chirico. What had once been the city's busiest thoroughfare was now a sulphurous shambles, its shops blown out or burnt to a skeletal front, behind which all else had fallen into dust. The demolition squads would soon be on the scene to knock down the tottering remains. As he continued towards the junction of Lord Street the air became so acrid and gritty that he had to tie his handkerchief over his mouth. Then he discovered the source of this drastic elemental shift.

What had once been the corner of Paradise Street and Lord Street was a jagged acreage of blackened brick and swirling dust, so much dust he could barely keep his eyes open to focus. A blizzard of burnt paper mingled with it, the flotsam of so many incinerated offices. On the south side not a building stood between here and the junction of South John Street. Baines, still in his rescue overalls and helmet, was allowed through the cordon and made his way up the street. A similar scene awaited him at the top. St George's Crescent, Preesons Row and the Goree Piazzas were gone, while a long vista of desolation led down South Castle Street all the way to the wrecked Customs House. But it wasn't just the historical landmarks he lamented; hidden, unchronicled nooks of the city had fallen to ashes and would be lost for ever. He thought of the little jeweller's where he had bought the cigarette case for Bella a few weeks ago – gone; the clockmaker's shopfront he had once asked Richard to photograph – gone. Whole streets looked amazed at their own shattered state, mortified at their nakedness amid pulverised bricks and sullen little fires. Still standing, however, was the Victoria Monument, and the public lavatories beneath it. Its survival was ironic, he thought, given how unloved the statue had been. He looked up at the Queen, still resplendent in bronze beneath her dome, and very much not amused by the view in front of her.

Firemen were still at their branches, cooling the ashen wastes with water that sizzled as it fell, and crowds gathered to watch them. There was an urgency in bringing the fires under control before night fell, otherwise their light would make a convenient flight path for the returning bombers. That they would return was now beyond doubt: the concentrated attacks on Merseyside had become an item of national news. By Tuesday, after five nights of raids, Baines heard the sirens' wail with a stoical sense of inevitability – it had become business as usual. Hackins Hey, as one of the few depots to escape damage, had become chaotic from the overspill of displaced rescue squads. At about eleven in the evening he spotted Richard across the room and waved, but he didn't appear to have noticed him. Just before midnight they heard the planes overhead, and a few minutes later a call came directing them to a fire in Abercromby Square. When they went down to the van they found a lively crowd of emergency workers milling about in search of a lift. Farrell pushed his way through them, and as he opened the driver's door an ARP warden stepped forward.

'Eh, mate – is this your van?'

Farrell nodded brusquely, and the warden asked if he had room for passengers.

'Could take a few in the back.'

Soon the unspecified few had become a surge of bodies piling into the van as if it were the last ride out of town. Baines found himself almost fighting for space on the bench as five became ten, then fourteen, until Farrell came round and barred the way to any further boarders.

'All right, enough's enough. This isn't fucken Dunkirk – yous'll have to wait for the next one.'

He slammed the back door, and soon they were bumping west, through streets pitted with craters and strewn with building debris yet to be cleared. Now and then the van would be thrown violently to one side as Farrell pulled the wheel to avoid a collision. Mike and McGlynn were facing Baines on the adjacent bench.

'Have you seen Liam?' he asked Mike.

'He called to say he'd be late – had to look after some neighbour who got bombed out.'

Baines noticed that McGlynn was more than usually withdrawn this evening; his face was the colour of unbaked dough. Mike had noticed too, and turning to him said, in a kindly voice, 'All right, Glynnie? You OK?'

McGlynn kept his eyes to the floor, and nodded almost imperceptibly. The nervous exhaustion of the last few days had evidently got to him, as it had got to others. Baines had overheard talk in the depot of a publican who had hanged himself rather than face another night of bombardment. The strain of waiting, of knowing that this night might be your last, could not but affect you – it was simply a matter of how you dealt with it. He considered the proximity of others to be the best psychological safeguard. One could feel terror in his heart, but two or three together could not show it. That was how it had been so far, but looking at McGlynn now he wondered if some had reached their breaking point.

They were almost at the crest of Mount Pleasant when they heard what sounded like a sack of spanners being emptied on to the van's roof. A few of them jumped, then looked around at one another.

'It's all right,' said Mike, 'it's just shrapnel fallen from the ack-ack guns.'

A few moments later the van pulled to a halt, and Farrell shouted 'Everybody out.' Baines noticed that as each man climbed out he immediately raised his eyes towards the sky. Now they could see what they had heard all the way there, formations of German bombers hovering as thickly as gnats in midsummer. Shells were bursting around them. The van had stopped at the foot of Oxford Street, aswarm with firefighters and engines and trailer pumps, all dazzlingly lit in the glow of burning buildings. Their path was blocked unless they went by foot. The ARP warden who had talked to Farrell at the depot raised his voice so that he could be heard above the roaring flames.

'There's a short cut to the square through Egypt Street – it'll be safer than goin' through that.'

As the others walked off, Mike called to Baines and Farrell.

'McGlynn's still in there.' He nodded at the van. 'I don't think he's comin' out.'

Baines quietly opened the door and climbed into the back. McGlynn was sitting in exactly the same position he had occupied during the drive, head bowed, hands clasped together, as if he might have been in church. Farrell climbed in after him, and they sat down on the bench opposite.

'All right, mate?' said Farrell. 'You comin' out?'

McGlynn kept his head down, and said nothing. Farrell cleared his throat.

'Been through some rough times, 'aven't we? But we've always got through it, you know – by sticken together . . . us lot against the world!'

His cajoling tone found no purchase with McGlynn, who only shook his head.

'Come 'ead, Glynnie, we can't leave you 'ere.' This was Mike, who was standing at the van door. He received no reply. Farrell turned to Baines, and with a helpless shrug gestured at McGlynn, as if to say, 'Your turn.'

Baines felt he had no better powers of persuasion than either of them. He looked at McGlynn's bowed head, the sand-coloured hair carefully wetted and combed – his side parting revealed the whiteness of his scalp. He didn't know a great deal about him, aside from that he was young, lived with his parents, wasn't altogether bright but had a good heart.

'Mark,' he said, realising he had never heard anyone address McGlynn by his Christian name before, 'I know it's tough. None of us wanna go out there, but there are people depending on us to help them . . . and Terry's right – we stand a much better chance of getting through it if we stick together.'

McGlynn had stopped shaking his head, and sat eerily still. After a few moments he said, in a low, decisive tone, 'I'm not goin' out there. So don't ask me to.'

Baines and Farrell glanced at one another, and there was silent agreement in their look: this kid wasn't going to move. Not now. Possibly not ever. They sat there for another minute, waiting, until Baines stood up and patted McGlynn on the shoulder.

'We'll see you later.'

Outside, the night sky was canopied in a pinkish-orange haze, like the last gasp of a Turner sunset. The whole day had been spent putting out fires and now an even vaster number seemed to have sprung up in their place. Baines glanced at Mike and Farrell, who had not said anything since they had left McGlynn in the van; there was something disheartened in the set of their shoulders. They reached the turning into Egypt Street, a narrow back alley entirely deserted but for two firemen who were holding their gushing hose against the wall of a Victorian almshouse, its high windows and parapet dancing with flames. They had just started up the alley when they heard an ominous swish behind them, and incendiaries began clattering on to the pavement. Then they were falling in front of them, too, bouncing and rattling against the cobbles.

'Fuck's sake,' shouted Farrell as they began to run. 'A lot "safer" this is!'

They hurried past the two firemen, who were perfectly oblivious to the fizzing cylinders and their greenish-white flames. They had only the fire raging above them in their sights. Baines marvelled at this sangfroid, and at the same time briefly registered the strange clicking noise that rose above the crackle. He almost instantly forgot about it as they continued dodging down the gauntlet of spitting magnesium flares. As they emerged from the alley on to Mulberry Street they were met by a familiar face – Mavers had just arrived with another party of rescue workers. He must have come straight from a dig, because his clothes were coated in plaster dust. He lifted his chin in greeting.

'You look done in,' said Baines, alarmed by Mavers' exhausted pallor.

'House collapsed at the end of our road – four hours diggen them out.'

'Then you need a lie-down.'

Mavers snorted ruefully. 'No chance of that tonight. Where's McGlynn?'

'Couldn't get him out of the van,' said Farrell. 'The kid's lost it.'

'We did try,' added Baines, seeing Mavers' brow darken.

'Where did you leave the van?'

Farrell sighed. 'Look, he's 'ad enough.'

'We've all 'ad enough,' said Mavers curtly. 'Where's the van?'

'End of this alley, round the corner.'

'I can't believe you left him there,' he muttered, and stalked off down the alley.

'Wait for me,' he called over his shoulder. They watched him run, weaving past the incendiaries, then past the two firemen, until he was lost from view round the corner.

'Is he tryin' to make us feel bad?' asked Mike. While they waited they dealt with the incendiaries crackling away on the pavement; most of them had burnt out, finding only cobblestones to feed on, but some had lodged in doorways, blistering the paint, then torching the wood. Extinguishing them was vital, for just one left unattended could set a whole building alight. They had retraced their steps to within thirty yards of the two firemen when Baines heard the liquid clittering again. He stopped and turned to Mike.

'D'you hear that?'

Mike nodded. 'Sounds like it's comin' from there,' he said, pointing vaguely to where the jets from the firemen's trailer pump were still going strong.

'Should they be spraying that wall so hard?'

'Dunno,' said Mike, 'but I'm not gonna be the one to tell 'em.'

Just then a coping stone flew down, narrowly missing the firemen as it crashed to the ground. Smoke was pouring from the windows. Baines watched the men briefly dip their heads together in consultation; he heard one of them laughing as they took a few steps back, steadying the hose. Beyond them he saw two more figures walking up the alley: through the gloom he could make out Mavers and McGlynn. Both of them were smoking companionably. That sardonic but friendly assurance of Liam's – he could imagine the way he'd joked with McGlynn, given him a cigarette, made him feel protected and necessary to the team.

'Tuh – look who's back in town,' said Farrell, with a grudging laugh. But Baines was listening to something else, the clicking had become a kind of grinding, and only then did he realise that what they could hear was the unstable chemistry of red-hot bricks and cold water. He should have known. Slates were now peeling away from the roof one after another and cracking on the street like dinner plates. He should have known. As he saw Mavers and McGlynn approaching the point where the firemen stood, Baines opened his mouth to shout 'Liam', but his voice was torn away by a monstrous rumbling – the wall bulged and suddenly, massively, began to topple. It fell as if in slow motion, though not slow enough for those below to escape the roaring avalanche of incandescent brick and plaster and glass. It fell, smothering all before it, and such was its impact that the earth vibrated beneath their feet.

'Liam,' he repeated, turning away from the huge black dust cloud that was rolling towards them.

'Oh Jesus, Jesus,' he heard Farrell cry, in a voice so forlorn it seemed that nothing could ever be right with the world again. They had staggered back to the end of the street, coughing from the smoke that had burnt up the air. Others had come running to see what had caused the crash, and soon he heard low muttered voices describing it. Minutes that seemed as long as years ticked by while they waited for the maelstrom of dust to clear. Baines felt his eyes streaming; he presumed it was from the acrid smoke, but then he wasn't sure. Mike had started walking towards the fallen building; he and Farrell followed on his heels.

'Oi, where are yous goin'?' A chief warden had overtaken them and was holding off Mike's advance. Mike stopped and looked at him.

'Our mates are lyin' under there – that's where we're goin.'

Sensing his mood, the warden became conciliatory. 'Look, I'm sorry, there's no way I can let you work on that. It's a dangerous site –'

Farrell interposed himself. 'We can see what the fuck it is, la'. Just get your lot to give us a hand.' But the warden's 'lot' were now ranged around him, blocking the way. A scuffle broke out as Farrell tried to barge past, and Baines realised that at this stage a fight was probably unavoidable. He was just bracing himself when out of the night another rescue squad materialised, and a voice called his name. It was Richard.

'Tell your friends – we can't work on this now. The brick is too hot, there's a chance of more collapses.'

'We've got two of ours buried under there.'

'I know. And it would take another three squads to dig them out.'

'I don't care how many it takes!' Baines said tightly.

'Listen –' Richard paused. 'You won't bring them out alive.'

The baldness of this winded him – it was so unlike something Richard would say that he knew it was true. Baines turned to Farrell and Mike, looking from one to the other. He swallowed hard.

'I'm afraid he's . . .' He couldn't manage anything else.

Farrell looked Richard up and down. 'Who are you?'

'Richard Tanqueray, a rescue squad leader.' He let that sink in, then continued. 'We'll dig them out – later. Right now we need to evacuate the Heart Hospital by Abercromby Square. There are fires all over the place.'

Richard had kept his voice low, but there was a decisiveness in it that even Farrell seemed to acknowledge. He really was a man for a crisis, Baines thought. He took one more look at the smoking rubble of the almshouse, around which the ARP men were setting up a cordon. In the distance they heard the clanging of a fire engine's bell.

'Let's go,' he said to Richard.

With the wardens and fire-watchers they now made up a team of about twenty, all hurrying towards the hospital. On either side of them the rooftops and chimney stacks were silhouetted against the torrid night sky, the result of fires that were outstripping the city's emergency resources. The frequency of explosions had stepped up to one every two or three minutes. As they entered Abercromby Square they felt a gale blowing in their faces; they could see fires burning fiercely, but what they didn't yet know was that these fires were devouring the oxygen at a startling rate. The vacuum created at ground level was producing a wind, which in turn whipped up all the flames in its path: this was the beginning of a firestorm. At the south-east corner they were accosted by a white-haired man, almost breathless with anxiety, whom Baines could now overhear pleading with the chief warden. The latter trotted over to Richard and held a brusque consultation. Richard, turning to the rescue workers, had to shout to be heard.

'The old man's come from the church over there. They're trying to put out a fire on the roof – if they can't they'll have to evacuate the whole shelter in the crypt.'

Baines knew the church immediately. It was St Catherine's, where the Eames family had worshipped eighty years previously. Cassie Eames had been married there; Frank Eames's memorial service had been held there. How often had he read its name in the journals?

'I'll go,' he said, and looked to Farrell and Mike.

'We're not lettin' yer go on yer own,' said Mike.

Richard nodded, and for a moment it seemed that he was about to continue with his squad to the hospital. Instead he took a couple of stirrup pumps, handed one to Baines and stood in readiness himself, having dele-gated the hospital evacuation to one of his men. In the time it had taken the old man to scour the street in search of help, the situation at the church had deteriorated. The vicar was standing beneath the stone portico as they arrived, his face a mask of weariness and sorrow. He led them inside, where fire was burning a bright hole through the dome and cinders were falling through the nave like confetti.

'Where's the fire brigade?' asked Richard.

'We called them half an hour ago,' said the vicar, with a despairing shrug. It did not even bear mentioning among them that the last few nights had left the fire services hopelessly overstretched. There were thousands of people ready to protect the city, they knew, but there were many more thousands of firebombs, rattling on rooftops, lodging in the eaves, bursting into fiery life. If they were going to save anything here Baines knew they would have to act quickly.

'Is there a ladder we can use?' he asked.

'I believe there's one in the mission hall,' said the vicar, pointing, 'across the yard at the back.'

'Right, Mike, you take a pump and see what you can do with the fire up there. Terry, you start getting them out of the shelter. We'll have to try and climb on to the roof.'

They dispersed. Led by the vicar, Baines and Richard emerged into the churchyard, where more fires were blazing in the wind. Flames leapt skywards, and the smoke made their eyes stream. As they reached the mission-hall door Baines could feel red-hot sparks stinging the back of his neck. Once inside they tried the lights, but the fuses had blown. He noticed the varnished parquet floor, the wooden chairs stacked at the side, the stage with its tatty velvet curtains – all perfect tinder. But no ladder. 'It must be in the basement,' said the vicar. Above them they heard another stick of incendiaries clatter across the leads. They waited for the vicar to unlock the basement door, and then, pointing their torchlights into the dark, the two of them made a cautious descent down the rickety staircase. The smell of damp and mould suffused the air. Their beams, butterflying haphazardly over the room, disclosed yet more stacked chairs, a bookcase of hymnals, a rusted bicycle. Richard had gravitated to the far side of the room, where a lawnmower stood and tools hung on the wall. He was examining something as Baines went to join him.

'Looks like the gardener's room,' Richard said absently, and picked up a spade.

'Or the gravedigger's,' said Baines.

At this Richard turned his face towards him, and with a cheerless little laugh said, 'You know, this would be a perfect opportunity . . .' His face was so deep in shadow that his expression could not be read.

'Opportunity . . . for what?'

'Well, a madhouse outside, fires everywhere, bombs flying down – you could literally get away with murder.' He seemed to be talking more to himself than to Baines, but his musing tone was not pleasant to the ear. 'I mean, with all this noise who would hear the blows to the head, or the screams as I did it? I could even use the spade to dig your grave.' *Your?*

'Richard, what are you – talking about?'

'I think you know, *Tom*,' he said, snarling out the last word. Baines started to walk past him, but in one swift manoeuvre Richard whirled the shaft of the spade through the dark and caught Baines on the side of the head. He felt so surprised that he almost laughed, but the blow had dazed him, and he sank to his knees. His torch rolled across the floor. He felt Richard's shadow loom over him. His voice came eerily flat and quiet.

'You must have taken me for such a fool – that offends me almost as much as what you did. With *my fucking wife*.'

He tried to focus, but his head was throbbing. 'Richard –'

'Shut up. All that time – you didn't think I knew. It's insulting, actually. That afternoon at the flat, you skulking in the darkroom, and she comes out of there, all la-di-da, *hullo, darling* . . . You got really careless. D'you think I didn't notice your cigarettes stubbed in the ashtray? Yes – *that* – number one in the dos and don'ts of sneaking around with another man's wife. You fucking fool –' He put his boot on Baines's chest and shoved him over. Baines heard him clang the point of the spade against the concrete floor, and wondered just how vengeful Richard's mood might turn. He now felt the steel blade pressing against his jugular.

'Is there any reason in the world why I shouldn't beat you to a bloody pulp?'

He said it in such a steady tone that Baines for a moment *couldn't* think of a reason. He knew that Richard had killed men when he was at the front all those years ago – he knew he had it in him. But back then he was a soldier fighting for his life, it was kill or be killed. Surely he wouldn't stoop to murder?

'Well? Any last words?' Apparently he would. Baines felt so undone by the suddenness of his predicament that he couldn't find any words, even the ones that might help him beg for mercy. His head twisted to one side by the steel edge, he saw the beam of his fallen torch trained on a spot along the foot of the wall, and wondered if this might be the last thing he ever gazed upon. Then he realised what he was looking at.

'Over there . . .' he heard himself croak.

'What?' said Richard, coldly.

'. . . by the wall.'

Richard, briefly nonplussed, directed his own torch sideways. The dim illumination picked out the cobwebbed rungs of a wooden ladder which had been laid lengthwise against the angle of wall and floor. Richard then shone the beam full in Baines's face as he silently considered his betrayer. The moments seemed to stretch out, until he snorted, and lifted the spade from Baines's neck.

'Looks like you've just saved yourself,' he said, and hurled the spade away. In the distance they heard a *whump* as another bomb exploded nearby. By the time Baines had risen unsteadily to his feet Richard was dragging the ladder towards the stairs; without another pair of hands it would be an arduous task getting it out of there. He watched while Baines picked up his torch, gingerly palpated the bruise on his head and then grasped his end of the ladder. As he did this Richard turned away momentarily and said, in a tone that now had only a baffled wonder in it, 'You know the most surprising thing of all . . . ? I'd always thought you – *liked* me.'

And he shrugged. The words cut Baines more painfully than anything else he could have said. In that moment he wanted desperately to protest against them, to plead with him and ask his forgiveness, but he hardly knew how or where to begin, and before he could open his mouth to speak Richard began hauling the ladder up the steps. Too late – and had he not forfeited the right to plead in any case? He had been merciless in his deception, and no apology, no act of contrition, could wipe that slate clean.

Richard opened the door at the top of the stairs and backed out slowly into the hall, guiding the ladder through. Just as Baines reached the top step the room convulsed in a blinding flash and the air around them split into screeching shards of metal. Simultaneously he felt a body slamming into him with a force so volcanic that it propelled him right back into the darkness from which he had just emerged. Something inconceivable had begun to suggest itself – *the one you didn't hear*. Familiar geometries were suddenly collapsing. The building seemed to have flipped on its side, the door he had just held open had leapt away and now the stairs were somersaulting past him; a flurry of jagged fragments whistled past his ears as the floor of the basement rose to meet him with a bone-crunching smack. Then a deluge of dust began raining down, filling his eyes, his nose, his mouth, until he thought he might choke to death on it. There was a keening in his ears, shrill and monotone; he hoped it would stop soon.

He had lost consciousness, for how long he wasn't sure – it could have been ten minutes, or an hour. When he awoke he could feel the most excruciating pressure on his chest; every breath he took seemed to poke a dagger against his lungs. He tried to move his arms, and found they were pinioned. He spat out some dust, and tried again. Some unearthly weight, cold and gritty, was pressing down on him. The air seemed to be eddying, as if some electrical charge had taken possession of it. He thought he might try to speak, but when he did all that emerged was a broken moan. Then he remembered something that had happened just before the world turned upside down. He had been carrying a ladder up the steps with – Richard? So where was he? He wanted to call out to him, but all he could feel in his mouth was a terrible dryness. He supposed Hell might be like this, the perception of a desire – to talk, to move – instantly rendered as its denial. He knew that there was something else, something absolutely vital, that he had to do, but he couldn't remember what it was.

The time, blank and busy, ticked on. Then he saw, from the very corner of his eye, something move; at first it was a rough shape, and seemed to crawl on all fours. A dog? As it dragged its way towards him he felt frightened. It was a dog, and that noise he could hear was its slavering jaws – it was bending its head down, about to fasten its teeth on his help-less neck. Oh God . . .

He must have passed out again, because he awoke to find Richard there, on his hands and knees, calling his name over and over.

'Tom? Tom? Oh thank God! . . . Thank you.' He was silent for a few moments after that. Baines could see the beam from his torch, but behind it Richard himself was a blur. He wanted to apologise to Richard for something – that he didn't mean to mistake him for a dog? No, it was for something else, but he wasn't sure what, and couldn't make himself understood in any case.

'Don't try to talk, old boy. Look, you've got this bloody great chunk of – *wall* on top of you. The bomb blew it right through. I'll have to try and –' Richard rose to his feet and staggered for a moment. 'Not so good myself, to tell the truth,' he said. It was too dark for Baines to see anything, but he could hear Richard muttering, and the crunch of debris under his boots. He was still finding a way to accommodate the pain in his chest. What distressed him more, however, was the loss of that thing he had meant to say to Richard. He was fairly sure he had to make an apology, but he couldn't for the life of him recall what he might be apologising for, and it goaded him furiously.

'Who'd have thought it, eh? After all the lucky escapes . . . we get one that lands right on top of us!' Baines thought he heard a slight vibration in his voice; there was something not quite right in the pitch of it. There followed long minutes of silence, and he wondered if Richard had fallen unconscious. Then from somewhere behind he heard the thin sound of running water, and footsteps slouching back towards him. Richard knelt down, holding a tin helmet that was slopping with water. He carefully guided it towards Baines's mouth.

'Found a privy at the back – sorry, only thing I could find to pour it in.'

Baines felt it trickle over and past his clotted mouth, then it was on his lips and – oh relief! – it swilled around his mouth. He tried to swallow, and choked. He could feel rivulets of water on his tongue, oh the mercy of water . . . I will show you fear in a mouthful of dust . . . Now he could feel Richard wiping the dirt and blood from his face.

'There – that looks better.'

Baines felt ready to try again. 'Richard . . .' It was no more than a froggy rasp.

'There we are! Back in the land of the living. Just hang on, my old mate, I'm going to try . . . and shift . . . this *fucking thing*.' He was straining heavily at the broken slab of masonry, but just as Richard seemed to get it clear it fell back on him again. Baines moaned as the daggers' points pierced him. This was agony more exquisite than he had ever thought possible. It was killing him, he knew. Dead wouldn't be so bad, really – it was the dying that was hard. He wondered if it would take long. But Richard had not abandoned the struggle, that was merely his preparation, and with quick grunting breaths, like a champion weightlifter, he heaved the torturing burden away. It fell with a dull thunk to his side. Then Richard too dropped heavily to the floor. For a few minutes Baines listened to the fractured rhythm of his breathing. Somewhere up above he could hear the raids continuing, the faint whistles and the distant explosions. Now that the pressure was off him his chest felt euphorically light, almost empty, and he attempted to raise himself on to his elbows. The stabbing pains had receded, though he could see that one of his legs was twisted in an unfamiliar way – he wouldn't try to stand just yet. He saw the gleam from Richard's dropped torch, and picking it up he poked the narrow funnel of its beam into the darkness. Richard was lying on his side, eyes closed, his face cut about with raw incisions and glistening blotches; he looked bloodier than Banquo.

Baines called out to him, once, twice, but received no answer. He hauled himself over on his back to where his companion lay, and gently shook him by the shoulder. Richard groaned and stirred.

'Richard, I wanted to talk to you,' he said, feeling his way towards something important. 'I wanted to say how sorry I am – for –' He thought by saying sorry the rest would follow, but he had led himself up a blind alley. What was it? What had he done that he was sorry for? Richard didn't appear to be listening in any case. He had sat upright, and now Baines could see through the treacly blood that matted his hair a stark white gash, like the white of fat on an uncooked pork chop. He decided he didn't want to look at that any more, and began patting Richard's leg instead.

'God, I feel tired,' Richard muttered. 'Think I must have dropped off just then . . . How are you doing, Tom?'

Baines considered. 'Not too bad – a bit cold. I wonder if they're going to send someone to help us?'

'Mmm, soon enough – they're just having a pretty hot time of it, up there . . .' His voice had started to slur. Baines thought he should keep him talking, otherwise he might peter out for good.

'I know you've been through worse than this. I remember you telling me – the noise of the shelling, at the front.'

'Hmm . . . I did tell you that . . .' He stopped, as though he might be trying to recall it for himself. Through the blasted doorway of the basement Baines heard a shrilling, not of a bomb but a whistle.

'D'you hear that? That must be the warden – they've found us.'

He saw Richard nod, slowly, but his mind had gone elsewhere. He mumbled something, and Baines, straining to hear, said, 'What's that?'

Richard's head had slumped at a drunken angle on his chest, but he lifted it slightly and said, '. . . to the very last.'

'I know, I know,' said Baines, patting his leg again. 'To the very last.' His voice had dropped to a whisper. 'Tom . . . I'm not sure –'

The sentence was not finished, and never would be in this life.

PART THREE

Searching
1944

It is my love that keeps mine eye awake,
Mine own true love that doth my rest defeat,
To play the watchman ever for thy sake.
Sonnet 61

15

As soon as she walked through the revolving doors Baines found himself unable to tear his gaze from her. It was the busiest time of the day in the Lyceum tea rooms, and the steadily thickening traffic of office clerks, leisured ladies and waitresses around the place might have obscured her entrance altogether. But there she was, seated at a table against the wood-panelled wall that offered him a most satisfactory vantage from which to spy. She was tall, dark-eyed, in her early thirties he supposed, and carried herself with an unemphatic indifference that beguiled him immediately. When the waitress addressed her the woman reeled off her order and completed it with a quick unnecessary smile. From the tannoy came the muted strains of a song he knew well.

The stars are still on high,
But they don't twinkle any more.
Why does it seem
They've lost their gleam?

He had been there for nearly an hour, and now had a focus to prolong his vigil. He had already made a study of the two American servicemen, eavesdropped on the proud but nervous parents with the son back home from college, speculated on the portly businessman whose sausage-like fingers kept drumming, annoyingly, on the table next to his. Until the woman had entered he had been preoccupied by an unarguably fetching waitress, the single junior of a staff that comprised matronly women no younger than fifty. When she had taken his latest order (he was on his third pot of tea) he had noticed her fingernails, bitten to the quick, and a certain harassed distraction that caused her to miss the wry lift of his chin he had intended as a gesture of sympathy.

He lit another Player's and tried to blow a smoke ring, a trick he had never quite mastered. The woman was closely examining her dark eyes in a little compact, and Baines took advantage of her absorption to have a good long stare. As he did so her eyes flicked sideways and suddenly he was trapped in the full, frank light of their gaze. He looked away, embarrassed. As a couple swished past his table towards the exit he used them as cover to retreat to the lavatory at the back, the panorama of the room flashing before him in the long horizontal mirror. The song trickled on beneath the hum of conversation.

Oh, there's a lull in my life.
The moment that you go away,
There is no night, there is no day.

The atmosphere in the Gents was rather less refined than the one he had just left. The tiled floor had recently been scrubbed yet failed to mask the stink from the urinals. He locked himself in the single cubicle, lit only by the filthy squares of frosted glass through which he could hear the noise of the street carrying on above. On the glazed brick wall beneath the cistern someone had scrawled I LIKE THE GIRLS WHO DO, and beneath it a respondent had added ME TOO. This little exchange had been crudely trumped by another hand, which had declared in incongruously neat capitals: I WANT TO FUCK THAT WAITRESS. There could only be one. The baldness of the language, and the ammoniac stench in his nostrils, stirred him – he found he was reluctantly, seedily aroused. He briefly considered . . . No, the prospect of a slow Wednesday afternoon spent fiddling with his cock in a cafe toilet would be too demoralising even for him.

He buttoned up and unlocked the door. In the smeared mirror above the basin he found a face with a sombre interrogative gleam in the eyes. Below the right one he could see a cicatrice, half an inch long, a result of the wound's inexpert stitching at the time. It did not have the glamour of a Heidelberg duelling scar, but he felt nonetheless grateful for its persistence. He returned to the room, careful not to let Dark Eyes catch him staring. After another ten minutes of his sidelong surveillance she paid her bill, gathered her things and got up to leave. Baines quickly called for his own bill and forty-five seconds later was pushing through the revolving doors on to the street. Crowds were streaming around him at the confluence of Waterloo Place and Central Station, but he saw the swing of her distinctive brown-and-blue checked coat as she advanced up Ranelagh Street. A rugged little March wind was blowing east and obliging people to clap a hand to their hats. Dodging awkwardly past an oncoming tram he kept a distance from the woman, who had stopped to look in a shop window before she turned into Great Charlotte Street, still a building site almost three years after the bombing had demolished its south end.

On St George's Place she stopped again and took out her compact for another quick primp. Then she turned into the Imperial Hotel, to meet the person, he supposed, for whom she'd been checking her make-up. This was perhaps the moment he should abandon his pursuit: he had no idea why he was following her anyway. With a sigh he walked into the lobby of the Imperial – and straight into her. The expression on her face wasn't friendly.

'Why are you following me?' she said.

'I wasn't, not exactly –'

'Don't lie. I saw you, at the Lyceum, and I've just seen you outside here.' He was just wondering how she had spotted him when she held up her compact, with its telltale mirror. *Canny*, he had to admit.

'I'm sorry . . . I just –' He thought he might as well say it: 'You reminded me of someone I used to know.' She pursed her lips in a sceptical pout, and Baines shrugged helplessly. 'I know that sounds like a line, but it's the truth. Look, sorry, I'm honestly embarrassed. I don't make a habit of following young women – sorry, ladies – at all, and if you don't want to talk I'll go right now and . . . not pester you again. Sorry.'

She looked hard at him for a few moments. 'Well, you can stop saying "sorry". What did you want to talk about?'

'. . . I don't know, really.'

She remained guarded, but he felt a slight thaw in her frostiness. People were passing through the lobby on either side, not even glancing at them. Now that they were up close he could see faint crow's feet about her eyes – was she a little older than he thought? With another appraising look she said, 'What happened – to your leg?' So she had noticed his limp, too.

'Er, I fell, during a raid. There was a double snap below the knee. Hasn't healed properly.' He hoped she wouldn't ask about the scar.

She paused again, then said, with a wary inquisitiveness, 'Do I really remind you of someone?'

Baines nodded. 'Very much.' She must have heard something in his voice, because her expression changed again.

'You said "used to know". She's not . . . dead, is she?'

He looked down, considering. 'It sometimes feels that way. I haven't seen her in a long time.' Now her own gaze fell, and she seemed to regret her directness. The war had given people a kind of permission to ask questions like that. He sensed that a moment had to be grasped. 'I know you must think me very odd, but I would so appreciate your company for a little while – just to talk. I wouldn't . . . try anything.'

The shadow of a smile passed over her face. 'I've heard that one before, too,' she said wryly, and glanced at her watch. 'You're in luck – I've got an hour before I meet someone off the train. So . . .'

'I know you drink tea,' he said, gesturing to the entrance of the hotel lounge with a hopeful smile. With a quick disbelieving shake of her head she murmured her assent, and they walked through.

That May, nearly three years ago, the planes returned for a seventh night of bombing. Then, the next day, just as the city seemed likely to be obliterated in this unrelenting holocaust, the skies were clear. Though they would return intermittently through 1941, the Blitz was over, and the Nazis turned their focus to the war in the East. At the time Baines had been oblivious to this or any other development. For three and a half weeks he was in intensive care, lost in a semi-conscious delirium, while the doctors and nurses of the Royal Infirmary laboured to keep him alive. The last thing he could remember from the night of the blast was Farrell lifting him clear of the wreckage, and his head being carefully cradled – then he had blacked out altogether. What followed was, he later realised, a coma, but it was not the kind of merciful oblivion that he had hitherto associated with the word. It was instead a wild and terrifying phantasmagoria from whose depths he would occasionally fight free, only to be plunged once more into its turbulent pit. Faces, real and imaginary, danced before his eyes, while in his ears a babel of voices clamoured for attention yet offered nothing to him of comfort or even coherence. Richard was the figure who stalked his dream life the most, often in the grotesque shape of an animal that had been savagely mauled in a slaughterhouse and then bizarrely allowed to roam free. A schoolteacher of sadistic bent – a figure who had not troubled his consciousness for thirty years or more – became vividly present, and revealed himself unimproved by time. More mysterious was the recurring image of a man he had never seen before; he was roughly of his own age, in a high collar and greatcoat, reaching out a hand in supplication but apparently unwilling to speak. He had the impression of falling through dark, liquid fathoms in the company of this man who, in spite of his plaintive expression, seemed to act as his protector; for some reason Baines knew that he would be safe with him.

Whatever paltry shelter his mind sought to hide beneath, he was defenceless against the tumultuous carnivals of pain that rioted through his body. He gradually pieced together what had happened to him that night. The HE which had speared through the roof and exploded in the mission hall had blown first Richard, then him, then half of the back wall down into the basement. His right knee, with the tibia and fibula below it, had shattered; his right wrist was broken; four of his ribs had snapped – the daggers he felt in his chest had been their sharp ends probing the tissue of his lungs. If Richard had not hauled the broken wall off him they would almost certainly have punctured the lungs and then collapsed them. In spite of other lacerations, he had been lucky. There was only bruising to his spine, the shrapnel had missed all of his vital organs and the loss of blood, though serious, was not fatal. Unlike Richard, whose wounds had killed him.

One of his most grievous torments in the aftermath of that night arose from the unlikeliest source. Adrift as he often was in the shadowlands between waking and dreaming, he began to hear a sound that made his flesh bristle and his heart crouch in fright; it was a slithery *clicking* that seemed to come at regular intervals of the day, and in his mind's fevered eye he saw a wall in slow, agonising collapse and great black clouds of dust suddenly closing in, choking the life out of him. The sound excruciated him, for he knew that he should have identified its cause and taken precautions – thus might he have saved lives. Liam. One afternoon he had woken to find May, who had been keeping a daily vigil by his bedside during the hospital's visiting hours. He could hear her whispered prayers, but there was something else there, too – the soft insistent clicking, so horribly like that brick wall just before it fell. At that moment he realised it was May's rosary beads that were clicking through her fingers, counting off the devotional quota she hoped might be the key to saving his life. He called to her, and as she dipped her face towards his he saw such a look of tender concern that he baulked at asking her to stop. When George came in the evening Baines explained in halting, broken phrases the anguish he was undergoing, an account so garbled to his own ears that he feared its point had been entirely lost. The penny must have dropped, however, because the next afternoon May was there, but her rosary beads were not. The matter was never mentioned between them; and the nightmare of that disintegrating wall slowly began to recede.

Of all his trials, however, the one that most oppressed him through his waking and his sleeping hours was the disappearance of Bella. Once he had clawed his way off the critical list he had expected, or rather he had hoped, that she would make an appearance at his bedside. He had been too close to the grave himself at the time to attend Richard's funeral, an occasion that would have been fraught enough even without the guilt of what he had done. The long days of convalescence dragged by, and still she didn't come. He wanted to write to her, but his wrist was broken, and dictating a letter was out of the question. Finally, when he could tolerate the suspense no longer, he yielded to the inevitable and asked Jack whether he had seen her. Baines had not told him about what had happened between himself and Bella – his natural close-mouthed instinct militated against it – so he had kept his tone as neutral as possible. He felt shabby about this, because Jack had been a Samaritan to him during his worst days, keeping him company and sometimes bringing Evie along when he thought the patient most needed cheering up. At his request Jack had gone to call on her at Slater Street and pay his respects to the grieving widow, but returned to Baines's bedside with the news that the studio was locked up and a notice to let hung in the window.

At first he was afraid that she might be dead; nearly fifteen hundred people had been killed during the May Blitz, and for someone in his febrile condition it required no great imaginative leap to believe she might have been among them. Jack had looked through the lists on his behalf and found no mention of her name, but as to hard evidence of her whereabouts he kept drawing a blank. The gallery assistants had been as mystified as anyone else: all they knew was that Richard was dead and Bella had vanished. In the end his facade of calm cracked, and having sought a refuge one afternoon in a distant corridor of the infirmary, he had raised his glistening eyes to find Jack standing there, looking down at him in his wheelchair. Prompted by shame and the relief of disclosure, he poured out the story, faltering only when he reached the account of his and Richard's Calvary in the rubble of the mission hall. It was the single time he had confessed it, how he had lain there trying – and failing – to remember the terrible betrayal he had visited on his friend, and the apology, however inadequate, he needed to articulate. The shock of the blast had short-circuited his memory that night, but now it had returned to harrow the long days ahead when it was too late for apology. Jack, squatting by the arm of the wheelchair, had listened as patiently as any confessor ever had, and when the penitent could speak no more he said in a voice that held both pity and an odd optimism in it, 'He did forgive you, though – by saving your life.' Baines nodded, his eyes stinging, but he was inclined to wonder if that act of forgiveness might not also have contained within it the slow-acting poison of revenge.

Was that what Bella had felt too? So complete was her vanishing act that he could only assume it was. As the weeks turned into months his conviction that she would at least send word began to fray. Disbelief slowly soured into frustration, and rage. Discharged at last from the hospital, he spent his early convalescence at the Elms, where George and May nursed him so attentively he wanted to scream at such unmerited kindness. He longed for solitude, and as soon as he could get up on crutches he asked George, over their protestations, to take him back to Gambier Terrace. There, at least, he could languish in his misery uninterrupted. Visitors to the flat seemed impressed by his resilience, which he himself knew was simply the effort required to conceal his monumental depression. Most days he sat for hours without opening a book, and his solitary walks, except when they took him to Jack's flat in Falkner Square, were aimless. The only time he felt roused from this torpor was that moment in the morning as he sat by his window, waiting for the postman's footfall in the street. As it approached he went out to the head of the stairs and leaned over the banister, listening for the snap of the letter box; if it went he would hobble down the stairs, ignoring the pain of the ill-knit bones in his leg, and examine the cage into which the post had dropped. Occasionally there was a letter for him – but it was never from her. One day, six or seven months after her disappearance, he had made his morning descent to check the post and, on finding nothing, had laughed at the clockwork monotony of his disappointment. That was when he knew she wasn't coming back.

But this did not prevent him from thinking about her, and he could pass whole afternoons absorbed in recreating conversations they had had in the very living room where he now sat. This was the sofa she had lounged upon, this was the window she had looked from, this was the clock whose chimes she had heard – and in the end it was the clock that had to go, because in those long vacant afternoons he had started to think he could hear the sound of her minutes, and the measuring of her hours. The raids, which had thinned out during the year, ceased entirely by January 1942, though not before three bombs fell one night around Upper Stanhope Street and killed fifteen people. A kind of normality slowly returned, both to his own life and to the city's. He had set about revising the text of his Liverpool book to accommodate the drastic changes the city had undergone in the last year and a half, though he had little appetite for the work. The streets were cleared, tramlines were repaired, and the shops began to fill again, but the pounding it had taken from the Blitz was not easily concealed. While a few bomb sites in the centre were enclosed by hoardings or else turned into a parking place for motor cars, elsewhere dereliction reigned, and mournful spaces strewn with bricks and broken concrete were now home to weeds and grass. This was probably the result of a native slovenliness, though Baines sometimes wondered if the city had deliberately allowed its desolation to remain uncovered, like an open wound – a reminder to all of its suffering.

Its broken demeanour rather suited his own mood. He traced in these ruined streets and levelled spaces a companionship of loss, and he felt more affectionate towards the place than ever. Indeed, it was the continuing survival of certain buildings that caused him the keenest pain; if he happened to be walking along Dale Street he would quicken his pace past the Kardomah, the cafe he always associated with the day they met. As for the Lisbon, scene of the last time they had dined in public, he would no more willingly have entered there than he would have thrust his hand in a fire. These things he could avoid. What he hadn't been able to suppress was a behavioural tic – it had lately become quite compulsive – of glancing behind him. It had first manifested itself as a blur at the corner of his eye, and he would turn in the expectation of someone, or something, just behind his shoulder. Invariably, there was nothing. At first he had dismissed it as a mere psychological reverberation from his injuries, and it did disappear. In the last few months, however, it had returned, and often, as he walked the streets, he would have the maddening sense of a shadow just out of view behind him. Reluctantly, it had become one with the name that had not ceased in three years to toll through his head. Bella. Bella.

The main bar of the Philharmonic was beginning to fill with a lunchtime crowd. A fire was crackling away in the grate, a counter to the whippy spring wind snapping the air outside. Baines, having arrived early to secure his favourite table in the smaller of the two dark wood-panelled snugs, idly turned his gaze from the pub's ornate ceiling to Jack's face as he stood at the bar waiting to be served. Having cultivated his thin and slightly spivvy moustache for three (or was it four?) years he had, without warning, shaved it off. Its removal had subtly altered his face, made his top lip seem somehow denuded, as though it had been exposed by chance rather than choice. Baines had delighted in mocking it during its tenure – the *gingeriness* was his principal goad – but now that it was gone he realised he might miss it, as one misses a familiar but unloved bit of furniture.

'What's the beady look for?' said Jack, as he placed their Higsons on the table, in the careful manner of a magician about to perform a trick. Baines shook his head non-committally, and lit his first Player's of the day.

'So – tell me about this girl you met,' Jack continued. Her name, he learned over their cup of tea at the Imperial, was Joanna, and she worked as a fashion buyer at Bon Marché. Even wartime deprivations couldn't sabotage the Liverpudlian passion for shopping.

'Oh, she's just . . . someone. We had a chat. She's got some feller, he's in Burma fighting the Japs.' Baines was already regretting his casual mention of her.

'Hmm. How did you meet, by the way?'

'Er, I saw her one afternoon in the Lyceum.'

Jack frowned in bafflement. 'Hang on, I thought you said you were drinking at the Imperial?'

'Yeah, I did. I followed her there.'

'You *followed* her? Why?'

'I hardly know. I liked her face. She reminded me . . .'

His eyes met Jack's, and the rest of the sentence was understood. Jack sighed ruefully. 'Oh, Tom . . . I mean, following strangers. I'm surprised the girl didn't call the police on you.'

'She might have done, but – I think she felt sorry for me. And she turned out to be a good listener, you know . . .'

'So you told her about – *her*?'

Baines nodded. 'I've never told anyone else, apart from you. It felt odd, really, talking about her, about Richard, after all this time. But it was easier, too, just *because* she was a stranger.'

'Will you see her again?'

Baines shrugged. 'Maybe. She said I could stop by the Bon Marché sometime . . . I wasn't sure if she meant it, though. And I don't know what we'd talk about now.'

They smoked in silence for a few moments. Baines shifted in his chair: the unseasonable cold was making his leg throb again. There was no forgetting, he thought, whether it was a woman's face or an ache in his shin – he would never be quit of that time. Fighting the tidal pull of his melancholy he began to ask Jack how his work was going. In the years since the Blitz he had been freelancing for the Corporation, assessing bomb damage and calculating which buildings needed to be demolished. The task of rebuilding, as he told Baines, would require many more years yet.

'Round by the docks it looks hopeless,' Jack was saying, 'like one mouthful of rotten teeth after another. You get to thinking it'd be better to knock down the lot and start again. If the city had the money I dare say they would.' He took a swig of his pint, and cocked his head in an attitude of reminiscence. 'Odd thing – we were doing a clearance this week on a warehouse in Norfolk Street. A bomb had sheared the whole front off and exposed this wonderful old brick wall – I had a look inside and found – I don't know what – might have been a church hall. It had these elaborate tiles and pillars, with oriels at either end . . .'

Baines, who had only been half listening, felt his attention snap abruptly into focus.

'A church hall – in the middle of a warehouse?'

'Well, I can't be sure what it is – but it's a shame it caught so much damage.'

'What will happen to it?' A bell had begun to toll from some distant avenue of his consciousness.

Jack shrugged philosophically. 'They'll probably pull it down.'

'Can I go and see it?'

'I should be back there next week . . .'

'No, I mean, can we go there now?'

Jack stared at him over the rim of his glass. 'I was quite enjoying –'

'Please – right now?'

Ten minutes later they had turned at the south end of Hope Street when Baines spotted a tram cresting the brow of Upper Parliament Street.

'Let's catch this,' he called to Jack, and as it was pulling away they hopped on to the platform like a couple of schoolboys. While they hung on to the straps inside the swaying car Jack eyed him curiously.

'D'you mind telling me what the hurry's for?'

Baines shook his head. 'It might be nothing at all. I just need to have a look.'

The tram turned right into St James Street, and they alighted at the church of St Vincent de Paul. Facing them was a grid of sloping narrow streets where Victorian warehouses loomed tall and gaunt, their brick-work a weathered motley of greens, browns, reds, mauves. Jack led the way down cobbled Norfolk Street, whose corner with Jamaica Street had been entirely masked by scaffolding and a baffle wall of corrugated iron. A workman's door stood to the side, armed with a heavy padlock to thwart trespassers. Baines turned enquiringly to Jack, who had already fished a janitor's ring of keys from his pocket; following a brief sequence of misin-sertions he sprang the lock and they were through. The immediate prospect was dispiriting: they were inside a dank grotto of tumbled blackened bricks, with bent rusted spindles sprouting from a half-shattered wall. Three years of rain had streaked the plaster and a steady drip echoed lugubriously against the floor. Jack walked over to a workbench and returned with a lantern, which he raised to illuminate the interior.

'So, this is one part the bomb destroyed, but see – it's only a partition wall. If you just step round here . . .' Baines followed him through the gloom, until they came to a further wall, this one of well-preserved sandstone, though all of its windows had been bricked up. Jack was now heaving open a metalled door.

'Now, through here . . .' he continued, 'is the hall I told you about.'

Unusual it certainly was, the walls beautifully tiled in cream and aquamarine, as might have adorned a late-Victorian municipal swimming baths, with a row of oriels set high at either end of the room. The stone flags underfoot were cracked here and there. Above them soared a rib-vaulted ceiling. Baines could see why Jack had thought it might be a church hall, but his instinct nudged him to doubt it – he sensed that it might be an atrium of some kind, perhaps an antechamber to a larger room. He felt his way along the sandstone wall, rimed with moss, until he felt it curve into an embrasure; arched double doors reared up, oaken, studded and faintly churchy, their twin handles cuffed by a looped iron chain of Promethean tenacity. Baines felt its cold weight in his hand, and gave it an exploratory rattle. He heard Jack approach, the lantern's light swinging before him.

'This is where old Harry would be useful,' he said.

Baines was surprised to recall Jack's ancient handyman. 'Good God – you mean he's still around?'

'Of course. And shows every sign of living for ever.'

It was an impasse. Without a pair of heavy-duty bolt cutters there was simply no possibility of getting through the door. Baines paused for a moment, probing the odds of his intuition being correct. There had to be another way.

'You know you said there was a lot of damage. Where else is it?'

'Round the corner on Jamaica Street. You saw all the scaffolding. That's probably where the bomb landed – blew a bloody great hole through the side.'

'Let's try it, then.'

Jack sighed impatiently. 'What are you looking for?'

'I don't know. I'll tell you when I find it.'

The canvas skin that had been stretched around the scaffolding rippled madly against the wind buffeting along its side. As the wooden platform wobbled slightly Baines had the disquieting impression of stepping along a ship's gangplank. The first and second ledges disclosed nothing but a tangle of rusty beams and girders. As they made their way up to the third he saw a window which had been boarded up rather than bricked. Closer examination revealed the plywood to have rotted at the edges. He prised a corner away, and the sound of splintering wood suddenly transported him back to the days of heavy rescue. Had he used his time as profitably since? Jack had torn away the remaining veneer, beneath which stared a dull windowpane, its glass warped and mottled by time. Baines picked up the lantern Jack had set down, and thrust its brass base against the pane; the glass made a high outraged twang as it cracked, then a second blow sent a shower of fragments pealing down. He removed his overcoat and laid it over the base where a few glittering shards still spiked the frame. His mobility now reduced, he accepted Jack's leg-up and clambered on to the sill, where he stood balanced.

'Careful, Thomas,' said Jack.

Baines peered into the near-darkness; he could make out the faint gleam of an iron gallery that ran along an enclosure. The drop to it was about ten feet, and before he could begin arguing with himself about the risk he jumped down, and felt a lightning flash of pain shoot up to his knee upon landing. He whimpered quietly, relieved at least to find that he could still stand. Jack had climbed on to the ledge and stood silhouetted against the light.

'Tom,' he called, 'are you all right?'

'Mmm. It's a longer drop than I thought.'

Jack's shadow flew down moments later and landed with a metallic thud, but he rose from his haunches quite nonchalantly, and he also had the lantern with him. The air within seemed sluggish from the years of accumulated dust and neglect. Jack swivelled the lantern through a half-circle; as far as they could tell they were on a second-floor gallery that skirted a long hall. They began to walk along its length, which eventually offered a right turn across the inky expanse of unstirring dark.

'There should be a staircase towards the middle, I think,' said Baines. His voice sounded small within the monumental stillness. His hand, which had been feeling the way blindly along the balustrade, now clawed only the space in front of him. He was two yards away from the top of a wrought-iron staircase.

'Have you been here before?' said Jack, the faintest trace of irritation in his tone.

'Never,' he replied, though he felt an anticipatory thrumming in his blood as he took the stairs downwards, one at a time. He suddenly had the image of himself as a pith-helmeted adventurer groping his way down the steps of a pharaoh's burial chamber, a flaming torch to hand. Would the treasure be intact, or had it been plundered by tomb robbers long centuries before? Down, down, their footfall clanged against the last few iron steps, and as the sensation of space appeared to expand around them he wondered if he could bear the disappointment of it *not* being the place he thought it was.

'Give me the lantern,' he said to Jack, in a voice more peremptory than he had intended. He held it aloft, and on either side they could see walls recessed with alcoves, with slender granite pillars ranged in between, their lower portion decorated with arabesques, while above them a frieze of mythological creatures – a busy menagerie of sea nymphs, griffins, dragons – stretched on into the shadows. Baines was wondering at this riot of elaboration when he noticed that the row of lovingly carved capitals beneath the frieze were all of the same figure, a young man seated, one leg crossing the other, reading a book. And that was the moment he knew. The young man was Frank Eames, the carving taken from a sketch by his brother, Peter Eames, who had redrawn it obsessively in his journal during 1868, the year he conceived the Eames Library – which was where they now stood. He felt the delicious horripilating shock of recognition, of certainty that something which had been lost had now been found. Lost? There had been no record that this building had ever *existed*, outside of a few feverish pages written near the end of Eames's all-but-forgotten journal. *I could not . . .* He remembered now the architect's final, uncompleted entry, the point at which his life seemingly began to fall apart. His wife discovered in adultery with his business partner, their separation, the collapse of his finances, the ruin of his hopes. Baines had assumed that Eames 'could not' have fulfilled his scheme to build the library, but he was wrong. How glad was he to be! In those last four years of his life he must have – Too many questions were crowding in on him, he needed to investigate the rest of the building, to find out how far exactly this legendary work had progressed. Yet it was a 'legend' no longer, he realised with a start; he was now standing on the same tiled floor (breathing the same air!) that its creator once had. He suddenly felt faint, and for a moment feared he might – appropriately, Victorianly – swoon. Handing the lantern back to Jack he stepped over to one of the granite pillars and leaned his forehead against its smooth unyielding cold. He would examine this granite, just as he would all the other stone and brickwork, the wrought iron, the Minton tiles at his feet, this vaulted ceiling above him –

'Are you all right?' said Jack, interrupting his reverie.

Baines turned to his friend's face, pale against the gloom. 'I'm fine,' he replied. He was relishing the prospect of telling him what they'd found – the magnitude of it – but for the moment he felt curiously fatigued. It didn't matter: after seventy-odd years of obscurity the building could wait a few minutes longer for an introduction. Baines thought again of the pith-helmeted adventurer, and recalled Howard Carter's thrilling account of that famous day in the Valley of the Kings in November 1922, when in flickering candlelight he first peered through the hole into the burial chamber of Tutankhamen. Well . . . perhaps their discoveries didn't *quite* bear comparison. Jack was sweeping the lantern's interested beam around the hall, and at length said, in a voice that seemed prepared for revelation, 'So – what are we looking at?'

Baines felt himself begin to smile. 'Wonderful things, Jack. Wonderful things.'

16

In the days following the discovery Baines felt a surge of nervous excitement that others, less guarded than he, might have called happiness. His
immediate urgency was to help Jack secure the Norfolk Street site, which
necessitated some tedious wrangling with Corporation officials whose
natural inclination was to tear the place down. The War Damages
Commission argued for this procedure on the grounds that it would provide
the city with 'short-term employment' – no matter the long-term loss of
its architectural heritage. Baines was appalled by this blithe justification
of civic vandalism, particularly in view of the scars still evident from the
Luftwaffe's pounding, but Jack had endured such bureaucratic myopia too
often to be surprised. The next task was to hire a crew of trustworthy
nightwatchmen to guard the premises against looters, who would otherwise
be preying on the building's riches of marble and mahogany and cast iron.
No change there, thought Baines, recalling Peter Eames's exasperation with
'bluey-hunters' who stole the lead from roofs to make quick money.

Even this precaution could not set his mind at rest, and arriving at the
site one morning with an old camera that Richard had once loaned him he
began to make a photographic record of the library's interior. The entrance
hall, with its swimming-bath tiles, had suffered the most damage, and the
south-west corner would have to be almost entirely rebuilt. But the solidity
of the sandstone at its front, and the cast-iron stanchions at its rear, had
preserved its structure remarkably. The main hall was the beneficiary of
this engineering, and once the place was properly illuminated it disclosed
the full extent of Eames's imaginative designs and the craftsmanship that
realised them. The architect's taste for Gothic decoration still flourished,
and the repeated capital of a figure, seated with a book, conformed to
Ruskin's principle that a building should speak the truth about itself. But
it was counterpointed by a freedom of composition and an extravagant use
of space that looked to the Arts and Crafts movement twenty years ahead.
News of the discovery was celebrated in specialist periodicals such as the
Engineer, which had maligned Eames during his short lifetime but now

took leave to acclaim him a pioneer in his use of cast-iron frames and curtain-wall construction. Its article on the Norfolk Street find would eventually be published under the title 'Victorian Visionary'.

In the midst of so much dutiful promulgation there was one person to whom Baines was especially eager to communicate the news – and whom he owed a personal debt for alerting him to Peter Eames's journal in the first place. One afternoon early in May, a few weeks after he had written to notify the Liverpool School of Architecture, Baines was continuing the clearance of the library's entrance hall when he heard a motor car pull up on Norfolk Street; he heard the engine idling for some moments, then the thunk of the doors closing. He went out and, as he had hoped, saw the frail but determined figure of Professor McQuarrie being helped along the temporary wooden gangway by a young man with brilliantined hair who, his supportive duty complete, nodded briefly to Baines, then returned to the car and drove away. McQuarrie, leaning on his walking stick, saw Baines's look of concern, and announced in his precise Scots burr, 'The approach is difficult. The retreat – desirable.'

It sounded characteristically gnomic. Baines went to offer his arm, but the old man waved him away, perhaps out of pride. In the years since he had last seen him McQuarrie had become quite shrunken, and turkey wattles drooped at his bristly neck; his eyes, which once were gimlet-sharp, now looked milky with age. He was wearing a greenish-brown worsted suit very like the one – was it the same? – he had worn the last time they had met five years ago. Once inside the main hall his spirits seemed to lift in contemplation of the scene, and he offered some drily approving remarks on the room's proportions and the standard of the workmanship.

'The patterning of light and shade is really very striking. Wherever there's tracery or screen-work there's always a window nearby to illumine it. And he seems to throw away the space almost deliberately.'

'Why do you suppose that was?' asked Baines, genuinely intrigued.

'Think about it, Mr Baines. The library was built in a poor quarter, for people who'd spent their whole lives in cramped cellars and gloomy courts. They'd never known *roominess* – not even in the pubs and the spirit vaults they went to for a change of scene. Eames made a gift of it to them.'

'It seems to have been designed on a much larger scale than he mentions in the journal. Do you think that was his mistake?'

'I suppose so. You only have to look at the entrance hall to sense how much it would all cost. But Eames never bothered with the economy of a thing. It's amazing that he got this far with it.'

'His extravagance may have saved it in the end.'

The professor raised an eyebrow. 'How so?'

'Well, I had to research the history of the place. At the end of 1872 Eames appears to have run out of money, and the work was put on hold. There was talk that he was raising more funds to continue, he was going to add another floor . . . But by the following summer it – well, he was dead. The building fell into abeyance – nobody was prepared to take it on – and the site was eventually put up for auction and bought by a building company, called Phoenix Properties.'

'Ironic name,' McQuarrie muttered.

'Anyway, the company wanted to use the site as a warehouse, but found that the library had been so solidly constructed that it would be more expensive to tear down than to leave alone. So they built a partition wall around it, then – seem to have forgotten all about it.'

'As did everybody else.'

They walked through the reading room, its wide bays ranged to left and right, and ascended the iron staircase to the mezzanine. As they looked out over the relic, magnificent in spite of its neglect, Baines stole a side-long look at McQuarrie's lined, worn features, his lightly trembling frame, and was struck by a realisation that the old man was probably of a similar age to the building itself, though he decided that it might not be endearing to point this out. The professor had turned his measuring gaze upon him, and said in a more confiding voice, 'And what of you, Mr Baines? I notice a limp – were you . . . ?'

'I worked in rescue. During the Blitz. I was lucky to survive.'

'Rescue, was it?' McQuarrie nodded, understanding, and made a small gesture that encompassed the room. 'Seems you have a talent for it.'

The stillness of the place enveloped them, but Baines, who would once have felt nervous in the face of his reticent tutor and perhaps have resorted to babble, had learned to live with silence – to enjoy it, even.

A quarter of an hour later they heard the slow creak of a car braking outside. McQuarrie lifted his chin in acknowledgement.

'That'll be my driver returned.'

'Your – son?' Baines had never enquired into the professor's family life; he knew only that he had been married.

'Nephew. He's been visiting, which is fortunate given my reduced mobility. You wouldn't know that I was once my college's champion sprinter, eh?' Baines smiled, privately bemused by the idea of McQuarrie as a young man at all. They emerged onto the street, and the old man extended his hand in farewell. 'I'll thank you for your time, sir. Keep me informed about your plans. And don't let this place slip away.'

'I'll do my best,' said Baines. When the car pulled away he waved to it, but the professor did not look back.

He had a second visitor that afternoon. He heard footsteps clunking around the entrance hall, and believing it to be the nightwatchman arriving early he went down to investigate.

'Ah, the Howard Carter of Toxteth!' drawled Adrian Wallace, and bowed deeply. How odd, thought Baines, that he too had thought of Carter on the day of his discovery. And how annoying that it should be this portly popinjay who had reminded him.

'Hullo, Adrian. To what do I owe the, er, pleasure?'

'You have to ask? Dear boy, I'm here on behalf of our city's favourite newspaper. This little discovery of yours is quite the sensation.'

Wallace, unlike the valetudinarian professor, had changed barely at all. His face retained its florid pudginess, and his wavy grey hair had not thinned. Baines made a quick inventory of his attire and found that this, too, adhered to the same flamboyant bad taste of old. The brown-and-cream correspondent shoes were fine, if you happened to be on a cruise down the Nile with Evelyn Waugh in the 1920s; the striped blazer was similarly anachronistic, a throwback to an Edwardian sports day, and it clashed horribly with the paisley ascot he wore at his neck. None of the clothes seemed to match, and what made it almost poignant was the evident pride their owner exhibited in them. His whole bearing spoke of one who considered himself well dressed. The man was preposterous. And yet, Baines could not deny to himself a reluctant pleasure in seeing Wallace again. Puffed-up and preening as he was, there hovered a spirit of gaiety about him that he found hard to resist.

'So,' Wallace said, as they entered the main hall, 'this was built by Peter what's-his-name in tribute to his dead – father?'

'Brother. And the name is Peter Eames.'

Wallace, nodding unconcernedly, took out a small notebook, licked his thumb and found a fresh page. He surveyed the room for no longer than a minute before turning to Baines. 'You found this . . . how?'

As he went through the story of Jack's work on bomb-damaged buildings and his chance mention of Norfolk Street, Wallace impassively took notes in shorthand, interrupting himself with an occasional grunt or nod: an old pro at work. After a cursory checking of dates and names, Wallace recapped his fountain pen, pocketed his notebook and yawned.

'Anywhere to drink round here?'

Baines was astonished. 'Is that it – I mean, have you got all you need?'

'Of course. Look, I'm sorry, but this will only be a small item. You may have noticed there's still a war on. That takes priority. But in compensation for your disappointment let me buy you an ale – on the paper.'

Baines, embarrassed by his own naivety, explained that he would have to wait for the nightwatchman, but he directed Wallace to a pub at the end of Jamaica Street and promised to join him presently.

Half an hour later he found the journalist seated at the bar and absorbed in *The Times* crossword, a haze of unfamiliar tobacco smoke wafting around him. His Turkish cigarette, parked on the lip of an ashtray, was raffishly affixed to an ivory holder. No, he really hasn't changed, thought Baines. Wallace glanced up as he slid on to the stool next to his.

'I'm stuck on seven down,' he said, tapping the newspaper with his pen. 'I think it's Wordsworth – "Suffering is permanent, obscure and dark, / And shares the nature of –" something, eight letters, probably ending n-i-t-y. I thought it might be "humanity", but . . .'

Baines shook his head. 'I'm pretty sure it's "infinity".'

Wallace scrutinised the clue again. 'By Jove – I think you're right. That fits with "paralysis" on ten across. Splendid!' He filled in the letters, then reread the quotation. 'Wordsworth, eh – that miserable sod.'

Having ordered them a round of Higsons and chasers, Wallace squinted at Baines through his smoke cloud.

'So, what'll become of your library?'

Baines gave a diffident shrug. 'I really need to find some institution that will take it on. I thought of applying to the Corporation –'

'Don't bother,' said Wallace, crisply. 'They'd just as soon knock it down.'

'Yes, but I thought, with it being a site of historical interest, they might want to preserve the place.'

'My dear chap, this is *Liverpool* we're talking about. "Preserve"? When has this city ever honoured the principles of culture or heritage above the cold brute urge to make money? You know as well as I do that the place has always been a mercantile centre – and if a thing isn't paying its way it's either knocked down or left to rot.'

'Well, what about the Walker Art Gallery? That's one of the finest –'

'Private investment. I don't deny that Liverpool's merchantmen have made philanthropic contributions from time to time. But now they're all moving out and taking their money with them. I'm telling you, it's all up with this place.' He paused to take a drag of his cigarette. Wallace's conversation seldom invited; he simply asserted and pronounced. Baines sensed that he was there only to provide an audience.

'Why do you say that?'

'Straightforward economics. It's relied on the port for too long. Once textile manufacture in Lancashire began to fail the writing was on the wall. Liverpool has never had any skilled industry to speak of – you've got generations who've only known casual labour. And that *won't last*. It's becoming the kind of city that people leave, in numbers.'

'Someone else once said that to me,' said Baines, distantly.

'Well, he was right. And once the war ends, if it ever does, you'll see even more following them.'

'I think you're wrong. I agree that there'll be economic worries. But you underestimate the people – their resilience.'

Wallace sighed loftily. 'Resilience, as you call it, will not create employment. It will not prevent the industrial centre shifting southwards. As for the people – your attachment is touching, but I don't think the rest of the country sees us quite so sentimentally.'

'I don't really care how the rest of the country sees us.'

'And that, if I may say, is an attitude typical of the native. Liverpool doesn't care – about anything. Resilience! That may have been true once – the transient population off the boats kept it going, the Negroes, the Chinese, the Irish. They had to look for work or else they starved. Now it's different. You've got a people born and bred here, and all I see in them is apathy and inertia. It would kill them to organise anything. Apart from a protest. You can almost hear it in the accent.'

'The *accent*?'

'Yes! Aside from everything else they can hardly be bothered to open their mouths to speak. The whole bloody city sounds like it's got a cold in the head. The dampness in the air is partly to blame – not to mention our unfortunate proximity to Wales and Ireland. But really, what other place could have fashioned such a hideous accent for itself? Nobody will ever take us seriously talking the way we do.'

Baines laughed at this. He noticed that when Wallace talked of Liverpudlians he kept shifting between his use of 'us' and 'them'. 'Where did yours go, by the way? Your accent, I mean.'

'My mother had the wisdom to send me to elocution lessons when I was at school. "Electrocution", as I so wittily called it. A teacher drummed most of it out of me, and I'm glad he did. Life's hard enough without a disreputable accent holding you back.'

Baines shook his head, feeling a sudden twitch of indignation. 'I have to say – I worked with fellers during the Blitz who had the strongest Liverpool accents you've ever heard, and there was nothing "disreputable" about them. They were brave, quite unimaginably brave, and they risked their lives to save people.'

'I was talking only about the perception of the accent.'

'Well, it's a misperception. However grating it sounds to your ear, it has no bearing on character. And as for "apathy", you'd think differently if you'd worked with a rescue squad during a raid.'

Wallace, realising he had hit a nerve, held up his hands as if he were patting an invisible wall. 'Dear boy, forgive. I don't wish to blacken the name of our good citizens. They've been brave as lions in this war, everyone knows that. It's *after* the war I'm worried about, because I tell you now, there'll be nothing left for them. The port, the jobs – kaput. If you have any sense you'll get out of here.'

'So why haven't you?'

Wallace sighed again. 'I've often meant to. Perhaps I've became complacent. I have an easy life, the paper pays me a decent screw ... it would require too much effort for me to leave now. There, you see – Liverpool apathy in a nutshell!'

Baines looked around the bar they sat in, drinkers huddled in twos and threes, pinched faces lit in the yolky pub light. An old man was shuffling about the room, selling the *Echo*'s late edition. As he passed them Wallace swivelled round on his stool and bought one. He briefly perused the headlines.

'Hmm. "NAZI SECRET WEAPON – MINISTERS' FEAR." Seems they've developed some kind of robot bomb ... London will have to batten down the hatches again.' He yawned, and continued riffling through the paper as if he were searching for something. 'Ah, here we are. *This Happy Breed*, opening at the Forum today. Reviewed by – Adrian Wallace.' He read it with unabashed interest, as if it might have been written by someone else. 'I'll have to post this down to Noël.'

'So you're still in touch,' said Baines. He had never quite determined whether Wallace's association with 'Noël' was an elaborately nurtured fantasy or not.

'Of course,' he said, not taking his eyes from the review. He chuckled, and read aloud, '"In the role of the mother Celia Johnson is an exemplar of enduring, resourceful womanhood. She has about her a peculiar refinement; she looks like the English Home Counties, or perhaps one might say the English Home Counties look like her."' Baines wasn't sure that the line merited quotation, but when its author looked to him he offered a wan smile of approval. When Wallace next spoke his tone had become more musing.

'I saw that friend of yours recently, by the way.'

'Who?'

'Bella – Bella Tanqueray? I almost walked right past her, actually . . .'

Baines felt his heart plunge headlong through a trapdoor. Its descent was so sudden he feared it must show on his face. He kept hold of his voice as carefully as a rider with a skittish horse.

'Whereabouts did you see her?'

'Oh, I was down in London – gone to see some bloody awful play. I was hurrying down the Strand when I spotted this face and thought – don't I know her? So I stopped and risked a "hullo". And then there was no doubt about it.'

Baines nodded, his mind racing in several directions at once. His longing to know – about her, about their meeting, about the last three years – pressed on him as an almost physical ache, but Wallace was not the man to whom he could betray that longing. Caution still governed his tongue.

'The Strand?' He registered his mind playing a trick of misdirection. 'How – is she?'

'Well,' said Wallace, with a shrugging laugh, 'I hardly had time to find out! She was with another lady, who had a child. She said she'd been living in London for a time – I didn't realise she'd lost her husband – ' He stopped, and turned a curious look on Baines. 'I presume from your questions that you've not seen her in a while?'

'No. After Richard died she just – disappeared. It must be –' he feigned a casual calculation '– three years since I saw her.'

A sly gleam had entered Wallace's eyes. 'Hmm. You know, I always imagined there was something going on between you two.'

Baines forced a disbelieving laugh that felt like ashes in his mouth. 'As you see, we're hardly close. Did she seem – very different?'

Wallace continued blithely, 'Still beautiful, I should say. She's one of those women who'd charm the grey off your hair. One can't imagine her languishing in widowhood . . .'

Baines looked down, and said nothing.

'I had a feeling she'd have liked to talk, but she was with a friend, as I said, and I was on my way to a matinee . . .' As Wallace proceeded to describe the play, Baines maintained the illusion of listening – a nod, a smile, a punctuating 'hmm' – while his mind tried to unknot its torturing coils of speculation, wonder and regret. Bella. After all this time . . . did the sight of Wallace cause her to think of him? If so, was she disconcerted, or indifferent? He was surprised at the intensity of his need to know. His ability to go for long periods without thinking of her had convinced him he had mastered that impulse, and even his awkward habit of glancing behind as he walked seemed to have receded of late. He had accepted the idea that he might never be able to expunge the memory of her, but had thought that to board it up in some dark chamber might be an adequate substitute. This too, he now realised, had proven unreliable. Wallace was talking on, charmed as ever by the necessary sound of his own voice, but after some minutes even he had noticed how quiet his drinking companion had become.

'It's worrying you, isn't it?' The question seemed so sudden and well aimed it caught him off guard.

'– Sorry?'

'The library,' said Wallace, guessing wrong. 'Look, I'll tell the editor we should go two columns on it – make a bit of a fuss. It won't persuade the Corporation to help out, but it might earn a stay of execution. In the meantime, let's get another one in.' He called to the barman, as Baines murmured his thanks.

By the time they emerged from the pub the street lamps were decanting their frowzy glare over the city. Wallace had kept up his inexhaustible chatter – he never seemed to talk about any given subject for less than an hour – and it satisfied both of them. Baines had no wish to talk, Wallace had no wish to listen. His meaty face flushed with drink, Wallace called Baines back as they were about to part and said, 'You should come and have lunch at the Lisbon – we'll continue our dialogue on the state of Liverpool. Cheer-o, then.'

He sauntered off, his dainty step rather at odds with his top-heavy bulk. Lunch at the Lisbon, thought Baines – not in this lifetime, friend. He walked on towards the centre, oblivious to the clangour of trams and buses heaving past. The place seemed to him subtly altered now that he knew for certain that Bella was elsewhere. He supposed he had always known, but Wallace's encounter with her down in London had made it an incontrovertible fact. She had never loved Liverpool; she had made that known the very first time they met.

These thoughts were preoccupying him when he looked up and noticed people shoaling around on the pavement in front of him. He was passing a cinema, its lights glaring in the dusk, and on impulse he stopped to check what was showing. The title signalled to him irresistibly: *This Happy Breed*. He smiled to think of Wallace proudly reciting from his review a couple of hours ago. The early-evening show was about to begin, and minutes later he found himself settled in the stale, tobacco-smogged dark amid dozens of faceless strangers. It was not an especially good film, for despite the sincerity of Coward's chronicle – twenty years in the life of an 'ordinary' suburban family – the underlying tone of condescension was too strong to be ignored. It was as if the writer were being the soft-hearted patron, instead of the beady-eyed artist. And yet Baines found himself absorbed by it. Just to surrender to the silver and black ghosts at play inside this glistening aquarium was enough to beguile two hours that would otherwise have been wasted in sorrowful moping. It was like a very abrupt holiday from the gravitational burden of being oneself. And Wallace – garrulous, conceited, amiable Wallace – was right about Celia Johnson.

Three days later Baines found it, halfway down page five of the *Echo*, under the headline LIBRARY DISCOVERED IN BLITZ RUIN. It was run over two columns, as Wallace had promised. A smudged photograph of the facade accompanied the article.

> The terrible destruction visited on the city by the Luftwaffe cannot be too quickly forgotten, yet a welcome surprise has belatedly emerged from those dark days. But for the bomb damage that befell a warehouse in Toxteth the existence of an 'unknown' library might never have been discovered. The library, begun around 1870, was only half completed when its creator, a little-known Victorian architect named Peter Eames, went bankrupt and was forced to abandon its construction. The building passed into the hands of a property company which had undertaken to clear the site but instead bricked up the library and used the shell as a temporary warehouse. The company itself went bankrupt some years later. And there the matter might have rested had not an HE landed on the corner of Jamaica Street and Norfolk Street one night in May 1941, destroying a partition wall and exposing the original fabric of the library within. This itself only came to light last month when war damage assessors stumbled on the find during a routine clearance. They handed on their discovery to an architectural historian, Thomas Baines, who quickly identified it as part of the 'lost' Eames Library, no plans of which are believed

to exist. Intricate tiled floors, vaulted ceilings, original plasterwork and stained-glass windows have been preserved in mostly
good condition, though damage to the west-facing wall is severe.
Mr Baines described its uncovering as 'miraculous', and said that
it enhances the reputation of Peter Eames as one of the most
innovative architects of his day. Even in its unfinished state, he
adds, it counts as a pioneering example of Victorian ironwork and
decoration. The architect, who also designed Janus House in Temple
Street, allegedly despaired of finishing the library and drowned
himself off Blundell Sands in 1873, aged only thirty-three. The fate
of the building now rests with Liverpool Corporation, which has
a poor record of looking after such properties. A spokesman
yesterday announced that no immediate decision had been made,
but conservationists fear the worst.

Over the next few days Baines received a handful of letters, forwarded
to him by the *Echo*, from assorted local historians, mostly of a pedantic
nature. One, from a society promoting 'Victorian interests', begged him
to send a catalogue of books. Another enquired as to its opening hours –
and was it a *lending* library? Ten days after the story appeared another
letter arrived, written in a tiny, crabbed hand and stamped with a Birkenhead
postmark. Its text was brief:

Ampthill Lodge,
Village Road,
Oxton

16th May 1944

Dear Mr Baines,
    I have read your article in the *Echo*, passed on to me by a very
dear friend. Thrilling news about the library, how CLEVER of
you to find it! Such an odd thing to have lost, a building, dont
you think.
    But you are quite wrong about drowning himself
    Yrs sincerely,
    Mrs E. Westmacott

When he had finally deciphered the handwriting he read it again, amused
first by the writer's rather dotty misapprehension ('your article'), then by

her enthusiastic praise of his CLEVER find. But it was the final sentence, the bald assertiveness of it, that snagged his attention. There had long been uncertainty over the exact circumstances of Eames's death: the contemporary accounts that Baines had read on yellowing newsprint when he first began his research had never agreed on the matter. Eames had been with his ex-wife and daughters, and another family, on an outing to Blundell Sands one afternoon in July 1873. He had gone out for a swim, and never made it back. Some reports had mentioned the possibility of suicide; others had described it as an accident. He realised that the obscurity of the life had helped draw a veil over the manner of the death – no biography had ever troubled to discover the truth, because no biography had ever been written. How then could this Mrs Westmacott be so convinced that the *Echo* article had misrepresented Eames as 'drowning himself'? There was, tantalisingly, no full stop after 'himself', as though she had paused mid-sentence, intending to explain, and then had decided against it. Or had simply forgotten to.

He dismissed the letter as an oddity. The handwriting and the unreliable punctuation suggested that the lady was quite elderly; it seemed quite likely that she was not in full possession of her faculties. She was doubtless some eccentric local historian who had inherited the story as gossip, then pickled and preserved it until it resembled the truth; there would be no profit in entering a correspondence with her. He decided to get on with other things, such as writing to his bank manager to request a loan. He still had a little money saved, an inheritance from his parents, but it would not be sufficient to keep the library site protected indefinitely. The Liverpool School of Architecture, his alma mater, wrote to him with an invitation to deliver a talk about Eames, whose reputation he had now seemingly been appointed the keeper.

And yet ... he kept thinking of Mrs Westmacott and her curious letter. *You are quite wrong about drowning himself.* He could not get the sentence out of his head. One afternoon he picked up the telephone directory and slid his eye down the Ws. To his surprise Westmacott, E. was listed, and on the ninth or tenth ring a woman's voice, younger than he had expected, answered. No, she was not Mrs Westmacott, she replied, but that lady's housekeeper. Baines explained himself, and asked if he might be able to talk to her in person. There was a pause, an echoey clunk of the telephone receiver temporarily put aside, and then receding footsteps; minutes passed, during which Baines wondered if his call had been forgotten, and imagined the telephone at the other end cupping its ear into the unpeopled silence. Just as he was about to hang up a scraping note sounded on the line and the housekeeper's voice returned from the void.

'Mrs Westmacott will be at home at two o'clock tomorrow, if that suits you.'

Silently digesting the formality of 'at home', he replied that it did, and rang off.

Standing on the top deck of the Birkenhead ferry, Baines leaned over the handrail and contemplated the sluggish, turbid waters of the Mersey slapping against the pontoons that supported the landing stage. It was a day neither sunny nor overcast; the sky was the worn white of a sheet that had been through the mangle too many times and now carried the faintest tinge of grey. A breeze, carrying a salty tang, chopped the river's surface into little hurrying waves. Alongside the landing stage two enormous liners were moored, dwarfing the ferry boat. On the other side a steamer mounted fore and aft with anti-submarine guns had recently docked, disgorging American troops clad in their grey-green waterproof jackets and steel helmets. He noticed other passengers crowding along the rails to watch their arrival; some of them waved and cheered. Then a shout came directly from below, the gangways were hauled back, the sliding doors of the ferry were run across, and the mooring ropes unloosed from the iron bollard and tossed on to the stern. These were caught, Baines noticed, by a crusty old salt who didn't even bother to remove the pipe from his mouth. The boat stirred and bumped against the stage, and, with a sense of reluctance, heaved away. The waters behind it began to churn, and by slow degrees the landing stage receded.

As the boat headed towards mid-river his gaze lifted to the uptilting panorama of the Pier Head and the trio of buildings that dominated the skyline, the Royal Liver, the Cunard, and the Mersey Docks and Harbour Board. This display of Edwardian imperial pomp – the city's gateway – was one that still made him swell with pride. How could Wallace look at such a waterfront and say it was 'all up' with Liverpool? These were buildings that indicated the very opposite of apathy and close-mindedness – they had swagger and scale. Surely this was a port that had no fear of the future . . . and if the largest transatlantic passenger liners now left from Southampton, well, what of it? There seemed to be more than enough traffic on the river and activity in the docks and warehouses to keep the place prosperous. Wallace's Cassandra-like prophecies of decline and collapse were merely the cynical jibes of a disillusioned old hack. He looked down at the churning dirty-white wake of foam, briefly absorbed by the flotsam that bobbed in it, bits of driftwood, bottles, ragged tresses of brown seaweed. He crossed the deck for a change of perspective, and there, downriver, he caught sight of a mast poking from the dun-coloured waves at a skewed angle. Next to it lolled buoys and a two-masted, anchored ship, a lighthouse to passing traffic. Along its hull, lettered in white paint, could be seen the word WRECK. Baines stared at it for a moment, then returned to his original vantage on the other side.

Arriving at Woodside he followed the straggling line of passengers disembarking down the gangway, and found a tramcar bound for Birkenhead. The Wirral peninsula remained something of a mystery to Baines, a place that he had gazed upon from across the Mersey for most of his life yet had seldom visited. The tram's route took him through streets still gap-toothed from the Blitz, yet amid the bomb damage he saw enough Victorian churches, coaching inns and opulent suburban mansions to make him repent his neglect. On receiving a nod from the conductor whom he had consulted for directions, he alighted at the brow of a long descending road and bent his steps towards the house of Mrs Westmacott. Village Road was a somnolent backwater on which stuccoed Italianate houses could be glimpsed over high sandstone walls and privet hedges. Ampthill Lodge, the grandest of them, peeped from the end of a bowered drive of tall chestnut trees. On either side of its wrought-iron gate twin pillars stood guard, each with a bell set inside a carved rosette; on the left was inscribed 'Visitors', on the right 'Tradesmen'. Amused by this quaint Victorianism, and then ignoring it, Baines lifted the gate's thin iron handle and walked up the drive.

He heard the old-fashioned bell pull ring distantly within the house, and while he waited he idly admired the door's handsomely plain fanlight, dating it to the 1850s. It was the kind of detail that occupied him. A shadow briefly hovered behind the stained glass before the door opened to reveal a middle-aged lady in capable tweed skirt, eau de Nil cardigan and a trim little brooch pinned to her blouse.

'Are you Mr Baines?'

She introduced herself as Mrs Fleetwood, and he recognised her voice from the telephone. At her invitation he followed her into the hall, where dark oak and brooding oil portraits had whelmed the place in gloom. From upstairs he heard a sprightly étude being played on the piano. Mrs Fleetwood, glancing over her shoulder, said in a conspiratorial undertone, 'She's in a good mood today,' as though they secretly both knew she could be a bit of a dragon. 'You can usually tell from the way she plays.'

She led him down a corridor of echoing parquet and, opening a door, ushered him into a study. Then she went off to fetch her employer.

Baines looked about the room, friendlier than the hall, high-ceilinged, with pleasantly rumpled sofas set around a fireplace. Books were stacked on shelves higgledy-piggledy, and a pile of newspapers mouldered in a wicker basket. He had been in houses like this before, when Jack had asked him along to help value the contents in a clearance – it might be an old dear who'd pegged out and left behind some monstrous-looking furniture, a couple of cats and the miserable odour of long-boiled vegetables. That wasn't the way here: all he could smell was beeswax; the floor had been swept and there wasn't a cat-hair in sight. French windows looked out upon a long lawn. He was examining a framed photograph on the mantelpiece when the door opened and Mrs Westmacott herself scuttled in. Once again his expectations were confounded. She was quite elderly and clad in a long bombazine dress, high at the neck with multiple buttons running down the front. But she was not the crazed Miss Havisham-type he had imagined meeting.

'Hullo there,' she almost called to him. 'Mrs Fleetwood said you were very young-looking.' She came forward to examine him more closely. 'You don't look that young to me!'

Baines laughed as he took the impossibly light hand she proffered. 'I'm forty-one.'

'Well,' she mused, 'I'm eighty – in August – so perhaps she's right. Are you impressed that I still play the piano?' There was a challenging gleam in her bird-bright eyes.

'I am indeed,' he replied, swallowing down the words, 'amazed, actually.'

She nodded complacently. 'Mm. I don't believe it *disgraced* Chopin.' Her voice had a flattened Lancashire burr, with something amused in its register.

'Will there be a celebration to mark your birthday?'

'Heavens – I hope so,' she said, with a quick smile. 'There should be some compensation for being this old.'

Baines laughed again – this one was a caution. She had an open face with reddish cheeks that seemed the result of natural high colour. She pointed to the larger of the two sofas and asked him to sit, then plumped herself down on a button-backed armchair at an angle to him. Just then Mrs Fleetwood entered bearing a tray with a teapot and a plate of biscuits that caused Mrs Westmacott's eyes to dart about in a near-parody of vivacious interest.

'Thank you for your letter – about the library article,' Baines began, wondering whether he should correct her impression of its authorship.

'Ah yes, the library. We were very pleased to read about that,' she said, waving vaguely at the departing housekeeper to explain the plural pronoun. 'We'd all assumed the place had been torn down years ago. Quite a turn-up! I dare say you've come expecting a treasure trove of – what? – *Eamesiana*, I suppose.' Baines heard a regretful note in the word, though he had not expected any kind of treasure, and wondered why she should think he had. Mrs Westmacott was daintily tapping the crumbs of her biscuit on to a saucer.

'Actually, I was just hoping you might explain something you said in your letter – about Eames not drowning himself . . .'

'Oh, they got that quite wrong. It's a very sad story. I tried not to think about that day for years, but as you get older, well, things start to come back to you.'

Baines sensed something unbelievable begin to take shape. 'When you say "that day", do you mean – you were *there*?'

Now it was her turn to look surprised. 'Of course I was there. Even the newspapers knew that much!'

'But I thought – I read that Eames went there for the day with his family . . .'

'Yes, he did,' she said, frowning at his slow-wittedness, ' – with my mother, my sister, Edward and me.'

Baines thought his scalp might lift off with the hair-raising shock of what he had just begun to comprehend. The discovery of the library was one thing, but *this* . . . Mrs Westmacott was now reading the belated real-isation on his stunned features.

'I'm sorry, Mr Baines, I thought you knew . . . Westmacott was my husband's name. I was born Eames – Ellen Eames.'

Baines felt the maddening pressure of questions – hundreds of ques-tions! – crawling over his brain like scorpions, but as ever, his mouth lagged some way behind. He found himself merely staring at her. Why had he not bothered to discover, of all things, whether Peter Eames's daughters still lived? His consciousness snatched randomly at a name.

'Rose?'

'My sister died in 1930. My mother and Edward died many years ago. But there are various Eames cousins still about, Aunt Cassie and Aunt Georgy's children – some in Scotland, and France, too. I believe I'm the only descendant still living in England.'

'I do apologise, Mrs Westmacott. I'm . . . overwhelmed. Could you bear to tell me about the day Eames, I mean – your father – drowned?'

She looked away for a moment, collecting herself. 'As best as I can,' she murmured. 'We were living near Blundell Sands by then. It was one day in July. I was eight, Rose must have been six. We'd gone to the beach for the day, with some friends. I think Pa arrived unexpectedly, because I remember being surprised to see him. Some friends of the family had come, and brought their boat, so most of the afternoon was spent taking turns out on the bay. Late in the afternoon Edward had taken the boat out with Rose and a friend of hers. I don't know how it happened, but Rose fell overboard – the first we knew of it was the sound of her friend making a commotion. Pa had been sitting with his sketchbook, and I saw him leap up and tear into the water, without even bothering to throw off his coat. He was a very powerful swimmer, I later learned. Much good it did him. We could see Edward dive in after, and some other boats in the area scudded over to help. Rose was saved, and they all came back – all but Pa. At first we couldn't believe it. Ma kept telling us he must have been taken up by some other boat, that he was safe. The next day word came that he had been washed up on the shore a few miles away. The papers –' Mrs Westmacott paused, and took out a handkerchief from her sleeve to dab her eyes. Even at a distance of seventy years the retelling of the story had the power to grieve her. 'The papers assumed there had been a scandal, and the idea that Pa had drowned himself just . . . caught on.'

Faced with her glistening eyes Baines observed a respectful silence, before curiosity got the better of him. 'Mrs Westmacott, was it not . . . strange that your father was there at all? I mean, after everything that had happened?'

Recovering a little of her natural bluff cheeriness, she swatted the question away. 'Well, he still wanted to see *us*,' she replied.

'Um, of course – but how could he bear to be in the company of Edward Urquhart? After what he did?'

She looked at him as if he were simple. 'I know you regard my father as a great architect, and that's very nice. But you have no idea of him as a man, so let me tell you. He was so – *obsessed* with his work that he didn't really have time for anything else. You've read his journals. You must have noticed how little he mentions us! And once he got started on the library we hardly ever saw him.'

'But he seems kind –'

'And so he was. He loved us, I'm sure of it, but he just wasn't *there*. Ma always said he felt a terrible guilt about it. He was shocked when my mother . . . did what she did – but he knew he was partly to blame. And that's perhaps how he found it in himself to forgive.'

275

'Really?' said Baines, doubtfully.

'Yes. He forgave Ma, and Edward. And somewhere along the way – I hope – he forgave himself.' She paused, and fixed her vivid gaze upon him. 'Can I tell you something I've learned, Mr Baines? Until you forgive yourself you cannot love anyone or do one bit of good anywhere.'

Baines bowed his head. The words sounded to him as if they might contain a kind of blessing. Glancing up at the mantelpiece he looked again at the photograph that had caught his eye before Mrs Westmacott had entered the room: it was of a young officer in uniform, a sepia relic of the Great War. Without having to be told, Baines knew that this was her son, and, just as surely, that he was dead. The war to end all wars . . . now here they were in the middle of another. Outside, the late-May afternoon was blurring towards sunset, and parallelograms of light were lengthening along the carpet. He sensed that Mrs Westmacott might be tiring.

'You've been awfully kind,' he began. 'I was just wondering – the Eamesiana?'

'That's another story, I'm afraid. We had a fire here many years ago, a great shame it was. Pa's papers went up in smoke, all of his drawings . . . Thank heavens we'd donated his journals to the Picton. I've nothing for you, Mr Baines. I'm sorry.'

She sounded as much. He knew he looked crestfallen, and tried to spur himself to a little gallantry.

'I can't be ungrateful, Mrs Westmacott, when I have his dearest legacy right before me.'

She smiled with regal graciousness at the compliment, and took it as a cue to dip into an exuberant flow of anecdotes about her father, and her family, that held him rapt for another hour. When he finally got up to leave and Mrs Fleetwood reappeared to show him out, Baines turned and thanked his hostess.

'Well – thank *you*! And I do hope you'll come again. We don't see a great many *young* people in the house, do we, Mrs Fleetwood?'

Baines carried away a strong impression that Mrs Westmacott might actually want him to return: that sort of gregariousness was difficult to feign. He walked back under the arching chestnut trees and started up the road towards the tram stop. As he neared the brow he sensed something come up behind him, and flinched. He turned to find – nothing. That was when he realised there was no longer any use in postponing what he had to do.

17

He woke with a start, disoriented for a moment by the darkened room in which he lay. Then its shadowy accoutrements began to coalesce into something more familiar, the narrow window, the melancholy flowered wallpaper, the sloping angle of his bed. It reminded him of a little hotel room he had stayed in, overlooking the esplanade of Llandudno, where he used to take holidays. But this was not there. The desultory rumble of buses and motor cars filtered into his fogged consciousness, and then he knew. He rose from the bed and pulled back the thin blackout curtain to let in the early-morning light. Through the window he could see the spires of St Pancras station poking over the adjacent chimney tops, and beyond that the drone of a vast metropolis was collected out of the air.

Baines had never much cared for London, and London, he soon realised, did not much care for him. He had arrived from Lime Street the previous week without anywhere to stay, his only tip a casual reference by Jack to the abundance of lodging houses in Islington. He emerged from beneath Euston station's vast triumphal arch and caught a bus to the Caledonian Road, where he spent an afternoon pounding the pavements in search of accommodation. It was not a delightful experience. From the top deck of the bus it reminded him a little of Smithdown Road in Liverpool, a long ascending thoroughfare lined with fish shops, cheap eating houses, furniture sellers, pawnbrokers, pubs – almost one on every corner – with frequent interludes of rubbled ground where bombs had fallen. But where the wrecked streets of his home town retained a poignant dignity, the life of Caledonian Road seemed to him drab, seedy and dispiriting, an impression only compounded when he stepped off the bus and began to apply at those houses that advertised rooms to let. He was not prepared for the London manner, which occupied a narrow range between hard-faced insolence and brute indifference, and the cawing, metallic voices that bit off words and spat them out half formed were a shock to his unaccustomed ear. He wondered how Wallace would enjoy such an accent.

After three hours of footslogging around some of the dreariest dosshouses he'd ever seen he decided to settle for the next place that offered itself. On seeing a 'Room to rent' notice in a house at the south end of the road he knocked at the door, only to be told that it had just been taken. The landlord apologised and directed him round the next corner to an address he described, with a genteel lack of irony, as 'respectable'. The house turned out to be in the middle of a tiny Victorian crescent just opposite King's Cross, so tiny, indeed, that it was not even marked on the *Bacon's Large Print Map of London and Suburbs* which he had bought at Smith's. Affixed to its front wall was a parish boundary stone, dated 1855, and the idea of being in two districts at once endeared the place to him. His fatigue gave way to relief on learning that the room he enquired about was still available. The landlady, large-framed, wall-eyed and of an uncommonly sympathetic demeanour, took to Baines almost immediately, their only awkwardness together being the moment he asked if he might have a shelf installed in the room for his books.

'Wot? You mean – *accahnt* books?' she said, apparently suspicious of the idea that her new tenant might be more astute in matters of money than she was. When Baines assured her that it was only a few novels and poetry collections he wanted to store she visibly brightened.

'Oh – *readin'* books!' she cried, as if the habit were a mild eccentricity she was happy to tolerate. It was an attic room with sloped walls around the dormer, slightly dowdy but reasonably clean. As he was unpacking she knocked at his door and presented him with a book of her own – a rent book. The landlady's name was Mrs Gorse, which Baines thought sounded about right. Once his suitcase was emptied, he took off his shoes and lay on the bed, its iron frame neighing in surprise. He lit a Player's and picked up the book he had started to read on the train down. It was a slim novel by Joseph Conrad, *The Shadow-Line*, which Liam Mavers had lent to him back in the Blitz days. He remembered him coming into the depot one night and, without preamble, handing the book over. ''Bout time you read this feller,' was what he said. After Mavers's death he had not known what to do with it, and was indeed half afraid to look at it. He wondered if that was because he could no longer return the thing to its owner; to send it back to his family without explanation felt somehow callous, and, not having yet read it, disrespectful to Liam. The nebulous air of obligation that hung about the loaned volume began to bother him, so he followed his usual instinct and hid it away.

Three years on, and more, he had found the book again, and now his principal feeling about it was not unease but curiosity. Opening it on the dedication page, he read:

To Borys and all others
Who like himself have crossed
In early youth the shadow-line
Of their generation
With love

He now recalled Liam telling him that Borys was Conrad's son, who had fought on the Western Front. His bookmark indicated that he had read two chapters. Perhaps he had not begun it at the required pitch of concentration (it had been a crowded train), or perhaps it was because he was new to Conrad, but so far – a young sailor in an Eastern port chucks in his job, then unexpectedly wins his first command of a ship – the story felt unequal to the portentous manner in which it was told. 'Chapter Three', he stared at the words, then closed the book. He had to take stock. He was in London, where he had neither friends nor a secure grasp of the geography. *Bacon's Map* unfolded teeming swirls and grids of names and streets and parks that sounded familiar yet daunted him in their sprawling multitude. He had last been here in 1934, when Jack persuaded him to make the trip down to watch Lancashire, in their Championship-winning year, play Surrey at the Oval. He had felt no particular urge to return. Now, ten years later, the purpose of his visit was altogether more quixotic. He had not the faintest idea of how to go about finding a missing person. But then Bella was not actually 'missing' at all. If Wallace was to be believed she was alive and well and residing somewhere in the city. Not missing. Only – missed.

Baines left the house as the bells of a nearby church were striking eleven o'clock. The morning air was still damp from last night's rain, and Mrs Gorse, arms folded and standing on the front step, shook her head sadly at the unseasonal cold.

'Can't 'ardly believe this is June,' she muttered with a shiver.

Sensing a need to be cheerful, Baines said, 'Perhaps I brought the weather with me, Mrs Gorse.'

She responded with an aggrieved sigh, as if there may indeed have been a link between his arrival and the dismal start to the summer. He walked on to the Caledonian Road and stopped at a little eating house around the corner. He liked the dark wooden booths, and the clatter from the kitchen which echoed indifferently off the room's tiled walls. The plate-glass windows wore a coat of condensation from the heat of the monstrous hissing tea urn at the counter. Settled into the mid-morning lull – there were only a few glumly silent customers – he drank overstewed tea and riffled through the newspaper, its headlines blaring reports of the Normandy landings. The mood of the editorials was cautiously optimistic; perhaps at last the war was beginning to turn the Allies' way. He felt in his breast pocket and removed a small notebook, into which he had copied the telephone numbers of every Garnett – Bella's maiden name – listed in the London area, on the chance that one of them might be a relative.

Finished with his tea and cigarette, he headed for King's Cross station, his pockets jingling with coins, and found a public telephone box at the side of the concourse. He then spent an hour going through the list, calling each number, drawing a blank every time. Then he remembered that Richard's parents lived in Maida Vale. If Bella had kept up with her in-laws, there might be a chance they would know of her whereabouts. He called the operator, who told him that there was a Colonel Tanqueray listed as resident in Hamilton Terrace. Baines asked her to put him through. As he listened to the peremptory repeated *brr-brr*, he wondered what he would say if the Colonel or his wife should answer. He had written them a letter of condolence three years ago in which he described, at some pain to himself, Richard's heroic conduct on the night of his death, but had received no reply. Perhaps they no longer lived there. The monotony of the unanswered rings was becoming hypnotic, and eventually he rang off.

Emerging from the station to find the sky darkly smudged with cloud he began to walk south, his mind dimly imprinted with the central slice of *Bacon's Map* he had studied the night before. He crossed Euston Road into Judd Street and thence Hunter Street, where he paid silent homage outside number 54, the house where Ruskin had been born in 1819. He turned right into Russell Square and past the two big Victorian hotels, the Russell and the Imperial, as solid and serene as a pair of old dowagers. He lost his bearings for a while in the backwaters of Bloomsbury before he joined the sluggish flow of traffic into Kingsway. Here and there he passed charred skeletons of buildings, but London had tidied up its damage much more efficiently than Liverpool; there were very few of the forlorn bomb sites you saw up there. When he reached the broad crescent of Aldwych he realised he was very near. Ever since Wallace had mentioned his encounter with Bella on the Strand Baines had been curious to go there himself, simply because *she* had been there so recently. After three years she had become, in absence, somewhat mysterious to him, and walking down this bustling thoroughfare, with its growling traffic and stolid air of business as usual, he found himself listening out for her invisible footsteps.

Having wandered without much purpose around the warren of streets north of the Strand he eventually caught a bus at Charing Cross bound for the Finchley Road. When he spotted Lord's cricket ground he stepped off and walked around its boundary wall, brooding on the irony that his first visit to the ground should coincide with the one period in its history when no cricket was being played. The streets bordering St John's Wood and Maida Vale, he noticed, were far quieter and leafier than most he had seen, and the gentility of Hamilton Terrace seemed a world away from the Caledonian Road. Here the scars of bomb damage looked almost surreal; blackened stumps that interrupted rows of imperial white stucco. Baines checked the address and, mounting the steps, rapped on the door. The sash windows on the ground floor were shuttered, while their blackish, glassy neighbours above stared down blindly. He knocked again, and something in the mere repetition of his tattoo told him there was nobody home. As he was turning away he heard a click and the creak of a door from below, and looking over the railings into the well of the basement he saw the face of an old lady peering up at him. Through the white candyfloss hair he could see her pink scalp.

'Hullo,' he called. 'Is this – the Tanqueray house?'

'Yes. But they're not here – the place has been empty –' She had come halfway up the steps, and paused. 'Are you a friend?' The voice was tremulously grand.

'Er, I was a friend of their son.'

'Oh, Richard. So sad . . . such a nice young man. It wasn't long after that the Colonel died too. Mabel went orf to the country a few months ago.'

'Do you have an address for her?'

'No, I'm sorry. You're the second person to ask me that lately – a young lady called here a few weeks ago, brought some flowers.' *Flarʒe*, she pronounced the word. 'She said they were for Mabel, to mark an anniversary. Well, I told her that she'd gorn, so she gave them to me instead.' She permitted herself a whinnying little laugh at the memory. Baines's mind was racing, calculating: a few weeks ago would have been Richard's anniversary, 7 May.

'Did this lady – was she tall, with dark hair?' he asked her.

'That's her! She seemed awfully upset that Mabel had left without her knowing.'

'Did *she* leave you her address?'

'Oh, no. We talked for a minute or two and . . . then she was orf.'

So Bella had been here, too. He sensed that he was getting closer, that the distance she had put between them was slowly shrinking. He was going to find her, whether she liked it or not. The old lady was still watching him. There was a faint loneliness in her gaze, and as they dallied over talk of the weather he wondered if the occasional word with a stranger might be the centrepiece of her day. After a few minutes they ran out of things to say; as he tweaked the brim of his hat in parting he felt rather sorry that he hadn't also had flowers to give her.

The following day brought rain, so he kept to his room and read *The Shadow-Line*. From being slightly bored with it he now found himself mysteriously enthralled. The narrator, still in the early days of his command, discovers that the first mate is morbidly obsessed with the previous captain, an unregenerate villain who filched the ship's store of quinine before he died. This act of treachery rebounds on his successor when, caught in a dead calm, the crew is laid low with fever. 'I have been decoyed into this awful, this death-haunted command,' writes the young captain, stricken with pity for his ailing men and almost despairing of their situation. Yet he finds hope in the steadying presence of Ransome, the ship's cook, whose grace and resolute character are the more admirable for his own personal vulnerability – a weak heart. As the crisis mounts their courage is tested ever more severely; the captain hardly knows how he will get them back to port. But it was Ransome, with his 'faint, wistful smile and friendly grey eyes' who preoccupied Baines, and brought unbidden to his memory the face of Liam Mavers. He had never known anyone so brave, and yet so unassuming in his bravery, and he realised that without his example he would not, could not, have endured the horrors of heavy rescue. He could not think about Liam very often, otherwise he would not be able to stop himself. He had not seen Mike Wo or Farrell since the May Blitz, but their faces, their voices, had never deserted him. Did they think of Liam? He felt sure that they did – we carry the dead with us.

He had set forth on another of his aimless perambulations one morning when he passed a newsboy on Euston Road excitedly crowing a headline. Bombs had fallen in London, but according to the paper they had not been dropped by a plane. He recalled something Wallace had said about a 'robot' missile which could fly over long distances. Could it really be launched from the other side of the Channel with any accuracy? The next few days proved that it could. By the middle weekend of June the suburbs of south London and Kent were under sustained attack, and casualties were mounting. (In his head Baines always doubled the number reported in the press.) On Sunday morning he was in Mrs Gorse's kitchen when he heard a low, growling noise that made the window hum in its frame; it sounded like a steam train dragging up a hill. He opened the door and went into the back garden, in time to see what looked like a burning enemy aircraft disappear across the sky with flames spitting from its tail. It must have been winged when it broke through the air-raid defences. He went back inside and finished off his breakfast.

He was reading the paper an hour later when Mrs Gorse burst through the door in a state of exhilarated outrage. Her meaty arms wobbled as she thumped her basket down on the table and stared at Baines, who tried to hold her divergent gaze. It was disconcerting not to know which of her eyes he was supposed to catch.

'Oh those *bleeders*! Only gone and dropped a bomb on the Essex Road.'

'You saw it?'

'Nah, but I 'eard it. I went down there to look. Awful it was, you could smell it a mile off. Bodies layin' on the street. Gawd knows 'ow many dead!'

'I saw something about an hour ago – I thought it was . . . a plane on fire.'

'Nah. Policeman says to me it was one of them new robot things. I says 'ow can they drop a bomb when there's no plane? 'E says, they're sendin' 'em from France an' they don't need no pilots or nuffink.' Mrs Gorse shook her head in a mime of scandalised disbelief. Baines felt for her, having heard the story of the raid that killed her husband, a fireman, three years before. Aside from a short spell in February London had been free of attacks since the May Blitz of '41. Now it seemed they would have to get used to them all over again. Those bleeders.

The next morning he went to his usual telephone box in King's Cross station in order to call May, who he knew would be worried by what was happening. The concourse was heaving with people, many of them trailing suitcases and an air of orderly agitation. In the distance floated the vacant sound of slammed doors and the shriek of whistles. While he waited for the telephone he watched the crowds milling about; exhausted-looking mothers half dragged their children towards the platforms, porters were scurrying about in a sweat and one queue at the ticket office had become distinctly rowdy. He thought back to the first week of the war and the evacuation of children at Lime Street. This time the mood was different: by now people had seen what bombs could do. Ironic, he thought, that he was getting settled into the place just as everyone else seemed to be abandoning it. He had got inside the telephone box when an argument he had half noticed at a ticket booth broke into shoving, and then into a fight; the glass blocked out most of the sound, and when a policeman waded into the melee it felt like he was watching a silent film. Jack picked up on the third ring.

'Hullo, stranger. Where are you?' He sounded pleased to hear from him.

'Still in London. King's Cross station. Right now I've got a ringside seat at a fight going on at the ticket office. There's a big panic here to get out of town.'

'I'm not surprised. I presume you'll be going with them.'

'Not yet,' he said. 'I still haven't found her ...'

He heard Jack sigh down the line. 'Oh, Thomas. What's the – have you ever considered that she might not want to be found?'

He had. A silence fell between them. Jack had pulled a sceptical face when Baines had first told him of his plan, but he hadn't tried to dissuade him; they knew one another too well for that. Jack cleared his throat in a businesslike way.

'Have you tried the Slade? The in-laws?'

'I've tried everywhere I can think of.'

'Then I see no point in your staying. These rockets – once the Hun find their range – '

'I saw one yesterday – passed right over the house. My landlady told me it fell about a mile away, so I went up there to have a look. Must have been quite a size, the blast area looked enormous.'

Jack snorted in exasperation. 'And you're staying put ...'

Baines paused. Hearing Jack's voice was making him homesick. 'I've got to find her. I can't get on with my life until I do.'

'But you might not –' Jack checked himself, unwilling to voice what he knew they were both thinking. Baines decided to muffle the moment with vagueness.

'I know, I'm tempting fate. Just do me a favour. Tell May I've tried to call her but couldn't get through. Tell her I'm fine –'

' – and that you'll be back home soon.'

Jack was never going to plead. They said their goodbyes, and he rang off. He stepped out of the telephone box to find the police re-establishing control of the scene, though there was little they could do about the creeping atmosphere of anxiety. It was as if the city were being visited by a plague whose touch fell on people – young or old, rich or poor, innocent or guilty – with terrifying haphazardness, a plague borne on the back of huge steel-winged locusts. This wasn't like the Blitz, that night-flurry of attack and counter-attack whose periods were marked by the sirens whining the all-clear. Back then the ack-ack guns and the roving fingers of searchlights at least furnished the illusion of a defensive front. This time there was no enemy up there to fight, they simply flew unannounced out of the clouds then nosedived towards earth. The sound of the rockets – 'doodlebugs' as they were being called – seemed to have been devised by a fiend. It was a low, vicious metal drone that would suddenly stop, and in the ten, twelve seconds of silence you would get out of the window's eyeline, hit the floor and hope the annihilating payload would pass you. The taut, apprehensive faces Baines passed in the street seemed to have found a middle ground between acceptance and helplessness.

Yet farce had not entirely exited the scene. Baines had gone for tea one afternoon at the Russell Hotel. The lounge where he sat reading had entered a slow mid-afternoon torpor, stirred only by the discreet clink of spoon on china. A waiter was clearing a table at the bay window that fronted the square when, from a distance, a steady buzzing drone gathered, approached – and stopped. The waiter, discarding his loaded tray with a hysterical clatter, had dived for the floor, and when the shout of 'Bomb!' went up the rest of the lounge's occupants followed suit, Baines included. He had time to brace himself, waiting in the awful pregnant silence, as he counted to ten, to twenty, to thirty . . . A full minute went by before he heard voices outside the lounge carrying on as normal. Then he saw the waiter – the canary in the coal mine – stand up and peer out of the window. The head barman was furiously upbraiding another of his staff, and people had started picking themselves up, quite cautiously, from the carpet. He heard a man's voice, half laughing, say, 'A motorbike – a bloody motorbike!'

An hour or more later he was wandering past the British Museum when sudden fat raindrops began to spot the pavement. In a side street of antiquarian bookshops and tiny galleries he saw the protective hood of a shop's awning, and hurried to take cover from the downpour. He stood there for some minutes watching the rain thrash the cobbles, filling the gutters so quickly that when a motor car swooshed by it sprayed the pavement and caused a woman passing too close to the kerb to shriek. For a while he browsed the outdoor tray of weather-warped paperbacks that seemed almost to beg to be taken away. Directly across the street a photographers' gallery had its lights blazing against the pewter-grey afternoon; he gazed idly at the prints spotlit in the window, monochrome society portraits, school of Beaton, mixed in with more gritty and realistic studies of urban life, school of Brandt. His eyes roved among them but kept returning to a smaller photograph in the window's bottom right-hand corner. It started out as no more than a shape, its detail blurred through the curtain of rain in front of him. There was something about it – the light, the composition – that nagged at him, like the lone fragment of a dream that just survives into consciousness before dissolving. It was still pelting down but curiosity made him hang on to his hat and dash through the puddles to the other side. The rain had formed long rivulets that streamed and broke at different angles over the window, and though it wasn't an ideal setting in which to examine it he now knew the photograph for certain.

He entered the gallery, setting off the tinkling bell over the door, and shook a few glistening raindrops from his sleeves. A young woman, invisible from the street, stood up to greet him; from the unpeopled stillness and her ingratiating smile Baines sensed it had been a quiet trading day. The photograph, plainly mounted in a slender beech frame, was removed from the window and propped on a dimpled leather sofa. The assistant took a few appraising steps back, as if she were belatedly revising its worth. The picture, taken at street level, was of a boy, perhaps six or seven years old, with a plump lower lip and a solemn level gaze that seemed to acknowledge the lowly background against which he stood – a dilapidated terrace, a charwoman on a step looking away from the camera, a dog trotting over the cobbles. Baines remembered just then that the child had worn no shoes.

'The photographer,' he heard himself say, 'it's Bella Tanqueray, isn't it?'

'That's right,' she said brightly. 'You know her work?'

'Yes. I was there when she took that photograph. Pitt Street, Liverpool – 1st September 1939.'

The woman looked at him, astonished. She walked back to the photograph and picked it up to examine an inscription on the reverse. 'You're quite right. *1st September 1939* is its title.' She handed it to Baines, who held it stiff-armed in front of him for a few moments. He was thinking of that day, the day they met, the wide-legged trousers she wore, the long talk they had at the Kardomah, the first time he heard her laugh. That

Germany had invaded Poland that morning seemed, in his fugue-like perspective, a mere footnote.

'We hope to do a show of her Liverpool photographs soon,' the woman was saying. 'Perhaps we could let you know ...'

Baines nodded absently. He still had the picture of the boy in his hands.

'You'll take a cheque for this?' he said to her. It was priced at four guineas. She really was making her way in the world. While the assistant trussed up the photograph with brown paper and string she chattered gaily on about Bella, whom she had got to know a little over the last couple of years – a real find for the gallery, and *such* a nice lady. As he signed the cheque he said, without looking up, 'Would you just remind me where she's living at the moment?'

The following morning, a Saturday, the sky was clear, and showed even a watery, apologetic sunlight. Baines had put on the one suit he had packed, and was now regretting it; he had wanted to look prepared, but the plain blue worsted made him feel like a solicitor, or a tax inspector. And what, in any case, was he prepared *for*? In his anxiety he missed the turning he should have taken off 'the Cally' (Mrs Gorse's diminutive) and overshot his route into Holloway Road. He turned right and began walking back south, taking out for the seventh or eighth time the compliment slip on which the gallery assistant had written down the address. Bella's address, there in his hand. When he had looked for it on his map the night before he was surprised to see how close it was, not much more than a mile between them. At any time in the last three weeks they might have passed one another in the street. He tried to imagine the look of astonishment that would have seized her. He was nearing the junction of Highbury Corner, and the sickness at the pit of his stomach seemed to have burrowed deeper. Trams were rumbling past him, clanging their bells. He saw a Boots chemist on the corner. Would a bottle of smelling salts be a good idea?

For a while he loitered among the crowds streaming out of Highbury station, its high dramatic blaze of finials and gables and turrets outlined sharply against the bluish-white sky. Now that he was here, dawdling near the street where she lived, he felt almost paralysed with indecision. Three years of wondering had led to this. He glanced at the faces of passing strangers, oblivious to his flutter of nerves, as strangers generally were. A news-stand board sombrely blazoned the headline MORE DEAD IN FLYING BOMB ATTACKS. He lit a Player's and dragged deeply on it, then began walking. Compton Terrace was a row of tall Regency houses that ran parallel to Upper Street, divided from it by a narrow strip of public garden and hedged around with railings. It had the air of a genteel neighbourhood that had fallen on difficult times. The brickwork looked carious, and weeds sprouted between the pavement flags. A clock stuck out its face like a nosy neighbour from the tower of the chapel halfway down. Number 33 had shallow steps rising to a pedimented front door. He tapped the dull brass door knocker against its plate and waited, like someone about to jump into a freezing pool. It was impossible, he thought, to knock uninvited at a door and not make it sound like an order. In the cloudy window before him a pair of net curtains hung, untwitched.

There was nobody answering. Just then, from the near end of the terrace a woman was approaching, with a young child stomping along at her side. Baines waited on the step while she drew nearer; she was tall, long-striding, and for a moment or two he thought it was Bella, much changed. He realised he was mistaken, yet in the same instant her face seemed oddly familiar to him, its chiselled contours, the bone structure. The eyes. He had come down from the top step, where his presence seemed to demand an explanation, for the woman had come to a halt. She looked at him uncertainly. Baines removed his hat and turned it nervously in his hands.

'Hullo, I wonder if –' He swallowed, and gestured at the door behind him. 'Does Bella Tanqueray live here?'

Her face relaxed, and she said, 'Yes, she does. You are – ?'

'Tom – Tom Baines. I'm a friend from – when she was in Liverpool.'

'Tom,' she repeated, blankly, and nodded. 'Hmm, I – I think she's mentioned you.' The vagueness of this cut him deeply, but he betrayed nothing in his expression. The woman had extended her hand.

'I'm Nancy. Bella's sister. We live together – with this little sprite! Say hullo, George.' She turned and ruffled the boy's dark hair. He giggled and promptly hid behind her skirt. Baines, trying to catch the boy's eye, raised his hand in silent salute. He now felt desperately awkward in the suit.

Nancy swept the child into her arms, and said, 'Would you like to come in and wait? Bella's been running errands this morning.'

This would be a surprise for her to come home to. 'Thank you. If it's not too much trouble . . .'

Baines followed a short way behind Nancy and the boy, who had wriggled out of her arms and was taking the stairs on his own, heaving himself up like a mini mountaineer. Their flat occupied the middle two floors of the building. In the living room long sash windows looked down on the tree-lined garden, through which the continuous honk of traffic could be heard. A large gilt-framed mirror over the fireplace turned its steady gaze on him, and sensing his intrusion he ducked out of its range. On the opposite wall he recognised, like an old friend, the Nicholson portrait of Bella. Nancy had gone into the kitchen to make tea, while George was busying himself in the far corner with paper and a quiver of coloured crayons. Occasionally he would turn and fix Baines with a frank interrogative stare.

Presently Nancy came into the room bearing a tea tray, and as she set it down said, 'So, you're just on a visit here?'

'Yes,' he replied, 'I – um, came to see a friend.'

With a sharp little glance at him she said, 'You picked a fine time to do it.'

Baines gave a kind of grimacing smile in acknowledgement of his implied stupidity. As she poured the tea he studied her; she was beautiful, too, but in a more severe way than her sister. There was a trace of flinty shrewdness around her eyes, and in her tone just now he had heard a slight acidity, the sort of tone that didn't suffer fools gladly. She had a brisk, practical air about her, acquired perhaps in the raising of a child by herself. She wore no wedding ring.

'Have you thought about – leaving London?' he asked, with a nod to the boy.

'Now and then,' she admitted. 'We've talked about it. But I'd find it difficult, with the job . . .'

'Your job?'

'Yes. I'm a doctor,' she said flatly, as though it were something she assumed he would know. 'I really thought we'd seen the last of the bombs, but . . .' She shook her head, and looked rather weary.

'I was at King's Cross the other morning,' he said. 'It's getting to be quite an exodus. You're brave to stay.'

She shrugged, not caring for the compliment, then frowned. 'So how do you know Bella? Are you one of her party friends?'

Baines wasn't sure what that meant. 'Er, I don't think so. I met her through Richard, when we worked together – he took the photographs for a book I was trying to write. They both did.'

'Ah, so that's how,' she said, returning a look of candid interest. 'You know those photographs are with a gallery in Bloomsbury now?'

'I do indeed. I bought one yesterday.'

Her face broke into a smile, and she gave a little clap of surprise. 'You did? Oh – she will be so *thrilled*.' Baines had a very strong intuition that 'thrilled' would not be Bella's immediate response. George, hearing her clap, had tottered over to offer the piece of paper on which he had scrawled a sequence of incomprehensible lines. Nancy examined it reverently.

'Darling, how lovely,' she said, turning the picture around, as if in an effort to make her estimation of it true. She added, archly, 'I think you may have your mummy's artistic nature.'

Baines took a moment to construe this remark. 'Sorry – did you say – are you not his mother?'

Nancy chuckled modestly at the idea. 'No, no. He's Bella's son. Can't you tell?'

He could not. He had not suspected it for a moment. And now, suddenly, his mind went plunging through furious calculations, starting from the likely age of the boy to the probable period of conception to the dawning possibility – He heard the slam of a door from somewhere below, and Nancy cocked her head in a casual reflex.

'That's her now, I think,' she said. The moment could not have been more exquisitely timed to unseat Baines's already faltering confidence. He should have left a note and waited for her to contact him. Or not, as she preferred. An occasion he had thought himself ready for was rapidly transforming itself into an ordeal. On hearing the key scratching in the lock, George abruptly hurried out into the hall. Baines heard the door swing open, and a voice greeted the boy. 'Hullo, you little terror!' Bella's voice, unaware of the ghost that awaited her in the next room. A merry smacking kiss was followed by some muffled words between mother and son. Nancy, listening too, flashed a quick complicitous smile at Baines. Bella was in mid-sentence, with George at her heels, as she walked into the living room and saw him standing there. She stopped, absolutely still, and he watched the colour drain from her face. Her eyes flicked in panic at Nancy, as if for a moment she suspected a horrible practical joke at work.

'Tom . . . what – what are you doing here?'

Baines, dazed by the moment, heard himself say, 'You have to ask?'

They stood staring at one another, about fifteen feet apart, like duellists, with Nancy an unwitting second in the middle. Even under its present mask of shock Bella's face seemed, if anything, more striking than he had remembered it; faint shadows beneath her eyes gave their lustre a poignancy, and the cheekbones stood out lean and sad. There was greying at her temples. The war had aged her, he thought; it had aged everyone. Nancy had perhaps begun to sense that this was no joyful reunion, and jumped into the silence between them.

'Tom's just bought one of your photographs, Bel,' she said brightly.

Bella, still frozen to the spot, didn't seem to hear her. She looked almost hypnotised with fright.

'I didn't know you'd had a son,' said Baines. This seemed to jolt her out of her trance. She bent down to pick up the boy, and held him protectively against the curve of her hip. Then her eyes were back on his, and as he looked at mother and child he knew – knew it more certainly than things which he had made a serious effort to know. He swallowed and said,

'Is he – is George . . . ?'

He had to hear her say it. Her mouth quivered, and her head dropped. Then, softly but clearly, she said, 'Richard – couldn't.'

He felt the room begin to close on him; there seemed less air to breathe. 'Oh God, God . . . Bella, what've you –' He sensed the chair behind him, and fell back into it. He thought he was going to be sick. 'What have you done?' He kept repeating these words, he couldn't help himself. He heard Nancy say to Bella with schoolmarmish impatience, 'Will you *please* tell me what's going on?'

George, alert to the sudden drop in the social temperature, had launched into an impromptu aria of dismay. Baines could hear Nancy and Bella talking in short, fierce half-whispers to one another, an exchange brought to a close when Bella hissed, 'Just *do it* – please,' and then he heard Nancy shepherding George out of the room. The door closed, but the recent heated words still charged the air. After some minutes Baines looked up. Bella was sitting on the sofa opposite, silent, her eyes glassy with tears. He didn't know where to begin.

'How old is he?'

Her voice sounded gluey in her throat. 'He'll be three, in November.'

He nodded slowly. 'Would you – were you ever going to tell me?'

'I wanted to. So many times – I – I wrote you letters. And couldn't send them.'

A thought jolted him. 'Did you think I was dead?'

She shook her head. 'I saw you in hospital – twice. You were still . . . not awake. The doctor I spoke to told me you were going to come through.'

'How nice of you to visit. Did you bring flowers?'

Bella bowed her head. 'I know you're angry –'

'Too right I'm angry. Where did you go? *Why* did you go?'

He had stood and taken a few steps towards her, and she flinched as if expecting him to strike her.

'I came down to London – Richard's parents wanted him buried here. A few days after the funeral I discovered I was . . .'

'Pregnant,' he supplied, baldly. 'And it just slipped your mind to tell me.'

She paused, resigning herself to his sarcasm, and said quietly, 'I wanted to tell you. More than anything. But I just couldn't go back to Liverpool, knowing what I'd done to Richard, and carrying your child. Can you try to understand that? The guilt I was – it felt as if I were being buried alive under it. And I thought that if I wrote to you –'

'– you knew I'd come and find you.' He could not keep the sneer out of his voice.

'I was always afraid that you would. And, I suppose, I . . . always hoped that you would. The whole time I was pregnant I longed for you to be there, I kept thinking – if only I could talk to him now. I imagined the look on your face when you saw it was a boy – our boy.'

This was too much. If she had put up a fight, met his hostility with some righteous fire of her own, he could have taken a miserable pleasure in grinding her down. But her quiet, cowed tone, and now this, a confession of maternal tenderness, were much harder to bear than an attempt to defend herself.

He felt winded by the sudden self-realisation: he was a father, and this was the mother of his child. That boy in the next room . . . a miracle! Yet still he sensed the venom stirring within his blood, provoking him, and he heard himself say, 'If you could know the kind of pain you caused me – if you could feel what it was like – I wonder how you'd manage to live with yourself.'

He watched Bella's face for a moment, and felt an appalled satisfaction as she trembled at his words. Then he scooped up his hat and said, 'I'll let myself out.'

He was through the door and hurrying down the stairs. This blasted limp . . . He hit the pavement and was moving as quickly as he could down Compton Terrace, oblivious to the traffic's roar as he dodged across Highbury Corner, the blood ringing in his ears. He was just going to keep walking, it didn't matter where. He wasn't even going to think about it. There was another long terrace abutted by a promenade lined with trees, and he had started along it when he heard Bella's voice calling him. He didn't turn round. After a few moments he heard her footsteps hurrying to catch up.

'Tom,' she called again, 'please stop.'

He kept walking. A couple passed by, their eyes first on him, and then over his shoulder at the person in his wake. Emerging from the bower of trees he now approached a sloping green, where people were enjoying a rare glimpse of June sunshine. She was now almost behind him.

'Tom,' her voice came, slightly out of breath. 'Please. If you ever loved me . . .'

That stopped him. 'What do you want?' he said, tonelessly.

'Please don't leave like this.' Her face was lit by an anguished radiance. He had never seen anyone look so beautiful and so pitiful at the same time. He wanted to say something vicious again, but he knew he had shot that bolt. Bella had looked winded by the cruelty of his words, and now he could no longer tell if he was angry or remorseful. Was it forgiveness that he sought, or the power to forgive? He thought of what Mrs Westmacott had told him about Eames – his magnanimity towards his betrayer. In the end you *had* to forgive.

'We did an awful thing to him, Bella.'

'I know,' she said, touching his sleeve.

'I was there. I watched him die.' His eyes tried to blink them back, then hot tears were running down his cheeks. She led him over to a wooden bench, its corporation-green paint flaking along the slats. They sat, and held each other for a long time without speaking. When he looked up she was gazing at him.

'Tom. I'm so sorry.'

Baines only nodded. His throat ached too much to talk. He felt her hand on his cheek, and thought of all the days and nights he had yearned for that touch. At times he had persuaded himself he hated her, and had rehearsed in his mind the brutal execrations he would heap on her for what she had done. But now here she was, holding his hand, and what he felt more than anything was a simple gratitude that she was alive. Alive, when others he loved, or might have loved – his mother and father, Alice, Liam, Richard – were not.

He felt her squeeze his hand suddenly. 'Tom, will you stay here, just for five minutes? Please?' Her face was close to his, beseeching. He shrugged, and said that he would, but having stood up she seemed afraid to leave him.

'You won't just – walk off?'

He looked at her, touched by her uncertainty. 'I'm not going anywhere.'

He watched her receding figure, an urgency in her long stride. That loping athletic walk he had admired the first time they met. As he sat on the bench, Saturday cyclists and promenaders passing in front of him, he considered the years that had separated them, the brooding, the useless waiting. Why had he waited for so long? Did he really believe he could forget? He was still lost in this reverie when he heard a child's shout from along the way. It was George, trying to grab at a pigeon; just as he bent down and reached out, the bird would strut ahead with a hurried little flutter of alarm. A short distance behind walked Bella and Nancy, amused by the boy's doggedness. He turned and waved at George, who seemed to be wondering where he had seen the man on the bench before. He halted on his stubby little legs and waited, until Baines waved again and called his name. Then with a wary expression he approached, walked right up to him and stared, with a child's artless candour. His eyes were a greenish-blue, with long, almost girlish lashes: his mother's eyes. He was still staring, transfixed by something on the stranger's face, and then Baines realised what it was. He took the boy's hand – as light and smooth as a plum – and gently helped his finger to trace the line of the scar beneath his eye. The boy's mouth, slightly ajar, broke into a gummy smile.

He smiled back. 'Georgie,' he said.

Before they parted later that afternoon, Bella had explained that she was going with Nancy and George to stay with old friends near Oxford for the weekend. It was a long-standing arrangement. They would get the train from Paddington that evening and return on the Monday. He was secretly distressed by this news, but then reassured when Bella insisted on his coming to lunch at Compton Terrace on the Tuesday – they would spend the day together. She gave him their telephone number (unlisted, it transpired) and told him to call on the morning, just to make sure that they had got back safely. On returning to his lodgings from Highbury Baines passed Mrs Gorse on the stairs and realised he was whistling.

'You're in a merry mood,' she observed.

'It's just being here with you, Mrs Gorse,' he said pertly, and drew an astonished shriek of laughter in response.

In the meantime he started on the final stretch of *The Shadow-Line*, convinced that Ransome, the only other man to have escaped the ship's fever, was about to be mortally felled by his weak ticker. For the captain-narrator the ultimate crisis comes when a blinding darkness envelops the unhelmed ship, and only a few stars glimmer against the sky. 'It was something I had never seen before, giving no hint of the direction from which any change would come, the closing in of a menace from all sides.' His crew by this stage have been reduced to shadows, 'ghosts of themselves', yet he urges them on to raise the mainsail, taking the lead himself. After an agonising wait – eighteen days of stillness – the breeze suddenly picks up, and the ship makes it to port, flying the signal for medical assistance. The captain had somehow crossed the 'shadow-line' from innocence to experience – or was it from arrogance to humility? – and lived to tell the tale. And Ransome, the 'priceless man', had survived! Turning back to the title page Baines noticed, beneath the title, Conrad's salute to the men of his ship's company – 'Worthy of my undying regard.'

He waited with impatient high spirits for Tuesday morning to come round. At ten o'clock he had hurried over to the King's Cross telephone box, oppressed by a dread that Bella might have changed her mind and bolted once more, never to return. He was still tormenting himself with this when her voice came on the line, and he smiled just to hear it. Yes, she and George had got back late last night – Nancy was staying on in Oxford for a few days.

'Come here about one,' she said. 'I've bought some lunch – and a bottle of champagne. We can have it in the garden if it stays fine.' Her attention was momentarily diverted, and he heard her talking to George.

'His nibs is very curious about you,' she explained. 'I'm going to hand you over.' He heard the muffled clatter of the receiver, and then a silent presence at the end of the line.

'. . .'

He said a few coaxing words to the boy, who had yet to grasp the two-way nature of the instrument. Bella came briskly back on.

'Sorry about that! But he does look adorable with the telephone pressed to his ear. We'll see you in a little while.'

The platforms at King's Cross were still a termitary of luggage-laden evacuees, pale-faced, a blindfold look in their eyes. Yet he barely registered the crowds as he nudged through the concourse and out to York Way. He was still humming the lines of a ditty he had overheard Mrs Gorse singing that morning:

> *I'm just about the proudest man that walks*
> *I've got a little nipper, when 'e talks*
> *I'll lay yer forty shiners to a quid*
> *You'll take 'im for the father, me the kid!*

He was too restless to go back to his room and wait, so he continued walking north and distractedly roamed the neighbourhoods of Kentish Town and Upper Holloway before swinging round and heading east towards Highbury. How different his mood from Saturday! A humid morning and his aimless footslog had left him rather dry-mouthed, and with another half-hour to kill before he could present himself at Bella's he looked around for a cafe. As he approached Highbury Corner he thought he might prefer a beer, and turning he saw the Old Cock Tavern, a giant Gothic companion to the station next door. A dray had just arrived and men were unloading barrels through a cellar-drop. Drinkers were standing at the pub's open doors. He passed a woman selling flowers from a stall. Inside the cavernous gloom of the back bar he shouldered his way through knots of office workers taking an early lunch break and ordered a beer. He took three swift gulps of it, and felt relieved. He picked up a newspaper left on the bar and retired to a corner table, idly eavesdropping on racing talk between two old boys, wearing matching caps. They were jawing on about a veteran jockey of their acquaintance.

'I 'eard 'e ain't been 'isself since that fall at Kempton,' one of them said.

'Yeah,' agreed the other dismally, 'and nor's the bleedin' 'orse.'

Baines kept checking his watch, willing the minutes away till one o'clock. He had just lit a Player's when the pub went quiet; it was like the moment at a dinner when a polite hush fell and someone rose to make a speech. Then he picked up the noise himself: it was a heavy whirring drone, like an engine running down, the same one he had heard in Mrs Gorse's kitchen. It could almost have been a plane flying too low. He felt it passing over them, the shudder of it, and seconds later it cut out. The whole room seemed to be holding its breath – but nothing happened. Baines caught the eye of one of the racing boys, who said, 'Phoo-hoo – missed us! . . . close one, though.'

Voices tentatively stirred around them. From the other side of the bar he heard someone laugh. He was thinking about the flower seller he had passed outside – what were Bella's favourites? – when an ear-splitting detonation shook the walls. They were still vibrating when a tidal wave of soot thundered out of the fireplace and turned day into night (he later realised it was the chimney coming down). Then a huge blast wave sucked the windows out in a sudden whoosh, the net curtains waving the glass goodbye, and the floor seemed to buck beneath his feet. The second rush of air as the vacuum was filled hurled him to the floor.

He could barely see in front of him, but he heard people coughing, choking inside the maelstrom of smoke and soot. Once he had crawled spluttering out of the door on his hands and knees he realised how lucky he had been to choose the back bar. The side fronting the street had taken the main brunt of it. Already he could hear screaming. Through the blinding pall of smoke he began to take in the effects of the blast, people wandering around dazed, some with their clothes half torn off and their faces scorched and bleeding. The men he had seen unloading the dray were lying dead, so too the flower woman, so too the policeman who had been on point duty at the crossroads. Other bodies lay pooled in blood, twitching out their last seconds of life. He walked through the moaning carnage as if in a dream, brushing past blackened shadows too stunned or too damaged to speak. He kept repeating in his head, for no reason he could fathom, *You'll take 'im for the father, me the kid!*

At first he thought his ears were ringing from the noise of the bomb; then he realised that it was an actual ringing, the sound of an alarm set off inside the bank just opposite. A car had been tossed on its side and smoke was pouring out of its engine. The alarm was still calling him forward. The railings that curved around Upper Street had been flattened as if by a tornado, and now, as he walked towards them, a horrific suspicion began to take hold. The missile had exploded not on the pavement of Highbury Corner but in the public garden on Compton Terrace. Which was now swarming with fire. Windows were bursting on to the street. He felt a hollow acceleration gather in his legs, and when the massive acrid clouds of smoke began to pour from the house he didn't stop, even though his eyes smarted and his throat gagged. He didn't stop.

PART FOUR

Ending
1947

18

Now he could hear the *tap-tap* of work starting up across the road. He had woken hours before in dull agitation, listening to the dawn chorus while grey light began to leak through the curtains. The sound of the builders meant it had just gone eight. (He hadn't needed an alarm clock for years.) They had moved on to the next stage in the construction of the Anglican Cathedral, a project begun in 1904. Forty-three years. That was slow going even by Liverpool standards. He was so used to the noise that most of the time he didn't actually notice it. But he would have welcomed a few hours of peace on a day like this. He rose from his bed and looked out at the half-completed church, the sight line criss-crossed with the long angled necks of cranes. Well, he could hardly rebuke them for the time they were taking, he who had spent his life on the shrinking margins of procrastination and delay. It was never likely that he was going to seize the moment, but somehow the moment had come along and seized him. Was it achievement he felt, or merely relief that a period of self-imposed servitude had come to an end? He couldn't tell.

He was sitting at the kitchen table in his vest, braces dangling limply over his trousers like a pair of black eels, when he heard a knock at the door. He knew that no one else would be in at this time of the morning, so he ambled down to answer the summons. On the step waited a woman whom he didn't immediately recognise.

'Tom?' she said, blushing. 'God, I'm sorry – you're not even dressed.'

She looked so exquisitely groomed – it was the forces-favourite style of Rita Hayworth – that he was still confounded by her familiar yet unlocatable face. Then the penny dropped: it was Joanna. He pulled the cigarette out of his mouth and smiled, amused by her embarrassment.

'Hullo! – pardon my, er, déshabillé.'

'I'll come back later –' she said, beginning to back away.

'No, please, come in,' he said, eagerly. 'I've just brewed a pot of tea. I'll put a shirt on, too, to make it formal.'

She looked uncertain for a moment, then shyly edged her way in. She was holding a carrier bag from Bon Marché, where she still worked as a buyer. They had met again by chance last year, one afternoon in Church Street, and since then had seen one another a few times, just for a drink. It was nothing serious. He led her through to the living room, then went to fetch her a cup of tea. He had put on a shirt by the time he returned, sensing that this might put her at her ease. She sat rather primly in her smart charcoal suit, knees together, as if she had been called in for an interview. As he buttoned up a shirt cuff he said, 'I hope you're still coming to this thing at lunchtime . . .'

She nodded with a head prefect sort of brightness. 'Oh, definitely! I was just on me way to work, though, and stopped by to – wish you luck.' He realised with a start that the Hayworth hair, the make-up, had perhaps been finessed not for work but for this afternoon's event.

'You make it sound like I'm getting married,' he said with a laugh in his voice.

'– and I wanted to give you this,' she added, abruptly covering another blush. She had taken out of the carrier a thin flat cardboard box, inscribed with a London–Paris–New York marque he vaguely recognised. He unloosed the ribbon, and took off the lid. Bedded inside snowy folds of tissue paper was a tie of slubbed silk, claret-coloured with a patterning of tiny silver fleur-de-lys. He stared at it for a moment, secretly wary of its fanciness, but openly touched by the unexpected gift of it.

'This is – lovely!' he said, beaming.

She looked at him anxiously. 'D'you like it? They'd just arrived at the shop . . . I can always take it back.'

'I don't want you to take it back.' He walked over and bent down to plant a dry kiss on her powdered cheek. As he did he glanced at the side table stacked with uniform copies of a book, their spines in serried repetition. Compliments of the publisher. He went over and picked one off the top, its pristine dust jacket in the familiar cream-and-sage livery of the series. The title was set in sober Roman type.

The Plover Guide to the Historic Buildings of England
LIVERPOOL
by Thomas Baines

It looked rather well, he supposed. The austerity paper on which it was printed couldn't be helped, but it had a nice weight in the hand and the accompanying photographs had a clean, professional crispness. It was almost incredible to him that it was finished, though the irony that parts of it were already out of date had not escaped him. Certain buildings he had documented in its pages had been recently pulled down. More would follow. Nothing lasted for long. He turned back to Joanna and handed her the book.

'I don't expect you to read this,' he said with a rueful smirk, 'but I'd like you to have one.'

He watched her as she smoothed down the title page of the book and made a very creditable effort to look enchanted by it. His thoughts turned to the day they had met, the guarded look she had given him as they stood in the lobby of the Imperial. No wonder she had been suspicious. He had not expected to see her again, but now here they were, exchanging presents like a couple of proper friends. Joanna had known heartache as well. She had waited for her man all through the war, and her prayers were answered when he returned from the fighting in Burma unharmed. But not unattached: he had met someone else during his service years, and later married her. Baines wondered if that was why she seemed much less sure of herself than he had remembered; something tentative in her manner. He liked that about her.

She looked up from the book with an enquiring frown. 'This line here under the title, "Worthy of my undying regard" – who's that for?'

'Oh, I stole that from a novel I read a few years ago. The author was a former seaman, and he wrote that in tribute to his ship's company.' He realised that this had not answered her question, but she didn't press him.

'I've never known anyone who's written a book before,' she said, wonderingly. 'Thank you.' She glanced at her watch. 'I'd better be off. But I'll see you later.'

'You know where it is, yeah – Norfolk Street?'

'I'll find my way,' she said, giving the book in her hands a little triumphant shake.

After Joanna had gone he went into his bedroom and, taking the jacket of his suit from its hanger, gave it a cursory brush. As he did so he saw the top of the envelope peeking from its inside pocket. He still liked to carry it there, for some reason. He took out the letter, written on wafery duck-egg-blue airmail paper, its US stamp franked and dated 2 p.m. March 16th, 1947. He had read it so many times now he could perhaps recite it. He discarded the jacket and lay down on the bed.

154 Spring Street, N.Y., N.Y.

March 15th

Dear Tom

I've lost count of the number of run-ups I've taken to this letter
– every jump so far has failed to clear the bar. The last one covered
eleven pages before I decided to spare you, purely on humani-
tarian grounds. Into the garbage it went. You could be annoyed
that it has taken me this long to reply, or you could regard it as
a compliment that I waited until I got it right – or as right as I
ever will. I hope you, as a past master in the art of postponement,
may understand. Though 'past' is now the *mot juste*, it seems, in
the light of your forthcoming publication! I was convinced you'd
finish it one day, even if you weren't. I am very, VERY proud of
you. And there was never a need, by the way, to worry about
getting my 'permission' to use any of those photographs – as far
as I'm concerned, they were always yours. I would only ask that
you send me a copy of the book when it's published. I know you'll
never let me forget what I said about Liverpool all those years
ago, but that doesn't mean I'm not fascinated to read it. So will
you – please?

I don't know what to tell you about the place I'm living in, as
I've only just moved here myself. It's a tiny apartment on the
fourth floor, with a leaky shower and no cooker. Cosy, though.
Downtown is less swanky than the 50s and 60s, there's a greater
sense of everyday toil down here, but it seems more of a neighbourhood too. Right now outside my window I can hear the truck
loading at the bakery door, and smell fresh-baked bread wafting
up. I don't know why, but that smell makes me incredibly happy,
– happier than I've been in a while. Rebecca, a new friend I've
made, says I should go into analysis – it's all the rage among her
crowd. Personally I can't think of anything more ghastly than
confiding my 'problems' to a complete stranger, but I suppose
that's just my Englishness coming out. Rebecca's also a photographer, and really has helped to get things up and running. I owe
to her the most fabulous stroke of good fortune; she'd bought
one of my photographs (a street scene) and hung it in her apartment where a gallery owner she knew spotted it and asked about
me. To cut a long story short, he's putting on a little show of

mine in a few weeks at his place on Bleecker Street, a few blocks away. So it's quite exciting!

Being busy again, being active – it's saved me, I think. About a year ago I had got to drinking more than I ought. I didn't notice it at first. They serve huge Martinis over here, from pitchers, and I developed a taste for them. Too much, I'm afraid. There were mornings I'd wake with a hangover so skull-splitting I couldn't even get out of bed to be sick. Of course I don't need to tell you what sorrows I was trying to drown. Remembering that day now – well, most of it's a merciful blank, but I still have in my head the awful moment I was lying on that gurney and asked you where George was. The look on your face that told me. That was the one and only time in my life I wanted to die, because oblivion felt preferable to the rawness, the shocking convulsion of that grief. I'd had intimations of it years ago when my parents died, but as a child one tends to be more resilient than is generally supposed. You live in your own world. When Richard died my overwhelming feeling was guilt, not just because of us – though that was bad enough – but because I'd never been the wife he'd hoped I would be. With George, I felt I was being punished for my selfishness. I'd never properly atoned for what I'd done – to Richard, to you – and now I was getting my deserts. You were so kind to me then, first at the hospital and in those months afterwards when I was stuck under that boulder of depression, so crushingly heavy I thought it would never move. When I think of how patient you were with me, after all that I'd put you through, I feel a lurch almost like vertigo.

I always thought I'd persuade you to come. There are alternatives which we hide from ourselves too convincingly for us to fear them. I *had* to go, and to the last minute believed you'd come with me. You once joked that your leaving Liverpool would be like a polar bear trying to abandon his ice cap. Yet sometimes I imagine you here in New York, wandering about the streets in that dreamy staring way of yours. You'd be amazed by the architecture, of course, the huge roaring canyons, the extravagant size of everything. Sometimes, when the fog comes off the river in the morning and the light slants at a certain angle, it reminds me a little of Liverpool. If this sounds as if I'm trying to tempt you into visiting some day, then – guilty as charged. Even polar bears need a holiday, don't they?

Talking of visitors, I have the imminent prospect of Nancy and David coming to stay. Heaven knows where I'll put them both – there's barely room here for me. Nancy's still in London and has met, rather late in life, a man that she likes. *Mirabile dictu*, as you would say. David has got someone, too, but he's much more secretive than either of us – I dare say he'll allow us to meet her in due course. When I've been feeling a bit 'blue' I try to remind myself how lucky I am. They've kept me going. Wherever I am – in a picture house on Third Avenue, or a bar (I haven't completely forsworn Martinis), or just the poky little bedroom where I write this – it's comforted me to know that you're out there. Even if it's the other side of the world. I once read, I can't remember where, that missing someone is a way of spending time with them. I'm not sure if that's true, but it's what I tell myself. Dearest Tom – I've left the enclosed till last. I hope you don't mind my sending it, but I just couldn't bear the idea of your not being able to remember him. Perhaps in time it will bring a smile to your face. Please know that it comes with all my love.

Bella

He lay on his bed, staring intently at the little glossy picture Bella had enclosed in the letter. It was a photograph, brownish, not much bigger than a cigarette card, of Bella and George in a garden. She is holding him forward to camera, her face smiling in profile as she seems to coax some engagement from him. George's face registers a subtle mixture of curiosity and surprise, his eyes wide and his mouth open, apparently on the verge of an exclamation. His hand, swiping the air, is blurred. Baines was glad that she had sent it, though she had been quite mistaken in thinking that he might not be able to remember him. We carry them with us. For a long time he lay there, without moving, as the *tap-tap* of the building work continued outside.

Of course he had left it very late, but then it would have surprised him to leave it any other way. The event began at one o'clock, which gave him about forty minutes: to be late for one's own party would look very shabby. He hurried down Gambier Terrace, the cracked Victorian flags glimmering from overnight rain. It had been a mild spring, after the atrocious winter of '46, but the sky had a lowering shifty look, as if it might launch a sudden downpour just for a joke. As he approached the junction of Upper Duke

Street he heard a tram, and made his customary hobbling dash for it, but it was already descending the hill by the time he got to the turning. He glanced at his wristwatch: half past twelve. The problem with running in public, he thought, panting, was the way it rendered you slightly pathetic, like a dotard, or a fugitive. He had been a cyclist for years until he came down one morning to find the wheels had been stolen from his Raleigh. He had never got round to buying another one. His reaction at the time was less outrage than bafflement. Who on earth would bother stealing bicycle wheels? He was slowing to a trot when he heard a taxi's engine chugging just behind him – deliverance! – and flagged it down.

As it tooled along Duke Street he wondered if he had forgotten the place. He had only been there once before, just after he came out of hospital in '41. Six years had slipped by without a single meeting. Perhaps it was the case that friendships forged in adversity withered in more tranquil conditions. It was the intensity that kept them going. Then through the cab window he saw it, Wo's, a narrow little front tucked into the middle of a terrace, its windows primly curtained against the daylight. He jumped out of the cab and with anxious steps entered the hushed gloom of the restaurant. A couple of tables were occupied, though smokers appeared to outnumber the diners. An elderly waiter stalked out from behind a beaded curtain and eyed him cheerlessly.

'Tabor for one?'

'Um, no,' said Baines. 'I was hoping – does Mike still work here?'

There was a minute slump in the waiter's shoulders as he turned and cawed incomprehensibly towards the kitchen. Then he continued past him. A few moments later another man swished through the curtain, his air unmistakably inconvenienced until he saw the reason for his summons.

'Hullo, Mike.'

Mike looked startled. 'Tom? Is it you?'

'Course it's me. How're you?'

'Er . . . bit shocked, to tell the truth.' He was staring candidly at him. 'What are you doin' here, like?'

'Oh, just wondering what the specials were today . . .'

'Crabs!' he replied brightly. They laughed, and he seemed to relax. Mike had put on weight in the intervening years; he was puffier around the face, jowlier, though he still carried himself with a certain bantam swagger.

'I know this is right out of the blue, but I wonder if – have you got an hour to spare?'

Mike looked at him awkwardly. 'Well, it's lunchtime . . .'

Baines resisted the temptation to gesture at the empty tables – maybe they filled up very suddenly about now – and looked him in the eye. 'Listen. You remember me telling you about the book I was writing – the one about Liverpool? Well, it's done. Finished. The publishers are having a little do for it, um, in about twenty minutes time. I'd really like you to – be there!'

'You don't give us much warnin', la'.'

'Yeah, sorry . . . I've got a taxi waiting outside.'

Mike exhaled, and scratched his head meditatively. He stared at Baines for a moment, then called to his old waiter. He barked to him in rapid Chinese, brusque little phrases that sounded impatient but might simply have been their everyday demotic. A younger waiter appeared, and then Mike was suddenly oscillating between the two, instructing the one in a long burst of Chinese and following it with a few choice words of Scouse. Baines watched this little confabulation in quiet wonder. Mike turned back to him.

'I'm 'ardly dressed for it,' he said, plucking at his kitchen whites.

'You don't have to be,' he replied.

Mike went back to the kitchen, and reappeared moments later shrugging on his civvies. Another querulous exchange with the old man, then they were out of the place and into the idling taxi. As the terraced streets slid by the window Baines couldn't help himself chuckling.

'Wha'?' asked Mike.

'Just listening to you and the old feller. I've never heard you speak Chinese.'

'He's me uncle,' shrugged Mike. ''e doesn't understand much English. And the young feller doesn't understand Chinese. But we get by.'

Baines offered him a Player's, and they sparked up together.

'So what've you been doin' with yerself?'

Baines sighed. 'Oh, not much. Finishing this book, mostly.'

'Not married or anythin' – kids?'

He shook his head. It would have taken too long to explain, and he wasn't inclined to burden Mike so quickly after their reunion.

'You?'

'Yeah. Coupla kids. The missus wants to move out of 'ere.'

'Where to?'

Mike gave a little snort. 'North *Wales*, la'. I'm not 'appy about it.' He seemed to brood on this, but then his face cleared. 'Eh, you'll never guess who I ran into.' His eyes were gleaming with amusement, and Baines thought he might be able to guess.

'Not Farrell?'

'Yeah! 'Bout a year ago, pub on Mathew Street. He 'adn't changed. Still called me Charlie.' Mike was enjoying the memory. 'We talked for a while, actually . . .'

'The old times.'

'Yeah. He was a fucken pain, really,' he said musingly. 'But it was . . . nice to see 'im again – you know?'

Baines nodded, and murmured, 'We went through a lot.' They had briefly stalled in traffic, and to their right the clank and thud of a demolition site made the car windows throb. Dust clouds were gusting from inside the shell of an old red-brick municipal building, and men in tin hats and masks drifted about, mute, incurious. Baines glanced at Mike, who was watching it too, and added, 'You sometimes wonder, though . . .'

The south-west side of the Eames Library had been reconstructed, though it still hid beneath scaffolding. The brickwork of the facade had been repointed, and the tiled floor of the atrium squeaked underfoot from its recent cleaning. Within, the reading room still bore the whiff of planed wood and fresh plaster, and motes of dust could be seen drifting in the funnels of light that poured down through the stained-glass windows. The walnut shelves had not been filled, but they soon would be. On a raised dais at the centre of the room a Mr Mowbray, editorial director of Plover Books in London, was winding up his muttered and rather pedestrian speech, unable to keep from his voice a faint note of astonishment that he was there at all. In the little cluster of people near the front Baines picked out Joanna, who smiled as he meaningly straightened the knot of his new tie. May and George were there, too, their faces bewildered with pride. Further back he saw Adrian Wallace, whispering slyly to a young woman. No change there. Then Mowbray falteringly invited his author to address the assembled.

Baines nodded his thanks, and stepped up to the dais. The nervousness he had felt on waking this morning had evaporated. He knew what he had to say.

'Thank you all for coming here today. I'm very lucky – we are very lucky – to be standing in a room which only four years ago was not even known to exist. Its architect, Peter Eames, spent the last part of his life trying to get it built, and you can see for yourself why his work exerts such a hold on the imagination. It's mysterious, and it's – very beautiful. I'm sure he would be pleased to know that his last great work has been saved, and what's more by a patroness whom he held in very high esteem. In fact, she's here with us today' – at this he looked over at her – 'Mrs Ellen Westmacott, Peter Eames's daughter.' He waited for the ripple of applause to settle before he continued. 'I'd rather not add to Mr Mowbray's kind words about the book, which was meant to take two years but actually took ten. That's a work rate even the builders at the Anglican Cathedral would disdain. My apologies to Plover Books, and my thanks to the late Professor Moray McQuarrie, who was an inspiring teacher. I'd also like to thank Richard and Bella Tanqueray for the excellent photographs of the town. And finally I'd like to raise a toast to the dedicatees of this book, the rescue men I worked with in 1940 and 1941. None of them is named there, but all of them, I should say, are worthy of my undying regard. Thank you.'

Later, as the waiters were ghosting among them, and the voices climbed and echoed around the vaulted ceiling, Baines went over to speak to Mrs Westmacott. Mrs Fleetwood hovered in attendance.

'It's looking rather grand, isn't it?' he said, swivelling his gaze around the room and then back to her. 'I'm so glad you took it off the Corporation's hands.'

'They were going to tear it down!' she said, with a little harrumph.

'That's why I'm glad you took it off their hands.'

'Well,' she said, 'it helps when you've inherited a lot of money.'

'You might have spent it on other things . . .'

'I'm eighty-two, Mr Baines. What else should I spend it on? And you made a very persuasive case.'

'The stock will begin arriving soon. I'll keep you informed – as your steward.'

'Yes! My *steward*,' she repeated, seeming to relish the word. 'Do your duties also include fetching me a drink?'

'Don't worry – I'll go,' said Mrs Fleetwood tolerantly. Baines bowed, in his new capacity, and withdrew.

He slipped out into the back courtyard, where he saw Jack and Evie sharing a cigarette. Jack had just said something to make Evie shake with laughter – her face was lit up by the delight of it. He paused briefly to watch them. They had married last year, and Baines had been the best man. Perhaps you didn't have to be alone. The sound of her voice – *her* laughter. That was one of the things he missed most. It was wonderful to make a woman laugh. Would she have picked up a faint New York burr by now? He hoped she wouldn't change, and then he half snorted at the absurdity of hoping such a thing. Jack had spotted him now and was calling him over. As he dawdled towards them he turned back to look at the banks of tall windows that formed the rear elevation. He saw in their reflection a jagged skyline of chimney stacks, a lonely church spire, the mauve brick walls of warehouses. Beyond them the surrounding hum of the city encroached, an infinity of pubs and back rooms and staircases and human appetites. The library had escaped the wrecking ball; other buildings would not. He'd heard that they were planning to pull down the old Customs House, which had stood by the river since 1829. It would be infamous – unforgivable. Whole streets and lanes were disappearing, their names remembered only by word of mouth, or in the forgotten folds of disused maps. These brief candles. They were blowing out their own past ... But maybe he'd got that wrong. Maybe you couldn't destroy history. You could only add to it.

Acknowledgements

I would like to thank Dan Franklin and all the team at Jonathan Cape, especially my editor Ellah Allfrey; also Rachel Cugnoni, Peter Straus and Sebastian Faulks. I am very grateful for the reminiscences of Keith Priestman, Bryan Perrett and John Quinn. Thanks also to the staff at Liverpool Record Office and Finsbury Library, London.

The following books were of invaluable help: Nikolaus Pevsner's *South Lancashire* (1969) and its successor, *Liverpool* (2004) by Joseph Sharples; *Merseyside at War* (1988) by Rodney Whitworth; and Quentin Hughes's magnificent and formative *Seaport* (1964).

I am most indebted to Rachel Cooke, my wife, for her steadfast love and encouragement.